RIVENNIA
A GAME OF WAGERS

RIVENNIA
A GAME OF WAGERS

JAIME URENCIO

SUNRISE & ROOSTER PRESS

Published in 2026
by Sunrise & Rooster Press
www.sunriseandrooster.com

ISBN: 9781919276403

Cover by Achiraya Jenjarrussakul and Xavier Comas
Text design by Clio Mitchell

A catalogue record for this book is available from the British Library.

Trigger Warning
This book contains depictions of suicide, sexual content, and violence, which may be disturbing to some readers. Discretion is advised.

For Fraser

Master of invention, he forges ahead,
at once to betterment, at another to ruin
Sophocles – *Antigone, Ode to Man*, 5th century BCE

Much learning does not teach understanding
Heraclitus – *Fragments*, 5th century BCE

PROLOGUE

GREN

Sixth Day of Month Ten, Year 500

The queen had asked for the anaesthetic to be administered before leaving the Royal Palace. I pictured her lying there, serene as the drug spread through her bloodstream, her eyes, once so fierce, slowly closing for the last time.

The bell marked eleven hours as I sat on the official dais, every muscle tensed to hide even the slightest sign of discomfort. Sweat beaded on my skin, and I once again clung to the dogma: *The greatest good for the greatest number.*

The screens came to life at half past. Twenty of them formed a ring along the middle tier of the arena. There was no way the audience could watch all of them at once. Ironic, since the only person at the centre of the stage would be unconscious.

Pigeons were everywhere – dirty, grey, purring and fluttering. They moved in waves, oblivious to the occasion. A flashing circle on the otherwise blank screens accompanied the queen's pulse, broadcast for all to hear.

Dum-dum.

Dum-dum.

She was no longer awake, but her heart continued its labour. Startled by the noise, the pigeons took off in chaotic flocks, only to settle back moments later, feathers scattering dust. I let out the breath I had been holding and managed to draw in another one. My wife Lorelei squeezed my hand, her touch barely registering.

At a quarter to twelve, the queen was brought in, her body lying flat on the floating platform. Her distinctive bun was unravelled, and the long white hair fell over her gaunt frame. My eyes were fixed on that hair, and a chill passed through me as visions of the Lodgers' wigs surfaced in my mind.

Slowly, the stretcher moved, coming to a stop above the pile of logs. The gap between each beat was so deep, I feared even the sound of my breath would disturb it.

Dum-dum.

Dum-dum.

It started with a spark. A flick of flint beneath the tree stumps. The crackling came before the flames, a wisp of smoke spiralling to where the queen lay above. I glanced at the crowd; some people were looking down, unable to face it, while others stared, eager to absorb every detail of the spectacle. No one but me knew, however, the reason behind her decision to go.

I turned my gaze back to the stage – to look away felt like a betrayal. It was her will to die here in front of all of us, and I owed it to her to watch, to bear witness.

Beside me, Lorelei began to weep as she gently stroked her rounded belly. But I found myself unable to comfort her as my own eyes stung with tears. The rising flames danced, wild, growing into a furious blaze that licked at the platform. Soon, the body was swallowed, and our queen became something not of this world.

When the heat reached me, acid rose in my throat.

What had started as a thin curtain of smoke became a thick, choking cloud. It was black and vile, spurting into the sky like some malignant spirit. The screens froze the moment the beating stopped, and a deep, terrible stillness fell over the arena.

'Time of death: twelve hours,' an automated voice announced with a mechanical detachment that felt abrasive. As the finality of the loss hit me, a sob escaped before I could pull myself together.

The greatest good for the greatest number. But I found no solace in the thought.

Lorelei reached for my hand once more, and tension gripped me. We can't choose what we desire. The woman I longed for wasn't my pregnant wife. One last time, I searched for her red hair in the crowd.

The silence in the arena carried a strange mix of grief and unease. People remained in their places, stunned into paralysis. Then there was the smell – earthy, rancid. A reek of wet goatskin and charcoal. A smell I knew would stay with me, precise and sharp, until the end of my days.

One-armed bots rolled into view; hissing, they sprayed foam over the dying flames. The fire sputtered and shrank, leaving behind only a smouldering circle on the stage. Movement rippled through the crowd as people made their way to the exits.

Every decision in my past could have taken me elsewhere, every fork in the road a chance to shape a different story. Though less than a year into my mandate, this was where I stood: at the brink of an ominous fate I never could have imagined, deprived of all possibilities but one.

The queen was gone. Now it was up to me to ensure her death would not be in vain.

PART ONE

Months One to Seven
Year 500

ONE

GREN

THE DRESSING ROOM WAS spacious but cosy. Soft, ambient lighting created a tranquil atmosphere, away from the chaos of live hologram broadcasting. A large vanity mirror, framed by round, bright bulbs, provided stronger light for makeup application. One beige wall was adorned with minimalist art, depicting the silhouette of Lacunfort, the tower city, as seen from neighbouring nations.

Beneath the mirror, the desk was cluttered with cases that opened into an assortment of trays, each holding foundation palettes, concealers, eye drops and sprays. Brushes, powder puffs and sponges were scattered around my nameplate: *Gren Moritz, Chief Minister.* After months on the campaign trail, I was all too familiar with these implements. It was precisely this familiarity that reminded me of how far I'd come. Here, in the heart of preparation, I felt steady; this was a well-rehearsed symphony, and I was its conductor.

Clara rose from the sofa in the corner.

'Keep it minimal and natural,' she instructed the makeup bot. 'Take the shine off, but don't overdo it.' Clara was always direct – almost blunt – but I'd learned to recognise the subtle care in her words from the very first day I met her, all those years ago at Varcega University. Being young and spirited, I hadn't been able to stop asking questions during her lecture: was it possible to have authority without coercion? Could democracy survive without equality? How could we reconcile universal animal rights with our nation's specific cultural practices? Her answers had been brief and polite until my fourth or fifth interruption, when she paused and stared at me. I braced myself for a reproach, but instead she gave me the faintest of smiles.

'What's your name again, young man?'

After class, I followed her to ask if she already had a teaching assistant. Perhaps to get rid of me, she recommended three books on political theory and told me that if I read any of them before the end of the week, I might have a small chance of qualifying for the role. By Friday, I had read all three. I handed in my reports with bags under my eyes and a grin on my face. Clara probed me with questions until she looked satisfied. That's how it all began.

Sometimes, I think our connection was inevitable. My grandparents raised me with love and care, but they couldn't instil the same curiosity and strength that Clara did. For her part, after years of preaching to deaf ears, Clara seemed to find renewed purpose in mentoring someone who shared her passion for a political theory rooted in traditional values. People often described us as having a mother-and-son relationship, but ours was more of a partnership. She lifted me up in ways that no one else did, and together, we achieved things that not only changed our lives but also, hopefully, those of others.

When I doubted my chances of heading the Student Government Association, it was Clara who scolded me for a lack of ambition. Her confused look every time I hesitated pushed me into roles I hadn't dared to imagine for myself: community organiser, policy analyst, city council member. Whenever I expressed doubt, she would cut me off with a firm, 'And why exactly not?' She had a way of making my imagined obstacles disappear with just a few words.

When it became time to appoint a campaign manager for my candidacy as People's Sentinel of Varcega, the choice was obvious. I don't think we would have secured victory without her. Then, as my Chief of Staff while I led Varcega's government, Clara made me believe I could become the first Varcegian Chief Minister of all nations in Rivennia. And now, we had done it.

The bot applied a lightweight foundation and a tinted moisturiser that blended flawlessly with my tanned skin, enhancing its natural radiance. A touch of concealer under my eyes erased any hint of fatigue, restoring the well-rested appearance I preferred. I never thought I'd be the kind of man who wore makeup before every public appearance, but at forty-two, maintaining my image was paramount. And I had to admit, I looked impeccable.

'Is this side even?' Clara asked, pointing at my hair. Her hand, now freckled with age, bore a dark, heart-shaped birthmark at the wrist – an ironic gift from nature for someone so indifferent to romantic frivolities. I used to tease her about that 'love tattoo', but she never gave me more than an eyeroll.

Clara and the bot stepped back simultaneously, tilting their heads to examine their work. The bot scrunched my curls and applied more hairspray.

There was a knock at the door, then a young woman wearing a glowing earpiece poked her head in. 'Five minutes?' she asked, looking directly at Clara. Clara nodded, and the woman disappeared as quickly as she'd come.

Clara crossed the room to the coffee table, stacked with printed magazines and newspapers. All their covers featured photos of me that, I had to admit, had turned out rather well. With the help of lighting and angles, I portrayed just the right balance of openness and strength.

Sighing, Clara retrieved her handheld and gave her notes one last glance.

'Nearly done,' the bot said.

In the mirror, I watched as Clara's hand rose to her neck, her fingers brushing against her skin as if searching for something to hold onto. Trembling slightly, she tucked a loose strand of hair behind her ear. It was the kind of hair that spoke of a life lived too busily to care for it properly – a wiry mass of grey gathered into a loose bun. She placed her handheld down on the table. As the bot finished with a light dusting of powder, it struck me that I probably wore more makeup in a single week than Clara had in her entire life.

'This will go well,' I reassured her, a rare role reversal for us.

'Keep your language simple,' she advised. 'Greta is the type to only skim the surface of policy. Try to avoid discussing the Coercive Sterilisation Bill unless she insists on bringing it up.'

I stood, enjoying the opportunity to stretch my muscles, and a thrill coursed through me. I had envisioned going on the Greta Andros show as the elected Chief Minister countless times, yet nothing compared with the reality. A live broadcast to Rivennia's largest audience was no small stage, and exactly where I belonged now. I glanced at Clara – this wasn't just my moment; it was ours. I only hoped she was savouring it as much as I was.

'Is Lorelei joining from the start?' I asked.

'No. She's still in hair and makeup. You'll have the first segment to yourself, and she'll join for the second.'

'Very well.'

Six months of marriage, and most of it spent apart – the realities of a campaign trail didn't allow for much else. Our union had been arranged, as was customary in Varcega, though it had served a political purpose too. Clara had made it clear from the start: a single man had never held high office, and we weren't about to test that precedent.

Another knock. 'Two minutes,' a man's voice called from behind the door.

Clara turned to me. 'We don't want you to be seen interrupting your wife when she speaks, but if things go off track, I trust you can steer the conversation back.'

'Is that what's making you nervous?'

'It's her first major appearance,' Clara admitted, adjusting her watch with a quick, deliberate motion. 'I'm not sure we prepared her enough.' Then her tone softened. 'She did spend the whole afternoon with a coach, though. I'm sure she'll be fine. She's very likable.'

'Exactly. That's why we chose her.' I checked myself in the mirror one last time, and Clara smoothed the creases from my jacket. 'How are my teeth?' I asked, flashing an exaggerated smile. Clara responded with two thumbs up, her ultimate sign of approval.

Gratitude swelled inside me. Clara's presence was as constant and vital as the ground beneath my feet. Today, we were stepping into a new chapter, walking into it together, ready to claim what we had built.

•••

I was escorted down a brightly lit, narrow corridor by the stage manager and her staff.

'Welcome to the Greta Andros Show, Chief Minister,' the stage manager said, her tone friendly but hurried. 'It's a real honour to have you here today.'

Hearing people call me by my new title still took me by surprise.

'Greta will do a short intro, then we'll cue you to walk on stage,' she continued as we approached the end of the corridor. 'We'll give you time cues once you're up there. You've got about fifteen minutes for the first segment. Greta might kick off with a question about tomorrow's inauguration, but feel free to pivot to your key points if needed. Your mic will be live as soon as you step on stage. No need to worry – just speak naturally.'

We stopped behind a door, and I could hear Greta's signature deep voice from the other side. A powerful hum came from the audience, slightly muffled by the wall. The sound vibrated through me, fuelling my anticipation. Moments later, the audience erupted into clapping and cheering. I squared my shoulders. I was ready.

'Cue in three, two, one,' the stage manager said, and the door slid open.

I reminded myself not to squint as the flood of stage lights hit me. Greta stood to the side, arms open in a welcoming gesture. She wore a cobalt-blue silk blouse with puffed shoulders and wide-legged black trousers. The signs of age on her face only added character, while her short, textured hair gave her a playful, edgy look. Her glasses – oversized, square, and glossy black – framed her eyes, which shone with a mixture of wisdom and warmth.

As I walked towards her, lively music rose from the speakers, amplifying the electric energy in the studio.

'Chief Minister Moritz, welcome to the show!' Greta's voice rang out. She gestured to the sofa. 'Please, take a seat.'

I sat down and waved to the audience, who responded with even more applause. Greta waited a few seconds for the noise to settle.

'We are *so* thrilled to have you here tonight,' she said, effortlessly capturing the room's attention. 'It's not every day we get to hear directly from the man of the hour. So, tell us, how are you holding up in all the craziness?'

'I'm very happy to be here, Greta. Thank you for having me, and for the chance to speak with your audience. It's been an intense few months on the campaign trail, and now we're honoured to have the opportunity to form a government for the benefit of the people of Rivennia.'

Greta beamed. 'Well, I hope you know how grateful we are that you've taken the time out of your packed schedule to join us. I can only imagine what your win means for people back in your home nation.'

She leaned towards the audience as if letting them in on a secret. 'Most people don't know this: I was born and raised here in Lacunfort, but both my parents came from Varcega. I spent election night with my father and, when the results came in, I saw him, this tough Varcegian farmer, looking at the news holograms with tears in his eyes.'

The audience chuckled as Greta mimicked her father's gruff exterior. 'He just couldn't hold back the emotion when he saw someone from his home nation elected to lead the *entire* global government.' She stretched her arms wide to capture the sheer scale of it.

A smile spread across my face. 'It's not just a victory for me as a politician; it's a victory for all under-represented nations. For Varcega in particular, it's an opportunity for the global community to better understand our people. We have deep cultural roots. Yes, we're more resistant to technology. We have arranged marriages. We farm animals for their meat, and most of us are theists. Though these traditions have value. We don't expect others to adopt our ways, but we do seek to preserve them.'

'Absolutely,' Greta's eyes twinkled as she turned back to the audience. 'And what a beautiful nation Varcega is. The fields just outside Gardonia are greener than *anything* you've ever seen. You feel like you're travelling back in time to a more untouched, natural world.'

The monitors placed around the stage displayed close-ups of audience members nodding in agreement.

'But with all this good news,' she continued, adopting a more serious tone, 'there are also challenges. You're stepping into government at one of the most contentious times in Rivennia's history. Your victory was razor-thin, and riots are still breaking out in some areas. There's a great deal of anger over whether and how we should enhance our bodies, as well as when and under what circumstances we should end our lives. Seeing that, is unity going to be your top priority?'

'Unity is vital,' I said, straightening my back. 'But I wouldn't call it our top priority. As many of our voters know, the rapid pace of technological advancement poses a significant threat to human survival. My primary focus will be protecting humanity from the rise of ultrahumanism. United or not, preserving the human race must come first.'

Greta looked thoughtful. 'Survival, for humanity…' Then her fingers drove through the air to punctuate each word: 'As we know it.'

'Exactly. We cannot afford to take risks with our genetics. Evolution has shaped us over millions of years, and it's irresponsible to tamper with that without fully understanding the consequences. Unfortunately, technology in this field has advanced faster than previous administrations could regulate it. Our current legal framework condemns illicit edits, but there is little clarity on what that actually entails.'

'I think we can all agree that, despite genetic treatments being considered illegal by most, people are still finding ways to access them.' Greta leaned in, her voice gentle but probing. 'But what about simpler cases? Let me ask you, for example... My father is colour-blind. He can't see red, green or brown. It's a common condition. Wouldn't it make sense to edit that gene and fix his sight? What could go wrong with that?'

I angled myself further towards her. 'It's a reasonable example, but things are much more complicated than they appear. We don't fully understand all the functions of each gene, and altering one might affect our bodies and our minds in unforeseen ways. In the case of colour-blindness, if we silence the gene causing it, we might unintentionally influence other traits, like insulin production or cancer susceptibility.'

The crowd stirred, whispering.

'A tragic example of this is the increasing number of women with neuronal enhancements who are having stillborn babies. It's a terrible reality. These women underwent treatments long before they even contemplated having children, hoping to enhance their own cognitive abilities. Sadly, the mutations introduced by these enhancements don't remain confined to the individual; they are passed down to their surviving children and subsequent descendants. Once a mutation enters the gene pool, reversing it becomes nearly impossible.'

I turned to the audience, who had fallen silent, bracing

myself for the inevitable counter-argument about women's freedom to choose. I could already hear it in my head: the noble defence of their right to bring full-term stillborn babies into the world as a routine exercise in personal liberty, all while irresponsibly contaminating the gene pool for new generations. I could almost see it – some of those polished and self-assured Lacunfort elites, likely scattered among the audience, nodding along to that narrative – even applauding, as though reckless self-destruction were a virtue.

But instead, Greta eased back, her expression thoughtful as she steered the conversation in a different direction. 'Are all mutations bad, though? Could some of them make us stronger, healthier... *better* in some way?'

I straightened my back. 'Rather than gambling on the unknown, we should cherish the miracle of the human body – a marvel shaped by millions of years of evolution. We already possess extraordinary potential. True progress should come from hard work, not from tampering with the very essence of who we are.'

The audience erupted into applause, and a wave of pride surged through me. I was among my kind of people.

'Now, Chief Minister,' Greta said, 'your views are well known, but many of your opponents argue you have been cagey on the details.' She shifted, sitting forward with a mischievous grin. 'Let me press you on one more thing before we move on. If my father, who is past reproductive age, wanted to undergo this treatment – with no risk of passing on the genes – would that be allowed?'

I paused briefly. 'Obviously, as an individual, I have my personal views. I'm deeply rooted in traditional values, and I respect the sanctity of the human body. It's not something I would want to compromise myself or see compromised in my loved ones. My duty as a politician, however, is to protect the human race. Beyond that, I'm not the morality police, nor do I want to be.'

Greta simply nodded, and I continued. 'So, to take your example: your father undergoing gene edits would ultimately be a personal decision between him and his physician. But there's one very strong caveat, which can't be overstated: *as long as those changes do not affect future generations*. That must be fully guaranteed. If there's any risk that the modifications could carry forward, the individual's freedom must stop where the potential to harm others begins.'

Greta arched her eyebrows and glanced at the audience. 'So, there's the catch, everyone. The government doesn't want to sterilise you, but if *you* want those gene enhancements, you have to choose sterilisation.'

I let out a soft chuckle. 'Yes, that's a fair summary. We're working on legislation to ensure that any potential risks are contained, but people do have the right to make decisions about their own bodies.'

Greta grew serious again. 'And that brings me to your first proposed bill. You're about to present a highly controversial piece of legislation to Congress, requiring permanent sterilisation for those who wish to undergo gene enhancement treatments. Many predict a catastrophic outcome, with the bill headed for a decisive defeat, while others have publicly suggested you could be ousted shortly after, making your mandate the shortest in Rivennia's history. Are you not worried that such a contentious bill might put the rest of your term at risk?'

'I'm not concerned about the success of my first bill.' Though saying that, I could feel a weight in the pit of my stomach. 'This is the right step to protect our genetic future. If people want access to gene therapies that alter their DNA, we must ensure those changes don't affect future humans. We are proposing permanent sterilisation for those who undergo these treatments to prevent unwanted mutations from entering the gene pool.'

Greta raised her eyebrows. 'That's going to be a tough sell – especially to those who value personal freedom. Many would say that it takes a real…*optimist* to push this agenda in the current environment.'

'I am an optimist, Greta,' I said, raising my chin. 'As anyone who's ever done anything worthwhile has had to be.'

There was sparse applause, and the audience murmured – some seemingly in favour, others uncertain.

Greta straightened in her seat. 'You certainly *are* an optimist, Chief Minister. That's one of the reasons your supporters like you so much. We'll be watching closely to see how this plays out.' She held my gaze for a second. 'Now, before we bring our next guest to the stage, I wanted to ask you about something else that's been making a lot of noise lately. It seems the number of assisted deaths in Rivennia, particularly here in the capital, has been rising sharply. And we're not just seeing this among the elderly or terminally ill. People of all ages are choosing to end their lives, especially after the recent modifications to the Right to Die Act and the rapid proliferation of Express Passing Centres, which are open to anyone. How do you feel about this? Have we made it too easy for people to take their own lives? Crowds protesting across Rivennia and the families of the deceased seem to think so. Should the government step in?'

'This is a deeply complex issue,' I said, frowning slightly. 'We are monitoring the situation closely. The rise in assisted deaths was anticipated when the scope of the Right to Die Act was broadened. As a society, we've given individuals more autonomy over their lives and deaths. But you're right; it's something we need to further assess to ensure the system isn't being abused and that people are making fully informed decisions.'

Greta's face was solemn. 'Well, thank you for sharing your thoughts on that, Chief Minister.' Then her expression brightened again. 'And now, the moment we've all been waiting for.' Rising to her feet, she turned to face the audience. 'Please join me in welcoming the First Lady, Lorelei Moritz!'

The music built once more as Lorelei stepped into view, her head held high. Greta extended her hand for a handshake, but Lorelei ignored it, choosing instead to blow kisses to the audience with alternating hands. She wore a modest black dress, her chestnut hair swept into a neat, low bun, pearls glinting at her ears and around her neck.

A familiar, half-hearted feeling stirred within me. Lorelei was, I reflected, *almost* pretty – charming in a way that no one would find intimidating. She possessed an understated appeal that resonated with people in the rural areas: a beacon of traditional values they could admire, seeing her as one of their own. The opposite effect, almost like a chemical reaction, occurred when she was set alongside the well-educated, affluent types that filled the capital.

I thought of Clara's earlier concerns about Lorelei's appearance on the show tonight and hoped she'd been wrong to worry.

Greta sat down, while Lorelei perched awkwardly next to me on the sofa, fiddling with her necklace.

'Lorelei, welcome to the show,' Greta said. 'This is your very first global appearance, isn't it?'

Lorelei bobbed her head quickly, her smile a little tight but still polite. 'Yes – first time.'

'And it's your first visit to Lacunfort too; is that right? Your new home.' Greta's look was both gentle and encouraging.

Lorelei nodded again, glancing briefly at the audience. 'Yes.

It's all…so different.'

The audience laughed faintly, and Greta leaned in as if to conspire with Lorelei. 'I'll bet it is. When my parents first moved here, they couldn't get over the city either. It's such a strange place, isn't it? So many things you don't see in Varcega.'

Lorelei's eyes widened. 'I know. Like the sky outside – it's not even real. They don't teach you that at school.' She paused, a hint of wonder in her voice. 'But it looks *so* real, with clouds and everything.'

A ripple of laughter spread through the audience, and Greta grinned. 'Exactly. Just a screen on the ceiling. It's impressive, right? It makes the city feel endless, but really, it's just layers upon layers. There was no room to expand into the lake, so the city had to grow upwards instead.'

'It's fascinating,' Lorelei said, faintly furrowing her brow. 'I've never seen anything like it. It's hard to imagine living somewhere this…vertical.'

The audience chuckled again, and Greta nodded kindly. 'It takes some getting used to, I suppose. It's definitely a unique world up here. What was your family's stance on technology when you were growing up?'

'Well, we weren't completely cut off from the world or anything.' Lorelei's voice was slightly hesitant. 'We had magazines and books.'

Her strong Varcegian accent coloured every word. I couldn't help but wonder how she was being received, particularly here in Lacunfort. The reactions in the studio were hard to interpret. Such thoughts made me feel ungrateful for my good fortune. I'd never thought of myself as the marrying type. But Lorelei was my wife now. My grandparents had gone to great lengths to find a suitable match within our circle, carefully balancing our traditions with the political necessity of presenting me as a stable, responsible, married man in the run-up to the election. This great-granddaughter of family friends seemed the perfect choice.

'No holograms?' Greta's tone was light and curious.

Lorelei shook her head. 'Nope. None of that.'

'No high-speed capsulas zipping through vacuum pneuducts?'

Lorelei's brows lifted. 'Oh, good God, no,' she said, laughing. But I couldn't miss the subtle shift in the crowd at the mention of a deity. 'We mostly walked or travelled on wheels.'

'That's quite a contrast,' Greta remarked. 'But I imagine it has its upsides. You must spend a lot more time interacting with the people around you and building close-knit community bonds.'

'Yes. Absolutely.' Lorelei's nervousness seemed to ease as she spoke. 'Family is important to us. You know…gathering, praying, celebrating traditions. We don't spend all our time glued to a hologram.'

There was a slight tightening in Greta's posture, though she quickly turned back to me with a fresh smile. 'What about you, Chief Minister? Did you grow up in a similar environment to the First Lady?'

'I grew up in Gardonia, which is more like the rest of Rivennia,' I replied. 'Though I doubt the rest of Rivennia would agree with me.' The audience laughed along, and the atmosphere relaxed a little. 'My parents passed away when I was a child, so I was raised by my grandparents. They were never too strict with traditions and were a little more open to technology than the average Varcegian. We'd travel to Lacunfort at least once a year.'

'You're both part of a new generation,' Greta said, turning her attention back to Lorelei. 'Mrs Moritz, you turned twenty-five last month, making you the youngest First Lady in Rivennian history. How does it feel stepping into such a public role at such a young age?'

Lorelei adjusted her posture, now radiating a quiet confidence. 'It's a big responsibility, but I'm excited about what I can bring to the role. I want to introduce a fresh perspective to Rivennia – not just in fashion, though I *do* have some beautiful outfits planned for our upcoming events.' She paused, her face lighting up. 'But more than that, I think it's important to find ways to bring people together. With everything happening, like the revolts, it's clear that people feel divided. Maybe we need more opportunities to connect, to celebrate what we share. Sometimes, a little joy can remind us of who we are as a group of nations.'

Greta played along. 'Count me in! Who doesn't like a good celebration?'

'I especially love the old holidays,' Lorelei said, her hand resting on her chest. 'They bring us closer to God and remind us of our spiritual values.'

The spark in Greta's eyes faltered. 'And as First Lady, how do you see yourself spending your time? Have you thought about any causes or projects you'd like to take on?'

Lorelei tilted her head as a pensive look crossed her face. 'I haven't committed to anything specific yet. People have suggested a few ideas, but I believe my main role is to support Gren and the work he's doing for Rivennia. He's worked so hard to get here, and we both feel incredibly fortunate to have this opportunity. God willing, Gren will achieve great things for Rivennia, and as First Lady, I hope to do my part by building a strong foundation for our family. Children are a blessing, and we're praying to be granted that gift in the near future.'

There was a brief, uncomfortable silence in the audience.

Greta's expression stayed professional, though a slight strain showed. 'Well, the Chief Minister is certainly fortunate to have you by his side. Do you see yourself playing a role in supporting his policy work?'

'Oh, absolutely,' Lorelei said, nodding with enthusiasm. 'My family back in Varcega supports him too, and I know his late parents are watching over him. Gren and I both believe in fighting ultrahumanism. People should accept how they're made – it's how God intended us.'

A sense of dread crept over me. People knew Varcegians were religious, but Lorelei sounded like an evangelical nun – and far too immature for her position. I should have seen this coming. Whatever coaching she'd had, it clearly hadn't been enough. We could have asked Greta's team to stick to a predetermined list of questions, but we hadn't. Clara and I should have rehearsed specific responses with her, drilling them until they felt effortless. But we didn't. There was simply too much to juggle. My new life had become a relentless storm of responsibilities – meetings, speeches, decisions – and sometimes, something this vital ended up overlooked. It was no excuse, but here we were.

This had been too much, too unfiltered for a stage like Greta's. In such a close battle for the head post, a misstep like this could have cost me the election just weeks prior. Once again, Clara's instincts had been right.

Greta wrapped up the final segment amidst a round of applause. As we exited, I took Lorelei's hand.

Clara was the first to greet us backstage. 'Well done, you two,' she said through tight lips, her face unreadable.

After Lorelei returned to her dressing room, all I wanted was to collapse onto a sofa, glass of whisky in hand, and go over a remediation plan with Clara.

'She's so young,' I whispered to Clara, shaking my head.

'Choosing a girl who didn't even attend university was a mistake.'

'We'll debrief in the morning,' Clara replied calmly. 'It's a big day tomorrow. We'll gauge the reaction based on what we see in the media. Comms is already on it. Nothing we can't fix.'

I nodded, feeling a bit dazed. 'Do we have anything else on the schedule for tonight?'

'Yes,' Clara said. 'A capsula is coming for you and Lorelei in five minutes. You've got a dinner reservation at Dario's on Platform 10.'

I shook my head. 'No, Clara, please. Not after this. We can't go out in public.'

'You'll have a private room.'

'Let's just cancel,' I said, exasperated. 'It's the night before the inauguration. I still need to review the final draft of the bill.'

'Gren.' Clara's tone was firm but measured. 'She's your wife, not just a political accessory. And you're not in Varcega any more. If you want her to be on your side, you need to treat her like a real partner. Spend time with her, get to know her. She won't cooperate if she feels like she's just there to play a role. You can't keep going through life like this – alone and detached.'

I sighed. 'One hour. Then I need to get back to the residence.'

'An hour is a good start.'

The private room at Dario's exuded luxury and modern elegance. A gentle glow from the lights bathed the sleek surfaces in a golden hue. Metallic sculptures adorned the walls on either side, glinting. The delicate scent of gardenias infused the air, mingling with the faint aromas of gourmet cuisine – earthy truffle, roasted herbs and a hint of sweet vanilla. A gentle breeze filtered in from the open windows behind us, bringing the fresh, damp-earth smell of the garden. A string quartet played somewhere in the background. The relaxed atmosphere eased my tension, and I took a sip of wine to calm myself further.

'Is that alcohol?' Lorelei asked.

'Yes.' My response came out more brusque than I'd intended.

'But...isn't alcohol bad for you?'

'It's not... If you drink it in moderation. You don't have to worry too much.'

'I see,' she said, though her uncertain expression didn't quite fade. She placed her hand on the white tablecloth and was startled as the surface lit up, displaying the menu. 'What is that?' she asked, drawing back.

'It's... the menu,' I explained. 'You can browse through it. I haven't been here before, but Clara said the food is excellent.'

'It's a short menu,' she remarked, glancing down.

'There's more. Look. Like this.' I demonstrated, moving my hand over my menu to flip the digital pages.

'That's *so cool.*' Lorelei beamed. 'Do it again.'

I obliged, and she tried it herself, giggling as she flicked back and forth through the pages.

'Anything good?' I asked after a moment.

'Oh! Sorry, I got distracted.' She laughed again, clearly embarrassed. 'I haven't actually read anything yet. Right, let's see...' She scanned the menu, murmuring, 'Lemon thyme chicken... Oh God, is that right? I thought they didn't do real meat here.'

'It's cultured meat, grown in a lab. No animals were harmed.'

She scrunched up her face, unsure. 'I think I'll stick to vegetables, if that's alright.'

'Of course.'

Then she brightened suddenly. 'Can you believe I just did my first live broadcast? I'm so gutted hardly anyone back home will see it.'

'Congratulations,' I said, trying my best to be cheerful.

'How do you think I did?' she asked eagerly.

Our food arrived, and I welcomed the pause, gathering my thoughts. The shadows cast by the candles danced across the table as I considered my response. Just as I was getting ready to speak, Lorelei clasped her hands beneath her chin. Eyes shut, she was saying grace in a long whisper, her lips twitching at high speed. Then, finally, she looked at me – back to normal.

'There are a few things you might want to keep in mind for future interviews,' I said tentatively.

Lorelei's eyes narrowed with curiosity.

'The most important one,' I continued, making sure my voice remained gentle, 'is to avoid mentioning God or religious practices too often. Outside of Varcega, it's best to steer clear of words like "praying" or "heavens", even as expressions. It's not your fault, of course,' I added quickly. 'We should have prepared you better.'

Lorelei's mouth parted, her cheeks flushing slightly. 'So... people want me to hide my faith just because they don't have one?'

'Not exactly,' I said. 'People know Varcegians believe in a higher power. It's just...when they see it in practice, it's unfamiliar. It creates a barrier.'

She blinked a few times. 'But the Human Order, in Lacunfort... Isn't it a religious organisation?'

'No, not at all,' I replied, choosing my words carefully. 'It may seem that way, but it's more about venerating science.'

'It looks like a church to me.'

I shook my head. 'The Human Order is a commercial

organisation with a social purpose. They want to maximise human potential through scientific innovation, not religious doctrine. They're a profit-making enterprise, operating independently from the government. But, as you've probably seen, they have *a lot* of influence in society.'

She frowned, considering this. 'So, no God, no prayers, just…plain progress for people to profit from?'

'Yeah. That's one way to put it. Nothing wrong with "plain progress" or "profits", though.'

'Do *you* have to hide your faith, then?' she asked.

'I… Look, I'm a little different in that sense. I do what I need to for my job. But I'm not…' I paused, struggling to pin down what was bothering me. 'I don't have to hide anything. I may be religious, but I don't practise much. I believe there's some kind of universal order. Sometimes I call it God, just because it's the closest thing I can name. But my ideology doesn't line up with the traditional religious view of God – not like yours, anyway.'

'You don't believe…' Her voice was nearly a whisper.

'Can we talk about something else, please?' I snapped. Then I sighed, frustrated – mainly at myself.

Lorelei's face fell, and she glanced down at her plate. 'Was I really bad, then – on the talk show?' she asked quietly.

'Listen,' I said, leaning forward to catch her gaze. 'People will talk. They always do. Especially in public roles like ours. You have to learn to tune out the noise. I don't want this to upset you. Promise me you won't read any news tomorrow or watch any holograms.'

'Why not?'

I grimaced. 'It won't be nice. And if there's any criticism, that's on me, not you. We'll make sure you have someone to help prepare you next time.'

Lorelei seemed lost in thought, her fingers absently tracing the edge of her plate. 'Greta asked what activities I'd like to focus on,' she said. 'What should I say when people ask me that?'

'We'll help you find some causes that matter to you. There are so many worthwhile projects you could support.'

'Could I help with your work?'

The muscles in my face tightened. 'I think it's best if you try a few things first, see what feels right. We'll arrange something for you. How does that sound?'

'OK,' she said, looking down. 'That sounds fine.'

She gazed out at the main dining room, a grand space filled with elegantly dressed patrons, their laughter and conversations muted behind the one-way glass. The sparkling skyline of Platform 10 stretched beyond, framed by the restaurant's floor-to-ceiling windows. We ate in near silence, and I worried I'd been too harsh.

Out of nowhere, Lorelei gasped. 'Oh, my Lord.' Her hands flew to her mouth. 'Oh... I'm so sorry, I just said it again.'

I couldn't suppress a smile. 'What is it?'

She pointed discreetly, forgetting that no one on the other side of the glass could see us.

'That's Primula Zhang,' she whispered.

'Who?' I asked, scanning the room.

'She's a supermodel...or *was*. I'm not sure. My sister and I used to make paper clothes for cut-outs of her from fashion magazines. I can't believe she's right there,' she almost squealed, her eyes bright.

I spotted the woman in question. She was striking, but there was something fragile about her, too.

'I have to say hello,' Lorelei declared, determined. She started to stand up.

'We can't,' I said, gently shaking my head and motioning for her to sit down. 'You're the First Lady now. No one knows we're here. It would create a stir.'

'I see...' she said, her excitement fading. 'I see.'

'And I think our capsula is ready. I've got work to do tonight.'

'Oh... I didn't realise...' Lorelei's voice trailed off as she glanced down at her wrist.

'What didn't you realise?'

She hesitated, then murmured, 'It's nothing.' Her fingers toyed with her bracelet, and I understood.

'Is the wristband reminding you?' I asked, lowering my voice. I wished I had the time and mental space for slow coquetry – the kind of attention a young girl like Lorelei truly deserved.

She nodded, spinning it to reveal the green bars. 'There's no rush,' she said quickly. 'If we miss this chance, we'll try again next month.'

I paused, then asked carefully, 'Are you comfortable with us trying unassisted?'

'Unassisted?' Her face flushed crimson. 'Oh... You mean...'

'Yes,' I said, just as flustered. 'Only if you'd like.'

She stammered, 'But, I'm your wife,' and her blush deepened.

'Of course,' I said hurriedly, feeling as awkward as she looked.

The butler's low voice interrupted us. 'Your capsula is ready, Chief Minister.'

We both stood, and in her haste, Lorelei caught the tablecloth, sending silverware clattering. The butler moved swiftly, righting everything while Lorelei muttered apologies.

Walking towards the exit, I leaned closer and whispered, 'I'll visit your room later tonight.'

Lorelei glanced up at me. Her face was a picture of uncertainty. She managed a small, uneasy nod.

•••

We had located the First Lady's bedroom in the south wing, away from the constant flow of staff. My room, in contrast, faced the north façade, with direct access through a lift to the press conference rooms downstairs and the administrative offices on the upper floors. While the idea of sharing a bed every night held a certain romantic appeal for most couples, I needed my own space and privacy if I were to keep up with the relentless pace of a Chief Minister's schedule.

Lorelei had already added her personal touch to the room. The walls, painted in pastel green shades, took on a more muted grace in the dim light. Delicate curtains framed the large windows, through which only the faintest glow from the city filtered in, casting gentle shadows on the antique furniture. A vase of fresh flowers sat on a side table, its perfume rising subtly, while a vintage mirror opposite reflected the glow of a nearby lamp. The stillness of the night offered a rare sense of calm.

Lorelei walked to the centre of the room, turned around, and looked at me before her gaze dropped to the floor. I took charge then, closing the distance, but I didn't kiss her straight away. Brushing my fingers through her hair, I leaned in to inhale the scent behind her ear. Her perfume was floral, delicate – almost too soft. I paused, letting the fragrance linger, then my lips brushed against her neck. She gave the faintest of whimpers, and a surge of heat shot through me. The space between us collapsed as I pressed myself against her. When she felt me, her breath hitched, quickening against my skin.

Grabbing her by the shoulders, I walked her to the bed, rolling up her dress and pulling down her underwear before guiding her to lie on its edge. The same whimper returned as

I entered her, and it grew louder with each thrust. It was only then that I allowed myself to kiss her, lips wet and tender. Her moans slipped between us as I deepened and hastened my strokes.

The contractions as I finished were intense but tasteless. I stood and stretched. The sound of my buckle clicking into place resonated in the room. Lorelei lay on the bed, chest heaving, one hand pressed to her forehead.

'I have work to do now,' I said as I strode towards the door.

On the morning of my inauguration ceremony, a large crowd gathered outside the Human Order temple, igniting in protest at the sight of my official capsula. Clara and I remained composed, but Lorelei glanced around, unsure. The three of us winced as the first rock struck the shatterproof glass with a muffled thud. More followed. I turned and caught a glimpse of them – men and women of all ages, fury burning in their eyes. And children. What kind of person brought a child to a protest to watch them hurl rocks at the Chief Minister's vehicle?

Soon after, the capsula entered the tunnel leading to the entrance, sealing us away from the chaos outside.

The temple had been designed to be awe-inspiring. As I stood on the threshold, its history pressed upon me. Inside, the cool air carried the scent of polished stone and ancient wood. The vaulted ceiling loomed over us. Beams of light slanted through narrow stained-glass windows. Unlike the religious temples in Varcega, these windows did not depict saints or halos, but instead celebrated scenes of human achievement: explorers planting flags on new worlds – all now united in a peaceful Rivennia – and scientists unveiling discoveries that reshaped our civilisation. Each figure was faceless, symbolising humanity's collective will rather than the glorification of any individual. The stone pillars lining the aisle were carved with symbols of progress: gears, books, open hands and human silhouettes encircled by five-pointed stars – the emblem of the Human Order. This place spoke to a profound part of me, an homage to what we humans were capable of achieving.

I sat at the front, facing a dais made of gleaming white stone. Lorelei would surely call that an altar. She sat right behind me, next to Clara. Further back, the rows filled with a gathering of Lacunfort's elite, the People's Sentinel of every nation, Congress members, and representatives of culture and the arts. Their faces were a blend of composure and barely concealed disdain. We had been told that the queen was not well enough to attend, but other members of the Royal Family were present to represent the monarchy.

The air was still, broken only by the faint shuffling of those arriving and the brethren preparing for the ceremony. Just then, holograms of my campaign promises appeared on long crimson banners hanging from the rafters. They captured the responsibility now resting on my shoulders: to safeguard humanity – our race and heritage, our individual fragility, and our collective strength. As I absorbed the grandeur surrounding me, I felt less like a man stepping into power and more like a symbol stepping into history. This ceremony was not just an ascension; it marked the dawn of an era that would be remembered, if I succeeded, for preserving the human race or, if I failed, for allowing its obliteration at the hands of a new, artificial one.

As the Supreme Leader entered, the chanting of low, resonant voices filled the temple. It wasn't a religious melody, but it felt sacred, swelling and echoing against the stone walls, drawing every eye to the great doors. Flanked by his closest confederates,

Igor Voychenko moved with slow, deliberate steps, exuding an air of commanding grace. Everyone rose. I stood with them, my heart quickening. I had seen countless holograms of the Supreme Leader, having followed his rise since my youth, but seeing him in person stirred a visceral excitement.

Voychenko was a presence. At seventy-six, his steps were steady. His white hair, neatly combed back, caught the light from the floating holograms, framing his face in a way that emphasised his aquiline nose, making him look like a predatory bird surveying its domain. He was serene, almost regal, his eyes seeming to take in the room without resting on any one detail for long.

I had always imagined that the burden of such lengthy leadership would visibly exhaust a body. But there was no weariness here. His gaze cut through the air like a scanner beam, his back as straight as the pillars lining the hall.

The Supreme Leader was known for his acute intelligence and directness with people. His position granted him no real power outside his organisation, but in reality, he carried an influence that we all acknowledged with respect. He possessed the kind of authority that wasn't granted by appointment, but earned over a lifetime.

As Voychenko reached the front, the chanting softened into silence. He ascended the dais with the calm confidence of someone for whom the temple itself had been built. In an instant, the ceremony began – *my* inauguration, where I would formally assume the mantle of government. The oaths of office unfolded with precise choreography; it was like watching from far away.

Then came my turn to stand on the dais. I'd been styled for the part – jacket firmly pressed and golden curls immaculate. In my speech, I made it clear that maximising human potential must never come at the cost of transforming ourselves into a new species.

'Our strength lies not in *abandoning* what we are, but in *embracing* it,' I stressed. 'Progress should serve humanity, not redefine it. We must advance with care, ensuring that our pursuit of innovation never comes at the cost of preserving the human genome.'

At the height of the proceedings, Voychenko raised his arms in the traditional gesture, his fingers splayed and his palms facing outward. His deep, formal voice resonated through the hall like that of an ancient patriarch. But who was this man to officiate such a moment? Who had granted him the privilege to initiate the head of the government?

The most natural answer would be the people of Rivennia – his billions of followers, along with the power wielded by the many businesses affiliated with the Human Order. An empire that controlled just over a quarter of Rivennia's economy.

As Chief Minister, I could resist the influence of the Human Order, or accept it and try to use it to my advantage. I knew which option I preferred, but it was too soon to tell how things would unfold.

'Hail Science,' Voychenko intoned, his words vibrating in the air. The congregation, myself included, echoed him, our arms raised in unison. 'Hail Science.'

'Science,' he continued, 'and only Science has the power to help us understand the world.'

'Hail Science,' we chanted once more.

Then Voychenko recited the litany we all knew by heart.

'By decree of the Human Order, we reject all beliefs in superior beings and supernatural forces…'

'Hail Science.'

'We accept the Scientific Laws of the Universe, in their

endless perfection, as the ultimate divinity.'

'Hail Science.'

'We believe our highest purpose is the continuous betterment of humanity, and we vow to ensure the perpetual survival of our race.'

'Hail Science.'

The chants rose higher and higher, repeating like waves until they reached a crescendo, then slowly began to fade. Applause followed, reverberating in the temple with a roar of approval. We remained in place, united under the same mantra. As silence fell once more, sealing the end of the ceremony, the moment carried me to a height where the entire world seemed to lie beneath me.

I had only taken a few steps when one of the brethren, a man well into his eighties, grasped my arm. He leaned in and whispered, 'The Supreme Leader wishes to see you in his office for a private audience.'

I kept my outward composure firm, but my pulse thudded as I said, 'Yes, of course.' I drew a slow, controlled breath, refusing to let nerves take hold. I had imagined this moment many times – speaking to Voychenko directly – but now that it was here, it felt different. Real. Immediate. His presence had filled the temple earlier, and now I was about to stand before him alone, without the protective barrier of the ceremony. But this wasn't a time for trepidation. I was, after all, the head of the government. No one sat above me.

I turned to Clara, explaining the situation briefly, trusting her to manage any prearranged commitments. Amidst curious glances, I followed the man to a lift at the side of the temple. He gestured for me to step inside, and as the doors hissed shut,

I was alone for the first time in what seemed like years. The feeling was peculiar – a glimpse of the lost independence I had once taken for granted.

When the doors opened again, the lighting outside was dim, the air musty. I stepped into a circular room, where floor-to-ceiling shelves held rows of old books, their spines worn with age. A sliding ladder ran along a metal rail. Glass domes displayed taxidermy birds under the soft glow of an old chandelier. In the centre of the room, two cracked leather sofas faced each other across a low table, but it was Voychenko at the far end who commanded my attention. Seated perfectly still behind an oak desk, his severe expression caught the dull, moon-like glow of a single lamp.

The wooden planks creaked beneath me as I stepped forward, and Voychenko's eyes lifted. His pupils were small against the pale grey of his irises.

'Mr Moritz,' he greeted me, rising from his chair. 'Welcome. Please, have a seat.'

'Supreme Leader.' I approached with purpose, meeting his gaze as I crossed the room. The atmosphere was charged with expectation, but I stood tall, letting no weakness show. Then I sat, facing him directly.

'Mr Moritz,' Voychenko repeated. His tone was even, but it was laced with something pointed. 'Congratulations are in order. Your election results were narrow, yet decisive – a reflection, no doubt, of the precise chord your ideas struck with the people of Rivennia.' His eyes lingered on me. 'Though,' he added, 'public sentiment is often fleeting. What resonates today may not endure tomorrow. This isn't meant ominously, of course.' He offered a subtle smile. 'But we both know that politicians must remain vigilant. This is merely the beginning of a long journey. A promising start, if one treads carefully.'

I reminded myself to lift my posture, keeping my tone respectful. 'Thank you, Supreme Leader. I understand that public opinion can shift, but I believe the mandate from our voters reflects more than just the present moment. I think it speaks to a deeper desire for human preservation. The people of Rivennia are ready for bold leadership, and I am committed to moving forward with responsibility, keeping the values of the Human Order at the core of our decisions.'

'Well, certainly the people of Rivennia are fortunate to have a man of your virtues heading the government through these difficult times.'

I couldn't help but wonder, with no small curiosity, what virtues those might be. But of course, it wasn't something I could ask.

'Thank you for your kind words,' I said. 'Your leadership has propelled our scientific thinking forward, and I intend to build on that foundation. I trust that my government and the Human Order can work together for the good of our citizens, and we will welcome advice where it is needed.'

'Providing useful guidance is both our purpose and our hope.' Voychenko's smile deepened, though I couldn't tell whether it was warm or condescending. 'There is something I'd like to show you. Have you ever been to the top of the main spire?'

'I have not.'

'Follow me.'

I walked behind him through narrow corridors and up a winding staircase. As we climbed, he described various features of the temple and their historical significance – the original stonework, quarried from the Astrin mountains, and the intricate carvings etched with ancient symbols. We eventually reached a platform lined with cages along its edge. Large birds rested behind the mesh wire, their dark eyes unblinking and watchful.

The stone walls here were rougher, unlike the polished grandeur below. Voychenko stepped towards a small cupboard set against the curve of the wall. He reached inside and pulled out a large, weathered leather glove, padded along the forearm. He slid it onto his hand with the ease of someone who had done so countless times. Next, he lifted a strange-looking device – a small leather hood with intricate stitching and tiny metal fixtures. He handled it with reverence.

'Let me introduce you to my falcons,' Voychenko said, full of pride. 'Years ago, we faced an unusual problem with pigeons. Their presence was desecrating the ancient stonework of the temple, their droppings eating away at the softer stone. Now, tell me, Mr Moritz, do you see any pigeons here?'

I glanced out over the view of Lake Lacun and saw none. 'No,' I answered.

'Oh, but they are there, always hiding. One must remain vigilant.' He opened a cage and placed the small hood over a falcon's head. The bird leapt onto his arm; its sleek, muscular body exuded power.

'Majestic creatures, are they not?' he asked.

The falcon's streamlined body seemed designed for speed and precision, every feather perfectly aligned. Even with the hood covering its eyes, an undeniable intensity emanated from it. Voychenko removed the hood, revealing a pair of keen eyes. With a quick upward motion, he released the falcon into the air.

'Hunt,' he commanded.

The falcon soared into the sky, its wings slicing the wind.

'These falcons are enhanced,' Voychenko explained. 'They come from my homeland, Gdynna. Twice as fast as unaltered varieties, and when they hunt, they devour the entire prey – bones and all – leaving no trace behind.' He glanced at me, amusement on his lips. 'Efficient, wouldn't you agree? Over time, the pigeons have adapted, but they will never outpace my specimens. You can learn much from watching what creatures will do to survive.'

I crossed my arms and held my tongue.

'What's remarkable, Mr Moritz, is that these falcons are hardly unique. Many species have been enhanced for humanity's benefit – rice, corn, soybeans, and even the cattle your fellow Varcegians slaughter in such numbers.'

I bristled at the comparison. Humanity's benefit – that was the key, wasn't it? Surely Voychenko wasn't equating the genetic tweaking of soybeans with the integrity of the human genome.

The falcon returned with a limp pigeon hanging from its beak. Voychenko directed it back inside the cage and laid the pigeon at its feet. As the bird moved towards its prey, something unexpected happened. The falcon jerked, its body tensing, feathers puffing unnaturally as an unseen force subdued it.

'A mild electric shock,' Voychenko explained, 'to teach obedience.'

There were no wires, no instruments. Just an invisible current that made the subject convulse. Whatever it was, it seemed cruelly effective.

'I wasn't aware such technology existed – to administer an electric shock remotely,' I remarked, steering the conversation away from gene enhancements. As much as I wanted to argue, this wasn't the moment for a heated debate over opposing views. 'I imagine it could have valuable applications.'

A hint of a smirk crossed Voychenko's face. 'You have no idea,' he replied.

When he finally gave a command, the falcon tore into the

pigeon, feathers flying as it ripped the flesh.

'Those who consume others thrive,' Voychenko said, with a mixture of playfulness and mischief. 'Wouldn't you agree, as a Varcegian?'

By the time we reached his office again, I was eager to conclude the audience, acutely aware of the unease Voychenko's earlier remarks had stirred in me. It was far too soon to jeopardise the fragile rapport we were beginning to establish. For my mandate to succeed, I needed the Supreme Leader as a partner, not an adversary. While I had expected many in Lacunfort to hold more progressive views on ultrahumanism than mine, I hadn't anticipated Voychenko to suggest so bluntly – and so early on – that my stance was overly radical.

'Please, take a seat,' he said, gesturing once again to one of the chairs before his desk. He sat down as well, steepling his fingers.

'I must commend your strategy – and your courage – in choosing coercive sterilisation as the subject of your first bill to Congress,' he began.

'Thank you,' I replied politely.

'How do you plan to ensure its approval?'

I chose my words with caution. 'My hope is that a clear and rational case, one that highlights the benefits of the sterilisation bill for Rivennia, will win the necessary support. It's a crucial first step in eliminating ultrahumanist practices that threaten our future. I've been working on this for months, and I reviewed the final draft last night. I believe we are ready.'

Voychenko's smile returned, faint and unreadable. 'Mr Moritz.' He paused. 'Such naivety is best kept hidden, not displayed.'

My muscles tensed.

'You will need allies,' Voychenko continued as though explaining something obvious. 'Many of them. Have you had the chance to meet with Her Majesty yet?'

'Not yet,' I admitted.

'It's no great loss. Her influence is almost non-existent these days. It will take her some time to warm to your administration, especially given your anti-monarchy stance during the campaign.'

I stiffened at the reminder. It was true – I had suggested that Rivennia could put the funds currently supporting the monarchy to better use. The statement had been a calculated move, designed to bolster support among the under-represented nations.

'You underestimate the resistance you'll face in Congress,' Voychenko said. 'It worries me that you seem to believe reason alone will sway votes. A rejection of your first bill could set you on a downward spiral, igniting more revolts, damaging your credibility. I've seen it many times before.' He shook his head slowly. 'Those who fail to pass their first bill rarely accomplish anything thereafter. And *your bill* is the most contentious ever to be brought forward as a first.'

His words landed heavily. There was truth in them, but it upset me hearing them expressed so plainly. I had been confident in my ideals, in the strength of my arguments. Now I felt foolish. My belief that a 'strong case' would suffice now seemed embarrassingly innocent. Voychenko's calm delivery only deepened my sense of unease. He was right. The path ahead was far more treacherous than I had realised.

'Of course,' he continued, offering a flicker of reassurance, 'victory is still within reach. And with it, a brighter future for your mandate. But we are far from Varcega, Mr Moritz. The political landscape here is tightly bound to the capital's elite. You must secure their support – and win it one person at a time.'

'How do you suggest I go about that?' My voice remained unshaken, though my mind was churning.

'That is why I brought you here – to offer my support. Your most vocal adversaries in Congress may need a subtle gesture of goodwill from you. This doesn't require any grandiosity – just something tokenistic.'

A knot tightened inside me. His words, smooth and calculated, carried an undercurrent I couldn't ignore. A *gesture of goodwill*? Something *tokenistic*? The implication left a bitter taste. I had known politics in Lacunfort could be ruthless, but I had hoped some lines would not be crossed. I stared at him, giving nothing away, though inwardly, I was appalled. When I spoke, my voice was more strained than I intended.

'Are you suggesting that I offer a bribe?'

Voychenko looked scandalised. 'A bribe? No, no, you misunderstand,' he said, raising an eyebrow. 'Nothing so crass.'

He fixed his gaze on me. 'Have you seen the condition of this temple? It may project grandeur, but it's far from pristine. The eastern facade is crumbling, cracks spreading deeper each year. The stained-glass windows in the upper chambers, magnificent though they are, have been worn down by the elements. Even the foundation is subsiding, showing signs of strain. This monument, like all valuable things, requires constant attention.'

I blinked, barely able to believe where this was heading.

'As Chief Minister, you have the power to approve grants for cultural preservation. A small sum could be allocated to the Human Order for these much-needed repairs. Of course, I would personally ensure that the funds are used as intended. Many in Congress are passionate about cultural heritage, and you might find them among your newest allies.'

I looked at my feet, considering my next words. 'I appreciate the suggestion, Supreme Leader. The preservation of the temple is indeed important, and I understand the cultural significance it holds. I will need to consider the options and ensure that any decisions align with the broader goals of my mandate.'

Voychenko's smile didn't waver. 'Of course,' he said. 'In the meantime, to help you navigate the intricate circles of Lacunfort's elite, I would like to invite you to an exclusive dinner. It will offer you the chance to meet with members of Congress and, more importantly, their most influential advisors in a particularly convivial setting.' He leaned forward. 'You must understand, however, that this event – and the identities of those attending – must remain strictly confidential. Not a word to anyone, not even your Chief of Staff. The individuals you'll meet are influential beyond their titles. They prefer to operate quietly, outside the public eye. Their acquaintance can be invaluable, but only if their participation stays unseen.'

He stood, signalling our meeting was over. 'There is one other thing,' he added, almost casually, yet with a trace of something I couldn't quite place. 'As a guest at this gathering, you may be asked to participate in a small game. It's nothing to be concerned about.' He waved his hand dismissively. 'Just a tradition; a formality really. All part of the ritual, you could say.' He paused to watch my reaction, then continued. 'It's a harmless exercise, but I would recommend that you go along with it. Show your willingness to engage. You'll find that the people you meet will appreciate your cooperation. It's best not to overthink it, Mr Moritz – just treat it as a gesture of respect to those who have been part of this for a long time.'

There had been rumours of such organisations in the capital, but as head of the government, I had assumed I was too much of an establishment figure to merit an invitation to a secret society. It seemed harmless enough, though the mention of that 'game' sparked a tingle of concern in me. Was it as innocuous as he claimed? Something told me this wasn't the moment to press further. I was restless, ready to leave, already searching my mind for an excuse to end the conversation.

'This is not to be discussed or shared. Am I clear?'

Though I bristled at being spoken to as though I were a child, a shiver coursed through me all the same. Beneath the unease, I must admit, I was curious. If these were the people who truly held sway, with the kind of influence that could make or break my mandate, wouldn't I want to meet with them? Part of me still recoiled at the idea of being drawn into this hidden world and making deals in the shadows. Even so, the thought that the Varcegian boy I once was could now move within such an exclusive circle – one operating beyond the usual bounds of power – awoke something in me.

Voychenko continued to watch me closely. 'So, Mr Moritz. Will you attend?'

Only a moment passed before I nodded. 'Yes, Supreme Leader. I will be there.'

TWO

PRIMULA

Just as the food arrived, Artur's handheld lit up with an incoming call. He answered without hesitation. Typical. He wouldn't know common courtesy if it slapped him in the face. With Artur, you could bare your bloody soul, and he wouldn't care. He'd be off in his corporate trance, too far up his own arse to listen. Or worse, he'd cut you off with one of his obnoxious alpha-male chuckles. That's how you knew he wasn't talking to you. He wasn't always so blatant about it. He used to pretend to be polite, back when I was his pet project. I'd once helped him rake in all that sodding ad revenue he worshipped. Now, though, he didn't know where to hide me – like some old trinket he was ashamed to keep but reluctant to throw away. Back then, I'd bent over backwards for him – no sleep, no breaks, starving myself thin for those hologram angles he loved. Honestly, I'd have jumped off a bridge if he'd thought it'd boost his ad numbers. Someone should have warned me that all those sacrifices would leave me bloody spent, irrelevant, and drowning in financial ruin by thirty-six.

I'd brought this near bankruptcy on myself without Artur's help, granted. I'd grown used to the reckless spending my old life afforded me, and now that things had slowed down, you'd need to add a zero to my total wealth just to cover my debts. Even if I sold everything I owned – down to the dress on my back – the bailiffs would still be breathing down my neck.

Dario's dining room used to be my territory, where people noticed me and whispered about me. Tonight, no one turned a head. Not the waiters, not the stuck-up couples at the nearby tables, not even the pair of giggly girls blocking the entrance, too busy chatting to notice – or care – that I was waiting behind them. Staying out of the public eye during my pregnancy had smothered whatever remained of my so-called career.

'Are you sure you're fine?' Artur was talking to me again.

'I am,' I answered, my fingers grazing the silver cutlery, uncertain of whether to start eating. 'Sorry, I'm not very hungry.'

He raised his eyebrows at me and swallowed. 'You know what I mean. Physically, mentally…as a woman. Are you recovered?'

I sighed. 'As a woman, Artur, I'm fine.'

But I wasn't, and hadn't been for a long time.

It wasn't his place to ask; not really. My wellbeing was none of his business. He was only meant to reintroduce me to all the pageants, give me that push I needed to make people notice me again. Instead, his question felt invasive, empty. He could have shown a hint of compassion. I'd have appreciated even the smallest gesture. 'I'm sorry this happened to you,' he might have said. But no one had expressed any sympathy. Not

Dr Greenville, not the midwife, not even the mortuary nurse. Pathetic, maybe, but with everything ripped away, all I wanted was for someone to bloody well care for once.

If no one else cared, if everyone was just doing their jobs, then it was left to me to bear the weight of it alone. And it had been too much. Pain in *all* its gleaming colours. From the moment I experienced that ring of fire on that hospital bed and I grasped how brutally accurate the name was. The burn only sharpened after it started, my body straining past limits I hadn't known existed. I screamed, desperate, cursing my decision to forego the anaesthetic. Even now, I could hear Dr Greenville's voice: 'If you're against surgery, we strongly recommend an epidural block.'

'I want to feel it,' I'd insisted.

The midwife, flushed and sweating, leaned over me. 'Stop pushing or you'll tear. Let your body take over.'

Two contractions later, my baby slipped out – a silent, lifeless girl. We already knew. She'd died a week before.

Time passed slowly in a daze as I questioned what could have gone wrong. But it didn't matter. If it did, it was only in the hope that finding a cause would somehow absolve me – make me a victim rather than a culprit.

The midwife clipped the cord, then removed the placenta. 'Do you want to see her?'

'Yes.' My voice sounded small and foreign.

She placed the tiny body next to me, her skin too pale, too fair. It ruled out the men I'd suspected, though it didn't matter. Nothing would change. I pictured, with a hollow ache, how things might have been different. I wasn't sure I'd have made a halfway decent mother, but I would have tried. I would have given it a bloody good shot. Instead, with nothing left to hold on to, I clung to the one thing I always knew how to do: asking someone else to look after me.

'Still getting nightmares?' Artur took another bite. 'Headaches and all?'

I nodded. 'I had a dream last night. Your father was in it.'

'My father?' His eyes widened, but I could tell he was feigning interest.

'Yeah, just standing there,' I muttered. 'I realised I wasn't wearing clothes, then woke up gasping like I'd been running.'

He chuckled. 'Not much of a nightmare though, is it?'

I narrowed my eyes. 'It was bloody terrifying for me. But, yeah, they do get much worse.'

He scraped his fork along his plate, eyes on me. 'It's all the stuff you put in your body. You know that, right? And you're fretting over not looking as radiant as you used to. Well, this lifestyle isn't going to help.'

My toes curled inside my shoes. I took a breath.

'Anyway…' My words tumbled out, surprising even me. 'Been meaning to ask. Is there anything out there for me?'

'Market's slow for your type. Everyone's after a fresher look… You know how it is.'

'Give me a few weeks. I'll be fit again. I just pushed out a kid, for fuck's sake.'

'I know, I know. You're resilient, no doubt. But long-term, maybe it's time we find an agent better suited to your style. Someone with the right connections.'

'Artur,' I said, a coldness spreading in my chest, 'you can't leave me. Not now.'

'Relax. I'm not ditching you. But I'm running the whole show now, and fashion's just one piece of it.'

'So you won't be representing any models yourself any more?'

He pulled a face, hesitating.

I bit back a grunt. 'This is unbelievable.'

'Come on, Primula.'

I leaned in, eyes locked on his. 'If you leave me now…no agent worth a damn will touch me. Don't act like you don't know what that means for me. You *can't* do this.'

He shifted uncomfortably, glancing around. 'I'm not leaving you, alright? Just saying, high-end clients are looking for new faces. But, listen, there is something. It's not the usual sort, but it's something.'

'What is it?'

'You heard of Skitto?'

I grimaced. 'You think I'm *that* desperate?'

He gave me a pointed look. 'They're rebranding, aiming higher, and they thought of you.'

'So that's it? From exclusive queen to a fast-fashion poster girl?'

'They want a fresh image and are ready to splash out for it. They've also got specific ideas about what they're after – think pink hair, ripped clothes. Edgy, urban.'

My hands went to my temples.

'And there's one other thing,' Artur added with a slight wince. 'They want…boobs.'

'They want *boobs*?'

'Don't we all?' He laughed at his own joke. 'No, but seriously, they want it all real. For live events, that sort of thing. It's so easy to have it done now, though. You're in and out in no time.'

I slammed my hands onto the table, almost knocking over my wine glass.

'I'm not some assembly-line doll they can just tack shit onto.'

As I spoke, a young couple started heading our way. A shred

of the old Primula lit up, imagining they might want their hologram taken with me. But as they stopped at our table, they bobbed their heads politely and addressed Artur instead.

'So sorry to interrupt. We just wanted to say hello,' the woman said, hands clasped.

I gave a polite smile, but they weren't looking at me.

'We're such admirers of your father's work,' she continued.

Artur's face glowed. 'Thank you. That's very kind.'

Her partner leaned in. 'He's done so much to bring real scientific rigour to our society. We're truly grateful for his leadership at the Human Order.'

'I'll pass that on to him,' Artur said, beaming.

As they left, the emptiness in my chest grew unbearable. I excused myself, fleeing to the bathroom. In my purse, I found two pills and swallowed them with a handful of tap water. By the time I returned, the city lights of Platform 10 outside the window gleamed brighter, a soft warmth brushing against my skin.

'Pink hair,' I muttered to Artur. 'Like some shitty carnival sideshow.'

He shrugged. 'It'd suit you.'

I pictured the hair, a delicate candyfloss colour, but Artur's impatient hand waved in front of me.

'Are you still with me?'

'Of course.'

'Good. I asked if you were up for a little adventure after dinner.'

I shot him a sly look. If I were honest, part of me had hoped he'd ask.

'The Dungeons?'

'Only if you're up to it.'

'I haven't been in ages.'

'It's all the same – nothing's changed.'

'Will you look after me?'

'When haven't I?'

Artur had been right: not much had changed at The Dungeons. Fresh tulips decorated the main desk in reception, and enormous, engineered orchids hung along the walls, each petal the size of a hand. There was the usual dim lighting, the faint sound of a saxophone, and the scent of oak firewood and pine. Walking in was like coming home.

'Prim! Good evening,' Fluvio called from behind the desk, beaming as he saw me. 'Just when I thought you'd gone all pure and virtuous, here you are, back like a salmon ready to spawn.'

'Can't a girl wear silver without being compared to a fish?' I ran my hands down my sides, showing off the glint of my dress. 'True enough, though. You know me – I'm always up for a bit of debauchery.' I rolled my eyes, and we both broke into laughter.

Artur had hung back a few metres, wandering in a circle, hands gesturing wildly as he took yet another call.

'I think you'll want the red chamber up the stairs,' Fluvio said.

I glanced back, trying to catch Artur's eye. He barely looked at me, just waved a hand to signal that I should go on. By now, the pills had kicked in, making me bold and electric. A raw energy ran under my skin, hungry for touch. Fluvio handed me a drink with a veil of rose-coloured mist rising from the surface.

'I know you like it strong,' he said with a wink.

I downed half the glass before I'd even reached the top

of the stairs. A door slid open at the landing, leading into a cosy room with a large square bed, a sofa, and a floating table. One wall, entirely glass, looked out onto a secluded garden where a cloud of fireflies circled above a bed of ferns. Every wall and every piece of furniture in the room was a deep red, the shades of crimson closest to the window fading to dark cherry in the shadows. No other lighting was provided.

A middle-aged man was already seated on the sofa, almost blending in with the furniture. He sat, ankles crossed, hunched forward. His mostly bald head had a darker strip of freshly shaved skin along the sides, his ears stretched slightly with age. His thick fingers were interlaced between his knees, and his face held an unexpected charm as he lifted his head to get a better look at me. Slurring his words, he introduced himself as Chuck. Of course, we both knew that wasn't his real name. Anonymity was part of the appeal here. But of all names, he'd chosen Chuck.

Before long, I had my face buried between Chuck's legs, his trousers bunched under my knees.

'Chuck smells like plums and cinnamon under his rags,' I murmured to no one.

Not long after, we tangled together, limbs knotted, gasping, our bodies a mess of heat and movement. The drink had loosened me, leaving me in that blissful, gliding state I craved. The lines on the walls began to curve, the red grew richer, and the fireflies seemed to multiply, scribbling neon trails through the dark garden. My skin became hypersensitive, every touch thrilling, my hair prickling like that of an agitated cat.

I wasn't sure how long we'd been at it when suddenly Chuck stilled and his body went slack beneath me. I straddled his fleshy thighs, leaning on his chest, but something made me sit up. Two figures silhouetted near the doorway were watching us.

Chuck scrambled to pull his clothes on, a frantic look in his eyes. I blinked, my vision slowly sharpening, and there was Artur, standing in plain sight instead of hiding behind the fake mirror, as he usually preferred, along with another man, unmistakably his father, Supreme Leader Igor Voychenko.

Chuck bolted past them, clutching the rest of his clothes.

'Have a good evening,' Artur said to him, smirking as Chuck rushed out of the room.

The sight was surreal. It was like I was observing some alternate version of myself from afar. I stared at the two men, the horror sinking in as I realised I was stark naked, exposed in front of the Supreme Leader. The adrenaline jolted me back to reality, and I hurried to gather my scattered clothes.

'Please.' Voychenko's voice was low but warm. 'There's no need to feel embarrassed.'

I managed to pull my clothes back on within seconds.

'Have a seat,' Voychenko said, gesturing to the sofa. 'I hope you don't mind that Artur invited me this evening.'

I turned to Artur. 'I…I do mind. Of course I bloody mind. Are you insane? Why didn't you tell me?'

'He only wants to help,' Artur replied. 'You need to relax.'

My head was spinning, and I wished I could shake off the drug's effects, just to think straight.

'She had a dream last night,' Artur said, amused, turning to his father. 'She dreamt she met you for the first time, and she was naked.'

'Is that right?' Voychenko said, a strange, satisfied expression spreading across his face. 'What a coincidence.' Then, looking at me, he asked, 'Miss Zhang, do you believe in coincidences?'

Hearing my name from his lips caught me off guard. 'Well,

I suppose I do now,' I replied, still flustered.

'I must admit…I do not,' he said, pausing. 'You see, the world is filled with connections between people and events. Nothing is left to chance. But these moments can still surprise us, reminding us how small the world really is.'

I didn't respond, trying to smooth my hair with my fingers, increasingly self-conscious of how I must look to him.

'And on that note,' he continued, 'I understand you know Dr Greenville, who happens to be a close acquaintance of mine. The world shrinks more every day, doesn't it? She wouldn't violate confidentiality, of course, but I did become aware of your recent loss. I'm deeply sorry for the passing of your child. You've been through more than anyone should have to endure.'

Of all people, it was the Supreme Leader who showed me the first hint of sympathy. Maybe it was the effects of the drug, but tears pricked at my eyes.

'Thank you,' I mumbled, my voice breaking.

'And the dreams,' he continued, 'I suspect they're all linked.'

'Linked? How?' I asked.

'I understand you underwent neuronal enhancements as a child. Is that right?' Voychenko asked.

'She didn't complete them, I don't think,' Artur said.

Normally, I kept this to myself, especially given some people's views on ultrahuman enhancements. But I wasn't about to lie to Igor Voychenko.

'That's right,' I said. 'I didn't finish.'

'If I may ask,' Voychenko went on. 'Why exactly not?'

'My doctor…was from Glossden.'

'From Glossden… I see.' He paused, as though turning the thought over in his mind. 'And that was in Lacunfort – correct? How many years ago?'

'Over twenty now.'

He tilted his head, contemplating. 'Was your doctor a victim of the year 480 attacks?'

'We could only assume,' I said quietly.

'And the nightmares…since then?'

I nodded.

He hummed in acknowledgment, his face thoughtful.

'We're getting Primula a new contract,' Artur chimed in, all pumped up like an idiot. 'She'll be the new face of Skitto. She'll be everywhere.' He gestured widely, as if presenting my future.

'Is that so?' Voychenko asked kindly.

'I haven't decided yet,' I said.

How was I even discussing this – in The Dungeons – with Igor Voychenko of all people?

'And what holds you back, if I may ask?'

'It…doesn't feel like me,' I admitted, uncertain even as I said it.

'There isn't always one version of ourselves,' he replied. 'Sometimes we find a side we never knew existed.'

'That's right,' Artur agreed, squeezing my shoulder. 'This will give you the visibility you need. And life's all about connections, isn't it, Father?'

'No one, however capable, stands entirely alone,' Voychenko said, turning back to me. 'Even the strongest are bound to others. And in Lacunfort, connections can make all the difference. Speaking of which,' he continued, 'I'd like to invite you to an exclusive dinner. As Skitto's new face, you'll mingle with prominent figures in all fields. It will be useful.'

'Thank you,' I said quickly, afraid he'd reconsider. I needed all the help I could get to claw my way out of this hole. 'It would be an honour.'

'There is only one condition,' he added. 'Complete confidentiality. Our guests value their privacy. I trust you, of all people, would appreciate that.'

Hearing such an invitation from the Supreme Leader himself was surreal. Could this be one of those secret societies people whispered about?

'Of course.' I'd experienced enough intrusions in my days of fame to know the importance of discretion.

'And as a guest, you'll participate in a small game,' Voychenko said.

'A game?'

'Nothing strenuous,' he replied with a polite laugh. 'More of a tradition. It's a ritual we maintain, mostly to show respect. Winning might even earn you a permanent seat. Fear not,' he added. 'I'll personally look out for you.'

Artur beamed at me, practically vibrating with excitement. 'What do you say?'

'Yes, of course. I'd be delighted,' I replied. 'Please count me in.'

THREE

SAM

THE NURSE BOT SWUNG THE DOOR open for me to step in. Mum lay in bed, a thin frame swallowed up by a satin cream quilt, her eyes blinking, a bit dazed. She squinted, as if she'd taken a second too long to work out where I stood.

'Hi, Mum,' I said, louder than I'd intended. I cringed; the walls were paper-thin. I cleared my throat, lowered my voice. 'Nice room, this, yeah? Loads of space.'

I checked the furniture. Even the lamp looked like an upgrade. 'Got your own sofa, look. And a proper desk with a fitted lamp. See that wall there? Just begging for some art, don't you think? And that window—' I hesitated, hoping it looked real enough to her. 'What a view. Fields full of flowers already.'

I'd tried to sound cheerful. Probably overdid it. She'd moved rooms three times in the last five months; I sensed the staff were getting fed up with her. This one cost more, and I'd already maxed out what my work benefits covered. No big deal, really. Just meant I'd tighten up on other stuff. Worth it if it kept her comfortable.

'Yes, yes. That's my favourite thing here,' she said, smiling faintly. 'Hard to find a room with a view these days. They're all snapped up.'

I grinned, relieved I'd got that bit right.

She shifted, stiffly, trying to sit up. I crossed the room in a couple of strides and offered her a hand. When she settled against the headboard, she narrowed her eyes and pointed a finger at the wall. 'Mary, next door. She got on at me yesterday. Said that wasn't a real window, that it's just a screen. Imagine that! Said they set these things up to look like the outside world. I told her, "Just look; that's no screen." But she kept on. Dared me to open it, to prove her point.' She scoffed. 'I told her no, didn't fancy breaking the rules just to humour her nonsense. And then, would you believe it, she laughed at me. All condescending, like I was a fool. So I said to her, "Well, Mary, my degeneration's 'moderate'; yours is 'well advanced'. Whose judgement are we trusting, then?" She didn't look too pleased, but I was fuming. Nurse bot came, and Mary stomped off in her cheap slippers, like she does.'

'Seen her since then?'

'Oh, she came in this morning. We both apologised, didn't we? But she still won't admit that's a real window. Jealous, she is. Kept talking about her kids, like they're something special – big shots and whatnot. I told her you've done alright yourself. You're working for the government, looking at them numbers. Made it right to the top.' She folded her arms and lifted her chin.

I bit my tongue. 'Well, I'm only a resource analyst, Mum.'

'What? Still? After all this time?' Her brows raised, just

enough.

'But,' I said quickly, 'I'm up for a promotion. Pretty much a done deal.'

'What'll they call you, then?'

'A senior analyst,' I said, feeling a little pride slip through. 'Only fifty of them in the whole Agency.'

She chuckled, coughing lightly. 'Only fifty,' she muttered. 'All that work, your father and me, all that money to get you to university. Wasn't cheap – I'll tell you that.' She sighed. 'It is what it is. Just doesn't look like we'll be raising any glasses in your honour at this rate. How old are you now? You thirty yet?'

'Turned thirty-five.'

'See what I mean?' She shrugged. 'You've done alright and stayed out of trouble. That's all that matters, I suppose.'

Then she frowned, as if something had just slipped her mind. 'Oh, meant to tell you – Samantha rang this morning. She's all about those modifications now; always going on about it. Kids these days don't ask what you think. You try to raise them to be little reflections of yourself, and they go off on their own path. But she's a good girl, that one.'

I just nodded, swallowing the words I wanted to say.

'You heard from her?' she asked.

I shook my head.

'Well, if you do, tell her to come by, will you?'

'She…' I began, but stopped myself. 'I will, Mum.'

After a quiet moment, I asked, 'And you? Doctor Khan says you're doing those…cognitive sessions. Been going?'

She looked away. 'Not talking about that.' Her tone was firm, but then she looked back. 'Samantha, though. Have you seen her? She's not been by.'

I exhaled just as the human nurse appeared in the doorway, her figure framed by the light behind her. We exchanged smiles.

'She's the human nurse,' Mum said, glancing at me proudly, pleased to show me she'd recognised her.

'I know, Mum. I've met her.' I softened my voice. 'Listen, I've got to head off to work soon. Want the news on?'

'Go on, then,' she said, settling herself, hands clasped over her stomach.

The hologram lit up, showing the Supreme Leader at a ceremony, welcoming the new Chief Minister from Varcega – some Gren Moritz. It was all banners and spectacle. I wasn't overly keen, to be honest, and I definitely hadn't voted for him. But Mum raved about the man.

'That's history, that is,' Mum said. 'A good man, Moritz. About time people woke up and started electing someone who wants to look after us proper humans, instead of giving everyone superpowers.'

The image changed to a red-haired woman called Fredrica Voychenko, a Civil Force Officer working on prison reform.

'That's the Supreme Leader's daughter, isn't it?' the nurse asked, refilling Mum's medications. 'Good they're finally focusing on prison reform. Maybe help people change instead of just locking them up.'

'They need to make them stop committing them crimes first,' Mum said, jabbing a finger at the hologram. 'Those Voychenkos are everywhere… Every spot of power.'

'The Leader's wife is actually my boss,' I said.

'Is she?'

'Well, everyone's boss, actually.'

'See what I mean?' Mum muttered.

'Her name's Galina,' I rushed to say, hoping to add credibility to my comment.

'Ever spoken to her?' the nurse asked.

'Not directly,' I admitted. 'But my supervisor talks to her, like…all the time.'

The nurse looked impressed.

'And I saw her once,' I added. 'Not up close, but yeah, it was definitely her.'

'Queen's looking old now,' Mum said, her attention fixed on the hologram again. The image had shifted to show Queen Brynhilda visiting prisoners, standing beside Fredrica Voychenko.

'They say she may choose to go soon,' the nurse said, but Mum had already started to doze off. It took only a few seconds for her to fall asleep.

I noticed the time and quickly leaned towards the nurse. 'How's she been?'

She lowered her voice. 'It's up and down, you know. I've got to say, though, your mum's strong. Won't touch gene treatments. Says she'll manage it old school, face it as it comes. But best you talk with Dr Khan.'

'Seeing him tomorrow.'

'Good,' she replied. But there was something in her look. 'I probably shouldn't say,' she added.

'Is anything wrong?'

'No, nothing like that. It's just… If I can trust your discretion…'

'Of course.'

'In strictest confidence,' she said. 'You know how it is. Please don't mention this to Dr Khan. But if your mother ever decides to opt for enhancements, to help with her condition, I may be able to...'

'She's dead against it.'

'I know, I know. Just wanted you to know that there is always that option.'

I thanked her politely, but a certain discomfort clung to

me as I left. Was it really that easy? Ultrahumanist treatments were on the rise, even though they were illegal, but I'd never seen the practice up close. A qualified nurse, casually offering black market enhancements to a patient who'd already refused? Madness.

The moment I entered Silas's office that morning, I sensed the news wasn't good. He started rambling about the sky-screens, going on about how absurd it was for them to choose grey skies when we lived in a climate-controlled city. I nodded along, biting back the fact that he'd said the same thing a dozen times before. He rocked in his chair, his plump little form reminding me of a garden gnome.

'Anyway, look,' he finally said. 'Update on the promotion. It's been competitive this round. Very tough decision, Sam, but we feel it's best you keep developing in your current role. Gives you a stable space to work on communication, assertiveness – all those development areas we've talked about.'

I swallowed, my mouth dry. *My assertiveness…* 'I thought…' I struggled to keep my voice from shaking. 'I thought I had a good chance this time. You said…and…I've been putting in all those all-nighters on the analytics.'

'You did. No question. Like I said – hard decision.' He flicked his wrist to check the time.

My mind went blank, the realisation sinking in that I could keep on at this for another decade and never get anywhere.

'Wanted to tell you before the new chart's announced,' Silas added with an air of benevolence. 'So you'd hear it from me.'

'Of course.' I bit my lip.

'Do you have any questions?'

'No. Thanks.' I was up and halfway to the door when a spark

of courage pulled me back. 'Actually, Silas, if I could ask…'

He looked up, already busy with something else, his face a mask of impatience. 'Sure.'

'Do you have any more feedback for me? I mean… What could I have done differently? How do I secure the promotion next time?'

He seemed caught out but managed a quick recovery. 'Look, you're doing great. Really. Maybe go the extra mile… Show leadership. Be the first to pitch in… Go above and beyond… Sell your work. And leverage the tools available to you. That's it. Does that make sense?'

'Yes, yes. Thank you, Silas,' I said, turning for the door. Just as I reached for the handle, I paused, swallowing back the tightness in my throat.

'Do you…want me to leave the door open? Or…should I shut it?'

Silas didn't respond, already absorbed in whatever document he'd picked up. I lingered for a second or two, my words having fallen flat in the silence. I took a steady breath and slipped out, quietly closing the door behind me as I went.

I spent the rest of the day working flat out to meet my usual deadlines, trying to ignore the conversation I'd had with Silas. As I updated the resource utilisation metrics, my mind spun with ways to show him I was going his so-called 'extra mile'. I threw together a quick algorithm to sum up resource utilisation across all platforms in Lacunfort, complete with per capita numbers and predictions on future needs. This was my field. I knew what I was doing, and there wasn't a soul in the department who could have come up with anything like it. Even if they got the promotions with all that polished talk and confidence, nobody touched me on the technical side.

But something was off. Across Lacunfort, most of the

platforms looked alright. The exception was Platform Zero, where the per capita numbers showed a steep spike near the Human Order temple. As far as I knew, nobody lived around there. I checked energy, water and waste separately, but the odd data held up. Couldn't make sense of it. Time slipped by without me noticing, and it was well into the evening before I realised I was still at my desk when Silas passed by on his way out.

'Time to go home, Samuel,' he called out.

'Yeah,' I replied. 'Just working on the resource metrics.'

He walked over and squinted at my screens. 'How's it looking?'

I explained the model, and right away, I could tell he didn't understand how I'd used factor analysis to simplify the data sets. Had to go over spatial interpolation basics for him. But when I got to the error around the temple, he froze.

'Who else has seen this?' Silas's gaze darted around the office. He pressed his lips together, fingers tapping a quick, uneven rhythm on the edge of my desk.

'No one,' I replied. 'It's just a model I built today. This bit's obviously wrong. I just need a little more time to work out why. Don't worry, I'll get there with another hour or two.'

'No,' he said, before slipping back into his usual, overly confident self. 'Just head home now. No need to stay up all night on it. Send me the work as-is, and we'll review it together tomorrow. Keep this one to yourself.'

'I don't mind,' I said. 'I'll fix it. I can do it tonight.'

'Send it to me and shut down, Samuel.' His tone turned firm.

'Yeah, no, you're right,' I said. 'I'll send it now and pack up.'

•••

Doctor Khan's office was just shy of cluttered. Stacks of books and magazines sat on every surface, with even bigger piles around the desk, leaving only a small, clear space in the middle. Instead of the usual display screen, the desk's surface held a scattering of handwritten notes, done in real ink. The air was musty, damp, reminding me of clothes left in storage for too long. The wall screens didn't glow like normal; they were matte, almost cardboard-like. One of them showed a list of names, and about halfway down, I found Mum's – Olivia Rosendale – with an odd line of symbols next to it that meant nothing to me.

I took the seat opposite Doctor Khan, who settled into his chair behind the desk. The leather gave a gentle squeak under his solid frame, and the ceiling lights glinted off his bald head as he leaned towards me.

'Doctor, hope you don't mind me asking… Are you a human physician?' I stumbled over myself almost immediately. 'It's just hard to tell these days.' Heat crept up my neck. 'You know what? Actually, forget I asked.'

Doctor Khan didn't flinch. 'I am, Mr Rosendale, and there is no need to apologise. Bots are taking over the medical field.' He paused. 'I'm not much for handing medical decisions over to bots, myself. You'll have seen nurse bots at this sanatorium – mostly for cost reasons – but they're limited to admin and menial tasks. I'm sure you know some of this, working in your field, but bots are easy to hack – a real safety hazard. Surprised me, honestly, when I read that the entire team attending to the queen is all bots now.' He shook his head in disapproval.

I was still searching for a response when he continued.

'Anyway, sorry. I know you're pressed for time and need to

get to work,' he said. 'We've tried various treatments – occupational therapy, cognitive behavioural therapy, approved and experimental medications to boost the messengers in memory and judgement. None of them has slowed your mother's decline.'

I took in his words, trying to think quickly. 'Any other treatments we could try? Maybe something with gene therapy?'

Doctor Khan's hands lifted slightly, and he grimaced. 'I probably wouldn't recommend that.'

'Of course, within what's allowed by law,' I added uncertainly.

He met my eyes. 'Our institution has a reputation, Mr Rosendale. It took years to build, and we wouldn't consider anything outside the legal requirements.'

I nodded, conceding. 'And my mother's completely opposed to the idea too.'

'Truthfully,' he continued, 'if you wanted gene therapy, we could probably apply for a legal concession based on her age. With proof that she's past her reproductive years, there's a small chance. The field's moving fast, especially under the new government. We could arrange it if it came to it, but legalities aside, I'd still advise against gene therapy in her case. The risks are too unpredictable. We can't be certain we'd do more good than harm.'

I forced myself to breathe steadily, using the calming technique I'd picked up. 'I understand. What are our options, then?'

Doctor Khan looked away, rubbing his jawline. I could hear the scrape of stubble.

'Your mother's firm on The Right to Die,' he said. 'She won't consider euthanasia.'

'Of course not,' I replied, flustered. 'She's not even eighty.'

'True, but her decline's faster than usual. Within a few months, we're likely to see worsening behaviour, physical issues, severe memory loss, even an inability to communicate.' He stopped, as though weighing his words. 'As of today, she's still of sound mind, but that won't last. She can record her wishes while she's capable. That way, she'll have control over what happens when the time comes.'

I shook my head. 'She won't.'

'In that case, once her judgement's compromised, the decision falls to her next of kin. Do you have siblings, Mr Rosendale?'

I shook my head again.

'Then it would be your responsibility.'

'How's that fair? How can it be my choice?'

'The Right to Die Act is specific about who decides for children, the elderly and the mentally unfit. We'd follow the law, as always.'

'And what if I refuse?'

'Refuse how?'

'Refuse to decide.'

'Then nothing would change. It's hard to predict how long someone with this type of late-stage degeneration might live. We have ways to extend life, sometimes for years, though in severe cases, most would consider euthanasia humane. Late-stage patients lose consciousness frequently, become agitated, restless. Many suffer seizures.'

I leaned an elbow on the desk, resting my forehead on my hand, trying again to control my breathing.

'I'm sorry, Mr Rosendale.' Doctor Khan's voice turned gentler. 'Nothing needs to be decided today. I suggest you have a conversation with your mother. See what she has to say. You may find some clarity.'

I sat back, fogged by everything he'd said, my eyes beginning to sting. 'Thank you, Doctor,' I managed. 'I'll speak to her.'

•••

I was late for work, and the first person I ran into was Silas. My pulse quickened; I knew how much he valued punctuality.

'There he is,' he said, grinning and pointing at me. 'How are you today, Samuel?'

'Yeah, good. Sorry I'm late. Had to go to the sanatorium to speak to my mum's doctor—'

'Don't worry,' he interrupted, waving it off. 'Listen, I looked over your analysis. It's good work. We need a sit-down. Can we meet in fifteen?'

'Sure, I'll come by your office.'

'No. Meeting room, upstairs.' He pointed upward. 'See you there.'

In all my years here, I'd never been invited upstairs. Right away, I was conscious of the flimsiness of my loose overshirt, wishing I'd dressed up a bit more.

I made it there on the dot, but as soon as I walked in, my stomach muscles clenched: Galina Voychenko sat next to Silas.

She stood to greet me, commanding the room. She said my name and shook my hand. My nerves flared, but beneath the jitters, I couldn't help picturing Mum's face when she learned I'd actually met Galina Voychenko.

We sat down.

'Silas shared some highlights from your analysis yesterday,' Galina said.

She was smaller than I'd pictured, but her presence made up for her low stature. Her dark red hair, cut just past her chin, was styled back neatly. Her face was angular, lined around her mouth and eyes – the look of someone who'd made hard calls for years without blinking. She wore a dark navy blazer with crisp lapels over a white blouse, a small, silver Agency insignia pinned neatly at the chest. It was nothing flashy, but her outfit made it clear she was in charge.

I mumbled something polite, feeling inadequate in my casual clothes.

'It's clear you've got some unique abilities. Your work shows not only an unusual mastery of mathematical analysis, but also a particularly refined skill in programming,' she said. Silas remained quiet at her side. 'Did you put this together by yourself?'

'Yes, Mrs Voychenko.'

She inclined her head slightly. 'For decades, I have worked with data analysts and statisticians, and I have to say – I've never seen anything quite like this. You've bypassed barriers in our network security to gather your data. Don't think I didn't notice. But given your prowess, I'm willing to overlook it.'

Heat rushed to my face. She was right – I had taken certain liberties to access parts of the network that were off-limits. The praise should have been gratifying, but all I could focus on was the fact that she'd caught me. I risked a glance at Silas, but he remained impassive.

'And have you shown this analysis to anyone apart from Silas?' Galina asked.

'No. He told me not to.'

She studied me for several seconds. Then she asked a series of specific questions, probing every detail of my methods. Her mind was razor-sharp. She asked how I'd selected factors to capture the most crucial points of resource utilisation. As I explained, my nerves began to ease; this was my territory, something I could own. I grew more confident with each answer. When we got to spatial interpolation, she raised a brow at my estimate for less populated areas.

'The high per capita numbers around the Human Order

temple – can those be right?' she asked.

I stumbled, saying it was an error, clearly wrong, and that I'd keep working on it.

'No need, Mr Rosendale,' she replied. 'We'll take it from here. In fact, we're moving you from resource utilisation altogether. We've decided to offer you a senior analyst role – in census. A good fit for someone with your analytical skills.'

I was stunned. While being a senior analyst was technically a promotion, everyone knew the census department was a dead end. Resource utilisation was where all the bright minds thrived.

'In line with data protection, we'll need you to turn in all your current work, and your system access will be reassigned.'

My mind raced. Silas and Galina's reactions weren't sitting right. A small part of me wanted to keep going, see what else I might find.

'One more thing,' Galina added. 'Given your contributions to the Agency and the extent of your capabilities, I'd like to invite you to an exclusive dinner. Our way to thank you for your hard work over the years.'

'Thank you,' I said, finding my voice. 'I'm honoured, Mrs Voychenko.'

'We ask that you keep this confidential,' she said. 'You'll have a chance to build some useful connections, especially now that you're a senior member of our team. Isn't that right, Silas?'

Silas gave her an eager affirmation.

'The attendees prefer privacy; it creates a safe space for them,' she added.

'Of course,' I said, though the idea of a large, private gathering left me anxious. Why such secrecy? She hadn't explained who'd be there, and it felt wrong to ask.

'We have a tradition at this dinner. A game,' she said, a hint of play on her lips. 'Nothing complex. Your mathematical skills might even give you an edge.' She paused. 'My advice for you is to cooperate and enjoy it.'

Still puzzled, I attempted a smile.

'When do you need my response?' I managed to ask.

She raised a brow. 'I'll have someone reach out with the details.'

'No, sorry,' I stammered. 'I meant on the role in census.'

She gave me a cool look. Silas tensed beside her.

'I see,' she said. 'Do you have any concerns?'

'No, it's just a big change. I'm grateful, truly. I'd just like to think it over, career-wise, before I give an answer.'

'Of course,' Galina replied, turning even colder. She glanced at Silas.

'Tomorrow,' Silas jumped in. 'We'll need your answer by end of day tomorrow.'

FOUR

LORELEI

My sweet, plant-loving, technophobe sister,

First off, please forgive me for not writing sooner. You can imagine how wild everything's been these last few weeks. I wish I could just sit down and tell you all this face-to-face, but since I can't manage to poke a hole through that anti-tech curtain of yours, I'll do my best here. I promise, as soon as life slows down a bit, I'll come visit you in Varcega for a proper few days – not just a weekend. I can hardly wait to see you, and I hope everything in the orchard is going well, especially now that the busy pruning season is starting!

Would you believe it's been exactly twenty-nine days since I became First Lady of Rivennia? I'm not sure I'll ever get used to the idea. Some days are such a mad rush that I don't even have time to think; I just go along with whatever's next. But whenever I do get a moment to breathe and think about everything, it's like a tiny jolt of panic rises up in me. Don't get me wrong – it's not all terrible, but it's definitely not all good either. It's just…a lot. A lot of everything, all at once. I feel like every little thing I do, or don't do, is being watched. I am still adjusting, but I pray that, with time, it will become more bearable.

Right after Gren won the election, the night before the inauguration, I joined him for this big interview. The interviewer, Greta, was actually very nice, asking me about how it felt to be in Lacunfort, coming from Varcega, and that kind of thing. I tried so hard to be proper and calm, and I thought I'd done well. But oh, was I wrong! Gren warned me not to read the news the next day, but I couldn't resist. The headlines were awful: 'Protocol Blunder by the New First Lady… The Kisses of Inexperience…' Mortifying, I tell you.

Apparently, there's a 'right' way to act at these events, and that is quite serious and official. But honestly, it was a talk show! People sat on a sofa and spoke. That was it. It wasn't like I was putting anyone's life at risk or anything – although that's what it felt like, judging by some of the reactions. Anyway, I rewatched the video (many times, I'll admit), and I did look a bit silly and over-eager. Lesson learned.

The coach they got me said I should always emphasise my belief in the fight against ultrahumanism, so I did. One of the few things I got right. They keep drilling it into me: condemn genetic edits. I understand how important this is to Gren's political agenda…but has anyone stopped to ask what I actually believe? I wish people around here would stop trying to teach me how to think.

Gren, by the way, has been nicer than we both thought he'd be, even though sometimes he's understandably stressed. You should hear him talk, though; he sounds nothing like a Varcegian any more. Most politicians try to sound like they're from Lacunfort, regardless of their origin, and I can understand why. I swear the moment I open my mouth here, I see heads turning in my direction, and I think to myself, 'Yes, people, it's called an accent. This is how I speak, and I'm proud of it.'

Gren comes by my room almost every night since we're trying to have a baby (my God, I'm blushing just writing that). I wasn't sure what to expect, but he's been gentle.

Perhaps one of the reasons I find this all so overwhelming is just how different Lacunfort is from everything we know. Gren used to come here a lot, so he knows his way around, but for me, it's like a whole new planet. The city is massive. You look up, and it's just wall after wall of buildings that seem to stretch up forever. They connect with bridges and passages, and there's something called a 'sky-screen' – a pretend sky, really, that's just a ceiling with clouds projected on it. It looks totally real, but of course, it isn't. And on top of every sky-screen is another layer of the city, stacked up like a pile of pancakes! There are 163 of these layers, if you can believe that. Yesterday, I was in Corin; I looked out across the horizon, and Lacunfort was just standing there like a giant tower. A tower of cities.

And the pneuducts – they're like little pipes that run everywhere, carrying people and goods around. They remind me of Mum's wisterias growing on the old garden wall, all twisted and tangled up. Honestly, I think you'd hate it here; it's so different from Varcega. But I still wish I could get you to visit. I'd protect you from all the strange technology, I swear. I'm figuring it out myself; half of it still makes no sense to me.

Life moves in such mysterious ways, but I like to believe that within all the chaos, there are moments of beauty. Maybe that's what we're here for – to gather as many of those as we can before they slip through our fingers.

Greta, the talk show host, asked me something that has stayed on my mind. She wanted to know if I had decided what I would focus on as First Lady. I wish God would guide me more clearly towards my purpose. I believe everyone has a calling – you've certainly found yours at the orchard – and I hope mine reveals itself soon. I know God hasn't forgotten me. I'm sure He will show me the way in His time.

For now, I must return to my duties. It seems every charity in the world is expecting a visit, and Gren believes it's wise for me to experience everything before I decide where to focus my work. No decisions yet – that much is certain.

Please write back soon and let me know how things are going with the orchard. I promise I'll write more often, too.

With all my love,

Lorelei

FIVE

GREN

SITTING ALONE IN MY OFFICE that evening, the strain of the day pressed down on me. It had been brutal in too many ways. Clara and I had recently started a daily recap, a ritual where, every evening, we'd review briefings, time-sensitive matters, and the following day's schedule. Often, we'd end up talking more freely, sharing lighter thoughts, or unwinding after hours of policy debates and meetings. As I waited for her, I removed my jacket, rolled up my sleeves, and kicked off my shoes.

My morning routine wasn't exactly set in stone, and it was rare to see Lorelei before we both headed out for the day. But that morning, we'd had breakfast together on the terrace at the Chief Minister's residence. The air was warm, infused with the scent of lavender from the nearby garden. Over coffee, fresh fruit and Corinnian pastries, we sat beneath the olive tree, its branches filtering the sky-screen light in a dappled pattern across our table.

The conversation began on a positive note. Confirming the pregnancy had been a happy moment for both of us. We shared a quiet joy at the thought of becoming parents and discussed names, weighing both Varcegian and Lacunfort traditions. But when Lorelei brought up her recent doctor's visit, she asked if we should consider in-utero treatments. She spoke easily about options to enhance neuronal capacity or reduce future health risks. Her suggestion left me speechless. I could only stare while a furious tightness gripped my chest.

I knew Lorelei was still adjusting to many aspects of my world, politically and otherwise, but I thought she understood, at least, the importance of eradicating ultrahumanism. To hear her raise this so casually, as though it were legal and simply a matter of choice, seemed like a betrayal of everything I stood for. Even so, I forced myself to keep calm, breathing deeply to stay in control of my voice. I didn't want to let frustration derail the morning, though anger rose inside me. At first, she didn't even seem to realise that the treatments she was talking about involved gene modifications.

'But…you said people in Lacunfort don't believe in God,' she replied when I explained my concerns.

'I don't see how that matters here.'

'Well, if I'm trying to adopt the Lacunfort way of thinking, then I can't rely on God to give me a healthy child, can I? But I'm also not supposed to take control myself. What does that leave me with? Can you guarantee our baby will be healthy? Fully able? And if not, why would you stop me trying to ensure just that?'

A few pigeons fluttered down nearby, pecking at crumbs scattered from Lorelei's plate. I drew a deep breath and repeated the explanation I'd delivered countless times in forums and debates – that gene enhancements carried irreversible risks, potentially introducing harmful mutations into future generations. The flock around us grew, their soft cooing fuelling the tension between us. Lorelei listened intently, narrowing her eyes as she absorbed my words.

'Future generations?' Her voice turned thoughtful, almost incredulous. 'What do I owe them? They're not here now. Our baby is what matters to me. Why should I protect people who don't even exist yet instead of *my* child?'

One of the staff came over and quickly shooed away the pigeons before directing me to my capsula.

'Three minutes behind schedule, Chief Minister,' he remarked with polite precision.

'I'm sorry, Lorelei,' I said, rising to leave. 'The answer is no. I will not turn my first child into an ultrahuman. I thought you'd have understood that without needing to ask.'

She folded her napkin silently, her reddened eyes downcast, then pushed back her chair, stood up, and walked away in the opposite direction.

At Congress, the day only worsened. I presented my case for the bill with precision, each argument laid out with the clarity I'd hoped would cut through the usual noise. But instead, the session devolved into mockery. My colleagues treated the bill as a farce, their laughter clawing at the edge of my restraint.

Sebastian Brown set the tone, leaning back with that infuriating smirk I'd come to despise. 'Sterilisation, Chief Minister?' he sneered with feigned surprise. 'Isn't that a bit rich? You're sounding more like Rivennia's new "Father of Family Planning" than a politician.' His words drew chuckles from around the room. He went on, hardly masking his disdain. 'Or is it eugenics we're flirting with now? The shaping of a so-called better breed? They may not teach history in Varcega, but let me tell you, that's never ended well.'

The roars of laughter that followed dug under my skin. Eugenics? The nerve. It was the gene therapies that would create a twisted hierarchy of the enhanced over the unaltered. I was fighting to protect humanity from precisely that, yet they twisted my intentions into something grotesque. My fists clenched, anger simmering, but I held it back. I wouldn't give them the satisfaction.

Helene Fallow from Daugresston spoke next. 'Forced sterilisation? Tyranny, from our Chief Minister? Why stop there? Perhaps we should issue breeding licences.' Her words fuelled the laughter, and my face flushed with fury. Every sarcastic jab was another blow to my pride. She went on: 'We said we would "never forget" after the ethnic cleansing of Glossdenians – the most terrible massacre in our history. And here we are again, with a new Chief Minister who thinks himself virtuous by deciding who is allowed to have children and who isn't.'

I pressed on, trying to steer the discussion back to facts, but it was clear they weren't interested. Another Congressman from Fubrikum taunted, 'What's next, Moritz? Genetic approval cards? A registry of the unfit?'

They laughed again. And, for the first time, I experienced the sting of genuine humiliation. All my work, my arguments, misunderstood and dismissed as naive idealism. What was the point of leading the global government if Congress was determined to throw obstacles in my way? As I walked out of the chamber, I thought of Voychenko's advice: allies. I'd brushed it aside, thinking that the strength of my ideas alone would carry me. Now, sitting in the dimness of my office, I saw my mistake with cold certainty.

Clara walked in briskly, apologising for her delayed arrival. Her grey bun swayed as she lowered herself into the chair across from me. She sighed and set down her files.

'Look,' she said, 'I know this feels bleak right now. But it's not the end.'

'The final deliberations are next,' I replied. 'I don't want to fall under that "first-pass curse". It might hold some truth. What if this sets us back beyond recovery?'

She held my gaze, her expression slowly softening until the faintest of smiles cracked across her face. 'A small whisky?'

I exhaled, unable to stop a smile of my own. 'Yes. We absolutely must.' What would I do without Clara?

I poured us each a glass, pausing to inhale the scent of oak and leather before letting the liquid touch my lips.

'Remember, you have a mandate from the people,' she reassured me. 'And you have all the under-represented nations backing you. They may not be as vocal, but they'll be there when the voting comes.'

We chatted about trivialities after that. I knew she was trying to help me relax.

Eventually, she glanced at the clock. 'Why don't we call it a night so you can get some rest? We have a gap to debrief at seven tomorrow.'

'Anything else pressing on your list?' I asked.

'Actually, one thing. An urgent request came from the Treasurer at the Human Order. They're asking for a grant for temple maintenance. It seems odd they're demanding an immediate response, and the amount of money they want feels excessive.'

She projected a view of the details on the wall, explaining, 'Some repairs are listed, but there isn't much context for the amount. Grant approvals for cultural preservation fall under your discretion as Chief Minister. We could offer half the requested amount as a goodwill gesture.' She turned to face me, eyebrows raised. 'What do you think?'

Finishing my drink, I hesitated, hoping Clara would see my pause as fatigue. After the day I'd had, the decision felt like stepping through a door I'd sworn to keep closed.

'Half, then?' she asked, studying me.

'No,' I replied, feeling my resolve harden. 'Approve the full amount. Strengthening our relationship with the Human Order could go a long way. I know they have no real power in government, but we can't ignore their influence.'

'Understood.' She made a note. 'See you in the morning?'

'Yes, thank you, Clara.'

'Get some sleep,' she said, a calm reassurance in her words as she left.

SIX

PRIMULA

What was it about breasts? I'd thought about it all day. It was ridiculous. Just some mammary glands wrapped in fat tissue, and yet some people lost their minds over them. Fat tissue. That was it. Beyond breastfeeding, what was the bloody purpose? How much of a woman's life was actually spent nursing, really? Just a fraction of it. But breasts were always there, making women feel sexy, proud, insecure, or just self-conscious. A whole mess of emotions because of them. And apparently, the amount of fat didn't even affect the quantity of milk, so why was everyone so obsessed with the size?

I never had big breasts, thankfully. I'd assumed I'd dodged that obstacle in modelling. My body was different – elegant and slim, made for high fashion, not for the vulgar curves pushed in the commercial scene. I wasn't some showy peacock; I was a heron, all grace and sleek lines. My appeal lay in a clean silhouette, the modest authority of good posture, not in curves that screamed for attention. But lately, the industry seemed to demand something I didn't have. It was clear elegance alone wasn't enough.

Boobs, then. That was what they wanted. And fucking pink hair, no less.

I displayed holograms of my younger self, strutting down catwalks like a feline. Back then, thinking of adopting a 'street look', like the one Skitto was proposing, would have felt like pouring tomato sauce on fine silk. The thought of wearing ripped clothes in the promos made my heart sink, but if I didn't start making money soon, I'd be stuck in bloody ripped clothes for real.

I projected a second hologram, layering in Skitto's suggestions piece by piece. My black hair, so famous for its sheen, transformed into a bright pink. The shock was surprisingly thrilling, like I'd crossed into some alien reality, unsettling yet oddly captivating.

Then came the clothes. Out went the tailored blazer and high-waisted trousers, and in came a battered leather jacket, scrawled over with graffiti-style patches, paired with torn fishnets and low-slung, frayed denim shorts. My polished heels became scuffed combat boots, turning my usual grace into something fierce and bold. Roar.

And then, the dreaded fat tissue. Except, it wouldn't be fat for me – more like a dense silicone gel, smooth and rubbery, injected to create curves where I had none. It's weird to be forcibly reshaped to fit someone else's vision.

Who was this new girl going to be?

'There isn't always one version of ourselves,' Voychenko had said.

I had no other option. The alternative was to fade out, to become an old woman on benefits, explaining to strangers who

I used to be. Skitto would find some other girl and carry on, and they'd forget they ever considered me.

The truth is, sometimes our choices are limited.

Staring at the holograms, I messaged Artur: yes to Skitto.

'Don't forget the dinner,' he shot back.

As if I would.

SEVEN

SAM

I CREPT INTO MUM'S ROOM, careful not to wake her. She lay on her bed, looking peaceful. But as I sat on the sofa, her eyelids flickered, and her head lifted a fraction.

'Samantha?'

'No, Mum, it's me. Samuel.'

'Ah, Samuel. Samuel…'

I stood, walked to the side of her bed, and held out a small box with a blue ribbon. 'I've got something for you.'

'For me?' She blinked hard, trying to shake herself awake. Her eyes settled on the box, and her face lit up.

'Buns,' she said. 'Are they cream or custard?'

'Both,' I said, grinning.

'Didn't think you could get them in Lacunfort.'

'You can't. They came all the way from Corin this morning.'

She cast a cautious glance towards the door. 'They say I shouldn't have sugar.'

I shrugged. 'I won't tell.'

She gave a mischievous little laugh. 'Well, go on then, hand them over. But help me up first.'

I took her hands, limp and fragile in mine, and helped her sit up. As she took her first bite, her eyes half-closed in bliss.

'Lovely,' she murmured, a bit of cream on her lip. 'Tastes like home, doesn't it? Proper Corinnian buns, just like the ones from Treva. Remember them summer walks along the shore? That was before the dam collapsed, so we weren't rationed then. Your dad always put Samantha on his shoulders, and she'd squeal like there was nothing better in the world. Full box of buns, we'd get. From that man in the beach hut. Heard he passed recently, the poor bloke. We'd sit there on the sand, watching the sun sink into the orange sky. That was the life, eh? Funny – when your dad stopped caring about his buns, that's when I knew it was serious. Nothing could lift his spirits near the end.' She shook her head, dislodging the memory, and let out a little giggle. 'But look at me now, chirpy as a dog with a bone.'

I chuckled with her, lost in thought. 'Mum, do you remember how, after Dad left, we kept saying it wasn't his time? We thought, even with the depression, there had to be some kind of cure. But...he'd given up, hadn't he?'

Her brow furrowed as she chewed and swallowed. 'Took all he had just to look at me by then, poor man. But he believed there wasn't a way out. Made it easier for him, in a way. Never was one for dithering, your father.'

'Mum... If it ever came to that for you, would you—'

She cut me off, frowning deeply. 'Don't be silly, Samuel. What I've got, this degeneration, it's nothing like what *he* had. I'm getting better, with the treatments and all that. You go ask Dr Khan. He'll tell you.'

I pushed down my unease. 'I know, Mum. It's different. But I'd want to make my own choice if I ever reached that point.'

'Well, I plan to enjoy every bit of life that's left in me. Don't talk nonsense now.' She seemed to have forgotten about the buns and busied herself with the hem of her sleeve instead.

I held back a sigh. 'Of course, Mum. But sometimes, it's worth defining what a good life means to us. So if…if it isn't that any more, we've got a choice. Dignity and peace, if we need it.'

She stared at me, her face serious. 'I don't want to die.' Then her eyes drifted down. After a moment, she spoke again, softly, almost to herself. 'They can keep your body running forever now, but they can't fix your mind when it starts going. Bit cruel, really.'

I took a breath. What was cruel was that some people, *maybe*, could fix her mind – with dodgy treatments, illegal and risky, bringing who knows what else along with them. But Mum had never wavered on her views about that.

She cleared her throat. 'Where's your father, anyway?'

I hesitated, trying to summon the words that always felt wrong. 'He…well, he…'

'Ask him what time he'd like us to have dinner,' she said, unperturbed. 'Don't want it to be too late. I've got work to do later.'

I nodded, pressing my lips together. Then I leaned down, placing my hands gently on either side of her head, and kissed her on the forehead.

'Will you stay for the news?' she asked, glancing across the room.

'I can't, Mum. I've got to get to work.'

She fixed me with a hard look. 'But surely you can be a bit late, now that you're a big cheese in that resource department…'

A familiar frustration bubbled up. 'I'm not, Mum. Well… I might be, but not in the same department. They've offered me a job in census.'

'Census?' Her look of disappointment was like a slap in the face. She glanced away, her shoulders slumping slightly. I hated that look, hated the sting that came with it.

Back at my desk, I stared at the resource metrics again. That error just wouldn't go away. There had to be a reason for it; something I'd missed – and maybe even an explanation for why Silas and Galina were acting so strangely about it. But I couldn't dig any deeper without slipping behind on my other work. Silas would notice that right away.

Another thought crossed my mind: could I take the data with me and find a way to look at it later, quietly? I knew I could. The real question was whether I could do it without leaving a trace. I'd seen gaps in the system, enough holes that anyone with half a mind could slip in, take what they wanted, and disappear. But would I leave any evidence? There was a master passcode that controlled the entire network, but getting my hands on that was too far a stretch. It changed every day, and Galina was probably the only one who knew how to derive it.

Accepting that I wouldn't get the master passcode, I shook off the hesitation and got to work. I backed up all the data and erased any sign it had been copied. Then I set up an invisible login – one I could activate from the census domain whenever I wanted. If they planned to cut me off, I'd still have what was required to get to the bottom of this.

It wasn't even five when Silas called, asking for my answer.

'Grateful for the opportunity and happy to accept,' I said. But really, what other choice did I have?

EIGHT

GREN

At Igor Voychenko's insistence, I travelled alone in a pre-programmed capsula, leaving my security team behind. Naturally, for my own safety, I had informed Clara of my plans, though I had little to share; the evening's details had been shrouded in secrecy. When the capsula finally stopped, I was startled to find myself at one of the discreet side entrances of the Human Order temple.

A bot welcomed me as I entered the hallway. 'Good evening, Chief Minister. The members of the Liffdom Lodges await your arrival. Please proceed to the lift; it will take you down.'

'Down?' I asked. 'Is there a basement at the temple?'

'Please.' The bot pointed towards the door.

The lift seemed to take an eternity to reach its destination. Fighting a giddy sensation in my stomach, I stretched my jaw in a wide yawn, trying to ease the pressure building in my ears.

When the metal doors finally slid open, I stepped into a

breathtaking chamber. It was spacious enough to accommodate at least a hundred people. Towering windowpanes – over five metres high – stretched up from the oval base to meet the intricate patterns of the ornate ceiling. There, faded but still imposing, were remnants of painted dragons – their elongated forms coiled and twisted, their scales worn and muted with age. Beyond the glass lay a solid darkness, a near-black indigo that only hinted at the profound depths of the surrounding abyss. We were deep within the saline lake.

The sound reached me before I could identify the source – a high, irregular rattle, like a malfunctioning drill. As I stepped into the ring of spectators and saw what lay at the centre, I stiffened instinctively.

The dogs were no larger than a hare, but there was something wild in the way they moved. Their unnatural musculature and oversized teeth could only mean they'd been enhanced. Bots held them back, the small faces of the dogs contorted with fury, their snarls rising to a fever pitch. Then, on some unseen signal, they were released.

A violent collision threw the creatures together, twisting them into a single, writhing form, their snapping jaws a blur. They barely paused between bites, a frenzy of motion and impact, until finally, one faltered, and the other wasted no time, seizing its advantage. A decisive move, then stillness.

Applause rippled through the crowd. The name of the winning dog's owner and the time taken for the win were announced. More clapping.

I forced a slow breath past clenched teeth.

'Mr Moritz.' Voychenko emerged from the crowd to greet me. His voice was smooth but imposing. 'I'm delighted you could join us this evening. Welcome to the Liffdom Lodges. This is the Beluga Room, our usual gathering place. I trust you've had the opportunity to meet some of our members outside the Lodges.'

I looked around, unsure.

'A reminder, Mr Moritz – this gathering is to remain strictly confidential. Do not speak of it when you leave, not even among yourselves.'

From a distance, I spotted a tight circle of people around a card table, recognisable figures from Congress, their expressions unreadable. Each held cards close to the chest, chips clinking as they changed hands. Someone fished in a pocket, drawing out another stack with a resigned sigh, while another smirked, raking in their winnings. My fiercest opponents from Daugresston and Fubrikum were there, though Sebastian Brown was nowhere to be seen.

A little further ahead, Fredrica Voychenko was with a group taking turns to throw knives at a board. It wasn't entirely surprising to see her here; I had already caught sight of Voychenko's wife and son in the crowd, so it was only natural that his daughter would be present as well. Despite her air of opulence, there was something about Fredrica that had always seemed out of place among the ruling class.

Her hair, just as I remembered it, blazed like a live fire against the muted tones of the room, a vivid red cascading in loose waves over her shoulders. Her blue evening dress clung to her figure with effortless grace. Even from across the room, her eyes shone sharp and glacial. Her freckled skin, untamed, seemed to defy the uniformity of the others.

That skin.

I knew the feel of it. I knew the taste.

I hesitated, uncertain of the best course of action. Should I approach her and exchange pleasantries? Or should I wait for an introduction, pretending we'd never met?

Even now, I couldn't quite define what we had meant to each other. Somehow, I had expected we'd carry on after she finished her work in Varcega. But she left, and I stayed. And that was it. Years had passed, and yet, seeing her again forced the question: what sort of memories did she hold of me?

Before I could dwell on the thought, her gaze swept in my direction. Our eyes locked, the room shrinking to just the two of us. But then, with the faintest flick of her glance, she dismissed me. Something at my core twisted and ached. She was a reminder of the kind of bond I'd once believed we could have, a hope I had long since abandoned.

It wasn't just Fredrica's indifference that struck me. As I surveyed the room, a wave of inadequacy began to form – unfamiliar and unwelcome. Despite my role as Chief Minister, and the polite cordiality of those I encountered, I sensed I was of little interest to anyone. My title carried no weight here. Only their betting games mattered. Who did these people think they were, cloistered in their underground society, basking in their self-importance?

Voychenko appeared at my side again. 'I must commend your decisiveness on the cultural grant, Mr Moritz,' he said quietly. 'We are deeply grateful for your contribution. Rest assured, the results will be evident soon.'

Looking around, I wondered how much of the temple lay hidden underground and what the cost of maintaining that portion might be. Why did they need a government grant anyway, considering how profitable the Human Order's enterprises were? I couldn't imagine it making any real difference. The recent expansion of the Express Passing Centres alone could have built Voychenko as many temples as he wanted.

The appearance of the first whale outside the glass window took me aback. Voychenko seemed amused by my awe. The whale's head was small compared to its body, with a narrow beak and a rounded forehead. Its black eyes were mere dots against the whiteness, alert despite their size, peering into the room, eager, inquisitive. Like a weightless balloon, the hefty body floated in perfect peace, making lazy tail waves as it advanced, inch by inch, occasionally rotating sideways to show off its flippers. Soon, a second whale joined, then another. Groups of them began to take turns keeping vigil on the humans inside the luminous chamber.

'Now, Mr Moritz,' Voychenko said. 'This is a significant evening for us. You will have the chance to take part in rituals of utmost importance to the Liffdom Lodgers. First, we shall bond over a meal. Afterwards, we will take your predictions for our traditional Game of Wagers – which, as you may recall, I've already mentioned to you. Please, walk with me.'

I followed him, discreetly glancing about, searching for more familiar faces.

'Before the evening concludes,' Voychenko continued, 'we will hold a ceremony to reaffirm our vows of respect and secrecy towards the Lodges. I trust it will be a truly memorable experience for you.'

'Of course, Supreme Leader,' I replied. 'I'm particularly intrigued by this Game of Wagers you mentioned. It sounds like an important tradition.'

Voychenko's face remained expressionless. 'Indeed, Mr Moritz.'

We stopped beside a man and a woman, the latter offering me a warm, genuine smile – the first I'd seen in this room. The woman was slim, her striking pink hair flowing long and straight, a vivid contrast to her porcelain skin. Her features were classically beautiful: dark eyes that carried a quiet, keen awareness. At first, I was distracted by the bold colour of her hair, but then recognition dawned: she was the woman Lorelei had been so thrilled to see at Dario's that evening.

Beside her stood a man with a strong, toned build. Corkscrew curls framed his face, and his light eyes stood out against his deep brown skin. He wore a jacket over a simple shirt, paired with trousers that were more casual than formal – an understated outfit that contrasted with the elegance of the crowd.

'I'm afraid I must leave you now,' Voychenko said. 'But before that, I would like you to meet your fellow players.' He pointed at them with an open palm. 'This is Primula Zhang, and this is Samuel Rosendale.'

NINE

PRIMULA

IT WAS THE CRÈME DE LA BLOODY CRÈME at the exclusive dinner. The Liffdom Lodgers were the magnates, media moguls, politicians and global executives you only hear about but never expect to meet. Not even at the height of my fame had I been in a room with this many power players. I hadn't quite got used to the pink hair – the boobs hadn't come yet – but people seemed to like it, and after my second glass of wine, I was loving my new self and ready to take on the world.

When I was introduced to the new Chief Minister, I thought he was a Lodger too, but it turned out he'd been invited as a guest, just like me. I must admit, it gave my little ego a boost; at least in this unconventional room, someone had placed me at the same level as the head of our government. This guy, Gren Moritz, seemed decent enough in person – one of those brick-house types, big and broad, built like he could tear down a wall, but still somehow wrapped up in that pristine politician's suit. Blond curls, perfectly arranged, like every strand had its unique place. His eyes were intent, always watching. I figured he'd come up from some backwater in Varcega, probably scraping by as a kid, and now he strutted around like he was part of the Lacunfort elite. But he couldn't fool *me*. I saw a rugged sort who'd put in the work to pass for refined – stiff and controlled. All in all, though, he was a likeable person.

Samuel, on the other hand, was nothing like Gren. Where Gren was all polish and bulk, Samuel was toned but smaller, holding himself quietly in a way that suggested he didn't want to draw any attention. His clothes looked almost deliberately unfashionable, like he'd thrown on whatever was closest without a second thought. He didn't carry himself like someone trying to impress. Maybe that was why I couldn't stop noticing him.

But the moment I paused to really look at him, an odd sensation curled in my stomach. I'd seen this man in my dreams the night before, standing just as he was now, slightly hunched as if trying not to take up too much space. It was unnerving, almost too surreal to be true, but it wasn't the first time I'd had one of those dreams, and it probably wouldn't be the last. There he was, in the flesh, looking exactly as he had in that hazy vision.

'So, Samuel, is that right? What do they have you buried under at the Agency?' I leaned in a little while Gren stood beside us, scanning the room like he was looking for something important.

Samuel scratched the back of his head. 'Oh, you know – just crunching numbers, telling people things they already know but don't want to hear.'

'Interesting. Try me,' I said.

'What do you mean?'

'Tell me something I already know but don't want to hear.'

I saw a spark of amusement in his eyes as he considered the question.

'Nah, not doing that.' He chuckled.

I couldn't help but smile at him. He glanced down, looking almost embarrassed.

'Well, it sounds thrilling,' I teased. 'What's the worst they've had you do?'

He looked up at me, the nervous tension easing a bit. 'Probably sorting resource quotas. Can't say it's glamorous, but it has to be done, I suppose.'

His tone was self-deprecating and honest.

'Glamour comes in many forms,' I murmured, holding his gaze a bit longer than necessary. 'I'd say your work is probably more important than anything the people around us do.' I shot the knife throwers a look and rolled my eyes.

His face relaxed, and, as he laughed, he showed a touch of pride. There was something about him. After years of meeting bland, pretentious people, this brief encounter was unexpectedly refreshing.

A bot standing awkwardly near us finally spoke.

'Players,' she said. 'I am here for your induction.'

'Induction to what?' Gren asked.

'For the Game of Wagers. Please, follow me.'

The three of us exchanged confused glances but trailed behind the bot as she led us to a quieter corner of the room. Four chairs were arranged in a neat square, facing each other.

'Please, sit down.' Her voice was pleasant enough, but it carried an artificial cadence, the kind that sounded almost natural but never quite was. 'I believe you've all been briefed on confidentiality?'

We nodded. She gave a perfunctory smile before continuing. 'Very well. First of all, Liffdom is comprised of three separate

Lodges. Each of you will be representing one of them in the Game of Wagers.'

'*First of all*... Can you tell us what this game is about?' Gren asked.

The bot raised a hand in a vaguely dismissive gesture while her polite smile held firm. 'This will be part of the induction.'

There was nothing overtly wrong with her – no glitches, no jarring malfunctions – but she seemed...off. An older model, maybe? Her movements were just a bit too deliberate, each step and gesture carried out with an eerie precision and a slight delay, like she was pulling them from an archive rather than generating them in real time.

'There is Portuatz, Lodge of the Arts,' she continued. 'Portuatz players are perceptive individuals with a strong inclination for creative expression. Primula Zhang, you have been selected to represent this Lodge.'

I raised an eyebrow. 'And what does that mean?'

The bot repeated the same gesture as before. 'This will be part of the induction.'

Annoying piece of hardware.

'There is also Hyender, Lodge of the Exact Sciences. Hyender players must be scientifically inclined, with an innate ability for complex analysis. Samuel Rosendale, you have been selected to represent this Lodge.'

Samuel shot a glance at Gren and me before giving the bot a small, wary nod.

'Finally, we have Grawledinn, Lodge of the Humanities. Grawledinn players are chosen for their passion to solve societal problems. Gren Moritz, we believe there isn't anyone better than you to represent this Lodge.'

Gren looked impatient, as though he had something to say, but this time, he held it back.

'The Game of Wagers,' the bot went on, 'is a tradition that dates back centuries. Tonight, Igor Voychenko will disclose the relevant event, and you will record your predictions as to when it will occur. While this is generally considered a game of chance rather than skill, many Lodgers believe the distinction is not always clear. The winner will receive the honour of a permanent seat at their supporting Lodge.'

I frowned. 'And what happens to the losers?'

The bot smiled, just as polite as before. 'That is *not* part of the induction.'

Gren scoffed. 'I'll attend the dinner and be gone before the game begins.'

'Your attendance this evening constitutes your acceptance to participate in the game,' the bot replied. 'I believe Igor Voychenko explained that.'

Gren crossed his arms. 'Why did they select us specifically?'

The bot took a long time to respond. Finally, she said, 'That is *not* part of the induction.'

Samuel hesitated before asking, 'So we'll be told about a future event and we'll have to predict when it will happen? Like a sweepstake?'

'Yes. That is correct,' the bot said, offering nothing more.

Gren leaned back, frowning. 'Why?'

'It's a tradition,' the bot replied. 'A game.'

'It doesn't make much sense,' Gren muttered.

'Human traditions often don't.' She stood. 'This concludes the induction. Thank you. You may now join the dinner.'

With that, she bowed her head slightly, turned, and walked off. Her movements, so stiff and artificial, were almost insulting. Couldn't they have asked one of the Lodgers to pause their betting games for a few minutes and speak to us instead?

Dinner could only be described as boring, and the moment

it wrapped up, the group dispersed. Then Voychenko's deep bass voice cut through the chorus of chatter: 'Welcome, once again, to our special evening. I trust everyone present is having a delightful time.' Roaring applause followed. 'Tonight, we will hold a dual event. What brings us together, primarily, is the initiation of our Game of Wagers.' He strolled in front of the group as he spoke. Another round of applause followed, more modest this time.

I sensed a rush of enthusiasm among everyone present.

'But we will also use this gathering for our sacred ritual of forfeiture, to correct the path of one of our brothers who has gone astray.' He raised his chin to get a better view of the Lodgers. 'I believe we have everyone in the room at this moment.' There was a mumbled assent. Voychenko took a sharp turn when he reached the far end of the room and continued his slow walk in the opposite direction.

'As is our tradition, the same tradition of all our Liffdom ancestors, I shall now unveil the event that will be the subject of our players' predictions. An event that most of us expect to occur within a year from today. The player whose date is closest to the occurrence will have the great honour of joining their supporting Lodge.'

The applause returned with increased strength. Was I meant to clap too? I started clapping when, out of the corner of my eye, I saw Gren and Samuel raise their hands, slow to join in.

Voychenko's next words were lost in the clatter. He raised a hand and waved away the noise. 'And the event we'll be playing for is…' He paused for suspense before making the final announcement: 'The death of Her Majesty, Queen Brynhilda of the Nations of Rivennia.'

This time, there was no applause, no cheering, or shouts of approval. The room filled with a mix of gasps and quick, furtive whispers. I was sure a smirk formed on Voychenko's face amid the Lodgers' escalating murmurs.

A few cheers rose from the crowd when Voychenko introduced us as the players, naming each of us with our supporting Lodge, just as the bot had described. Then he called my name first. I looked up to meet his gaze, and the room turned morbidly silent.

'May we take your prediction?' Voychenko asked. 'We must obtain three numbers from you, consisting of a day, a month, and a year – in that same order.'

My mind blanked for a second. What day was it? I'd never wasted brainpower wondering how long the queen might hang on. She was ancient, of course, and honestly, it was a miracle she hadn't gone years ago. Still, she'd kept at it, tottering along like some indestructible relic. You had to hand it to her – persistence, or sheer bloody stubbornness. Either way, I had to admit, it felt a little wrong to be guessing when she might die.

The silence grew increasingly distressing, suffocating me to the point of feeling an urgent need to speak.

'Twenty-fourth day...of month five...year five hundred.' Although my conviction hung by a thread, I thought I'd spoken with enough aplomb.

'A bold move from the Portuatz player,' Voychenko exclaimed. 'That is a mere three months from today. Primula Zhang,' he said, looking into my eyes again, 'do you confirm that your prediction for the death of Her Majesty is the twenty-fourth day of month five, year five hundred of our era? Please answer before the Lodgers.'

'Yes.'

A loud string of mutters broke out, buzzing with agitation and surprise. I couldn't tell if people were scandalised, annoyed, or just enjoying the drama. My prediction had clearly poked a hornet's nest. For a second, I felt a twinge of alarm – had I said something wrong? But I shrugged it off. It was only a game, wasn't it?

Voychenko moved on quickly, eager to steer the turmoil elsewhere. Samuel and Gren offered their guesses – safer dates, a little further off. Probably trying not to rile anyone the way I had.

With all the predictions recorded, the Lodgers herded themselves back to their posts.

'Lodgers,' Voychenko's voice resounded again, 'please be ready to attest our forfeiture ritual. We shall commence in fifteen minutes. I remind you that we must all observe this ritual in our traditional attire.'

Like actors frantically changing costumes between scenes, everyone scrambled towards the gates, where a line of bots dished out blue gowns and white wigs. The transformation was cult-like – a sea of identical faces framed by long, heavy wigs that belonged more to a haunted house than a high-society gathering. The whole thing appeared theatrical, like the prelude to a fashion shoot, and I just couldn't bloody believe what I was seeing.

To mark us out as players, Gren, Samuel and I got gowns in ochre. I copied everyone else, pulling the whole thing on, pins and wig cap included. The wig practically glued itself to my head, draping long white strands down my back and smothering my ears.

The cloak, at least, was a pleasant surprise. Velvety, thick but not suffocating, it swayed with a kind of regal grace. I almost convinced myself I looked dignified, until I caught sight of the wigs again.

'Our forfeiture ritual will commence in three minutes,' Voychenko said.

Everyone stood in perfect alignment. As players, we were instructed to take our places at the front. I grew increasingly uncomfortable, sensing that what had already been an unusual evening was about to turn even more bizarre.

TEN

SAM

I'D NEVER BEEN GOOD WITH crowds or fancy dos, but this was on another level. It took all my energy to try to appear normal, pasting on a grin and pretending I wasn't having a terrible time. Too many people. Too much small talk. All that pressure to say something interesting and funny… Not my thing at all.

I wasn't dressed for the occasion, but I had worn my smartest clothes. The only interaction I genuinely enjoyed was with Primula Zhang, the model. I had seen her before, I was sure, but she looked different now. Less girly, maybe? Her hair was pink, like one of those dolls you'd see in a toy shop, and I didn't think it had been that way before. Anyway, she was the only one who talked to me like I was an actual person, not some awkward bloke who didn't belong in that place. She was nice, yeah – dead nice, actually – and, well, stunning. Proper stunning.

It turned out the new politician from Varcega was also a

guest; go figure. He wasn't too bad, I suppose, but he seemed a bit out of his depth, not as comfortable as I'd expected someone like him to be. And maybe a bit annoyed, too. Not sure why.

Famous faces were everywhere, and they kept saying we couldn't tell anyone we'd been there.

By the end of the night, things had got properly weird. Everyone threw on these cloaks and white wigs, making them look like some ancient priest gang. Primula, Gren – the politician guy – and I stood at the front of the crowd wearing yellowish cloaks and the same wigs. Igor Voychenko announced the start of a ceremony – some kind of important ritual.

Then, a pair of bots wheeled an elderly man into the room. The bots wore only black and had their hoods pulled low to obscure their faces, if they even had faces at all. It was strange to see the man in the wheelchair without a wig like everyone else. His cloak was dark with a wide hood that was crumpled around the back of his neck. It wasn't until they brought him closer that the straps became visible – tight plastic ropes wrapped around his wrists and ankles.

The wheelchair was rolled out to the front, right where the crowd could get a proper look at him. The guy sat there, scanning the faces as if he was trying to find someone he knew – or anyone who'd look him in the eye, really. His beard was patchy and grey, like he hadn't shaved in weeks, and his hair was an unwashed mess. Up close, you could tell he wasn't that old – early sixties, maybe. But something about him made him seem worn down, like life had taken a bit too much out of him.

Voychenko moved with small steps towards the wheelchair. 'Before us sits Thomas Locke,' he said. 'Once one of us. A brother. A Liffdom Lodger.'

The man's lips trembled, and his eyes turned glassy. He could just about use his fingers enough to fidget with the loose end of a strap.

'Following severe accusations that Mr Locke breached the sacred concealment of our Lodges, our judiciary board has concluded its investigation and come to a resolution.'

A faint whisper rippled through the crowd. Voychenko raised his voice over it. 'The board has determined that Mr Locke intentionally and maliciously shared, outside our guild, confidential information regarding the existence of the Liffdom Lodges. A serious violation of our vow of secrecy. To assist in granting Mr Locke's redemption, the object of his forfeiture has now been defined.' He paused, scrutinising everyone slowly before continuing. 'By decree of our Lodges, Thomas Locke has been sentenced to forfeit his humanness. This ritual will aid in his transition, allowing him to remain part of this universe, though from today onwards, it will be in a different form.'

A murmur rose like a flutter of startled moths around the room. My head pounded. What was going on? I couldn't make sense of all the muttering and tense faces. Looking around me only made me more jittery. Palms clammy, I rocked back and forth, trying to find my centre. Something about this felt very wrong.

What were these people all about? They'd pulled us into this odd Game of Wagers, and now this? Galina and Silas hadn't warned me it was going to be *this* mad.

'Our board, in its infinite mercy, has allowed the use of a painless method this evening. Mr Locke will be in the company of his brothers and sisters, who, by virtue of this ritual, agree to forgive his offence.' Voychenko turned to the bots. 'Please, proceed.'

The injection took only seconds.

Voychenko leaned down, speaking softly into the old guy's

ear – but loud enough for those of us up front to hear. 'This is the time, Mr Locke, to share any final words with the Lodgers.'

Then he stepped back, leaving the poor man and his wheelchair alone under the lights.

Minutes crawled by before Thomas said anything. You could see the anguish all over his face. When he opened his mouth, he made a small sound, almost like a whimper, and finally, the words came out.

'I did not have a chance to say goodbye to my wife.' His voice was a shaky drawl. 'I urge those of you who know her to offer comfort in her grief and help her accept that my disappearance is permanent. Help her move on.'

He got no response from the crowd.

'I want to thank all of you for your compassion, my brothers and sisters, and especially our leader, Igor Voychenko, for allowing me to see you before my departure, and letting me go without pain.'

The calm dignity in Thomas's words struck me like a stone. He looked drained – sad even – but there wasn't a hint of panic in him. I kept waiting for someone to step in and shout that this was wrong and it didn't have to happen. But the crowd just stood there, silent. That's when I realised I might've been the only one hoping for some kind of change. I couldn't tell if the others had seen this coming or if they were just as blindsided.

'I see blue…' Thomas said, his voice trailing off. 'I see blue in the air.'

At first, I assumed he was referring to the Lodgers' gowns.

'And pink,' he continued in a high-pitched voice, 'the most beautiful pink.' A faint smile crossed his face. 'Oh, and green now. You all should see it. This green...'

I spotted a glint in Thomas's eyes, and what looked like joyful tears began to form. His grim expression transformed into one of happiness. It became clear that he had entered a trance, a state of elation. His eyes closed. He swayed his fingers from side to side and began to hum a melody.

The bots returned, carrying a big glass structure – a rectangular box, like something between a display case and a coffin. They didn't rush as they untied the man from his wheelchair, pulled off his cloak, and lifted his slack body, setting him gently inside. Thomas didn't fight them. He just kept humming as they moved him. His limbs hung loose, and a thin line of frothy drool trickled from his lips.

I spotted two vats beside the box just before the contents were poured in. A black, glistening stream spilled out, pooling around Thomas's body and creeping over him, inch by inch. It took me a moment to realise – it was insects. Thousands of them, crawling and writhing together. I broke out in a hot sweat. Beside me, Primula's shallow, anxious breathing matched my own.

I couldn't tell exactly when the humming stopped, but it wasn't long before Thomas disappeared beneath the black mass, thick and clinging like tar. The crowd stood motionless, eyes locked on the box as the minutes dragged on. Every part of me wanted to turn away and spare myself the sight. I wanted to stop it from etching itself into my brain, so it couldn't haunt me later. But somehow, that wasn't an option. It would've been unthinkable – a breach of some unspoken rule I was only just beginning to understand. We weren't mere bystanders; that much was clear. The three of us were meant to stand there, watching like everyone else. Whatever this was, we were supposed to learn it too.

As the insects slid away, the black mass thinned, turning slick and fluid. Bit by bit, white shapes emerged – naked bones, horrifically clean. By the time it was over, nothing remained but a skeleton: a grinning skull with hollow eyes and limbs stripped smooth like birch twigs.

I feared I might faint right there on the spot. My legs wobbled, but I pulled myself together. I needed every bit of my strength to get out of that place. Fast.

ELEVEN

LORELEI

My dearest sister,

I can't tell you how happy I was to get your letter. While I'm here, caught up in this strange new life, I can still picture you in the orchard with everyone else, weeding and watering, tending the trees. Sometimes, I close my eyes and it's like I'm right there with you, as if nothing has changed. I feel the Varcegian sun on my skin, and hear the tinkle of the stream behind me. You live in such a beautiful place, my dear sister, so close to nature and the grace of God – please, never take that for granted.

Now, they say I'm not supposed to tell anyone yet, but of course, I'll tell you. Just promise to keep it a secret. People here can be so funny about, well, just about everything.

But here's the exciting news: I had a positive pregnancy test! Isn't it wonderful? A true blessing, really. They say we're to wait until the second trimester before announcing it, so only you know for now.

I feel fine, maybe a bit tired, though it's hard to tell if that's the pregnancy or just life here. I've had a touch of nausea, but nothing too bad. I can hardly believe it's real.

I've started seeing a gynaecologist who's supposed to be the best in Lacunfort. Dr Greenville is her name. They say she cares for all the politicians and their wives. She doesn't seem to have much time for niceties, but if she's the best, I suppose she can afford to be a little brisk. Her staff, though, are very kind, and they confirmed the test at my first appointment, which was a relief.

Dr Greenville mentioned some potential treatments for the baby – life enhancements, they call them. Apparently, there are all sorts of in-utero options for ensuring the baby's health. Some can even double the number of synapses in a child's brain by the age of ten. It feels strange, but the truth is, if everyone else is doing it, would I be putting my child at a disadvantage by refusing?

I spoke to Gren about it the other day, and he flew into a rage. To him, these are gene enhancements, and his whole political stance is built against that sort of thing. I do understand that, truly – but for me, his work is one thing, and the wellbeing of our child is quite another. I can't possibly be expected to make family decisions based on what pleases Congress members I've never even met. And the way he spoke to me – so rude and condescending, like it was his decision alone. He simply said no, and that was the end of it. I'd assumed we'd talk it through and come to a decision together, but no.

You know full well, my dear sister, even when all people see in me is a sweet girl, I'm not one to be pushed around. I might not have Gren's air of sophistication or fit in quite like the rest of his staff, but I'm catching on quickly. I can think for myself, and I will make my own choices.

Dr Greenville was quite clear that if we decided to go ahead, any life enhancements wouldn't be included in the standard fees;

they wouldn't even bill the Chief Minister's residence. Varcegian notes or a non-traceable transfer would suffice. It doesn't sound so bad, really – just a common precaution, something to be on the safe side. With Gren's blessing or without it, I suppose we'll see how things unfold.

As I was leaving, one of the nurses, Julian, stopped me. He's a lovely man, about my age. We always chat – he compliments my clothes and makes me a lovely cup of tea. He treats me like I'm just a normal girl, which, of course, I am – though these days, people don't always act that way around me. Anyway, Julian must have overheard part of my conversation with Dr Greenville because he caught my arm as I was leaving and said, 'I really need to talk to you about that next time you're here.' He was whispering, but I think that's what he said. Then we heard footsteps, and he let go quickly, acting as though nothing had happened. I can't lie – it's made me curious. I suppose I'll wait to hear what he has to say before making any final decisions. I'll let you know what comes of it.

Now, aren't you thrilled? You're going to be an auntie! It's a bit hard to wrap your head around, isn't it?

Keep writing, my sweet sister. You know how much I adore hearing from you.

With all my love, always,

Lorelei

TWELVE

GREN

I HADN'T SLEPT A WINK THE night before. Now, each time I closed my eyes, the ceremony at the Liffdom Lodges surged back with horrifying clarity. I had witnessed no ordinary death – it was something much more sinister. The Supreme Leader, his family, half of Congress, the heads of the Civil Force, and nearly every luminary of Lacunfort society had been there, watching in solemn rows. They didn't flinch. Not once. They regarded the proceedings as though they were part of some hallowed tradition, not a barbaric execution.

In the morning, I requested a hologram audience with Voychenko. Within the hour, the appointment was confirmed. He appeared in my office, projected in a vibrant image, calm and composed, as if nothing unusual had occurred the night before.

'Supreme Leader,' I began, forgoing the usual pleasantries. 'I find myself struggling to reconcile the events of last night.'

'In what way, Mr Moritz?' he asked, tilting his head ever so slightly.

'We saw a man die before us.'

'People die every day.' His tone remained casual, as though stating the obvious.

'Not like that. Not in public executions.'

'You might want to choose your words more carefully, Mr Moritz.' Voychenko's face darkened. 'You, of all people, understand that assisted dying is allowed by law; it is a kindness we extend to those otherwise destined to suffer beyond endurance. Many choose to pass in the presence of their loved ones. It's a transition; nothing more.'

Destined to suffer beyond endurance. The phrase, deliberate as it was, hinted at depths of cruelty I could hardly fathom. I swallowed my arguments, realising they would lead nowhere, and turned my focus back to the reason I'd requested the meeting.

'Supreme Leader,' I continued, 'after what I witnessed, I am compelled to inform you that I've decided to suspend the cultural grant for the preservation of the Human Order temple.'

He smirked, making me feel exposed despite my efforts to hold firm. 'That won't be possible, Mr Moritz,' he replied. 'The funds have been transferred and are already in use for their intended purpose. Trust me, in the long run, you'll see their benefits. Don't forget, it's the success of your entire political agenda that's on the line here.'

'I don't want my government associated with the Liffdom Lodges.'

He raised his eyebrows. 'Perhaps you misunderstand, Mr Moritz. The ceremony's purpose was to demonstrate our commitment to secrecy. There will be no association of the Liffdom Lodges with your government, or with anything that touches the light of day. Not now, not ever.'

He paused, then added, 'Of course, I could always request an audit of the Human Order's Treasury. Such an audit might uncover the trail of the grant money, approved by you alone, leading directly to the pockets of certain members of Congress who have lately grown supportive of your ideas. Imagine my disappointment in discovering that the Human Order was used as a vehicle for dishonest transactions without my knowledge.'

The trap snapped shut around me with startling precision.

Voychenko kept talking, right through my silent horror. 'Shall we imagine what would happen then? Picture it, Mr Moritz: an investigation, a trial, and you – the first Chief Minister to endure such a spectacular fall from grace. Your sterilisation bill? Forgotten. Your whole agenda? Buried. Now, I'm not entirely certain how many years one might face for bribery and legislative interference, but as it happens, my daughter is quite invested in prison reform. I'm sure she could find the perfect accommodation for you, should it come to that.'

He chuckled – a low, rasping sound that made my jaw tighten until my teeth ground together. 'I trust that you will come to your senses. After all, this is Lacunfort.'

I held my tongue, knowing that speaking my wrath would only make things worse.

'You made the right decision with the grant,' he said, his tone one of finality. 'Never underestimate the importance of alliances. And now, Mr Moritz, lighten up. Soon, we'll be hosting a gala dinner in honour of our players on our very own Liffdom island, and I expect to see you there. You will receive the details shortly. Needless to say, confidentiality is paramount. We'll consider that a lesson learned. You have a good day now.'

He vanished, leaving me alone in the office, like a storm-wrecked village assessing the damage.

I forced myself through the day – back-to-back meetings on health and environmental reports, a policy briefing, a press conference – feeling like a pressure cooker about to blow its lid. One report, ironically, highlighted the rising rates of assisted deaths in Lacunfort, a statistic that now carried a deeper resonance after the events of the previous night. But the blow had struck, and its torment lingered.

It was late in the evening when Clara, deep in a rundown of market fluctuations, suddenly stopped. 'Something's wrong,' she said. 'What is it?' Her tone was clipped, her gaze searching. Clara knew me too well to be fooled by any excuse. I couldn't keep this from her – not her, the only person I could trust to understand.

I took a breath and poured out every thought, stumbling over my words in a rush to get them all out – from the truth behind the cultural grant to the events of the night before. I described Voychenko's trap, his veiled threats, and my disillusionment as reality sank in. Clara listened, her face calm, but I could see the concern in her eyes.

'So, the rumours are true,' she said finally.

'You've heard them too?'

'People talk about a secret society in Lacunfort. Whispers about their "rituals" – betting games, eating live animals, bizarre ceremonies – but most dismiss it all as nonsense. Until now, I assumed it was just talk.'

I blew out a breath. 'Hard to believe.'

'Why do they care about the queen's death?' She brought a hand to her chin.

'I have no idea. Maybe it's just another thing to bet on. I won't lie – I'm still shaken. I didn't imagine for a second that last night would end the way it did.'

'It's natural to feel that way. But this isn't your doing. From the sounds of it, the Lodges have been around for a long time. All you've done is stumble into their world, and I don't think that's something you could have avoided. You're just beginning to understand.'

'Yes, only just beginning…'

Clara folded her arms across her chest. 'But now that you know this, the question is, what will you do?'

'That's precisely what's been haunting me all day. I can't go up against Voychenko – not if I want my government to have any chance of success. I need him to think I'm in his camp. And he has me cornered with this grant threat.'

'I agree,' Clara said, rubbing at her temples. 'If he and the Lodges have their claws in the Civil Force and Congress, turning them into enemies would be the quickest path to failure.'

We sat in heavy silence, turning over Voychenko's motives. Why bring me into the Lodges at all? The answer seemed obvious: by reeling me in with the grant and the subsequent blackmail, he could keep me firmly under his control. Was his intention to dismantle my anti-ultrahumanism efforts, or did he simply find them irrelevant?

'I have to get close to them,' I said finally. 'I need to learn what they know, what they value. I don't see another way.'

Her voice softened. 'I know you're compromising more than you expected. It's not just hard work and good intentions that get us by.'

'My principles...'

She let out a faint huff. 'You may find that clinging too tightly to a moral code isn't something you can afford, if you want to achieve your goals.'

'I want to protect the human race,' I said, the words solidifying my conviction. 'If that means adapting, then so be it. My morals feel like a luxury when the stakes are this high.'

The way forward began to crystallise in my mind. I would learn everything I could, immerse myself in their world until I understood it completely. To lead in Lacunfort, I had to see it for what it truly was. Voychenko believed he held all the cards, but he underestimated me. And he had no idea what I was capable of.

THIRTEEN

PRIMULA

The room was stark white, blinding, with walls that seemed to close in. There was nothing in the space except a single chair in the middle, and on it sat a man. He looked wrecked – bloodshot eyes, haunted like he'd seen things no person ever should. His lips moved, reciting numbers in a broken rhythm: 'One thousand six hundred and three… Seven hundred and twenty-five, nine thousand eight hundred and eleven…'

The string went on for what seemed like hours. I could barely breathe. My heartbeat drowned out his words. Something terrible was waiting. I wanted to reach out, shake him, tell him to stop. But I couldn't move, couldn't even open my mouth to scream. I was trapped – an unwilling witness.

'Twenty-one, three thousand two hundred and forty…'

He hesitated, and a piercing buzzer shrieked. The sound shot through me like a dagger. The man's face twisted in agony as his body convulsed, writhing under an invisible torment. His fingers curled like claws, and a tortured scream tore out of him. An electric current reverberated through me, and I realised my hand was pressed against my chest, my breath coming hard and fast. There was nothing I could do to stop this.

When the shock ended, the man looked half-dead. Gasping, he clutched at the flimsy black cloak that covered him. His trembling hands pulled it tight around his body, like he was trying to hide from the horror of what he'd just endured.

'Number one hundred and eighty-one in the series is three thousand two hundred and forty-two,' came that cold, dead voice from somewhere behind the wall. 'Please restart.'

The man gave a nod; obedient, but his eyes were vacant. 'One thousand six hundred and three… Seven hundred and twenty-five, nine thousand eight hundred…' The silence stretched until it became unbearable.

His lip quivered. A tear slipped over his cheek. And then the buzzer rang again.

I gasped, jolting awake. My heart slammed against my ribs. I was drenched in sweat, still gripping the sheets like I was hanging on for dear life. Another bloody nightmare. I could still feel the panic in that poor man's face.

It took a few minutes for my pulse to stop hammering. The nightmares were routine by now, like an unwelcome guest that had decided to move in. They'd told me they wouldn't ever fully go away, but eventually, they'd stop haunting me so badly. Eventually, they'd feel almost normal. *Almost* normal. What a bloody consolation prize that was.

The physical discomfort after the procedure wasn't much fun, I had to admit, but the mild swelling and bruising faded in no time. At first, I thought my new breasts sat a bit too high on my chest, but apparently, they only needed time to 'settle', and I should just let good old gravity do its job. I hadn't been too keen on the idea in the beginning, but now, looking in the mirror, I saw a body with that classic hourglass shape. A generous bust and hips complemented my narrow waist, giving me a new feminine allure I hadn't realised I wanted. I felt sexy and powerful – a bloody wonderful feeling for someone who'd recently feared she'd be put out to pasture.

Skitto was moving fast. I still couldn't raise my arms above my shoulders as I sat in the bright boardroom, bombarded with sketches and lectures about the campaign's vision, goals and all the rubbish those marketing types live for. Honestly, I'd rather get ten more boob jobs than sit through another meeting on 'brand identity' and 'target markets'. Even though I was right there, they kept referring to me as 'the model', talking about 'alignment' with my 'public persona'. Apparently, part of my job was to sit there with a straight face and act like they weren't talking total nonsense, like they were actually having a smart conversation. I thought I did pretty well.

Early on, I'd learned the trick of asking questions. You can nod along, thinking about your shopping list, and when you've picked up enough of their marketing jargon, you recycle it into a question. They bloody *love* that.

'Quick question,' I cut in, watching as all eyes turned to me. 'To ensure we're fully leveraging my brand presence and optimising engagement, what's our strategy for maximising omnichannel touchpoints?'

They lapped it up. All of them started talking at once, buzzing for another half hour while I pretended to be interested.

But I perked up when they started talking media. The strategy had all the usual stuff – standard publications and holograms – and they had planned these retro-style billboards all over Lacunfort, tens of metres tall on nearly every platform. That's how massive this was. Campaign shoots started the next day, with a rollout planned for the following week. My face would be on every major fashion magazine, splashed across Lacunfort billboards, and flooding every social media feed. I'd be inescapable – at least for a few weeks. Skitto wanted 'iconic', and I was prepared to give them exactly that.

The launch included a string of appearances and celebrations to make the campaign unforgettable. First up was the rooftop unveiling party, held at Lacunfort's Platform 163, out in the open – the real outdoors. I'd stride onto the stage at The Cap, the swankiest skyline venue, after a live runway show, shimmering in Skitto's pieces. Influencers, celebrities and top-tier fashion editors would be there, each with a perfect view of the night-lit city and the surrounding nations beyond Lake Lacun.

Within days, my life transformed. My face was everywhere, stamped across every feed, trending like wildfire. I was back. Luxury brands that wouldn't touch me a month ago were suddenly sending gifts, hinting they'd love me to flaunt their things in public or post about them. They could all sod off. My messages were flooded with people who'd vanished when my fame slipped away – people who hadn't been there when I'd hit my lowest, when I'd bled and screamed, alone, forcing my dead baby into the world with no one beside me. They could rot for all I cared. They weren't real friends. But then again, who was?

Invitations to high-status parties and events poured in. The one I had my eye on was the biggest, most exclusive gala, held in some place called 'Liffdom Island'. I'd been so preoccupied with the campaign prep that I hadn't thought much about the Lodges. What I'd seen there was horrific – a message I couldn't afford to ignore. What mattered was making sure I'd *never* end up like that, drooling in a glass box and fed to the bloody ants.

But I couldn't trust myself – not when I was under the influence. I'd cried to strangers in bars about my baby, told random people that my agent was a Voychenko and how he'd look after me. I doubted anyone I spoke to remembered much, but the answer was clear. Stopping was survival. I'd allow myself the odd drink, maybe, but no hard drugs. Now that I was back on top, I'd be a fool to go to sex parties and hand the media an excuse to rip me apart. No sex is *anonymous* when your face is plastered across the city. That was it: the new me would be sober and sensible. I'd had my fun. Oh, had I had my fun! But now, I knew what a slip-up would cost me.

When Artur called, asking me to The Dungeons that evening, I declined without a second thought. 'Can't,' I said. 'Got a line-up of pop-ups in Platform 50, first thing.' I wasn't going to explain how much I'd rather be out all night or how terrified I was of blurting something about his father's secret society mid-coitus to some random. My life had changed, and I wasn't going to mess it up.

The new me made a mint tea, ran a bath, and went all in: eye mask, jade roller, cuticle oil – the full works. And when the shivers hit, even though half a pill would have stopped them, I clenched my fists and marched off to bed like a bloody martyr.

Asleep before ten. Who even was I?

FOURTEEN

SAM

THE CENSUS DEPARTMENT hadn't changed much. Still the same old place, just a bit more rundown than I remembered from my internship years ago. The carpets looked tired and threadbare, patches and stains telling tales of spilled coffee and rushed footsteps. The white walls had faded to some dull, murky colour, somewhere between beige and grey, as if they'd absorbed every weary sigh and stale breath in the place. Even the cubicles looked battered, their sagging dividers ripped, with panels missing.

Still, I couldn't complain. I was a lucky bloke now – a senior analyst with my own office. Five whole square metres of pure privacy, with an actual door to shut. And the cherry on top: my window looked out onto one of those massive Skitto billboards stretched across an entire building.

The first time I saw it, I nearly stumbled. She was there, towering over the platform, looking down the street like she owned the whole city. Primula Zhang, with her new pink hair, as bold as anything, staring out of those fierce eyes. She was dressed head to toe in urban get-up – layered jackets, sleek cargo trousers, chunky boots with a metallic sheen – giving her an almost otherworldly look. And her face…breathtaking. On my way in, I just stood like an idiot, gawking. I wanted to tell every rushed passerby, 'I've met her, you know.'

The job at census was easy, though – too easy. No challenge, nothing to keep my brain going, so it drifted back to my resourcing work. In maths, there are times when things need to be exact, and if they're not – even if they're close – it's often a sign of a deeper issue that shouldn't be overlooked. A result that's 'close enough' might seem fine on the surface, but it's a warning that there could be hidden problems underneath.

Just like my unresolved numbers in resourcing, and a lot of the recent events.

A few things didn't sit right. One felt outright terrible, like a kick in the gut – the business at the Liffdom Lodges. I'd lost most of my appetite since that night. Couldn't finish a meal without thinking about the insects and feeling sick. I didn't care about their ceremonies or their weird games. Didn't want to be anywhere near that. Part of me was almost relieved they'd stashed me in this dusty corner, out of their way, where they could do whatever sick things they were planning without me interfering. But what else was I supposed to do, stuck here with nothing more than the basics to tackle? So I turned down the blinds, pulled up the resource data, and used my secret login to access the restricted servers. I was glad there was no need for a master passcode this time.

The Lodgers meeting in those underground spaces seemed like a step towards an answer, but it didn't match up with the sheer scale of resource use and waste my algorithm had picked up. There was something else, something I couldn't nail down. I promised myself I'd find the root of it. There had to be a way to explain the strange results around the temple. It was possible – I knew that much. And now, at least, I had plenty of time on my hands.

I'd managed to craft a solid list of reasons to give Silas and Galina for skipping the gala they were so hyped about. I wanted nothing to do with those people or their messed-up rituals and planned to stay as far away from them as possible. Besides, social events had never been my strong suit. I was always rubbish at knowing what to say, how to act. Just thinking about it set my heart fluttering, and it only got worse as the day crept closer.

But then, when I hinted I'd back out, Silas shut me down. He told me straight, I had to be there. And, just as casually, he brought up my benefits. They'd agreed to keep covering the main fees for Mum's sanatorium. They'd *agreed.* Like that was ever up for debate. Why would a promotion mean fewer benefits instead of more? Still, he locked eyes with me, turning cold, and said he'd make sure that arrangement ended if I wasn't 'facilitative'. Like some kind of psychopath, he finished with a grin and said he looked forward to seeing me on Liffdom Island.

That's when the real fear hit. A creeping, suffocating dread. I was stuck. They had me. What did they even want me for?

I went as far as looking up symptoms for common illnesses and hacking into the GP's system on the ground floor to generate a proper medical note. I was on the verge of pulling out.

But I thought about Mum. There was nowhere else for her to go. Then I looked at that Skitto billboard outside my window. And I hesitated.

There she was again. I cursed myself for even wavering.

Would she talk to me if I went? Would there be a chance to steal a moment alone? Probably not. She'd likely be swarmed all night. But…would it be worth it? Just to try?

I stretched my arms and ran my hands through my hair, tugging slightly. Then I pulled up my virtual assistant and asked, 'What does one wear to a gala? And how much is that gonna set me back?'

FIFTEEN

LORELEI

My dearest sister,

I've just returned from my check-up, and I'm still in shock. Don't worry, there's nothing wrong with the baby. The little one is healthy, and they tell me she's the size of a nectarine now. So, whenever you see one in the orchard, think of your growing niece.

It's not the baby that's upset me, but rather what happened at the clinic. A new nurse greeted me today. She was a middle-aged woman who didn't seem very cheerful, though she did her best to be polite. When I asked after Julian, my usual nurse, she ignored my question and led me to the examination room. She was halfway through spinning a hologram of my placenta when I couldn't help myself and asked again.

'Where is Julian?'

Julian had been so keen to speak with me at this appointment – a tall, gangly young man with a booming nasal cackle that just wouldn't quit, the kind that made you want to laugh along. That's how I knew he was human – no bot would ever carry on like that. We'd become friendly over the visits, and he even confided once that he was planning to move out of Lacunfort with his partner, another nurse. So, when the new nurse's face tightened, I knew something was wrong.

'Is he alright?' I pressed.

She calmly shut off the hologram and stepped closer.

'He's no longer with us.'

I didn't understand what she meant at first, so I asked her to explain.

'Julian went missing a few days ago. No one heard from him; not even his partner.'

She hesitated, watching me, unsure how much to reveal.

'He was seeing someone here – one of the staff,' she said.

'I know,' I replied. 'He mentioned that to me. What happened?'

'After not hearing from him for days, his partner decided to check the Euthanasia Register, and he found Julian's name there.'

If I hadn't been lying down, I think I might have collapsed. I couldn't believe it. Julian was so full of life; a happy guy. And he was so young. You hear of older people or the very ill making that choice. But someone like him? Why would he affront God's will like that? It didn't make sense.

Lacunfort has a heartless way of turning even something as delicate as assisted death into an efficient business. There are these 'Express Passing Centres' dotted around the city. According to the register, Julian went into one of them. These places offer quick and private services for those who want to pass. They're owned by the Human Order – a church-like organisation that people say is definitely NOT a church, and somehow has its fingers in almost everything, including this. Apparently, these centres are very profitable. People who want to die don't tend to haggle.

I can hardly bear to think of Julian walking into one of those small cabins. From what I've read, he would've signed all the necessary forms on a display screen, and when he was ready, they would've had him lie down on something like a tanning bed. With the press of a button, the machine fills the chamber with anaesthetic gas to make the person sleep before releasing a lethal mixture. After death, the same device even takes care of the cremation. The whole process is over in two hours without any human involvement. How cold and horrible is that?

I thought maybe there'd been trouble between him and his partner, but the nurse assured me the poor man was just as shocked as everyone else.

After that, I was left waiting for Dr Greenville, feeling numb. Her office was spacious; all shiny, with a large desk. I thought there might be a bathroom behind one of the doors, but when I opened it, I found a strange sort of wardrobe with scrubs, a few white coats, and the oddest blue cloak lying next to a white wig on an old wooden mannequin. I was scratching my head, trying to figure out who would wear such a thing, when Dr Greenville entered. In her blunt way, she asked me to close the door and ordered me to sit down.

Now, you know I'm not overly fond of her, but I might actually consider some of the treatments she's suggested for the baby, at least the preventative ones. After visiting all these charities, I've become more aware of all the things that could…you know…go wrong, and I just want my little girl to be healthy. I'm not sure when or how to tell Gren. He's always so busy, and sometimes I feel more like I'm a colleague than a wife. I know I wasn't promised love, so I shouldn't complain. Still, he hasn't visited my room since the pregnancy was confirmed. I suppose, now that his duty is fulfilled, there's no need.

I'm sorry for the gloomy tone, dear sister. I have no one else to confide in, and I don't want you to worry. But today has been hard, and sometimes, it's difficult to keep my spirits up. If only God would show me my calling. I long for some kind of meaning in what often feels like a pretty empty life.

There is one more thing to share, though – something a bit brighter. With all these charity visits, I found one place I truly like. It's a centre for the deaf and hard-of-hearing, a place where people can connect through sensory experiences without sound. I suppose Gren expected me to be seen there, playing the part of the First Lady, but I keep going back because it brings me peace. Free from noise. I feel like I can connect more deeply without all that pressure to talk, talk, talk. You would like it, sister – the DC, they call it. Short for the 'Deafness Centre'. It's a nice, calm place in this bustling city.

I met two lovely ladies there, Sara and Rosa. They want to have a child of their own someday and made me promise to bring the baby to visit once she's born. It's a comforting thought that people like them are here, quietly doing good things and just being normal.

Anyway, I'll leave you now, my sweet sister. Your letters always bring me so much joy, so please, write again soon.

With all my love,

Lorelei

SIXTEEN

GREN

As I ploughed through a visit to a new energy station in Lacunfort, only one thing was on my mind: that evening's gala with the Lodgers. The last event had tested the limits of the unexpected, and there was no telling what this one might bring.

Later, in a closed-door cabinet briefing, I approved the construction of several large-scale health infrastructure projects across ten nations, firm in my belief that better access to care would reduce the lure of black-market gene treatments.

Before I was due to leave, I sat through another press-free meeting. This one focused on public sentiment analytics and opposition movements. Not much had changed, but there were murmurs of former detractors in Congress who had recently spoken favourably about the sterilisation bill in public forums. I couldn't help but think of Igor Voychenko's machinations, while the rest of the team received the update with a sense of well-earned optimism.

But the most important piece of intelligence on the opposition wouldn't be mentioned in that meeting. Keen to adopt the political ways of Lacunfort, I'd asked Clara to commission a top-secret investigation into Sebastian Brown. I figured that if I could find a way to bring him down, it would be like cutting the oxygen to a fire – and he was the one fanning the flames.

'The report is ready,' Clara whispered as we left the room.

My capsula was due to depart in less than thirty minutes, but curiosity pulled me into a side room, where Clara shared the highlights.

'Any skeletons?' I asked.

She shook her head. 'Nothing useful, really. But the man's an odd character – that's for sure. Collects dolls. Obsessed with obscure stories set in fantastical worlds. He's created several identities for hologram gaming – a fairy, a crow, an elf, a princess. Hooks up anonymously with young women and men, but they're all of legal age.'

My eyebrows shot up. 'Odd indeed.'

'And it seems his other obsession is…you. For at least five years, he's followed every article that mentions you and kept a photo archive.'

The thought of Sebastian Brown tracking my every move with such devotion was unsettling – an obsession that felt personal rather than political.

'What's that face? Don't be so disgusted,' Clara said. 'Aren't you doing the same here?'

Her eyes were red with fatigue. Her shoulders curled inward as she gathered a pile of documents, holding them close as though they might slip away. I wanted nothing more than to help her rest.

'Thank you for this,' I said. 'I hope you've planned an evening off.'

She blew air through her lips. 'Hardly.'

'You need to take a break. Have a proper rest. I'm sure whatever's pressing can wait until tomorrow.'

'Tomorrow's busy. I've only got tonight to sort out the correspondence triage.'

'Scrap it. If anything's important, it'll come back to us.'

'And there are diary clashes,' she added. 'The First Lady wants to host a charity lunch for the Deafness Centre on the same day you're scheduled to visit Liffingham.'

'One evening off won't do any damage. I'm asking you, as a favour to me, to rest.'

She looked at the floor, thinking for a few moments. Then she lifted her gaze and gave a light sigh. 'Fine.' Her smile didn't quite reach her lips, but it reached her eyes.

My capsula sped through the transparent walls of the pneuduct, skimming over the ink-black surface of the outer ocean as it carried me towards a remote location. Every map in Rivennia showed only water where Liffdom Island was meant to be. One more secret to keep.

The hidden island, a sliver of land lined with palm trees, came into view just seconds before the castle emerged on its shores. The structure grew larger with every passing moment, its turrets and archways exuding an air of ancient power. Through the clear duct walls, the entire place gleamed. Golden windows flickered against the dark water below, their reflections greeting me with the allure of a promise. Or the edge of a warning.

As we drew closer, a thrill stirred within me, laced with curiosity and something more precise: a cautious determination. This was the realm of privilege, of secrets long hidden from men like me. Awe had no place. If I were to cross this threshold, it would be on my terms. I wasn't just stepping into their world; I was here to find my way through it.

Inside, I was engulfed in a world of luxury beyond anything I'd known. The grandeur lay not in gaudy displays but in subtle craftsmanship: hand-carved banisters, high ceilings adorned with frescoes that seemed to dance in the light, and marble floors polished to a mirror-like sheen, reflecting the guests as they moved. Around me, Rivennia's elite had gathered, their faces set in casual indifference, as though this lavishness was routine.

The air was rich with the scent of fresh flowers arranged in large displays throughout the hall, mingling with wood smoke and a sweet undertone that I couldn't place. Breathing it in made me light-headed.

The Lodgers wore clothes that seemed more like treasures than mere garments. The men's tailored suits were cut with such precision that they appeared sculpted, their collars and cuffs embroidered in patterns discernible only to an attentive eye. The women's gowns swept the floor, each a masterpiece of elegance, crafted from silks and brocades that shimmered in subtle, undulating waves. Their jewels sparkled – not ostentatiously, but as quiet symbols of wealth.

I glanced down at my suit, well-tailored but unadorned. It was the attire of a public servant: practical and restrained. Appropriate, even dignified. Still, it was a reminder of the gulf that prevailed between their world and mine. But I was the head of the government now, and I wasn't going to let anyone make me feel small.

There was a pattern each time I crossed paths with a Lodger: brief eye contact, a polite smile, and a few pleasantries. 'Good to see you here, Chief Minister… Did you have a comfortable trip?' Eventually, a gentle incline of the head would signal a temporary farewell. This wasn't the time for long conversations; only enough interaction to acknowledge one another before moving on.

At the far end of the entrance hall, a grand staircase led up to a tall stained-glass window, backlit and casting a crimson light over the room. Beneath it stood Igor and Galina Voychenko. Igor seemed calm, a pleased look on his face as he surveyed the crowd.

Stepping into this place brought the wealth and power of Lacunfort into sharp focus – the kind forged in its highest seats. I straightened my posture, meeting the moment head-on. This night wasn't just an open door; it was my chance to thread myself into the Lodgers' fabric. New power is never given – it's taken, gradually, from those who already hold it.

In the grand hall, three long tables stood beneath banners representing each of the Liffdom Lodges. These were no mere dining arrangements; they were declarations, crafted to reflect the prestige and purpose of their respective orders. It wasn't something thrown together in haste. How had so much tradition taken root in such seclusion?

The first table was for Hyender, the Lodge of the Exact Sciences. Its banner was silver and midnight blue, a double helix intertwined with gears and compasses embroidered across its surface. Small orbs along the table cast a cool, blue glow over the guests.

Next was the table for Portuatz, the Lodge of the Arts, draped in deep crimson and gold. The emblem – three hands holding a paintbrush, a lyre, and a stylus – was sewn with elaborate detail. Candlelight flickered in sculpted metal holders, casting an amber glow over the ornate plates and glassware.

Finally, there was the table for Grawledinn, the Lodge of the Humanities – the one I was meant to join – marked by a banner in regal green and ivory. Its emblem depicted an open book flanked by laurel branches, symbolising wisdom and the pursuit of truth. The table exuded a stately, scholarly air, with heavy candlesticks and engraved silver place settings.

The chairs at each table matched the colours and fabrics of the tunics the Lodgers had worn at the previous ceremony in the Beluga Room. At the centre of each table, a single ochre-draped chair stood apart, reserved for the Lodge's player in the Game of Wagers.

The sight of rich, red hair stole my attention. Fredrica Voychenko was seated at the Grawledinn table, opposite the ochre chair. A satin emerald dress delineated her elegant figure. Taking a deep breath, I moved towards my chair, placing my hand on the backrest before sitting down. I offered a courteous smile to those nearby. 'Good evening,' I said, receiving the same in response. No one rose, so I took my seat. I was considering how best to formally greet Fredrica when she spoke.

'Welcome, Gren,' she said, striking a balance between familiarity and authority. Her use of my first name in front of others felt daring, yet somewhat refreshing. 'Fredrica Voychenko. I'm the First Lodger of Grawledinn. It's an honour to have you at our table tonight.' I took in her appearance, the familiar freckles scattered across her nose, the angles of her cheekbones, and the ice-blue eyes framed by striking gold eyebrows. Her face still held its youthful edge, but I wondered how the past few years might have shaped her, and what sort of person she was within this world I barely understood.

She spoke again, louder this time, drawing the table's attention. 'Grawledinn Lodgers, please welcome our player for this Game of Wagers, Gren Moritz.'

'Welcome, Gren Moritz,' the others roared in unison.

Bots paraded in, laying out drinks and an array of lavish dishes. Each course was announced formally: 'Roast swan with yellow pepper. Ostrich neck. Puffin stuffed with dolphin blubber…' A wave of unease twisted through me. As Chief Minister, feasting on outlawed foods with a group of strangers was an obvious risk.

'Ever tried alpaca, Gren?' a man two seats over called, his napkin tucked at his neck and his mouth half-full. 'One of the most flavourful camelids.' He pressed his greasy fingers to his lips before spreading them in the air. 'Lean and tender.'

'I haven't,' I replied, keeping my voice cautious. 'Is this farmed or lab-grown?'

Fredrica leaned forward, amusement curving her lips. 'Nothing of that sort. These are *wild* animals, all of them. What we're doing here is no different from what our ancestors did for thousands of years. Tonight, we invite you to cast aside the outer world and join us in our Liffdom rituals, connecting us to our primal roots.'

A violin played somewhere, lending a touch of elegance to the atmosphere as hands reached for the platters of food, Lodgers picking portions with evident relish.

'Is this really dolphin blubber?' I asked.

'Delicious,' Fredrica said. 'Try some.'

When I hesitated, she added, 'No one does more for human advancement than the Liffdom Lodges, even if a few laws are bent for our members. Outside, life continues as it should.' Then her smile turned sly, her eyes issuing a gentle warning. 'And as you might have gathered, indiscretions are punished severely.'

'I understand,' I said, while my gaze drifted to Primula, in the distance. She was laughing, her head tilted back. I tried to spot Samuel, but his table was too far away.

The meats were, surprisingly, some of the most enjoyable foods I'd eaten in years, each mouthful bringing rich flavours that transported me back to childhood weekends in Varcega, smoky scents wafting from our garden grill. But there was more – a thrill in tasting something forbidden and watching everyone around me do the same. I'd seen how swiftly breaches of conduct were punished here, and as morbid as that memory was, it assured me I was safe in this moment.

'We're proud to have you as our player, Gren,' said a middle-aged woman seated beside Fredrica. 'It's a shame you've come to Liffdom Island for the first time after dark. This place is paradise – much better appreciated during the day. Perfect weather, clear turquoise waters, white sand beaches. Beautiful villas are scattered across the ten thousand acres, each run entirely by autonomous bots. You'll *love* it here.'

'Perhaps,' Fredrica said, looking directly at me, 'once you become a Lodger, you might use these facilities as an escape from your stressful life.'

'We'll get you a blue gown!' shouted a man further down, his fists pounding the table in celebration. Others copied the gesture, and silverware clattered, adding a strange, merry rhythm to the cheers.

I leaned towards Fredrica. Lowering my voice, I asked, 'What is all this? What is the game about?'

'The Game of Wagers,' she said, serving herself a spoonful of some mysterious paste, 'is a centuries-old tradition. Our most important game. Didn't you have an induction? The winner becomes a permanent member of one of the Lodges.'

I raised an eyebrow. 'Is that something I should aspire to?'

She held my gaze, a mischievous glint in her eyes. 'Trust me, Gren…' She picked up a heavy-handled knife, driving it through a thick cut of meat with a force that belied her poised demeanour. 'If you want to stop the radical ultrahumanists – or accomplish anything, really – it's not Congress you need on your side. What you need is a blue gown.'

Something sparked inside me. Her magnetic presence carried an allure that was simultaneously dangerous and inviting.

'I don't suppose you've seen the pond outside the castle,' she said casually. 'Perhaps you'd join me on a walk after dinner?'

The front gardens stretched out in carefully trimmed symmetry, with hedges that looked like green velvet blocks from afar. The path was paved with textured tiles in shades of beige and reddish grey, woven with patches of carpet-like grass cropped to a perfect centimetre. At the end of the path was a majestic pond with a fountain at its centre. Lanterns hung from the trees, their light spilling over the water in soft amber hues. We followed a narrower trail that encircled the water, lined with weeping willows that swayed gently as we walked.

The quietness of the evening was interrupted by a splash.

'What was that?' I asked, squinting at the ripples spreading across the water.

'A night heron,' Fredrica said. 'They're nocturnal hunters. Fascinating birds.' She moved a little closer. 'Look,' she whispered. 'There it is.'

Her shoulder brushed against mine, and her scent sharpened my memory of her in that way only smells can. My lips remembered every inch of that neck, the soft, tender place behind her ear. Why hadn't I tried to find her after she left her assignment in Varcega? Why hadn't she tried to find me? Her breath was warm, and it took all my focus to keep my attention on the bird she was so eager to show me.

At last, I spotted it: a white creature with a black crown, its slender neck stretching as it swallowed its catch in sharp, jerking movements before giving a decisive snap of its beak.

'They're remarkable,' Fredrica continued, her voice returning to normal as we resumed our walk. 'Not just hunters – they're bait-fishers. They'll drop objects or food to lure fish close, increasing their odds. They say those who consume others thrive, but this takes intelligence, don't you think?'

'Incredible,' I said, genuinely impressed. 'And the self-restraint not to eat the bait before the fish come is a feat on its own.'

She grinned. 'True enough. Not that the fish appreciate it. Imagine being fed regularly and never knowing if it's from a well-meaning keeper or a heron with ulterior motives.'

'Well, we all feel a bit like that sometimes, don't we?' I replied jokingly.

She met my gaze and gave a gentle laugh. 'Fair point. I must admit, I felt like one of those fish listening to your campaign promises.' She raised an eyebrow in jest.

'My campaign promises?' I asked, smiling but curious. 'There was no bait involved. Whatever I offered was for everyone's benefit.'

She looked at me, gauging my sincerity. 'So, this fight against ultrahumanism...is that something you personally believe in?'

'More than anything else,' I replied without hesitation. 'Why would you question it?'

She shrugged. 'It's just not something you ever mentioned to me before. Then again, we didn't spend much of our time discussing politics back then. And I realise it was a different time.' She gestured loosely, as if clearing dust from the air. 'I'm not doubting your integrity – it's just that the anti-ultrahumanism stance, while divisive, drew strong support from conservative voters, especially from those traditional families outside the cities. That likely gave you the edge. You know that.'

'It's no secret where my supporters are based.'

'True. I just wondered how much of it was strategy versus

personal belief.'

'I hope I can convince you one day that I'm a man of real beliefs,' I said, studying her. 'May I ask about your views in that regard?'

'On whether you're a man of real beliefs?' she teased.

'No.' I gave a small chuckle. 'I'm well aware of your doubts there, so I'm guessing I didn't win your vote. I was asking about your stance on ultrahumanism. Are you in favour, or do you oppose it?'

She sighed, taking a moment. 'I'm somewhere in the centre. I agree that having unchecked mutations spreading through the population is reckless. But I also think controlled research and gene modifications can help address some of society's issues. In my work on prison reform, I see the genetic factors that often predispose people to criminal behaviour. I'm not suggesting we rush to "fix" these traits without a full understanding. I just believe we should pursue knowledge instead of shutting down any exploration of genetic engineering.'

I recognised in her pragmatism a sort of gateway argument – the idea that a little flexibility here could lead to a future where humans controlled their own evolution for the better. But to me, given humanity's long history of war, power struggles and atrocities, trusting people with that kind of power was out of the question. As I considered whether to press my case, another splash interrupted my thoughts, and we both jumped.

We shared a laugh, breaking the brief tension.

'It's the price to pay for such a beautiful view,' I said. The pond and garden, softly lit by the lanterns, had a peaceful, intimate charm. But it wasn't just the setting – it was Fredrica. Her hair glowed like molten copper in the lantern lights, and her skin cast a gentle warmth. A bold spark flickered in her eyes. She held me captive.

'Well, nothing's ever free,' she replied, shrugging.

'Exactly.'

'If you enjoy this,' she said, 'I'd recommend a walk around the pond in Lacun Park. It's quiet and peaceful at night.'

'I wish I could.' I pursed my lips. 'It's hard to go anywhere in public these days.'

'I often go at midnight,' she offered. 'Not a soul there. If you ever need space to think, I'm telling you – it's perfect.'

'Mmm,' I said, thinking of the impossibility of it, hoping I didn't seem dismissive.

We made our way back to the castle as the evening wound down. When we reached the entrance, we exchanged polite goodbyes.

'Gren,' she called, stopping me as I turned away.

'Yes?'

'I *did* vote for you.' Her voice sounded almost playful. My smile widened, and an unfamiliar joy swelled in my chest.

SEVENTEEN

PRIMULA

I LEANED BACK IN MY CAPSULA, sinking into the plush cushions as it took me home. Tonight's gala had been something else – grand, ostentatious, the chandeliers sparkling as though they'd never known dust.

Funny how fast the winds change. At the last event at Liffdom, I was practically a ghost; tonight, I was the centre-piece. People couldn't get enough of me, and I couldn't help but smirk. Artur made sure to remind everyone he was the one who had landed me the Skitto contract, even though he was ready to ship me off to a different agent just a few weeks ago. But fine, I'd let him bask in the credit if it helped keep me in view.

Gren vanished immediately after dinner, but Samuel was there. I spotted him across the room, dressed in a tuxedo that fitted him perfectly, giving him a smart look that still couldn't quite mask his unease. He appeared tentative, like he wasn't quite sure what to do with himself. He moved towards a shadowed stairwell, presumably trying to disappear, and without thinking, I followed him.

I found him on a small terrace overlooking the manicured gardens below. 'You don't exactly strike me as a gala type,' I said, leaning against the balustrade.

He started, then recovered, running a hand over the back of his head, his lips curving into a faint smile. 'No, I'm not.' He chuckled, a low, self-conscious sound. 'But you, on the other hand, you're like a fish in water here, aren't you?'

I laughed. 'I suppose I've had some practice.'

He looked surprised. 'Have you been here before?'

'Oh, hardly,' I said, rolling my eyes. 'I mean, the usual vapid events, yes. But nothing like this… This is truly unique.'

'It's mind-blowing,' he said, making a small gesture with his hands like his brain was exploding.

I turned to look at the garden. 'Big personalities everywhere, aren't there?'

'Oh, come on,' he said, grinning. 'You can't talk, you know. Do you have any idea what I see from my office window?'

'What's that?' I asked, turning back to him.

He pointed at my face.

I raised an eyebrow and touched my chin. 'This?'

'Uh-huh.' His expression was serious, but his tone was playful.

I raised my chin in mockery. 'Well, lucky you then, Samuel.'

'Didn't say I wasn't lucky.' He shrugged. 'Just that you're part of this big club of "personalities", that's all.'

I put a hand to my chest, feigning outrage. 'How dare you? I'm nothing like those egomaniacs.'

He shook his head, laughing. 'Right, of course you're not.'

'In there, I'm disposable,' I said, meeting his eyes. 'I'm just another asset they can chew up and spit out.'

He looked down. 'So we're both just players in this weird game, are we?'

'*Fellow* players.'

He leaned on the railing, gazing out at the maze of hedges below. 'And these people are all…murderers and who knows what else.'

His words shattered the illusion of glamour, the fantasy I'd let myself slip into for a few hours. I forced a steady breath. 'I try not to think too much about that.'

'Yeah, I try not to either,' he murmured, still staring at the garden. 'But it's hard to shake.'

Something in me cracked, and the words slipped out, unguarded. 'I've been scared. Very scared, actually. More than I've let myself admit.'

His eyes searched for something in mine. 'And what happens when we lose? Where does that leave us?'

'Without a chance of becoming one of them. That's for sure,' I said, catching myself and lowering my voice. 'But what else can they do? What we saw in that ceremony – it was all intimidation, a warning not to talk even *if* we lose.'

Samuel exhaled. 'But Gren… Gren's safe, right? They won't lay a finger on the Chief Minister.'

I swallowed, searching for conviction. 'No one's going to end up like Thomas Locke. They don't need to go that far…'

His gaze dropped to the floor again. 'Yeah, well… I've been scared too.'

'Then let's make a promise, Samuel. We'll be fine. Nothing bad will happen to us. Because we've decided it, right now. And we'll look after each other. We'll stay well. That's it.' I held out my hand to seal the pact.

He hesitated, then smiled and shook my hand. The touch

of his skin, softer than I imagined, was electric. 'Alright. But if we're "fellow players" now, you can't be calling me Samuel.'

'Sam, is it?' I teased. 'What a privilege.'

He gave a faint grin. 'Yeah, that's what my friends call me… the few I've got.'

'Oh really? Is that what your other half calls you as well?' I cringed the moment it left my mouth – but he didn't flinch.

'I have no other half.'

'Same,' I said, a bit brighter than I meant to. 'It's just me. Everyone just calls me Primula.'

Before I could say more, Artur's voice rang out behind us. '*There* you are.' He gestured to two men, already fawning over me, eager to meet 'the Skitto girl'. I barely registered their names, my attention caught by Sam as he hesitated at the threshold, his hand lingering on the doorframe. He glanced back just once, his eyes flicking to mine, before he ducked his head and slipped down the stairwell, disappearing into the shadows.

That night, I lay in bed, letting my hair spill loose around me, strands of pink fanning out across the pillows. I could still feel the pulse of the evening – the laughter, the music, the thrum of a night still alive in my veins. My mind kept drifting back to Sam, to the way he looked at me, like he'd caught a glimpse of the real me. Something true in a world of masks. Such a rare thing.

But then the ache crept in: the prickling restlessness under my skin, the faint shiver that no blanket could warm. My teeth began to grind. My hands clenched the edge of the mattress as the need called, first in whispers, then in screams. Sleep wouldn't come. There was only the hollow pull of the drugs.

And the sweat. But I'd come this far. This wouldn't last forever. I wasn't about to throw it all away now.

When I finally drifted into sleep, images came out of nowhere – a white room, sterile and bare. A woman in a ragged cloak. She was running, but it wasn't really running – more like her body was being dragged along. The floor moved beneath her like a treadmill, pushing her backwards, even as her legs pumped forward. The lines on her face – deep, jagged wrinkles – stood out like scars. A jolt of recognition shook me; a strange feeling, like her desperation was my own.

Just a drink of water. Dry mouth. Just water.

I could see the effort in her eyes, her mouth stretched wide as she gasped for breath, her skin sagging and blotchy. Her feet pounded the floor in a dull, relentless thud. I shuddered, noticing the shape of them – her big toes splayed out, thick nails curving like corroded blades.

'Three miles to go,' a voice announced.

A cold dread crept through me as she collapsed, her frail body hitting the ground with a thud. Her hands clawed at the floor; fingers scraping, bleeding. The thirst tightened further.

Then, a loud buzzer sounded. 'The task was unaccomplished. Water is not granted. Please prepare to restart,' the voice said.

My eyes shot open, that last echo still resounding in my mind. *No water.* I reached for the glass beside my bed, gulping it down in desperate, greedy swallows. But the fear remained.

EIGHTEEN

SAM

I'd never tried a stunt like this before – not even close. The whole thing had started as a half-baked idea, and I didn't think I'd have the nerve to pull it off. But I'd read up on enough network security to know the basics: fake identity, mirrored login, delete the trace, and you're in. I wasn't breaking into Skitto directly; they'd outsourced their event through some exclusive media company.

So much for their 'Class-A Security' – within minutes, I was on the guest list for Skitto's launch. I couldn't help but laugh when I got their official message:

Welcome to the Skitto Launch Event at The Cap, Platform 163. We can't wait to indulge you in an unforgettable evening of innovation, luxury and exclusivity. Prepare to experience the future of fashion like never before. Dress sharp. Be curious. And most importantly, be ready to push boundaries alongside our signature star, Primula Zhang, who will be there in person to make this night unforgettable.'

Push boundaries. Exactly what I was doing. Hacking the system had been simple, but blending in with a crowd like this was a different challenge. These were the types who'd size you up with a single look, casting silent judgments before you could blink. I didn't know if I could handle it. But every time I looked up from my screen, there she was, her face filling the building across from me. Something real had happened between us; I wasn't imagining it. There'd been a connection, and I needed to see her again.

I couldn't shake the memory of that first event at the Lodges either. It had left me feeling twisted up, out of place. No one else would understand what that night had done to me. Only Primula. Being near her was the only way to set things right.

Dress sharp. Easier said than done. After way too much deliberation, I ended up with a tailored charcoal blazer, crisp white shirt and dark trousers. I wasn't sure if it looked 'sharp' or just like I was trying too hard. I even splurged on a pair of leather shoes, a step up from my usual trainers. I figured the cost could go on the credit – six monthly payments wouldn't kill me. I checked my fitting hologram one last time, the projection spinning to show how the outfit would look on me. The image still gave the impression of a kid dressed up in borrowed clothes. But maybe that was the point.

On the day, I was jittery from the start. Could barely focus at work, my mind spiralling through every way this could go wrong. Just thinking about stepping into a place like that left me feeling off balance. Still, something in me pushed through the doubt. I was tired of letting the good things in life pass me by.

The venue was all neon lights, sparkle and glitz. Guests strutted through an archway where bots in feathered head-pieces greeted them like futuristic aristocrats. I put on my best confident face, raised my chin, and strode through. The light turned green as my biometry was scanned. I was in.

A red carpet stretched out ahead of me, flanked by people in metallic jackets, asymmetrical cuts and glistening fabrics. It was like walking into a magazine spread, only I was like everyone's dad, stiff and plain by comparison. Cameras flashed, names I'd never heard of were shouted – people doing their best to be seen. It was all a bit full-on, so I kept to the edges, hoping to go unnoticed.

I passed a woman in a cape that trailed behind her like smoke. She snapped into her comm bead, 'Tell Marcus if the hem's even a millimetre off again, I'll slit his skirt myself.'

Someone else – shirtless under a blazer, glitter stuck to his chest in neat little triangles – laughed to an interviewer: 'Oh, this? No, darling, it's not fashion, it's rebirth.'

The interviewer blinked. 'Right. And who are you wearing?'

'I'm wearing my regrets, sweetheart.'

Nearby, a cluster of teenage girls was swooning over someone's sunglasses.

'Are they real diamonds?'

'No, babe, they're simulated. Real's a bit desperate, isn't it?'

I edged further back. Someone air-kissed over my shoulder without clocking I was there. A tall bloke I was sure I'd seen before, with holographic sparkles twinkling in his beard, said, 'No, no, no. I'm not *in* the industry. I *am* the industry.'

It was like I'd walked into a parody. Had any of them ever looked in a mirror without posing first? Did they even realise how daft they looked?

I snagged a seat in the third row, far enough back not to

attract attention but close enough to see everything. The crowd thickened, and after what seemed like an eternity, the lights dimmed. A deep, atmospheric bass filled the room, thumping through the air. When the first models appeared, a high-energy techno beat took over, the perfect backdrop for the stylised, futuristic outfits on display. Each model walked with a cold, detached elegance, their clothes shimmering as if alive.

The music slowed and came to a stop. There was a soft bang, a puff of floral-scented smoke, and there she was – Primula. The crowd seemed to hold its breath, then everyone burst into cheers. She wore a sparkling, form-fitting gown that seemed to send flashes around her. Her pink hair was slicked back, accentuating her features. Her gaze swept the crowd. Intense. Daring anyone to look away. She was here, so close. Everything I'd gone through to sneak in was worth it.

Then, with a swift movement, she dropped the gown, revealing a bodysuit underneath. The fabric had a swirling texture that looked like liquid metal. Delicate chains were draped over her shoulders. She let the audience absorb the transformation, and a hint of a sneer touched her lips. I was transfixed. My mind blurred.

The show carried on, each outfit more daring than the last. Every time Primula returned onstage, the crowd erupted. At one point, she reached the edge of the runway, and her gaze landed on me.

It was quick, barely a heartbeat, but in that instant, we saw each other. I felt it. There was a spark of recognition, a glint in her eyes, and then she turned away, resuming her cool, collected poise. But that brief moment stayed with me. I hadn't imagined this connection. I was certain of it.

When the show ended, the crowd turned into a frenzy – everyone pushing and pulling. Laughter, shouts, glasses clinking. I tried to make my way to the exit, caught in the storm of bodies. Suddenly, a hand grabbed my arm, and I turned to see a staff bot dressed in black, who silently handed me a note. It read: *Gate 3.*

I scanned the signs for the gates. Heart pounding, I decided to see this through.

Gate 3 was nearly deserted except for a group of teenage girls engrossed in holograms from the show and a few bots carrying equipment. Just as I was starting to doubt the whole thing, I heard my name. I looked up and spotted a narrow white door camouflaged in the wall. Primula's face peeked out, signalling for me to join her. My hands shook as I walked towards her.

Before I got there, the girls spotted her too and squealed, rushing to crowd around the door. Primula raised a finger to her lips, then leaned in to pose for a hologram with all of them at once. As soon as they'd got their shot, she motioned me inside, the door clicking shut behind us. The hallway was dim, shadows spreading along the walls. Primula was now in shorts and a loose t-shirt. A soft light cast a glow across her face as she turned to me.

Without a word, she wrapped her arms around me in a gentle hug. Her scent was soft – something warm and deliciously mysterious. I wanted to breathe it in deeper. I hugged her back, and the feel of her against me quieted the last of my nerves.

'I can't believe you're here,' she whispered.

'Yeah… I can't believe it either,' I mumbled, trying to laugh.

'Did you get a pass through the Lodgers?'

'No, nothing like that.' I hesitated, then admitted, 'I, uh… technically wasn't invited. Managed to add my name to the guest list. And here I am…'

She laughed. A loud, carefree sound. 'Well, I am very glad

to see you here.'

My cheeks went hot. 'I am glad to see you too.'

'Are you staying for the after-party?'

The thought made me cringe, imagining the crowd, the noise. I hesitated.

'You're not the party type, I know.' Her attention flickered, and she looked away, thoughtful. 'What are your plans?'

'No plans.' I shrugged.

'Perfect,' she said, grinning. 'Well, I'm not feeling well, so I'll have to skip the afterparty.'

'You're not well?'

She gave me a playful nudge and laughed. 'That's just what I'll say, silly. Let's go somewhere else.'

'Somewhere quiet,' I said, half to myself.

'Yes, away from *all* these people.' She tapped her chin. 'I'm just five platforms down. I could have a capsula here in ten minutes.'

I stammered an agreement, still in disbelief.

'Brilliant. I've got some lovely wine.' Her eyes shone. 'Don't you go anywhere. I'll be right back.'

NINETEEN

GREN

Of all the engagements I'd handled as Chief Minister, I hadn't expected this to be the one to test my nerves. The first thing that struck me as I crossed the front archway of the Royal Palace was the profound sense of its history. I cleared my throat twice before responding to the butler who greeted me. Suddenly, I was just a provincial upstart from Varcega, surrounded by a legacy that only served to underscore how little I belonged.

The woven carpet was plush beneath my feet. The butler, a tall, severe figure with a measured gait, led me up a grand staircase, lecturing me on royal etiquette.

'Never speak to Her Majesty unless spoken to,' he instructed. 'Always address her as "Your Majesty" instead of using "you" or "yours". I assume you've practised your head bow, Chief Minister.'

'I have.'

'May I see it, please?'

I performed a modest bow, as rehearsed. 'That's quite enough,' he said, sounding only partially satisfied. 'A few additional reminders: do not turn your back on Her Majesty, refrain from asking personal questions, and, above all, do not make physical contact with Her Majesty under any circumstances. It would also be wise to avoid any signs of nervousness or excitement.'

I offered a brief nod, as if his advice was all I needed to finally centre my thoughts before meeting a living relic of Rivennia's history. The pointed remarks I'd made about the monarchy's relevance during the campaign now echoed uncomfortably in my mind. And then there was the Game of Wagers. I couldn't stop thinking about how we'd placed bets on when the queen would die. Standing in the palace, it dawned on me just how disrespectful that was – to make a game out of the death of an elderly woman who, good or bad, had dedicated her life to Rivennia.

'Any questions?' He looked down his nose at me, eyebrows raised.

'No,' I mumbled, keen to end the conversation. His entire demeanour had only magnified my sense of inadequacy.

The study room was larger and loftier than I'd imagined, with crimson and gold wallpaper, marble columns rising to elaborate sculpted vaults, and chandeliers that descended from each vault like glittering conifers. The butler gestured towards a chair by a heavy mahogany desk. I lowered myself into it, running my fingers over the raised velvet brocade. The detail and craftsmanship were astonishing, but I barely absorbed any of it; my mind was too preoccupied with the upcoming meeting.

Across from me, a grand fireplace dominated the wall. Above

its mantel hung an oil portrait of a young Queen Brynhilda, painted perhaps a century ago. Her high cheekbones and thin, unsmiling lips were distinctive features, even then. Her skin appeared smoother, still plumped with fat. Her hair, now a snow-white bun, had once been a dark, lustrous black. Even in her youth, she bore that inscrutable expression we so often associate with elders.

Without warning, the queen entered, gliding silently on a floating board. It seemed out of place against the traditional elegance surrounding us, an almost grotesque clash of eras. I stood up abruptly, feeling a jolt as I remembered the bow I'd been taught. I lowered my head in a quick but respectful gesture, and when I looked up, she was watching me intently. Her signature stand collar framed her withered neck, and below it, jewel-encrusted shoulder pads sat atop a cream-coloured dress.

'Chief Minister,' she said. 'Please, take your seat.' She turned to the butler. 'Thank you. You may go.'

The butler left.

'The sky-screens are particularly bright today, wouldn't you say?' Her voice, though frail, still reached every corner of the room.

'Yes, Your Majesty,' I replied. 'A fine day indeed.'

Silence grew between us. I resisted the urge to break it, recalling the butler's warnings. Then at last, she spoke, her eyes fixed on me.

'Fifteen,' she said, offering nothing more.

'Fifteen?' I repeated, hoping I didn't sound as lost as I felt.

'Fifteen Chief Ministers I have had the fortune to meet during my mandate.'

'That is a large number, Your Majesty. I am honoured to join that line and hope to carry out my duties with the same rigour and dignity as my predecessors.'

'I'm sure you will. I have no doubt.'

A trace of a smile flickered across her face, though it might have been a trick of the light.

'If pressed to guess, Chief Minister, what would you say is the single most important trait for the head of our government to possess?'

I had never been fond of this type of guessing game as a way of introducing a concept. 'I wouldn't presume to know the answer, Your Majesty,' I replied.

'Detachment,' she said. 'The single most important trait is detachment.'

I held her gaze, unsure how to respond.

'You see,' the queen continued, 'I am certain you wish not only to be a good Chief Minister but also a good man, a good husband, a good grandchild, and, one hopes, a good father someday. You may indeed be all those things, but your actions cannot be driven solely by that wish. The responsibilities laid upon you demand that you do the work – and do it well – without letting the desire to perform interfere with the performance itself. The path of your work must instead be guided solely by the welfare of our citizens. This is where detachment is essential. A Chief Minister must ensure their agenda is rooted in sound, objective knowledge, setting aside personal conjectures. Public servants must understand that one's own experience is but a drop in the ocean, influenced by countless variables and plagued by unreliable memories.'

'I understand, Your Majesty.'

'I am glad you do.' She took a moment. 'I do not offer this advice lightly. You are a passionate speaker – a truly gifted one indeed. Yet one can't help but notice a certain thread in your ideology. And while I, of course, believe that the fight against ultrahumanism is an honourable pursuit, I do hope that your conviction is grounded objectively. Personal experiences must not dictate a political agenda, especially one that will shape the lives of billions, and of those who will come after them.'

The queen's words stirred something I'd tried to bury.

Those dark days. The darkest of all. My father had been the first to die, barely a day after returning from the clinic. There had been no warning – just a high fever, then seizures; all side effects the doctors had described as typical of longevity treatments. I had hidden behind a heavy curtain, blocking out the world. The smell of stale dust filled my nose as I pressed myself against the polyester fabric. In my newly found refuge, there was no one treating me with condescending pity, no one trying to tell me that things would be fine. Even at age seven, I knew things would not be fine.

Varcega was in chaos. The bombs that tore through the capital had targeted the politicians everyone called the 'Ultracons', a name I barely understood at the time but would forever associate with fear and destruction. Many of them lay buried in rubble, their deaths a grim reminder of how radical conservatism could ignite violence. Hospitals were overwhelmed, their doors closed to anyone who wasn't bleeding or broken. I remembered my grandfather's face, pale and still, as he sat by the radio, the static crackling. The streets were unsafe, the clinics unreachable, and no ambulance would come. I didn't need to be older to understand his helplessness. The explosions had shattered more than buildings; they had shattered any hope of saving my parents.

Through the thick folds, I could hear the adults in the next room. 'He'll come live with us.' It was my grandfather Rolan's voice amidst the broken sounds from the woman who had once been my mother. She was beyond grief, beyond shock;

something inside her had broken, and when she died a few days later, all that remained was a cold sack of flesh, emptied of the woman she had been. My real mother, like my father, had been taken the moment that treatment robbed them of who they were.

It was an irony that sneered at us all – a therapy meant to prolong life had severed theirs, turning a quest for betterment into a permanent tragedy.

'Do you understand me, Chief Minister?' the queen asked.

It seemed easy for her to speak of detachment, sitting upon a throne. The queen had endured personal tragedies, yes, but could her suffering compare to mine? And what did it matter if my convictions were rooted in my own losses? Surely, a man could use his past as fuel, as purpose. To pretend otherwise – to claim some sterile, objective stance on the question of humanity's future – felt more like denial than wisdom. If my personal history had led me to this cause, wasn't that just proof of its importance, of the need to protect humanity from repeating such mistakes? But debating with her would serve no purpose.

'I assure you, my beliefs are rooted not in personal grievances but in universal truths. My goal is to protect the human race and its unaltered genome.'

'As is mine,' she said. 'But remember, yours is the power to govern as you see fit. My role is only to advise.'

Without further words, she turned her floating board away, gliding out with the same quiet grace. But her message remained, needling at me. I resisted the feeling, unwilling to let her doubts – or anyone else's – cast shadows over my convictions.

•••

With only minutes before I was due to leave for Congress, Clara and I paced around my office in restless circles. A noise like muffled ocean waves filtered through the glass as protesters gathered in the square below, hardly setting the calm atmosphere I needed before the final deliberations. Some were even settling in tents, prepared to camp overnight. Pigeons gathered around them, pecking at scattered crumbs.

'Test me,' I told Clara.

She raised her voice like an actress on cue. 'Chief Minister, your views on gene enhancements are outdated and anti-progress. Why are you so stubbornly taking Rivennia backwards?'

'My views aren't anti-progress,' I replied. 'They're about protecting people from a technology we don't really understand. I am not going to sit by while corporations tamper with humanity's future, completely unaccountable. We've already seen the cost of charging ahead without—'

'A bit defensive.'

I exhaled, reining in my temper. 'You're right,' I conceded. 'Progress doesn't mean greenlighting every new idea. Sometimes progress is about knowing when to say no.'

The approval in her eyes eased my mood, but only just.

'I hate this,' I said, pressing my hands to my temples. 'The whole game is rigged. The rules are so twisted that, even if we win, we'll still be left wondering why.'

Clara looked me in the eyes. 'We'll know why, Gren.'

'There's almost no point in preparing any more, is there?'

'Would you like me to stop?'

I groaned, though I knew she was right. Anticipating and preparing for all possible arguments was the only thing that might save me from the circus out there.

'When you approved that grant,' she said, 'you knew where this was going.'

I stiffened, taken aback by the edge in her voice, as though she were accusing me. Coming from Clara, it stung more than I cared to admit.

'I thought it would help.' My jaw clenched. 'I thought aligning with the Human Order might establish a stronger foundation for us.'

'So it's done, then. And now, we have to live with the consequences. If we win, we win. That's the goal, isn't it?'

Her tone was that of someone explaining life's harsh truths to the uninitiated. She knew the full story; she knew I'd been misled and cornered, yet her words held no comfort.

'What I didn't know,' I continued, forcing strength into my voice, 'was that Voychenko would blackmail me, and that this could threaten my entire government. I didn't know about his clandestine society or their twisted practices.'

Clara looked me straight in the eye again. 'You're not normally one to lose your nerve, Gren. Don't start now. What's done is done with Voychenko. Worrying won't change it.'

I sank into the sofa, rubbing my eyes. Clara joined me.

'What's done is done,' she repeated. Her voice was stripped of understanding, leaving me feeling exposed and isolated. 'Voychenko is up to no good. I don't know what, exactly, but he wants you too tangled up in it to escape. This way, if anything goes public, you'll look like one of them, part of his circle. And that will keep you quiet; bound to secrecy.'

I sighed. 'I understand the risk,' I said. 'But keeping close to the Lodgers is the only way to stay a step ahead. Standing against them outright would be the end of us.'

Clara offered me a gentler look, but it did little to dispel the effect of her earlier words. 'It's time to head off,' she said.

We rose, both pausing to breathe in. Clara adjusted my collar and patted down the creases in my jacket, a familiar ritual that propelled me to action. When she wished me luck, I saw the sincerity in her, along with a rare glimmer of vulnerability in her otherwise unshakeable demeanour.

The chamber was alive with the usual prelude to deliberation. Members of Congress shuffled to their seats, murmuring final off-the-record comments, verifying final facts, and glancing through their well-studied notes. It was more like the atmosphere before a battle than an examination. From my seat at the sunken centre of the auditorium, I had a clear command of the room – every speaker in view, and all eyes on me when I chose to speak. I adjusted my cuffs and sat straighter. Today had to go perfectly.

The front rows were filled with Congress members – some guarded, some charged. Beyond them, the audience ranged from People's Sentinels and Nonpartisan Assembly officials to media representatives and select invitees.

Earlier that morning, Clara had briefed me on the timeline. Voting would take place an hour after the session ended, with results expected by dusk. For the Coercive Sterilisation Bill to advance to the legislative phase, we needed at least seventy per cent support. I couldn't help but question whether any newly converted allies, secured through Voychenko's influence, would be enough to tip the balance in our favour.

Weeks of debate had reduced the bill to its nickname, 'The Freedom Bill' – a mocking jab coined by Sebastian Brown. He and others like him argued that the measure undermined personal liberty. I fought to suppress a snarl as I recalled their rhetoric. This wasn't about freedom. It was about the conservation of our species.

The session began with my address. I rose, ensuring my voice came out calm and clear. 'Esteemed members of Congress,' I began. 'We stand at a crossroads today, where progress demands responsibility. We have seen the dangers of unchecked genetic tampering. Families shattered. Lives irreversibly changed. My bill ensures that treatments altering genetic traits are confined to the individual and do not enter the genetic pool, preserving humanity's integrity for future generations.'

I delved into the data – evidence of stillbirths among women with enhancements, studies linking experimental therapies to long-term health conditions. Anticipating Sebastian's objections, I emphasised the point of personal agency. 'This is not a restriction,' I said, meeting their eyes. 'It is an assurance. Those who choose enhancements will retain full autonomy, but they must agree to prevent heritable risks.'

I could almost feel a pulse running through the room as I continued. The data spoke for itself, but data alone wouldn't win this political battle.

When Sebastian took the floor, his booming voice rang out, gripping everyone's attention. 'What have we become,' he began, pacing, 'if we cannot trust ourselves to care for one another? What are we, if in our most vulnerable moments, we turn to sterilisation as a solution?'

He spoke with a gloss of assurance, a mask of certainty. 'We cannot allow ourselves to be reduced to commodities. Human dignity is not something we trade for promises of safety.' He gestured expansively, raising his voice. 'We cannot forget about our individual freedom!'

The murmurs in the chamber grew louder. His theatrics were working, and I could see doubt creeping into the faces of many of the Congress members.

I analysed his every move, every intonation, and it was then that something about his performance struck me as off. He was always passionate, but today, his mannerisms had a touch of wildness – sudden jerks of his head, overdramatic gestures. Adrenaline, I assumed at first. But as he descended from his seat and approached me, the air in the chamber changed.

'We can't forget our freedom!' he shouted.

His face was now inches from mine, his breath hot and stale. Then, in a sudden, shocking motion, he grabbed my face with both hands and pressed his lips to mine.

Gasps erupted around the room. I jerked back, stunned, but Sebastian only chuckled – a hollow, almost maniacal sound. 'We can't forget!' he shouted again, stepping back. Then, before anyone could react, he began stripping off his clothes. His jacket slid to the floor in a crumpled heap, followed by his shirt. Then came his trousers, pooling around his ankles, and finally the rest, until he stood completely naked under the chamber's merciless lights, his pale, wiry frame stark against the varnished wood, arms raised in defiance.

The chamber was in chaos. Security bots descended, their protective metal suits moving swiftly towards Sebastian. He continued shouting as they restrained him, his voice now a monotone chant: 'Freedom! Freedom!'

I stayed rooted in my seat, my mind racing to process what had just happened. It wasn't merely an outburst – this was calculated turmoil. A disruption designed to destabilise. However, beneath the shock, I was aware of something else: opportunity. Sebastian had overstepped, and in doing so, he had handed me the moment I needed.

As the bots escorted him out, I rose to my feet. The room fell silent, all eyes on me. I straightened my jacket and addressed the assembly with a calm but firm voice. 'What we have witnessed here today,' I said, 'is a reminder of the very dangers my bill seeks to address. When passion outweighs reason, when impulse overrides responsibility, we put not only ourselves at risk, but the future of humanity itself.'

I scanned the room, meeting their eyes one by one. 'This bill is not about control; it is about safeguarding our species. Today, we have witnessed the consequences of unchecked emotion and how unreliable individuals can become. We must not let such instability dictate our decisions.'

There was a subtle but significant shift in the room's energy. When the session adjourned, Clara was waiting for me outside the chamber.

'That was...unexpected,' she said.

'To put it mildly.' I took off my jacket and rolled back my sleeves.

'You handled it well.' She frowned slightly. 'But don't let your guard down. This isn't over.'

'I know,' I said, exhaling. 'But today, we took the first step.'

As I pushed through the throng of shouting reporters and surging crowds towards my waiting capsula, I could see that the road ahead would only grow more unpredictable.

The capsula hummed to a stop just shy of midnight, and I stepped into the cool night air at Lacun Park. I made the ten-minute walk to the pond flanked by a retinue of security bots. Their torch beams carved narrow paths through the dim, uneven light, catching the wet sheen of dew on the grass. The distant murmur of the city blended with the chirping of insects and the occasional rustle of something unseen.

When I reached the pond, I let my steps slow. The setting radiated tranquillity, the water smooth and black. I could easily picture this place under the sky-screen light: families strolling along the tiled paths and children laughing as they raced past the benches. For a moment, I let myself forget the challenges ahead, the battles still waiting to be fought. I wasn't thinking about Congress, the Lodges, or even Fredrica.

And then I saw her.

Her silhouette emerged from the darkness, fluid and graceful. It struck me all at once how vividly I remembered her from before – the way her presence had stolen my breath then, just as it did now. In this quiet, private moment, she wasn't merely beautiful; she had an energy that drew me in without effort.

'I told you it was nice here,' she said.

The sound of her voice made her real, broke the spell.

'I believe you now,' I replied, smiling despite myself.

I gestured to the bots behind me. 'Please, stay here. I won't go far.' They acknowledged the instruction with a nod, their gazes fixed forward.

Turning back to Fredrica, I asked, 'Mind if I join you?'

'Please.'

We began to walk, side by side, our steps falling into an easy rhythm. There was something about her that made the world feel smaller, more manageable. For a fleeting moment, it was as though this was all that mattered – her company, this path, the quiet night.

'I guess congratulations are in order,' she said, glancing at me.

I chuckled. 'Thank you. What a day it's been.'

'Ninety-two per cent, no less. That must be a record.'

'One of the highest, certainly.'

'I guess we got just the right amount of crazy there. Any more, and perhaps the votes would have been suspended altogether,' she said, huffing out a laugh.

Her words carried a trace of agency I hadn't anticipated, making me pause.

'*We* got...?'

'Oh,' she said, waving a hand, brushing it aside. 'Don't worry. It's just a figure of speech. I meant you and me. My father doesn't know a thing, if that's what you're worried about. And of course, you weren't in on it either; you couldn't have been. Going into that chamber, you had enough to focus on without extra distractions.'

I stared at her. 'It was *you*?'

Her eyes widened slightly, as if gauging how much to reveal. 'I only wanted to help.'

'And you did,' I admitted, though my voice carried a note of hesitation. 'But how?'

'A mild psychedelic. Completely safe and undetectable,' she said.

I held my breath as I processed her words. 'But...how did you know it would work?'

'I didn't.' She smirked. 'I certainly didn't expect him to kiss you.' There was a hint of real amusement in her. 'We simply allowed him to express his true feelings more freely.'

The audacity of it all startled me. It was bold; reckless even. The shock remained – but alongside it, a spark of admiration. 'Is that fair, though? His career is ruined now.'

She stopped walking and turned to face me, calm but rigid. 'Fairness... It takes a Varcegian to believe in such a thing.'

What was she expecting me to say to that?

'If fairness matters,' she continued, 'then let's call it fair that one career was a small price to pay for taking the first meaningful step to protect humanity. Don't you agree?'

My moral compass spun wildly without finding its bearing. She was a force of nature.

'I did this for you,' she said, stepping closer. Her perfume drifted between us, rich and intoxicating. It was the same fragrance I remembered from before – but tonight, it had a heightened intimacy, a memory wrapped in a vivid sensation, like reliving the past. My heart quickened as she came closer still.

'Thank you,' I whispered. Before I could second-guess myself, I leaned in. Her lips brushed mine, tentative at first. Then the kiss deepened, slow but consuming. My hands found her waist, pulling her closer, and her fingers traced my face. It was a moment I couldn't have resisted, one as inevitable as breathing.

When she pulled away, the world came rushing back. She resumed walking, like nothing had happened, leaving me to gather my thoughts and catch my breath.

'Have you met with the queen yet?' she asked. Her voice betrayed nothing of the moment we'd just shared.

'I have,' I replied, still reeling.

'Good,' she said. 'We must ensure you win the Game of Wagers.'

There was a severe undertone in her words.

'And if I lose?' I asked.

Her pause was brief but telling. 'Let's not even consider that.' She sounded determined, but there was something else I couldn't identify – fear, guilt; perhaps both.

'Fredrica,' I pressed, my voice rising. 'What happens if I lose?'

For the first time that evening, her gaze faltered, sliding off mine before returning with sudden force. 'Just focus on winning.' She was quieter now, almost gentle, but her words left me more unsettled than reassured. Winning a wager – a prediction – seemed absurdly abstract. Was that truly what she meant? Was she suggesting something else? The notion was too morbid to entertain but too persistent to dismiss.

Before I could shape my confusion into words, she smiled – abruptly, disarmingly. 'We should do this again,' she said, brushing away the tension.

And then she was gone, slipping into the darkness, vanishing so completely it felt unreal. The lingering taste of her kiss was the only proof that I hadn't imagined the entire encounter.

TWENTY

PRIMULA

THE DULL THROB IN MY SKULL signalled the start of a headache – one of those nagging ones that dared to ruin an otherwise decent evening. I grabbed a mild sedative, popped it dry, and told myself it didn't count as breaking my promise to stay clean. Just a nudge to get my head in order after the gruelling week of prepping for the launch pageant. That event had drained me, body and soul, and I was glad to have it behind me.

Sam looked a bit out of place across the living room, perched on the edge of one of the oversized sofas, as if uncertain whether he should be sitting there. The fire opposite us wasn't even real – just a high-tech illusion – but it gave off heat, smelled like oak, and could probably burn your hand if you got too close. It was all unnecessarily clever, but I couldn't help finding it a little silly.

'If it burns and crackles like fire, and it scorches your fingers to the bone when you touch it, what's not bloody real about it?' I said as I kicked off my shoes, letting them clatter onto the marble floor. He flinched slightly but gave a polite laugh, fiddling with his shirt cuffs like they'd suddenly grown too tight.

Men had sat in this room before – plenty of them – and they'd all blended into one unremarkable mould. I wasn't stupid; I knew most of them wouldn't have been there if it weren't for my fame. Sam wasn't quite like them, though. He definitely wasn't here for a glimpse of glamour or to bask in my fading spotlight. And that put me on edge more than I wanted to let on.

'My house bots are out of service,' I said, striding towards the kitchen. 'So, I'll fix us some drinks. What's your poison?'

'I'll help,' he said, jumping up quickly, like a student desperate to please.

'Brilliant,' I called over my shoulder, gesturing for him to follow.

The kitchen, with its polished granite and chrome, was cold compared to the cosy living room. Through the wall-length glass panes, the lawn stretched out like a crafted background, the cypress trees standing in perfect alignment under the soft glow of the floodlights. Sam stood by the window, mesmerised by the view, his silhouette outlined against the garden.

'What about some wine?' I opened a cabinet and pulled out a dusty bottle. 'This one's from Astrin. Year 495. It's meant to be nice.'

'Sounds good,' he said, easing himself onto one of the stools at the island. His movements were stiff and deliberate, like he didn't trust himself not to knock something over.

I poured the wine, sliding a glass towards him as I perched across from him. My hand brushed his back, and his muscles under my fingers tensed slightly. Seeing him wound up so tight only made me want to unravel him.

'Relax,' I said, leaning back. 'The kitchen won't bite, and neither will I.'

That got a laugh out of him. He ran a hand over his corkscrew hair, looking down at his glass. 'I'm not used to...this kind of place. Or this kind of company.'

'What kind of company is that?'

He gestured vaguely. 'The kind that lives in this type of place, and doesn't spend half their life worrying about bills.'

'You think I don't have my worries?' I said, keeping my tone light but letting an edge slip through.

He looked at me then, really looked, his eyes searching mine in a way that made me brace myself. It wasn't the usual look men gave me, the hungry, hollow stare of someone wanting to *take*. Sam's gaze was curious, almost tender, like he was trying to understand me. It was unnerving.

'What do you worry about, then?' he asked.

I hesitated, the words catching in my throat. 'Losing what I have,' I said eventually. 'Losing...myself.'

It wasn't the kind of honesty I normally allowed, but there it was, laid bare. He didn't push, but the kindness in his eyes suggested he understood.

'And lately,' I added, swirling the wine in my glass, 'I've been worrying about the Lodges and their sick games. And about what happens to people like us when we lose.'

He blew out a breath. 'You and me both.'

I studied him, his unease still present but gradually dissolving under the wine and our conversation. There was something raw about him, something real. He wasn't bothered to put on a show of confidence or pretend to be anything other than himself.

'You're not like the others,' I said.

'Guess I'm just not like most people.' He tilted his head

in a small, dismissive motion. That self-deprecating charm of his brought more warmth to the room than any fake fire ever could.

'No, you're not,' I said quietly, perhaps more to myself than to him.

I wasn't used to silences like this, ones that didn't need filling. And for the first time in years, I didn't experience the need to put up a front or play a part. I just let it be.

'You're different too,' he said after a moment. 'Not what I expected.'

'And what did you expect?' I rested my chin on my hand, locking eyes with him.

He paused, his shoulders rising and falling awkwardly. 'Dunno. Someone who didn't care.'

'Care about what?'

'About someone like me, for instance.'

I opened my mouth, searching for a clever reply, but the words didn't come. His honesty had somehow disabled the defences I tended to rely on. There was no quip, no performative charm – just me, sitting across from someone who seemed to want to take the time to see more of me than most ever bothered to.

'I don't buy into that,' I said after a moment. 'This idea of "people like me" and "people not like me". People are just people. Aren't they? Someone told me recently that we don't have just one version of ourselves, so perhaps there's a version of me who cares about a version of you, and vice versa.'

Sam gave me a gentle smile, and for the first time, I noticed the faint dimples on his cheeks. Something about him made the storm in my mind settle into a strange kind of calm.

Then, the headache returned, intensifying rapidly, reminding me that calm was never my state for long. A pulse behind my eyes that made me wince. I pressed my fingers to my head, closing my eyes briefly.

'Are you alright?' Sam asked.

'Yeah, just a headache,' I said. 'They come and go. Nothing new.'

He didn't look convinced, but he let it rest.

'You look nervous,' he finally said. 'You know, you can tell me if it's something more. I'm good at listening.'

It wasn't what I'd expected to hear. I debated telling him to drop it. But something about the way he said it – his earnestness, without the usual undertone of expectation – made me stop and reconsider.

'It's…a little complicated,' I started, my voice lowering slightly. 'Not something I tell just anyone.'

'You don't have to tell me,' he said quickly. 'Not if you're not ready.'

That made me laugh. 'If I waited until I was ready for anything, I'd wait my whole life.'

He smiled, but didn't interrupt.

'Alright,' I said, exhaling slowly. 'Here's the thing. I'm not… normal. Not completely, anyway.'

His brow furrowed, curiosity lighting up his eyes. I continued before I lost my nerve.

'When I was a kid, my parents had this bright idea to give me neuronal enhancements. It was supposed to make me smarter, more capable – whatever... But the treatments were experimental, and halfway through, the doctor disappeared. He vanished without a trace. This was back in 480. Do you remember the ethnic cleansing attacks against Glossdenians? No one took credit for those, but they were rampant in Lacunfort. My doctor was from Glossden, so…it must have been that, poor guy. And since everything was done under the table, there was no way to find someone else to finish the job.'

I paused, glancing at Sam to gauge his reaction. He didn't look disgusted or even surprised, just thoughtful.

'So, I'm left with this half-done enhancement, whatever that means,' I went on, motioning loosely. 'And now I get these migraines, and these nightmares that feel too bloody real. And on top of that, I'm afraid I'm going to be labelled "ultrahuman", which may as well be bloody leprosy according to some people around here.'

The words tumbled out fast, in a torrent of bottled frustration that I rarely let escape.

Sam was silent for a few moments, slowly processing my words. 'That's rough,' he said finally. 'But…you didn't choose that. It doesn't define who you are.'

I scoffed. 'Oh, it does. If people knew, they'd probably see me as some gene-tampered freak.'

'Good thing we've already established,' he said, his lips twitching into something close to a grin, 'that I'm not like most people. And I don't think you're a freak.'

I looked away, suddenly uncomfortable under his gaze.

'I get it, though,' he added. 'The labels, the assumptions. It's exhausting. People don't know half of what you've been through, but they think they've got you all figured out.'

'Exactly,' I muttered, my fingers curling around the stem of my glass. 'They don't know. And frankly, most of the time, they don't even *want* to know.'

'But *I* do,' he said. 'I would want to know.'

That brought my eyes back to his. There was no judgment there, no pity. Just Sam. Quiet, solid, truthful. The ache in my chest eased, just a little, and for the first time in what felt like forever, I let myself believe that maybe someone could see me for more than what I'd been made into – and accept all of me.

I squared my shoulders, shaking off the vulnerability threatening to take root. 'Enough about me,' I said, lifting my glass. 'Your turn. What's your biggest secret, Sam?'

He hesitated, then began rubbing the side of his jaw. 'It's not… I mean, it's not the same as yours, but it's…' He trailed off, his words faltering.

'Spit it out,' I teased, trying to lighten the mood. 'Come on, it can't be *that* bad.'

He gave a small, nervous cough. 'You might need more wine for this.'

I broke into a hearty laugh, natural and unforced. Perhaps this evening would turn out better than I'd expected.

TWENTY-ONE

SAM

PRIMULA'S QUESTION PULLED me back to that hospital bed.

My body was tender and unfamiliar.

'Samantha Rosendale?' the nurse bot called from the hallway.

I looked up from the reclining bed as the backrest hummed, adjusting upward. 'Yes.'

'May I come in?'

'Yeah, sure,' I replied, my voice catching slightly.

'Post-op, age eighteen?'

I struggled to speak but managed a mumbled, 'Mm-hmm.'

'How are you feeling this morning?'

'Bit thirsty.' My voice was raspier than I expected. 'Hurts to raise my arms.'

She moved to the bedside table, her hand hovering just above the cylindrical container as a scan flashed across its surface. 'Still some left,' she said. A thin tube extended with a soft click, and she clipped it to my collar like it was routine. 'Drink up.

You'll need the fluids.'

It had been nearly two years since the Corin dam collapsed, and water scarcity had turned rationing into a way of life. The sound of the liquid moving through the tube made me both excited and remorseful. My mouth was rough like sandpaper, but still here I was, sipping easily, while most people in Corin were queuing for their daily share, hoping the pumps hadn't run dry again.

The water was cool against my tongue, but it left a bitter taste behind. I couldn't shake the thought that every sip came at someone else's expense, while babies and the elderly were dying of dehydration.

The nurse's tone turned gentler. 'I'm going to inspect you now, Samantha. Have you looked at yourself since the operation?'

I shook my head. The name didn't sit right, but I let it go, focusing on the task ahead.

'You'll notice some bruising and swelling. That's perfectly normal. There are drainage tubes on either side of your chest. They're there to help the healing process.'

I forced myself to listen, imagining the worst. Still, the thought of a life without binders, without hunching or hiding, kept me going. This was the beginning of something better.

'Let's change the dressing,' she said, stepping closer.

I straightened cautiously, every movement a negotiation with pain. The sting sharpened as she removed the bandages. I tried and failed not to wince. When the last strip fell away, I hesitated, then looked down.

My chest was bruised, the skin blotched with angry shades of beetroot and mustard. The incisions were smaller and less offensive than I'd expected, though thin streams of blood seeped from one of them. The drainage tubes curved awkwardly, like frowning faces, but none of it mattered compared to the flatness – an absence that spoke volumes. For the first time, I wasn't betrayed by my body. The relief was overwhelming.

Hair would grow back, scars would fade, but this was freedom.

A year into the hormones, my body was already taking a different shape. My voice had deepened, the scratchy rasp now second nature. A faint shadow of stubble teased my jaw, and my muscles were denser, more solid. Even the unexpected changes – the new-found angles in my face, the coarser texture of my skin – were welcome signs that I was becoming myself. The strangest part was the hunger, constant and insistent, as though my body was recalibrating every cell. It wasn't just food; it was touch, feelings, life itself. Every sensation felt heightened, more alive.

The nurse had just started applying a fresh dressing when the door opened. Mum stepped in, her face giving nothing away.

'No, not on my budget,' she snapped. 'If he reckons I'm footing the bill for that, he's got another thing coming.' Her words were brisk, each one landing like the tap of her heel on the floor.

'She's not talking to us,' I whispered, noticing the device tucked in her hand.

A blunt, 'Fine. Later, then,' ended the call, and she finally looked up, her eyes skimming over me.

The nurse finished securing the new bandages, and Mum tilted her head, appraising the sight.

'Is it what you wanted?' she asked.

'It's sore, but yeah. Once it heals, I think it'll be perfect.' I tried to add a note of confidence, but it came out uneven.

'How long's that going to take?'

'A few weeks, they think.'

'And this is just a knife job, not changing them genes, are they?' She shot me a severe look.

'None of this is an enhancement.'

She nodded, her earrings swaying. 'Good. Well, I can't stay long, but I'm glad to see you're managing.' Her eyes darted around the room. 'Need anything? Got enough water?'

Her words sounded more like obligation than care. If she'd listened to me years ago, let me start blockers when I'd first asked, all of this might've been avoided. Instead, I was here, dealing with what should've been dealt with long ago.

'I'm alright,' I said, swallowing the knot in my throat. 'But, yeah, actually, I think I just ran out of water again.'

She turned to the nurse. 'Can my son have more water, please? If there's not enough, I'll order some from Lacunfort myself.'

'Yes, it's not a problem,' the nurse said, stepping out of the room.

It took me a moment to register what she'd said. My *son*. That word hovered in the air between us after all the others had dissipated. I blinked hard, my eyes threatening to well, my chest tightening in a way that had nothing to do with the surgery. It wasn't an apology, but it was something. A validation. Somehow, the day didn't feel so heavy any more.

'Like being a teenager wasn't hard enough,' Primula said.

I glanced at her, angling my face upwards. 'It's all much better now.'

'You're a man,' she stated – neutral, but searching.

'Always was,' I replied, holding her gaze. 'Just not…visibly so.'

She leaned in slightly. 'Well, I'm not sure how to say this, but…I really appreciate you telling me. I'm glad you felt like you could.'

'I wouldn't have, if I didn't think you'd understand. I don't hide it, but I don't go around broadcasting it either. I'll always tell if I'm asked.'

'Fair enough,' she said, leaning back. 'People make too big a deal of all sorts of things these days. But I get what you mean – it's never easy to know when to bring up something like that.'

'Say it too soon, and you're oversharing. Say it too late, and you're hiding something. Feels like a lose-lose sometimes.'

Primula didn't reply, but she gave me a look like she agreed. Later that night, as silence settled over us, I lay beside her, watching the rise and fall of her chest, its fullness as graceful as the rest of her. Vulnerability and strength seemed to intertwine in a way I couldn't quite fathom. For all the fame and glamour, Primula longed for the same things I did: safety, love, and a place to belong.

Gently, so as not to wake her, I pressed a kiss to her shoulder and let my eyes close, feeling, for the first time in years, that I wasn't alone.

The sun made my skin tingle like it'd been slapped raw. I sat watching Primula slice through the water as though she'd melted into it – not a single splash. Her hair streamed out behind her like ribbons unravelling; a bright pink streak against the blue of the pool. She moved with the ease of someone born to it. I felt like the luckiest bloke alive just being there with her. It hadn't been that long, but nothing in my life had ever hit me this hard. Not even close.

When the heat got to us, we moved to the shade and plonked ourselves down, still dripping, our skin hot to the touch. Beyond the terrace, the Astrin Sea sprawled into the horizon. A deep, shimmering blue. Its constant waves were a reminder of how vast the world was – and how insignificant we were in it.

Primula flipped on the hologram display next to the table. A newsfeed flickered to life, showing a reporter outside the Royal Palace. He spoke of Queen Brynhilda, whose health had once again become the topic of hushed speculation. They'd rolled out more medical bots to keep an eye on her, all of them taking orders from some Yunnia D – the fanciest bot yet, apparently. Then the footage cut to inside the palace, showing Yunnia D in what looked like a proper posh medical suite. If you didn't know better, you'd swear she was human. Smooth skin and eyes that blinked and locked onto things like she was alive. She wore one of those spotless white nurse uniforms: blouse buttoned right up, neat skirt just below the knees, and the royal crest stitched on her chest. In the background, the voice-over droned on as Yunnia D waved her hands about, directing the other bots like she owned the place. Every move was so natural – it was like watching a real person give orders.

'Look at that.' Primula gestured towards the display. She gripped her glass of water, knuckles turning white. 'She's got an army of bloody bots keeping her alive now. The day of my prediction is tomorrow.' She stared at the hologram, her lips pressing together.

'You could still win even if she hangs on a bit longer.'

Primula's dark eyes narrowed. 'What do you mean?'

'The winner's not whoever guesses the exact day. It's whoever's closest to the actual date.'

She sipped her drink, the ice rattling softly in the glass. 'Closest date. That's right.'

'So,' I added, 'if she dies after your prediction but before

Gren's, you're still in with a chance.'

'Huh.' She crunched a piece of ice between her teeth, her gaze distant and troubled. 'That makes sense. I've got more time than I thought.' She gave a brittle laugh, like she was trying to convince herself it was all fine.

When she invited me to spend the weekend at her house in Astrin, I wasn't sure whether to accept. My backlog of work from analysing the resource puzzle – not to mention how little I could concentrate after the Liffdom fiasco – was enough to keep me buried in census data for weeks, even if the work itself was straightforward. But I wouldn't have been able to focus properly anyway, and the thought of swapping it all for the sea – and Primula's company – had been too tempting to pass up.

The house was every bit as extravagant as her place in Lacunfort. High ceilings, marble everywhere, and rooms so vast they seemed designed to dwarf anyone inside. The terrace offered a perfect view of the sea, with the pool perched just high enough to make it look like it spilled straight into the endless blue beyond.

'When's Gren's prediction again?' she asked, interrupting my thoughts.

'I think the twenty-third day of month six,' I replied. 'Mine's later – the nineteenth day of month one, next year.'

She frowned, her fingers tapping against the glass. 'So it's me and Gren now, isn't it? A proper showdown.'

'Do you even want to win?' I asked. Then, before I could stop myself, I added, 'I don't. The thought of having to see those people forever unsettles me more than anything.'

Primula sighed, brushing a damp strand of hair away from her face. 'Mainly, I just want it to be over,' she said, sounding drained. 'Maybe it won't be as bad as we make it out to be?'

She was trying to sound casual, but it didn't land that way.

She stared out at the sea, her fingers idly tracing the rim of her glass. When she spoke again, her voice was thinner. 'Do you ever think about what your life's been about, Sam? Like, really think about it?'

'All the time.'

She nodded slowly, fixing on the horizon. 'This might sound ridiculous, but I always thought I'd be a mum someday. Not that I had a plan for it or anything. I just thought it'd happen, like it does for everyone else. But now, I'm well into my thirties, and well…' She shrugged, her movements stiff, like she wanted to push the thought away. 'This game – it's grim, it's morbid, and the whole Thomas Locke thing terrified me. But craziness aside, the Liffdom Lodges could give me a shot at building some useful connections. Connections that could free me from begging some idiot like Artur Voychenko for scraps of attention until I fade into nothing.'

Her voice cracked just slightly, though she hid it with a sip of water. I didn't know what to say.

'Why do you think they only want one of us?' she asked suddenly. 'Or why wouldn't they just invite Gren to join them and be done with it?'

'They'd probably want you over Gren. Have you considered that? You're probably underestimating your pull,' I said. 'You've got reach. The young look up to you. You can change public opinion in ways that Gren can't. That's influence.'

She snorted softly. 'But that only lasts for as long as I'm the *pretty* one.' She sighed and swirled her drink again. 'I can't stand their rituals. Those wigs, that horror show with the ants. It's enough to make anyone want to run away.'

I grimaced, my insides clenching at the memory. 'I deleted everything. Calendar notes, files. Didn't want a trace of it left.'

'We've got to be careful,' she said, her fingers brushing

against mine on the table.

'Yeah.' I gripped her hand. 'We do.'

She let out a slow breath, her eyes meeting mine before she turned away, refilling my glass from the jug.

I held her hand tightly as we walked down the carpeted hallway. Our footsteps seemed louder than normal in the stillness. 'The door at the far end. That's her room.'

Primula stopped abruptly, pulling me to a halt. 'Wait.' Her voice had the force of a command. From her bag, she drew out a small device, flipping it open with theatrical precision. A white glow lit her face, defining the angles of her cheekbones and casting shadows beneath her eyes. She studied her reflection, her perfectly shaped eyebrows rising ever so slightly as she tilted her head one way, then the other. She tucked loose strands of hair behind her ears in a practised motion. Then, to my quiet amusement, she stretched her upper lip over her teeth, inspecting them with such focus that I had to fight the urge to laugh.

'How do I look?' she asked, finally snapping the device shut.

'Magnificent, as always,' I said, unable to stop the smile spreading across my face. I didn't care if the staff were watching. She deserved to hear it, and I meant every word. Her confidence drew people in, magnetic even when it appeared a bit rehearsed. But it was at moments like these – when she let her guard slip without realising – that I loved her most.

Primula smoothed the silk blouse spilling from her lapels. Her tailored trousers hugged her legs perfectly, and her heels lifted her calves, giving her the poise of a demoiselle crane. She was every inch the elegant, untouchable beauty, but beneath her composure, there was a restlessness I wasn't used to seeing.

'This is ridiculous,' she muttered, brushing invisible lint off her jacket. 'Why do I feel all flustered? I'm a bloody embarrassment, even to myself.'

I gave a short laugh, hoping to ease the tension. 'She's probably more nervous than you are.'

Primula shot me a sceptical glance. 'And you?' Her tone turned mockingly accusatory. 'Why are you so calm? It's not fair, watching me get all fidgety while you strut around like it's no big deal.'

'I'm not nervous,' I admitted. 'I know you, and I know her. You'll get on just fine.' It was strange, feeling calm for once. Because this time, I actually believed what I was saying.

She rolled her eyes, but her look was more teasing than harsh. With one final, deliberate tug at her jacket, she straightened her posture and looked at me. 'Fine. Let's do this.'

I offered her my hand again, and her fingers slipped into mine with an ease that made me feel I was hers completely. As we neared Mum's room, muffled voices drifted out from one of the slightly ajar doors further up the hallway.

'Goodness me, it's her!' came a whisper.

'Let me see,' another voice said, faint but excited. 'Move over!'

I turned my head just in time to see the door click shut. I sighed and leaned closer to Primula. 'That's Mary,' I said, keeping my voice low. 'She's the one who tried to convince Mum her window wasn't real.'

Primula's lips parted in feigned shock. 'The bloody nerve.' She shot an icy glare at Mary's door, her fingers tightening around mine.

I chuckled. 'And, by the sound of it, a fan of yours.'

'Shut up,' she whispered, elbowing me playfully. She lowered her voice further, pointing at the next door down. 'Is this it?'

'Yes, this is Mum's,' I replied, tapping on the door twice. I wasn't expecting a reply, but almost instantly, my mother's voice called out, clear and melodic.

'Come in.'

The sound took me by surprise. She hadn't sounded that lively in months.

I opened the door, stepping inside with Primula close behind me. Mum was seated on the sofa, a book propped open on her lap. She put it down delicately, like a treasured artefact, making a show of its placement. It struck me as odd – Mum had never been much of a reader. She used to scoff at books, calling them the indulgences of people with too much time on their hands. Still, here she was, treating it like it was something precious.

Her appearance stopped me short. She'd powdered her face, softening the dark freckles that normally spanned her cheeks. Her hair was neatly combed, a scarlet ribbon tied around it, matching the cardigan draped over her shoulders. It was the most effort I'd seen her put into how she looked in years.

'Hello, Samuel,' she said, her face glowing.

I gestured to Primula. 'Mum, I'd like you to meet someone. This is Primula.'

Primula stepped forward, her movements uncharacteristically reserved. 'It's lovely to meet you,' she said, bowing her head slightly.

Mum clasped her hands together, eyes shining. 'I never dreamt I'd meet you in the flesh. This is a true honour.'

Primula smiled. 'The honour's mine. Sam speaks so fondly of you. Thank you for inviting me into your home.'

The tension in the room eased, bit by bit, as the conversation found its rhythm. They talked about life in Corin and Lacunfort, trading stories and laughs like old friends. I kept quiet, happy just to sit back and watch the two most important women in my life find a way to connect.

At some point, Mum said to Primula, 'That's a nice outfit, love. You look smashing.'

Primula's smile widened, and a rare tenderness softened her features. 'Thank you. I'm flattered. And may I say, you look absolutely radiant too.'

Mum giggled. It was a sound so rare it made my heart ache.

It wasn't until Doctor Khan interrupted us that the atmosphere dissolved. Primula's demeanour changed the moment she saw him. Her face went pale. Her body froze.

I glanced between them. 'Everything alright?'

But before anyone could answer, Primula moved awkwardly, bumping into the small medicine tray and sending it clattering to the floor. Pills scattered in every direction, a few rolling under the bed. Her face turned red. She dropped to her knees straight away, her hands unsteady as she scrambled to gather them, mumbling apologies under her breath.

I crouched beside her, placing a hand on her shoulder. 'Prim, leave it. It's alright.'

She looked up at me, her eyes brimming with tears, and then bolted for the door.

'Prim!' I called, but she didn't stop. Without thinking, I ran to catch up, the sound of her footsteps growing quieter as she turned the corner ahead.

I found her in the bay window at the end of the corridor, three flights down. Something terrible had caused her to flee, and I had followed as best I could, careful not to cause a commotion. By the time I got there, she was crumpled in one of the upholstered chairs, her face buried in her hands.

The chairs looked older than both of us put together, and

they were scratched all over, like someone had let a cat loose on them. I sat on the chair across from her, leaning forward with my elbows on my knees. For a long moment, the only sound was the soft hiccups of her breathing.

Finally, she lifted her head. Her eyes were red-rimmed, her face blotchy – rare for someone who always looked so flawless.

'I'm sorry,' she said. 'I'm so embarrassed.'

I didn't know what to say at first. She rarely let her guard down like this, and it gutted me to see her so broken. 'Prim, whatever's going on, we'll sort it. Just talk to me.'

She met my gaze but didn't speak right away. Then she sniffed hard, her shoulders rising and falling as she steadied herself.

'That doctor…' Her voice shook, and she looked away before meeting my eyes again. 'You know him?'

'Dr Khan? Yeah, he looks after Mum. Why?'

Her hands twisted in her lap, gripping her trousers like she wanted to tear the fabric. 'He was one of them. At The Dungeons. Called himself Chuck.' Her voice dropped to a whisper. 'Artur brought him there. To…to have sex with me. While he and his father watched.'

The floor seemed to tilt beneath me, and my thoughts scrambled to make sense of what I'd heard. I stared at Primula, but she didn't look back at me – just kept speaking like she needed to get it out, words pouring out faster now. 'I was completely out of control back then. Drugs, sex – it didn't matter. I didn't care about anything. I'd take whatever would numb me. But it wasn't just that.'

Her voice broke, and she swallowed hard, her hands trembling. 'I lost my baby, Sam. A little girl. And I can't stop thinking… What if it was my fault? The things I was taking back then, the things I was doing – it all adds up, doesn't it?

Even if the doctors say it was the enhancements, I know I didn't help.'

The last word came out as a gasp, and she collapsed forward, covering her face with her hands while sobs shook her entire body. Her tears were deep and full of pain, the kind that clawed their way out because there was no other place for them to go.

I didn't know what to do – only that I couldn't just sit there. I would have given anything to ease her pain. Sliding off my chair, I knelt in front of her and gently took her hands in mine. 'Prim,' I said. 'I'm here. I've got you.'

She didn't respond. Her shoulders heaved violently. I stayed there, grounding her as best I could, wishing I could pull her grief out of her and carry it myself.

'Prim, listen to me. None of that makes you a bad person. You weren't in a good place. You were hurting. And I don't think for a second that you meant for any of it to happen.' I squeezed her hands. 'You're not alone in this. I'm here, and I'm not going anywhere. Whatever it takes, we'll face it together.'

She stared at me, her eyes filling again, but this time they didn't overflow. She nodded, and a trace of that stubborn determination I loved so much came back.

'I don't deserve you,' she said.

'Don't say that. You deserve to heal. You deserve to have someone who loves you, and I do. I love you. I always will.'

Her lips quivered as she fought to hold herself together again. I stood and gently pulled her to her feet. She was still shaky, but she let me guide her, her fingers tightening on mine.

'Prim, I want to show you something. It's a tradition from Corin.' I took her hand and placed it against my wrist, guiding her fingers to wrap around it. Then I wrapped my hand around her wrist in return. 'It's called a Corinnian life bond. I've never done it before. It's deeply symbolic and meant only for your soulmate.'

Her brow furrowed slightly, her lips parting as she listened.

'This is how it works,' I said, demonstrating. 'We each hold the other's wrist like this.' I made sure our grips were firm but not tight. 'It's a symbol of strength – a promise.'

I lowered my voice to a whisper. 'Then we bring our foreheads together, like this, and close our eyes. It means we trust each other completely. It's a bond that's supposed to last a lifetime.'

Her skin was warm against mine as we clasped each other's wrists. We leaned closer, our foreheads gently touching, and I breathed her in.

'Now, repeat after me.' Keeping my eyes shut, I inhaled deeply. 'I vow to stand by you, in moments of light and shadow.'

She repeated, 'I vow to stand by you, in moments of light and shadow.'

'I hold dear all that makes you who you are.'

'I hold dear all that makes you who you are,' she said quietly.

'Together, we are unbreakable, through all that life may bring.'

'Together, we are unbreakable, through all that life may bring.'

The world faded. It was just us, our breaths mingling. When we pulled back, her eyes shimmered with calm reflection.

'A lifetime, then,' she whispered.

'A lifetime.'

TWENTY-TWO

PRIMULA

EVEN UNDERWATER, THE MAN had to wear the wretched cloak. This one was strapped to his body so the fabric couldn't float free. The water in the cube reached about five feet from the floor, enough that he had to strain his neck and stand on tiptoes to keep his face above the surface. Standing normally brought the waterline to his eyebrows, which forced him to alternate between standing tall and bending his knees, arms thrashing just to stay afloat. Either way, it was clear neither position could be maintained for long.

No food. No rest. His only escape was a morbid choice – to stay submerged, flood his lungs with water, and let the bright lights of the cube blink out forever. That, I somehow knew, was the purpose of the experiment: to answer the question that hung over it all – how long before the body gave up, after the synthetic enhancements?

The water rippled in eerie silence. My heart ached just

watching him. But was I watching, or was I him? The lines between us blurred until his exhaustion, his hunger, and the terrible resignation were mine too.

Then the alarm drilled into my skull. I gasped, flailing out of bed as the noise receded into the background.

Sam's voice followed, paired with a gentle kiss on my forehead. 'Morning, Prim. It's just the alarm.'

I groaned, stretching stiff limbs, trying to shake off the nightmare. 'News service,' I shouted. 'Look up: Queen Brynhilda.'

The familiar monotone of the invisible gadget started at once: '*Then and Now*, the new documentary about the queen's life across the early and modern eras, now available in hologram—'

'Skip.'

'A new statue was unveiled at the heart of Platform 37—'

'Skip.'

'An exclusive interview with the staff at the Royal Office and a peek into the monarch's—'

'Shut down,' I snapped, rubbing my eyes.

Sam stood by the bed, his smile faltering at the edges, though he quickly masked it. His eyes darted to the wall display before meeting mine. 'She doesn't seem to have died yet,' he teased with forced lightness. 'It's the ninth day of month six. The next prediction will be closer now.'

'No shit.' My voice came out rougher than intended. He kept his calm, though his fingers fidgeted briefly at his side.

'I'm sorry,' he said. 'I know you thought joining Liffdom could help you. I'm sure there will be other ways. They chose you for a reason. You're exactly what they need – it's just bad timing.' He cleared his throat. 'But you shouldn't let this stop you, if joining is what you want.'

The words were kind, but my mind had already wandered. As Sam continued getting ready, the wall display blinked to life with my messages, one standing out in urgent red. A sudden pang hit me as I skimmed it. Igor Voychenko wanted me at the Lodges that evening. The instructions included a cryptic mention of a pneuduct gate – no explanation, just coordinates. Punctuality was 'imperative', as usual. My heart began to race.

'Sam!' The sound of my voice echoed through the house.

From the bathroom came a muffled reply. Moments later, he emerged, drying his hands on a towel. 'What's wrong?'

'Did you get a message from Voychenko?'

'I don't think so. Did you?'

'Check.' I tried to steady my voice, but it trembled anyway.

Sam squinted at the wall as he scrolled through his messages. 'Nothing here. Let's not jump to conclusions, though. Are you feeling alright?'

'It's because I lost, isn't it?' My breath came faster. 'They're going to tell me I'm out. And then?'

'Stop.' Sam came closer, his presence quieting the storm inside me. 'You've done nothing wrong. They only care about breaching secrecy, and you haven't done that. Just go, hear them out. There's no need to panic. This is all protocol for them.'

'I could pretend I didn't read it. I'll ignore it, delete it. I'll say it got lost.' The idea felt absurd even as I said it.

'They'll know you've read it.' He wrapped me in his arms. The solid weight of him helped a little. 'It's best to go. Message me when you're on your way there and back, alright?'

'You're right. I'll go,' I said, though my heart wasn't in it. 'It's a shame I didn't win.'

Sam said nothing, pulling me gently into a tighter embrace, his silence somehow more soothing than any words could be.

•••

The capsula hissed open, revealing an all-white cube. Sterile. Blinding. Empty.

It was disturbingly familiar.

'Please exit the capsula,' came a voice. It wasn't welcoming – it barely sounded human.

I squinted, scanning the space, but there was no one there. Just the glowing walls. I stepped out hesitantly, heels clicking against the cold floor. Behind me, the capsula door slid shut with a soft thud, and before I could turn, it was gliding away through the pneuduct.

Cold crept through my skin. There was no exit. No way back.

'Primula Zhang,' the lifeless voice said.

'Hello? Is someone there?' My voice sounded weak and pathetic.

The voice ignored me. 'You were granted an opportunity to play at the Game of Wagers. It is now clear that your prediction was inaccurate. As of day nine of the sixth, you are now pronounced a Servum in the name of the Liffdom Lodges.'

That word was a punch to the gut. *Servum.* It rang in my ears, dripping with menace. *Servum.* It looped through my mind; an echo from somewhere.

My eyes darted around the room, desperate for more information. That's when I saw it: a box, barely noticeable against the white walls. It sat in the far corner, camouflaged like a predator lying in wait.

'Please open the box,' the voice commanded.

I hesitated, feet glued to the floor. But then my legs moved of their own accord, carrying me across the room. My fingers brushed the lid before I pulled it open, the hinges letting out a low groan. Inside lay a single garment, folded with precision – a black cloak that was coarse and heavy. The sight of it drew my hand back.

'Please extract the cloak,' the voice said.

Tensing, I pulled it out and held it up, the fabric scratchy against my fingers. It had an oversized hood and loose sleeves. A wave of nausea rolled over me as full recognition hit. This was no ordinary cloak. It was identical to the one Thomas Locke wore at his execution – and the one I'd seen countless times in my nightmares.

My skin flushed hot, the dress clinging damp at the base of my back.

'Please remove all your clothes and put on the Servum cloak provided,' the voice instructed.

My legs shook beneath me. 'I want to speak with Igor Voychenko,' I said, clutching the cloak tighter to stop the trembling. 'He's the one I'm here to see.'

The voice didn't falter. 'Please remove all your clothes and put on the Servum cloak provided.'

I dropped the cloak back into the box, turning to step away.

Then a sudden, searing jolt of electricity vibrated through me, starting at the base of my spine and radiating outward in waves. My muscles seized, trembling forcefully as the current pulsed through every nerve. A hot, convulsive pain. I collapsed to the floor while my body continued to shudder. When the shock finally subsided, I lay static, panting, the hum of the current still pulsing in my bones.

'Please remove all your clothes and put on the Servum cloak provided,' the voice repeated.

I swallowed hard, forcing myself to sit up. My fingers fumbled with the toggles of my jacket, and I shrugged it off, letting it fall to the floor. The delicate zip of my dress resisted as my shaking hands struggled to undo it. Eventually, the fabric peeled away and fell around my feet. I stepped out of it, shivering in the cold air. Finally, I slid the cloak on. The rough material grated against my skin as it settled over my shoulders. The hood cast a shadow across my face, swallowing me in darkness until I pushed it back.

'Please remove your jewellery and hair accessories. Deposit all personal items into the box.'

I unclasped my silver bracelets and dropped them all into the box. My fingers hesitated at the comb in my hair, the last remnant of my elegance. With a reluctant tug, I pulled it free, and my long hair came tumbling down. It felt like I was shedding a part of myself, piece by piece.

When the last item was placed inside, I stood motionless, waiting for what would come next. My heart pounded in my ears, and once again I tried to suppress the trembling that had overtaken my entire body.

'Please proceed to the far wall in front of you,' the voice finally said.

I turned and walked slowly across the room. My mind raced with a tangle of questions I didn't dare ask aloud. What had I done to deserve this? And what in the world was waiting for me beyond that wall?

TWENTY-THREE

SAM

It wasn't that I wanted to die. But I wished life came with an on and off switch – a way to slip out of existence and escape the act of feeling, even just briefly. I stood, locked in place by another ceremony I never asked to be part of, while my head throbbed with this dull, dragging ache. What I witnessed didn't feel real, no matter how long I stared.

The members of the Lodge of Portuatz moved around in flowing red robes. They crouched low with hoods pulled over their heads. Their natural hair was sometimes visible underneath as they whipped themselves with leather straps, the ends studded with bits of metal that tore at their backs, slicing through cloth and flesh. Their chants were guttural, rising and falling with the violence of waves crashing against rocks.

I wanted to close my eyes and shut it all out, but I was paralysed. Whether from fear or exhaustion, I couldn't say. Maybe I was too caught up in the sheer madness of it all by now. The crack of the straps kept coming, over and over.

Was I hallucinating? Lack of sleep could do that. I hadn't managed more than a few hours in the last two days. The night Primula disappeared, I'd just tossed and turned, sweating into the silken sheets and staring at the ceiling. The room was stifling, the air too thick. I glanced at the clock: 03:00 changed to 03:01.

Primula hadn't replied to any of my messages. That wasn't unusual – not entirely. She was unpredictable, bursting into the room at all hours of the night. Sometimes she'd come in bawling a cheerful greeting, loud enough to wake the dead. Other nights, she slipped in quietly, barely ruffling the sheets before her soft snores began. It was always the same, especially after those fashion events I couldn't stand. She claimed she hated them too, but somehow, she always stayed until the very end. Surely, her meeting at the Lodges would be no different.

But doubt gnawed at me. Could she have had a relapse? She'd told me stories of her past – things I didn't like imagining. I pictured her caught up in something sordid, her body on display, surrounded by strangers. I squeezed my eyes shut, trying to banish the image, but when I opened them, the clock had barely moved. Three minutes had passed.

What if she didn't come back? The thought gripped me hard. I couldn't go to the Civil Force. What would I even say? Disappearances were always taken seriously, though if I so much as hinted at the Lodges being involved, any trail would be wiped clean. Still, I clung to the hope that she'd walk in, like she always did. Any moment now.

I took a deep breath, catching her perfume on the pillow. Sweet, sensual. The scent brought memories flooding back: the warmth of her skin, the plush softness of her lips, the way her mouth tasted. She would come back. She had to.

Unable to bear lying there any longer, I got up and started pacing. That's when I saw it – news alerts stacking up. The headlines made no sense: *Model Primula Zhang Dies by Euthanasia.* My heart stopped. I tapped through, desperate for details, but the articles gave none. They only said her name had appeared in the Euthanasia Register at an Express Passing Centre in Lacunfort. No witnesses. No explanations. Just a statement that she'd chosen to die. Why? Because she'd lost the game?

It wasn't true. It couldn't be. She'd gone to see Voychenko. She wouldn't have wanted to die. I was certain of that. Part of me still expected her to burst through the door, laughing at the absurdity of the news reports. But she didn't.

And now, here I was, watching as the Lodge of Portuatz put on their grotesque display, mourning Primula and marking their loss in the Game of Wagers.

'A real tragedy,' Igor Voychenko said to Gren and me. He stood tall in a blue gown, the long white wig cascading down his shoulders. Gren and I were just off to the side in ochre tunics. The colour hierarchy had imposed itself on me quickly, and in that moment, I felt diminished.

'She didn't want to die,' I said, meeting his eyes.

Beside him, his son Artur tilted his head, his face solemn. 'It's heartbreaking,' he said, 'but sadly, not unexpected. Her struggles with addiction were well-documented. Perhaps this will serve as a cautionary tale for her young fans.'

They walked off. My fists clenched so tightly that my nails bit into my palms. I turned to Gren. 'I don't believe it,' I said. My voice shook. 'She didn't kill herself. I don't even think she's dead. I think they have her.'

I needed Gren to take me seriously. He was the only other player left, and I couldn't afford to lose his support. But he didn't react. His eyes stayed focused and calm.

'Many people end their lives without warning,' he said slowly. 'The Right to Die Act protects their choices. It's not for us to question their motives.'

'She had no motive.'

'You can't know that for sure.' His voice was measured, careful.

'I can,' I snapped. 'We'd become...close. We spent most of our evenings together. Last time I saw her, she was on her way to meet Voychenko.'

Gren didn't respond immediately. His silence was maddening, but I caught a flicker of something – acknowledgement, maybe, though it didn't feel like enough. Before I could press him, a woman in a blue gown approached. She was younger than the others, her face dotted with freckles. Gren gave me a polite nod, then turned to speak with her, leaving me alone among the crowd.

Being at home by myself only amplified the emptiness, so I spent most evenings in the office, hoping the constant buzz of work would drown it out. One night, as I stared blankly through the window, a team dismantled the massive billboard on the building opposite. It was a clean job, stripping away Primula's image and replacing it with the grey monotony of a real estate ad promising 'Luxury Living' in buildings as soulless as the message itself. The city's pulse seemed to slow, its energy duller without her.

I turned back to the screen. The resource data glowed in the darkened office, staring back at me. I'd spent hours recalculating, validating, cross-checking – each attempt ending in the same frustrating result. The anomaly refused to budge. It was infuriating, like trying to solve a crossword puzzle for a word that didn't exist.

Still, I couldn't let it go. If I could just find the answer, maybe it would unravel something that might finally make sense of the Liffdom Lodges. That the error was at the Human Order temple seemed too precise to be random. I scribbled down ideas, only to cross them out moments later. My thoughts churned in endless loops, the anomaly standing firm. It felt impenetrable. A dead end.

Just as I was about to give up for the night, something clicked in my head – a new way of thinking, something I hadn't considered before. What if the error wasn't an error at all? The thought hit me like a slap. I'd dismissed it as a mistake from the start, convinced my approach had been flawed. But what if it wasn't? What if the anomaly wasn't a glitch but a clue?

Silas and Galina had brushed me off before, their reactions too strong to be normal. They weren't just uninterested – they were hiding something.

The numbers seemed to realign before my eyes, taking on a significance they hadn't had just seconds before. The resource utilisation figures near the Human Order temple were far higher than they should have been. Far beyond what even the Lodgers and their visits could explain. The amounts suggested something much bigger. The idea was terrifying. And then, the thought of her crossed my mind – Primula. My heart hammered in my chest. Could she be there? Was she part of whatever this was? If those resources were being used, someone had to be there. So where were they? And more importantly, why were they hidden?

Then another thought occurred to me. I'd already checked the Euthanasia Register for Primula's name, so while it was still open in front of me, I searched for Thomas Locke. His name came up, but what made me pause was the date on his record.

He'd died on the tenth of month three, but the register listed his death at the start of month one. The world had believed he was dead for nearly two months, while he'd been alive – kept captive.

A prickling unease crept over me as the pieces began to fall into place. The implications were staggering; almost too much to process. Ideas collided in my head. I tried to control my breathing. There was only one person I could talk to who might help me make sense of it – Gren. I didn't know if I could trust him. But I didn't have anyone else. He was the only one who knew about the Lodgers without being one of them. I needed to speak to him, somehow.

The office around me was too quiet, too still, as the enormity of the revelation sank in. I pushed back from my desk and stood. If I was right, this was bigger than anything I'd ever come across. And if I was wrong…well, I didn't have much left to lose.

TWENTY-FOUR

GREN

FREDRICA'S FLAT WAS NOT AT ALL what I had imagined. It appeared to be a study in contrasts, much like the woman herself. The space was sparse but nicely decorated. A mix of industrial steel and soft, warm tones created an oddly harmonious tension. The faint aroma of roasted coffee wafted in the air as I leaned against the counter, observing her.

'Do you take it black?' she asked, glancing at me over her shoulder. Her red hair was tied in a ponytail, a few strands falling free.

'Yes. As strong as you can make it.' I replied. 'Thank you.'

Her lips twitched in that way I had come to recognise – half amusement, half calculation. She activated the coffee machine with a light touch of the sensor. Its gentle hum filled the space between us. I was watching her too closely.

'What is it?' I asked finally, unable to hold back.

She let her hair fall loose before gathering it into a bun,

securing it with an elastic in a motion both unhurried and precise.

I tried again. 'It's obviously something.'

Fredrica didn't respond right away. Instead, she placed a steaming mug on the counter between us and leaned her weight onto her forearms, studying me with those matter-of-fact eyes. 'I realise this is the first time we've had coffee together. And I was just thinking... I hadn't pictured you as the *super-strong* black coffee type. You seem more like... I don't know. A latte guy, maybe.'

'Do I?'

She laughed softly. 'Don't take it the wrong way. You're the Chief Minister, so obviously stress is part of the job. But still, I imagined you'd take your bitterness elsewhere.'

I shook my head. 'No bitterness here,' I said, tapping my chest. But it wasn't entirely true, and we both knew it.

Fredrica took a sip of her coffee and gave me that same half-smile again, the one that made me feel like she knew something I didn't. She gestured to the mug I held but hadn't yet drunk from. 'Go on – taste it.'

The coffee was scalding hot as I took a careful sip. It was strong, with an earthy edge. As I placed the mug back down, I decided to steer the conversation where it needed to go.

'Primula Zhang,' I began, watching Fredrica closely. 'Do you know where she is?'

'Where she is?' Her reaction was subtle but telling. A shift in her eyes, a slight change in her posture. 'Well, she decided to end her life, didn't she? What do you mean, *where* she is?'

'It doesn't make sense,' I said. 'Someone as prominent as she is doesn't just walk into an Express Passing Centre and go through with it unnoticed. And it happened right after she lost the game.'

Fredrica sighed, cradling her mug between her hands. 'Gren,' she said, 'things like this happen more often than you'd think.'

'I'm not sure I believe that,' I pressed. 'Do you know if she's still alive?'

Her response came slower this time. 'You'd be better off not asking those kinds of questions.'

'So you're admitting the Lodgers had a hand in her disappearance?'

'I'm not admitting anything,' she replied, and this time her gaze didn't waver. 'But I am telling you this: Primula's situation is not unique. The world is full of tragedies.'

'So, no intervention by the Lodgers? No wrongdoing at all?'

'Wrongdoing,' she repeated, considering the word. 'That makes me feel like I'm at work. *Wrongdoing…* They love that word at the Civil Force, did you know that? As if things can be either *right* or *wrong* without the relevant context. If only life were so simple. Personally, it's not a term I like to use. Maybe because I don't see all forms of "wrongdoing" as something that should always be avoided. You know, sometimes, harm is necessary to achieve a greater good.'

'So if enough people benefit from someone's death, murder is justified?'

'If the benefit outweighs the harm, then yes.'

'You're twisting your ethics.'

'There's nothing twisted about it,' Fredrica said with a shrug. 'This is the kind of ideology you'll have to embrace when you become a Lodger. Believe me, you'll lose your mind otherwise. And frankly, you'll need it as Chief Minister too. Every decision you make has a cost. Think of the days when wars still happened – what would you have done then? It's all about the greatest good for the greatest number.'

'The greatest good for the greatest number,' I repeated. 'I

wish I knew half as much as you do about what it takes to be a Chief Minister.'

She rolled her eyes.

'It's the only practical goal,' she said. 'The greatest good for everyone is a fantasy.'

'Even if it's difficult in practice, shouldn't that still be our aim?'

'Oh, Gren.' She sighed. 'Aiming for the impossible doesn't make you noble – it makes you impractical. In the real world, someone always pays the price.'

'I disagree... You have ten hungry children and one loaf of bread. You divide it evenly – no one pays the price.'

'The world is more complicated than that,' she said. 'Imagine ten children and two loaves, one laced with poison. You don't know which one is safe. What would you do? Let all ten starve? Or ask one to test a loaf, knowing their sacrifice might save the others?'

'I'd test the bread myself.'

Fredrica laughed, though her eyes held a strange sadness. 'Of course you would. Because you're a *good* man. But if you die, who will protect the others? In this scenario, the best option to secure the greatest good for the greatest number is to consciously choose one victim.'

'And who should that be?'

'That is the most difficult decision to make. And I'm afraid those who become leaders cannot escape that responsibility. In many ways, you have already decided who should suffer to bring good to others.'

'So what's your point?' I asked, fixing my eyes on her. 'That leadership is about choosing who gets hurt?'

'Sometimes, yes. You're in a position of power, Gren. You don't have the luxury of idealism. If you try to save everyone, you'll save no one.'

I looked down at the mug in my hands, its contents now lukewarm. 'Is that why you joined the Lodgers?' I asked after a moment. 'To make sure you're never the one who gets hurt?'

I caught the faintest shift in her, something unguarded that wasn't there before. 'You make it sound like I joined by choice. I am Igor Voychenko's daughter…'

She seemed to regret that immediately, stiffening back into a more formal tone.

'As a Lodger,' she said, 'I believe in shaping the future, not standing by while it crushes us.'

'And Primula? What about *her* future?'

Fredrica's gaze dropped to her hands. 'Primula made choices. We all do.'

My voice rose before I could stop it. 'So you're saying she deserved whatever happened to her?'

'I'm saying that you can't save everyone. Not Primula. Not Samuel. Especially not if you want to save yourself.'

At the mention of Sam's name, I became more alert. Clara had told me just the night before that he had been trying to contact me. I'd planned to return his call later that day.

'What exactly do you mean by that?'

Fredrica hesitated, as though she were choosing her next words with precision. 'Just...be careful when you talk to Samuel. There are ears everywhere. Samuel is a good man, but he's also a player – your last opponent. And it's you who has to win this game.'

Her warning gave me an icy dread. *Ears everywhere.* Was my office bugged? The residence? I wouldn't have been surprised. I finished the coffee and set the mug down. The clink of ceramic against steel echoed in the kitchen.

'Maybe he will win instead,' I said.

Fredrica's face turned stern. 'The stakes are too high. We can't talk about this lightly.'

'If you're trying to protect me, Fredrica, then tell me how it is. Tell me the truth.'

She looked at me for a long moment. Then, with a faint, bittersweet smile, she said, 'I already have.'

The queen's friendliness caught me off guard.

'It was with much delight that I heard the announcement of your wife's pregnancy, Chief Minister. Goodness be praised.'

I blinked, startled. In all our previous meetings, she'd been nothing but professional. But here she was now, speaking to me not as a monarch, but as a person.

'Thank you, Your Majesty,' I said, recovering quickly. 'A very happy occasion indeed.'

I reached for my handheld, intent on the agenda. As I prepared to address the first topic, she interrupted, faintly reproachful.

'I don't suppose you have more important matters to discuss today.' She tilted her head, and I couldn't tell whether she was disapproving or only thoughtful.

'More important, Your Majesty?'

'More important than the imminent arrival of your firstborn, of course. Let us not pretend that you will remain unchanged by such an event. Having a child is a profound disruption to one's life.'

'A disruption,' I said, unsure whether I was agreeing or questioning.

'Indeed. Twelve times I have given birth. Trust that you are hearing from experience.'

'I would never presume there is a single matter where Your

Majesty is inexperienced.' As the words left my mouth, I realised with dismay they might be misconstrued as sarcasm.

'Oh, please, do not flatter me,' she said, and there was a glint in her eyes that reassured me I had not been imprudent. 'Parenthood will change you. You might think the intense love you feel at first will wane, but it only deepens as the years go by. And with it comes worry, for that is the nature of being a parent. I've often spoken of the impermanence of all things in life, yet this worry does seem to be eternal. Even at my age, I remain a mother first, worrying every day about my children's wellbeing.'

I found myself smiling. 'Perhaps that is why the world knows Your Majesty as "The Mother of Rivennia".'

The queen's lips tightened almost imperceptibly.

'That title is undeserved,' she said. 'Absurd, even. There is so much I could have done, so much I *should* have done, to protect the people of Rivennia. I fear that only in hindsight will my mis-steps become clear, and by then, the path we're on will be irreversible.'

Her words contained an unexpected openness. I felt privileged to witness this moment, but still inadequate to respond.

She met my eyes. 'If I may burden you with a question, Chief Minister, in your honest opinion, have I been a good monarch to this world?'

I straightened, unsure what to say without falling into platitudes. But as I spoke, and despite my earlier criticisms of the monarchy, I believed my words. 'Your Majesty, Rivennia could not have wished for a better queen.'

She gave a small nod but looked away. 'I often wonder if my devotion to my children stole too much from the people who needed me most. Did I fail humanity by putting my own family above all else?'

In an instant, our roles had inverted. It was now the queen who was seeking, if not my advice, at least my opinion.

'Your Majesty,' I said, choosing my words carefully, 'you have shown kindness beyond measure. No other figure in our history commands the respect and admiration that you do.'

Sorrow passed over her features, though it vanished as quickly as it came.

'Six of them,' she said, almost to herself.

I knew what she meant, but dreaded hearing more.

'Six of my children chose to end their lives. Children should not go before their parents. And yet, here I stand, having witnessed the unthinkable.' She paused, and her grief cast a shadow over the space between us. 'I assure you, Chief Minister, there is no greater torment than losing a child.'

I sat frozen, my mind racing for something to say.

'I am truly sorry, Your Majesty,' I began. 'I cannot imagine—'

'Could it be,' she interrupted, 'that my attempts to save humanity doomed my children instead? And then by narrowing my focus to my family, did I not only fail the world, but also those I sought to shield?'

'Save humanity?' I asked gently, seizing the pause. 'Your Majesty, I understand the depth of division, the revolts, and the rise of radical ultrahumanists. But I remain optimistic. May I ask, what is it that Your Majesty sees as the greatest threat to humanity?'

Her gaze bore into mine. 'Chief Minister, I hope the threat is not as dire as it seems. And when I reflect on my children's choices, on their abrupt departures…I hope they are truly free of pain and anguish.' Her voice faltered.

I couldn't find adequate words, so I let silence take hold. My thoughts drifted to Primula, and my throat tightened.

Then, regaining her composure, the queen blinked a few

times and raised her chin. 'Do forgive me; I am hardly making sense now. Please forget everything I have just said. An old woman's rambling, that is all it is.'

'Your Majesty—' I began, but she cut me off, her tone brisk once more.

'Will you be so kind as to show me the latest projection of your child's scans? Surely you have one with you.' She raised her eyebrows twice in a subtle, urging gesture. 'Go on – take out your handheld. Let us see.'

I obeyed, my hands suddenly heavy.

TWENTY-FIVE

SAM

MUM CLASPED HER CUP OF TEA, dunking the teabag over and over. I stared at the cup, watching the colour spread into the water. My sadness made every breath feel forced. If Mum asked about Primula, I didn't know how I'd answer without falling apart. My fingers curled beneath the edge of the table, hoping she wouldn't bring it up.

'Doctor'll probably say it was a bad seizure. You know how they are.' She spoke matter-of-factly, now squelching the teabag against the cup. 'Truth is, though, when you're in the middle of one, it's not as bad as people think. Not pleasant, mind you, but you just get on with it. Like most things in life. You know what I mean?'

I was unsure how to respond. She sipped her tea, then licked her lips with a small, deliberate movement. She seemed so fragile, almost swallowed up by the chair.

'You sure you don't want a cup of tea?'

'No thanks, Mum.'

Her face crumpled. 'What did you call me?'

'Mum,' I said again.

Her eyebrows shot up, and her eyes scanned my face. Then she relaxed, letting out a breathy laugh. 'Oh, of course. Aren't I daft? Thought you was one of them nurse bots for a second.'

'It's me, Samuel,' I said, leaning forward to touch her shoulder.

'Yes, yes, I see that now,' she muttered, like she was talking more to herself than to me. 'And you're sure about that?'

'I'm sure.'

'Good. Well then,' she said, sitting straighter. 'These seizures, though… They don't stop once they start. That's what they told me. Said they'll only get worse. Not exactly encouraging, is it?'

I forced a smile, but it was brittle, ready to crack. Nothing I said could fix this. Still, I figured I might as well give it a go.

'Mum,' I said in a hushed voice. 'Maybe it's not too late to think about an enhancement, you know?'

She looked at me like I'd just told her the world was flat. 'What? And turn me into one of them ultrahumans, with who knows what other mess? Nah. You've lost it, I swear. Don't want to hear no more of that from you.'

'Fine,' I said quietly.

Then she widened her eyes and gave me an intense look. 'You don't think that seizure was caused by, you know…'

'What?' I blinked, caught off guard.

She mimed holding something up with both hands and taking a bite of it with exaggerated caution.

'Oh, you mean the buns?'

'Shh!' She glanced around like someone might overhear. 'They're not supposed to know.'

'Mum, I don't think anyone's listening.'

'Still,' she said, her finger wagging. 'Do you reckon that's what caused it?'

'No.' I shook my head. 'And if you like, I can ask the doctor about a dispensation for you. Get you some proper treats.'

Her face lit up, then settled into a frown. 'Nah. Doctors won't let me eat anything but those tasteless peas and that dry chicken they grow in labs. But if it wasn't the buns, then there's not much I could've done to stop it, is there?'

'No, Mum,' I said, my voice as gentle as I could manage. 'Your diet didn't cause it. We knew it was part of this condition.'

She nodded slowly, lips pursed. A minute passed before she spoke again.

'In the grand scheme, I can't complain,' she said eventually. 'Had a good life. Nothing to sniff at. Just wish this…thing could've waited a bit longer, that's all. But what's the point in crying about it?'

'You've had a life many people would envy.'

She gave a small laugh. 'Maybe, maybe. But there's been confusion lately. Memories coming and going, you know? Some good, some not so much. I try to hold on to the nice ones and toss the others aside. That's all you can do, isn't it?'

'Yeah,' I said, and in that moment, I felt something warm and overwhelming. I wanted to reach out and hold her hand, but I didn't.

'Mary next door,' she went on, 'she's not been round in weeks. Her seizures are getting worse, poor thing. Can hear it all through the walls – nurse bots rattling down the hall, doctors shouting orders. It's awful. No one should live like that.'

'I feel sorry for her.'

'Me too. Don't wish that on anyone, not even her. And I've been thinking…' She paused, her voice catching a little. 'Don't reckon I'll let it get to that for me. You tell Doctor Khan, yeah? When it's more than one a day…that's enough. And I don't want *any* fuss,' she said, shaking her head. 'No ceremonies, nothing. You don't even have to tell me in advance for all I care. Alright?'

I was too choked up to say anything.

'Alright?'

'Alright.' I swallowed hard. 'I'll let the doctor know.'

'Good,' she said, a quiet calm settling over her face. Then she leaned forward. 'But while I'm still here, dispensation or no dispensation, I want those buns. Not just cream – custard ones too. I like them both.'

I managed a shaky smile, feeling my lashes wet as I blinked. 'I'll get them for you, Mum. Promise.'

TWENTY-SIX

LORELEI

My dearest sister,

I'm sorry I didn't reply to your note from Thursday. As I write this, I am finally alone, tucked away in a quiet capsula, heading back to Lacunfort after two days visiting Leeram, Delpovan and Flovya. I must admit, the novelty of this lifestyle has almost completely worn off. All that remains is the hard work it demands. Still, I manage, and I dare say (but only to you) that I'm getting quite good at it. Life is like that, isn't it? Once you learn the rules and endure the struggles, you find a way to carry on. And that's what I've done – just got on with things, no matter how hard.

I made this trip alone. Gren has been so busy lately. But, and I don't know if I've said this before, there's something else about him I can't quite name. He's distant in a strange way, as though he's always thinking about other things, even when he's speaking to me. I've known from the start that ours would never be the sort of marriage others might imagine. Deep down, I accepted that long ago.

Even so, I hoped Gren could at least be a kind of friend – someone to rely on amid the endless crowd of hypocrites and backstabbers fluttering about. But even that feels like a dream slipping further from my reach.

I don't mind if Gren has something going on with another woman, or a man, or even a bot, for that matter. I truly want him to be happy. I do. This wasn't the kind of union anyone enters looking for love, after all. So if we can't find love with each other, isn't it only fair to hope we might find it elsewhere?

Still, I can't help feeling a little silly for holding onto that tiny, stubborn hope that maybe, with time, some version of love could grow between us. Have I ever mentioned Clara, Gren's assistant? She helped me settle in when I first arrived, and I'm grateful for her kindness. But there's something about her – something that makes me feel as though Gren belongs to her and I'm intruding. The way she fusses over him, tidying after him, keeping him perfectly on schedule. The way she decides who gets to speak to him, and when. Her every movement is so precise, so purposeful. She's a soldier on duty.

Curiously, though, Clara herself is always dishevelled. You can tell when she's brushed her hair, because it doesn't happen often. Her clothes are expensive but old, and they hang off her like they belong to someone bigger. Despite all this, I doubt there's anything romantic between them. Gren loves her attention and care, I'm sure, but I don't think he sees her that way. She's quite a bit older, too. But still, the thought crosses my mind now and then – not out of jealousy, really, but maybe only because I feel so lonely. I have no mission to speak of. God is taking His time in showing me what my true calling is meant to be.

I have God to thank, though, for Sara and Rosa. They're my only friends in Lacunfort – or anywhere, really. Isn't that sad? Remember how many friends I used to have when we were young?

I suppose that's life. We drift apart as we grow up.

Sara and Rosa keep me sane. Sara works in logistics. She once tried to explain the details of her job to me. I pretended like I understood, but honestly, it all flew over my head – not because of her signing, mind you, just the complexity of it. Something about ducts and vacuums? Maybe. Whatever it is, it sounds like the kind of thing you'd need a very specific brain for. She keeps her blonde hair cropped short; it's a bit thin in spots, so much so that you can see bits of her scalp if you're paying attention. But Sara's not the sort to feel self-conscious about something like that. She owns who she is.

And then there's Rosa, the scientist. Where Sara is solid and straightforward, Rosa is...well, just different. She's got this willowy frame, the kind you see in old oil paintings of women who look like they spend their afternoons reclining on chaises longues. Her long, black hair is so smooth it could almost pass for silk. She's always perfectly made-up, and she carries this scent of roses that's like a whole garden's worth. Her nose is long and sharp, almost too much for her face, but somehow it works. I wouldn't call her pretty – not exactly. She's got something more elusive than that – a sort of magnetic femininity that feels effortless.

Not that Sara isn't feminine. She absolutely is. But her version of it is different. Sara's the type who's at ease in any room. And I think she'd scare the hell out of most men if she wanted to.

Anyway, did I tell you about their baby plans? They've decided to find a sperm donor who's congenitally deaf, so their child can grow up as part of their community. They will use Sara's eggs, but Rosa will carry the pregnancy. It's all settled, except for one thing – the sperm donor! Somehow, in a moment of half-joking chatter, I ended up agreeing to ask the DC Director if he might consider... you know. I'm laughing as I write this! How did I get myself into such a situation? He's tall, handsome, probably in his late forties, with perfectly wavy silver hair. He's been on my mind ever since he explained that only hearing people understand silence as the absence of sound. Being born deaf, he doesn't know what sound is, so he doesn't think of his life as a 'silent' one. I have a meeting with him next week to discuss government grants for his department. From what I can tell, he's quite desperate for funding. The poor man seems to be juggling far more than anyone should, and the strain is starting to show.

Now, before you say anything cheeky, I'm not planning to use the government grant to sway him, you wicked sister. I'll simply mention it as a way to ease into the conversation and see if he might be open to…a different kind of donation on his part. So, wish me luck!

Turning to my own plans, next week I'm meeting with Dr Greenville to run feasibility tests on life enhancements for the baby. We'll see what the results say, but if things are viable, I'll go ahead with it. I haven't mentioned this to Gren. I doubt I will. He was furious the last time I raised it, and truthfully, he hasn't seemed particularly invested in me or in our future family for some time. Politics will always come first for him. Which means, I suppose, this is a decision I am forced to make alone.

My capsula is nearly at its destination, so I must say goodbye for now.

Lots of love,

Lorelei

TWENTY-SEVEN

SAM

THE MORNING AIR SLAPPED against my face as I stepped off the pneuduct at Platform 99. The Government Office stood ahead, smug and enormous, its base swarming with people weaving in and out like ants around a sugar spill. Up close, it was even more intimidating – a giant pyramid stretching up so high it made my neck ache just looking at it, the tip bent like someone had yanked it mid-build. This was where the big shots pulled the strings that ran our lives. I felt like a speck of dirt in a pristine world.

Crowds poured out of the ten massive pneuduct gates surrounding the square. The air buzzed with voices, footsteps and the occasional hum of a drone. Over on the north side, tents flapped in the breeze where protesters had set up shop. Their static signs blinked in and out, clear even from where I stood. *You Can't Stop Human Evolution*, one declared. Another said, *Shut Down Express Passing Centres*. My mouth went dry as I spotted a larger placard. *DEATH TO GREN MORITZ = LIFE TO US ALL*, it read in crude, blood-red strokes. The letters looked slapped on in a hurry, but they carried a threat so sinister they seemed to crawl under my skin and stay there.

I wiped my damp hands on the sides of my trousers. What was I even doing here? Talking to Gren had seemed like a good idea, but this wasn't what I'd imagined. My head was still tangled from the call the night before. He'd sounded clear enough, but stiff, like he was putting on a show or holding something back.

'Good evening, Mr Rosendale,' Gren had said. His tone was oddly formal, rigid, as if we'd never met before.

'Good evening. May I...ask who this is?' I played along, unsure of what to make of it.

'This is Chief Minister Moritz.'

Hearing him call himself that, so stiff and distant, set me on edge. Gren wasn't exactly a close acquaintance, but this didn't feel like him. His words seemed rehearsed and fake. A faint, metallic buzz on the line made me question if it was a bot using a cloned voice.

'It's good to hear from you,' I said carefully, a little less assured than I wanted to be. 'I've been trying to reach you. Need to talk with some urgency… Wondering if this line is secure?'

'It's good to talk to you too,' Gren interrupted, brushing past the question. 'I apologise for the late call. Do you have a minute or two? I promise I won't take very long.'

'Of course,' I said, shifting slightly in my chair.

'There are areas where your organisation and my office could work together.' His words came in quick bursts. 'I've been reading about the new initiatives at the Census Office – the survey design, the data collection processes. Fascinating work.

We'll need to discuss it further, but let's do that in person.'

'Yes… When would—'

'Tomorrow, first thing,' Gren interrupted again. 'Meet me at the Government Office at seven o'clock in the morning.'

Before I could respond, the line went dead. No goodbyes, no clarification. The abruptness of it left an itch of doubt I couldn't scratch away.

Now, standing in front of the building, I wondered if I'd made a mistake. Who walks into the Government Office of the Chief Minister and asks to see him? Did people actually do that? I half-expected someone to grab me by the scruff and toss me back onto the street. But I didn't have much choice.

At the entrance, I stammered my explanation to a bored-looking security guard, hoping I sounded more confident than I felt. Thankfully, he let me through. The hallway inside was clean and minimalist, with muted colours and thick sand-coloured carpets that muffled my footsteps. Trimmed palms in glossy pots lined the walls, standing in perfect symmetry. Signs hung at every turn: *Ministry of Education, Northwest Wing, ROE: Rivennian Office for Euthanasia, Basement Bureau.* I shuddered at that one.

The lift ride was short but unnerving. When the doors opened, I found myself in a huge reception area. A bot greeted me. She looked like a young woman in her thirties, but the lapel tag gave her away. Blue. Not real. Still, if you hadn't known, you might've mistaken her for flesh and blood.

'Samuel Rosendale?' she asked.

'Yeah,' I said, focusing on my breathing. 'That's me.'

'Please, follow me.'

Gren's office was like another world. The circular room was encased in curved glass, offering a panoramic view of the platform. Light from the sky-screen filtered through, bathing everything in a soft morning glow. It was almost too perfect, like a simulation.

Gren stood at the window, his back to me. His desk – a massive thing with raised and tilted surfaces for different displays – looked more like a control panel than a workspace. He turned to face me, pushing up the glasses perched on his nose. I hadn't seen him wear them before. They suited him, adding to his air of seriousness, like he was some sort of studious scholar.

'Mr Rosendale.' His smile looked sincere. 'Thank you for coming. It's a beautiful morning, isn't it?'

'Good morning, Chief Minister.'

'Come here.' He beckoned, gesturing towards the window. 'Have a look at this view. Isn't it great?'

I joined him. Platform 99 sprawled out below us in layers of pneuducts and towers. It was a breathtaking view.

'Except for them, of course,' Gren said, pointing at the protesters below. 'See the group in the far corner?'

I squinted. 'Yeah, I can see them.'

'Can you read their signs?'

I focused, narrowing my eyes. 'The big one says, "Freedom of choice".'

Gren raised an eyebrow. 'Good eyesight. Most people would need smart contact lenses for that.'

'I've never worn contacts,' I said with a shrug.

As we spoke, I was relieved to see that the morbid sign I'd seen earlier was now discarded on the ground.

'Even more impressive,' he said, his tone light but his eyes calculating. He glanced at a sliding door embedded in the central column of the room, and I followed his gaze. A moment later, it opened with a faint hiss.

Gren stepped inside and motioned for me to follow. As the door closed, he waved a hand over the control panel. Then he pressed a finger to his lips, and I nodded, understanding immediately. My pulse quickened. Something about his deliberate, calculated movements set me on high alert.

As the lift plunged, my stomach rose like it was trying to meet the drop halfway. Whatever was waiting for us below, I wasn't sure I was ready to face it.

Gren led the way into a capsula. It was a cramped two-seater with no windows, leaving me clueless as to where we were headed. He met my eyes briefly, raising a hand, palm down, in a calming gesture while shaping a silent 'shh' with his lips. He settled into his seat across from me, his hands clasped on his lap. Words formed in my mouth more than once, but each time I swallowed them back down. Gren was the type to have a plan. If he wasn't talking, it meant there was a reason. I decided to trust him and let him make the first move.

When the capsula came to a halt, Gren held up a hand, indicating once again that I shouldn't speak. He opened a compartment beneath his seat and pulled out a small box. Inside were two sets of identical linen trousers, knitted jumpers, and slip-on shoes. Then, he reached into his pocket and produced a stylograph and a piece of paper. He leaned forward, scribbling quickly before holding the note up for me to read:

DON'T TALK.

STRIP DOWN COMPLETELY.

LEAVE EVERYTHING HERE.

PUT THESE CLOTHES ON AND FOLLOW ME.

I read the note twice, then I nodded. Gren underlined the word *EVERYTHING*, his eyes hard as they met mine. I nodded again, more firmly this time. He crumpled the paper into a ball and, to my astonishment, shoved it into his mouth, chewing it like food. The sight was both absurd and disconcerting.

I took a deep breath, trying to focus. This wasn't the time

for modesty. But as I began unbuttoning my shirt, a hot shame rose to my face. The last time someone had seen me like this was Primula, and even then, we'd talked about it beforehand. Now, under Gren's inescapable gaze, I felt exposed in a way I hadn't in years.

Gren was already out of his clothes before I finished unbuttoning mine. He stood, unbothered as a statue, his thick, sandy hair covering his entire body. He held up the linen trousers, inspecting them as though working out which side was the front. His complete lack of self-consciousness only made my awkwardness worse.

I peeled off my shirt and trousers, leaving me in just my underwear. The packer sat like a rubber lie against the fabric. I should have left it at home. My hands shook as I reached for it, yanking it free and letting my pants fall in the same motion. A deeper flush crept up my neck, and when I glanced up, Gren's eyes were on me. He'd seen. I looked away, quickly pulling up the linen trousers and throwing on the jumper. The shame was irrational but strong, taking me back to my teenage years when glances were filled with judgement.

Once dressed, Gren opened the capsula door and we stepped outside. The air was cool and fresh, filled with the chirping of birds. I blinked, taking in the sight before me: an endless expanse of birch trees, their white bark dappled with cracks and knots. Moss-covered rocks lay scattered among flowering shrubs, where slow bumblebees drifted between their multi-coloured petals. The forest seemed to stretch on forever.

Gren finally spoke. 'This is where I come when I need an escape.' There was something close to sadness in the way he looked at me. His tone turned serious. 'You're certain you've left everything behind? No implants, technoparts…and you're sure about the lenses? Nothing in your eyes that could be hacked?'

I shook my head. 'Nothing.'

He glanced at me as we started to walk. 'I figured this was the only place safe enough to talk. Away from bugs and the prying ears of the Lodges.'

'You think they'd bug us?' I asked, startled.

'I have good reason to believe they might.'

I let his words sink in. 'I've been looking into what the Lodgers might be up to,' I began to say, watching him closely. 'There's something I need to share.'

'Is it about Primula?' Gren's voice dropped, but there was an edge to it. 'You don't think they've…'

'I don't think she's met the same fate as Thomas Locke,' I interrupted. 'At least, I want to believe she hasn't. But it was Locke who gave me the first clue. His name was in the Euthanasia Register months before we saw him.'

'I see,' Gren said, his jaw tightening.

'There's more,' I continued. 'I found data – validated it myself – that shows massive resource use and waste production near the Human Order temple. It doesn't make sense. There's hardly any population in that area.'

Gren pressed a hand to his forehead, his posture stiffening as he processed the information. 'How many people would justify that level of activity?'

'I'm not sure yet,' I admitted. 'A few hundred – perhaps more. But I dug deeper and found another name: Doris Ekcol. She used to be Isabel Locke, Thomas's widow. After his death, she changed her name, sold her shares in his company, and tried to erase her tracks. Not long after, she left Lacunfort for Nova Rhumya.'

Gren turned to me with a sudden intensity. 'She must know something. She's hiding. Running from the Lodgers.'

'It looks that way,' I said. 'But if she posed a real risk to them, I doubt they'd have let her leave. Whatever's going on, she holds pieces of the puzzle we're missing.'

Gren was quiet, his thoughts clearly in motion. 'I'm scheduled to visit Nova Rhumya next week,' he said cautiously.

'I know. Your schedule is public. That's why I needed to catch you now,' I said. 'We need to find her and get her to talk. If the Lodgers are bugging us, it has to happen in a device-free space with no traceable interactions. You'll be there on official duties, which makes it the perfect cover. If I go, they'll notice, but you can probably meet her without raising suspicion.'

Gren glanced around the forest as though weighing his options. 'The schedule's packed, but I'll find a way,' he said finally. His voice was even, though I could sense the uncertainty beneath it.

He turned back to me with a look that made it clear he wasn't taking any chances. 'Can you give me a specific location? Coordinates? Something exact?'

I drew in a breath, then pulled my shoulders back and looked him in the eye. 'Yes. I'm almost certain I can. The data I found pointed to a precise area. I'll make sure you have it – securely – before you leave.'

Gren studied me, then gave a curt nod. 'Good. That's what we need.'

TWENTY-EIGHT

GREN

The car swayed on its springs as it wound through serpentine country roads. Three headlights carved cones of light into the night, revealing sheets of water that fell in torrents.

A capsula could have reduced this journey to minutes, but the pneumatic arteries of Nova Rhumya bypassed places like this – fewer than a hundred pneuducts branched out of the capital, and none ventured into the depths of the Rhyss forest. To reach this remote corner, I had no choice but to endure three hours on uneven ground roads.

I fidgeted in the back seat, unable to sleep. My departure from the Rex Royal Hotel had been orchestrated with care. I had stripped to nothing in the cloakroom, changing into the bellboy uniform Clara had prepared.

'The things you make me do,' she'd said.

She was trying to lighten the moment, but the worry in her eyes gave her away. Once again, she'd gone to absurd lengths to help me. No one else would have done this. There was no one else I could trust.

My clothes and personal items remained in my suite to maintain the illusion that I was resting in bed. By the time I returned, just before dawn, no one would suspect otherwise.

The brimless cap and waist-length jacket of the uniform had served their purpose. I removed the cap, tossing it onto the seat beside me, and loosened the brass buttons on the jacket. I inhaled deeply, summoning a sense of focus as the car rattled forward.

Out of the darkness, two glowing dots appeared, hovering a metre above the ground. I held my breath as the car continued towards them. A million droplets swirled and leapt in the beams. Then the lights revealed the unmistakable shape of a fox, its fur a striking red, its eyes gleaming like honey. In an instant, the animal bolted, vanishing into the forest. I exhaled slowly, the momentary panic dissolving into relief.

'One mile from your destination,' the car announced.

Gravel crunched under the tyres as we entered a clearing framed by towering pines. The forest loomed, giant trunks standing firm against the restless wind, while the bushes below whipped in all directions under the rain. At the far edge of the clearing stood a solitary house. As if on cue, a light blinked on in one of the windows, beckoning me forward.

The car came to a stop, and the door slid open with a quiet swish. Cold rain pelted my skin as I stepped onto the gravel. The smell of damp soil and pine made me feel far from everything. I pulled my jacket close, hunching against the wet gusts as I made my way to the porch. At the door, I raised my hand to knock, but the sound of locks turning stopped me. Chains rattled, and the door creaked open, revealing Doris Ekcol.

Her gaze was cautious, scanning the porch and the clearing

beyond me. Only when she was certain I was alone did she gesture for me to enter.

The room, though sparse, was warm – a stark contrast to the chill outside. Uneven wooden floorboards groaned underfoot. A worn rug stretched across the space, its frayed edges curling upwards as though it had only recently been unrolled. The scent of burnt wood and dampness made the air feel stagnant. Doris moved with a quiet urgency, her white dress brushing her ankles as she led me to a table by the fireplace. She pulled out a chair and gestured for me to sit, then took the seat across from me.

'I appreciate your courage in meeting me,' I began. 'This visit was not without risk – for either of us.'

Doris inclined her head but said nothing. Her eyes lingered on the bellboy jacket, perhaps reassured by the lengths I'd gone to maintain discretion.

'I'm truly sorry for what happened to your husband,' I said, with as much tact as I could manage. 'Thomas spoke of you before...the end. He wanted you to know that he went in peace.'

Her eyes flickered briefly, and she looked down.

'I don't mean to reopen wounds,' I continued. 'But your knowledge is invaluable. If there's anything Thomas shared with you – anything that could help us – please, I need to know.'

Doris hesitated, then opened her mouth, revealing a wet, flat stump at the back of her throat. It moved slowly, up and down – the remains of a severed tongue.

'I'm...so sorry,' I stammered, pressing my hand to my heart. 'I didn't know.'

Doris's eyes glistened, but no tears fell. Instead, she rose and moved to the hearth, gathering cold cinders into her hand. Returning to the table, she picked up a piece of charcoal and paused. She drew a single line on the wooden surface, then rubbed it with her fingers, leaving a dark smudge. Inspecting the mark, she seemed satisfied and set to work. Each stroke of the charcoal was deliberate and firm, her focus unshaken as the words began to take shape: *'Lodgers... Must... Stop... Torture.'*

'Torture?'

She nodded, her hand trembling as she continued. *'Thomas... helped Servums.'*

'Servums,' I repeated slowly, pressing for clarity.

Her next words struck me like a blow: *'Human slaves. Prisoners. For experimentation.'*

I leaned back in my chair, my lungs robbed of air. Her movements quickened, urgency overtaking hesitation as she wrote: *'Ultrahumans. A city of Servums. War will begin.'*

'War.' The word sat like ash on my tongue.

Doris's hand tightened around the charcoal as she gripped my arm with her free hand. The charcoal hissed against the table as she scrawled her final plea: *'Servums need help. A Lodger. Thomas now gone. YOU must help.'*

Before, infiltration had been a strategy – a political tactic aimed at advancing my goals. But with Doris's information, it had taken on a new urgency. The horrors I now knew only underscored how passive I'd been until now. *War* – that's what this was.

'I will,' I said, my words an instant vow. 'I swear it.'

A noise from another room shattered the moment. Doris froze, her eyes round with fear. She darted to the door, fumbling with the locks. My pulse raced as I followed, a sense of dread clawing at me. Someone – or something – was here with us.

The chain jammed, drawing a whimper from Doris. Pushing her aside, I heaved with all my strength until it came free. When the door flew open, she dashed into the drenched forest.

Her figure was swallowed by the darkness within seconds. I stood on the porch, water soaking through my clothes as the car raced towards me, its lights once again piercing the storm. Every second seemed to stretch endlessly; it was like the world itself had paused.

The car door opened, filling the interior with a soft blue glow. I could feel a presence behind me, but I refused to turn, afraid of confirming my fear. Instead, I climbed in and slammed the 'Close' button with a forceful thump of my hand.

'Destination: Rex Royal Hotel. Levan, Nova Rhumya. Would you like to start the trip?' the car asked.

'Yes,' I shouted.

The vehicle sped up, and I glanced back, my panting breath fogging the window in uneven bursts. On the porch stood a tall, motionless figure. A humanoid form cloaked in black. My skin crawled as I recognised its eerie resemblance to the bots that had dragged Thomas Locke into the Beluga Room.

I turned away, trying to collect my thoughts, but Doris's warnings pressed in, drowning out everything else. This was no longer about belief or theory, no longer a battle waged through legislation. We had moved beyond the bounds of rules. The Lodgers were breeding ultrahumans, experimenting on people.

Suddenly, it seemed obvious. There was strong demand – we all knew that. So why follow the law when there was so much profit to be made? Why submit to clinical supervision when they could run clandestine experiments unchecked?

Very few of the Lodgers shared my conservative views on what human progress should mean, but I hadn't expected them to stand so perversely opposed to those ideals, or to be so deeply involved in dismantling them.

They thought themselves above the law – but I would be above them. There was no turning back.

PART TWO

Months Eight to Twelve
Year 500

TWENTY-NINE

PRIMULA

THE BEEPING JOLTED ME AWAKE. It always began like this. I had ten seconds to get up before the shock came. I'd learned that the hard way on my first morning here. The pain searing through me was a cruel lesson I couldn't forget. Never again. I scrambled off the creaky mattress. Cold air bit at my skin as I reached for the cloak hanging on the wall. It barely qualified as clothing, but it was all I had.

Six weeks had passed. I'd counted the cycles – the dark hours that marked the passing of each day. My life had become an endless, monotonous loop of blinding lights, mechanical voices, and the dread of not knowing what came next. Time was a formless thing here; it bled into itself, smothering any sense of reality.

The room was bare – four walls, a bed, a metal flap for meals, a hole in the ground to be used as a toilet, and the cursed door that led to the places where they did things to me. The voice decided when it opened, and its orders were unavoidable. I hated that bloody voice. Sometimes, I imagined it belonged to someone human, someone I could punch. Deep down, I knew better. Day to day, this place ran itself, but somewhere out there, I assumed, people had designed it – the same people who decided, perhaps, what would ultimately happen to me.

When the voice told me to leave the room, I obeyed. There was no choice. Occasionally, it led me to the so-called garden – a sad parody of the outdoors. A painted sky, fake breeze, and plastic plants that somehow made the lie worse. It was both a reprieve and a reminder of what I'd lost. Even there, the machines lurked – faceless things with metal arms and wheels that prodded, shaved, and injected. They'd carved things into my skull, leaving a bald, throbbing patch as a souvenir. The memory made me shiver; I forced myself not to think about it.

The metal flap screeched open. Breakfast had arrived. Blocks of food that could've been anything – eggs, carrots, cabbage? The flavours were muted, designed to sustain, not to satisfy. I ate slowly, staring at the scratched surface of the tray. Its dull reflection caught my eye, and I tilted it, searching for myself. Somewhere in there were my eyes, my nose, my lips. But the blur offered no certainty. Would I even recognise my face when I saw it again? After enough time here, would looking in a mirror feel like meeting a stranger?

I missed human contact – so much that I talked to Sam – not out loud, of course; for fear that the voice might hear. But in my head, I told him everything. I spoke to him about the food, the machines, the endless dread. I told him to run, to stay far away from whatever had trapped me here. He didn't answer at first, but eventually, my mind filled in the silence. I imagined his voice, always so sweet and caring, telling me to be strong and promising we'd be together again.

When my tears came, they were a reminder that I was still human enough to feel this pain.

'Please prepare to leave the room,' the voice commanded.

I wiped my face, bracing myself. The door opened, and I stepped through.

By the second week, they had me staring at apples. Row after row of the bloody things.

The first was red, polished to perfection, drops of water clinging to its skin like it had been plucked from a tree on a dewy morning. Then came a green one, smaller, sour-looking. A yellow one followed, a sorry thing. The wall display spat out hundreds more – round ones, squat ones, some sliced to show their cores, others with bites taken out. Apples with spots, stripes, patches; a nightmare tailored by some sadistic bastard just to push me over the edge.

After a while, I turned my focus to the floor. It was smooth and featureless. But of course, they wouldn't let me rest my eyes. The buzzer rang.

'Do not stop looking at the images on the display,' the voice from nowhere said.

I snapped upright, forced my gaze back to the screen. Another apple. This one had a bruise on its side. My eyelids fluttered involuntarily, but I snapped them open each time, terrified of the punishment. I didn't want another shock.

They wouldn't even give me a real apple. Just this visual feast of torment. My mouth watered in spite of myself. I imagined sinking my teeth into one of those glossy skins – the crunch, the burst of sweet, sharp juice. The rhythmic crush as it softened between my teeth. My stomach twisted in protest. I hated myself for wanting it. But I would have been less miserable, perhaps, if they'd just given me a bloody apple to eat.

And then it all stopped.

The wall went back to its white void. I let out a shaky breath, relief mixing with fear – because it was never really over.

'Please shut your eyes,' the voice ordered.

I squeezed them tight.

'Now, picture the objects you just saw.'

As if I'd ever forget those sodding apples. They were burned into my brain. No effort required.

'Return to your room.'

I stood, legs shaky, and made my way back to that sterile little box they dared to call a room. Every step was like a march to nowhere. This was my life now: apples, orders, and a hollow silence where my sanity used to be.

The days dragged on, and the images never stopped. I sat there, wide-eyed, taking it all in, always careful to keep my gaze fixed where it needed to be. Other fruits came after the apples, then they showed me chairs, flowers, butterflies and trees. I took in every detail, just as the voice commanded.

I broke the moment the first human face appeared on the wall. A dark-skinned man, grinning. His mouth stretched across a porous skin. His teeth were crooked and sparse, like stray kernels of corn on pink rubber. But there was a warmth in him – real, human warmth. It was ridiculous, but I wanted to talk to him. He looked like he'd listen. Like he'd save me from the voice.

'Please, contain your emotional response,' the voice said.

I wasn't just crying, I was sobbing out of control. The spasms came in waves, gripping my chest and wringing me out. A guttural wail tore out of me. I sobbed for my misery, my loneliness, my fear of the future. Everything I'd buried surged in a torrent I couldn't stop.

'Please, contain your emotional response,' the voice repeated. 'Focus on the image.'

I tried to pull myself together, forcing a deep breath, but it only unravelled me further. Another wave crashed over me. My grief grew until it became unstoppable. I doubled over, trembling. I wanted to hold on to some sliver of strength, but it slipped through my grasp.

Then, the buzzer.

Terror shot through me. I had seconds to prepare myself before it hit. I couldn't do it. The shock was blinding, more pain than I thought a body could endure. My mouth opened in a scream, but no sound came out, just the horrible convulsions wracking me senseless.

The second shock was worse – longer and more punishing. I barely registered the coldness of the floor pressed against my cheek. There wasn't anything left to break in me.

Then came darkness.

And then peace. Silence. But the absence of pain was also cruel. It had become a reprieve that only deepened the fear of its return.

I stared at the wall, hardly blinking, as another set of faces appeared. This time, the topic was human emotions. Excitement, awe, sorrow, fear – all paraded across the display. It was the tenth day since the images had started. By then, I'd spent most of my waking hours with my eyes glued to that glowing surface. Better than the bots, I told myself. Better than their pricking and prodding. And better than being confined in that desolate room of mine.

The images were something, at least. Some moments, I even found them entertaining. No two were the same. The faintest flicker of anticipation stirred in me each time one image faded, replaced by the next. A habit, perhaps. Or insanity. Probably both.

Then something changed.

Instead of a single image, three objects appeared side by side: an apple in the centre, a fish to the left, and a flower on the right. I studied them as I always did, instinct guiding my eyes to their details.

The voice spoke. 'Apple.'

I froze, unsure what it wanted. Was I supposed to say something? Do something?

I stared at the apple.

'Apple,' it said again.

A black ring formed around the apple. The wall brightened, and new images replaced the objects.

A cat. A dog. A bird.

The voice waited longer this time, but it came again. 'Cat.'

My eyes lingered on the cat first. It sat upright, looking smug. That was the kind of look that would've had me cooing once, long ago. But not any more. Then my attention flitted to the bird. It was small, frail, its feathers painted in exquisite detail. I could almost feel the texture of its wings. Beautiful. My mind drifted as I marvelled at the red triangle of its beak, the colour of a ripe strawberry.

The buzzer stunned me back into focus. My heart jolted as I swung my gaze back to the cat.

'Please focus on the cat,' the voice ordered, and I did as instructed. My eyes drank in its details, every strand of fur, the lazy curl of its tail. When the black ring appeared around the cat, relief flooded me. No shock this time.

The task seemed simple. Match the word to the image. All I had to do was look. But then it got trickier. If I didn't truly concentrate – if I didn't see the image, down to the grain of it – nothing happened. I tested it, half-looking at an image while thinking of something else. No ring appeared. It wasn't until I filled my mind with the object, until I really *felt* it, that the ring came.

I hated that I was getting good at this game. Hated the way it seeped into me. 'Tree,' the voice said. I glared at the tree but pictured the fish instead. Nothing. I switched – swaying branches, silver leaves in my mind – and the ring snapped into place.

Then came the faces. Three of them, all the same person, each with a different expression. One looked pained, the next wide-eyed, the last drooped and tired. My jaw clenched as the voice returned. 'Surprised.'

Closing my eyes, I summoned the face I'd glimpsed – the one with raised brows and a gaping mouth. Nothing happened. Still, I held it in my head. When I cracked my eyes open, the display had already refreshed. No buzzer. No command.

I'd done it. Without even looking. I'd picked the right image using only my mind.

Goosebumps prickled along my arms as the realisation sank in.

I didn't understand how it worked, but I knew one thing: they weren't just training my eyes. They were rewiring my mind – and doing a bloody good job of it.

The nightmares returned. They always did, like parasites burrowing into my brain. The fear was so familiar; the only constant in the chaos.

Sam sat next to me. His chair was positioned as though he belonged there, a guest in my torment. But his clothes didn't fit the scene – soft cords and a plain jumper, like he'd just come in from a quiet evening at home. No ominous shroud. Just him, watching, his eyes reflecting the sterile light of the cube. I was the one trapped in the nightmare, and he was the audience.

'Don't look away,' he said. But I couldn't stop myself. I was beyond caring. Exhaustion had stripped me bare. Weeks of this sickening grind. 'Sam, I can't,' I murmured, though my voice felt detached, like it came from someone else.

He didn't understand. How could he? The voice roared at me, a growl that morphed into an electric buzz. Pain slammed into me, stronger than usual, breaking through the fog of my fatigue, like a thousand blades piercing me at once. Was I bleeding? I gasped, struggling for breath. Frantic. Desperate. Sam's shout was the last thing I heard before I was ripped from the nightmare.

I woke with a start, the sheets tangled around my legs. My chest heaved as I sucked in deep breaths that pulled me back to the dark stillness of my room. The nightmare's grip loosened, but the fear remained. I waved a hand in front of my face, searching for any sign of light in the oppressive blackness, but it was like looking into a void. Was I blind? I blinked hard, but the darkness didn't change.

Then came a whisper, faint but unmistakable: 'Hands.'

I froze. 'Hello?' My voice cracked.

Silence.

The word came again, surreal. Not a sound; not really. But it was definitely there. I snapped my fingers, needing the contrast of a sound I could actually hear.

The whisper persisted. 'Hands…comfort.'

My hand flew to the back of my head, fingers brushing the

scar concealed beneath the regrowth of hair. Memories of what they'd done to me surged. I pushed them back, concentrating instead on forming a thought, a question.

'Who are you?' I sent the question out, shaping it in my thoughts, visualising the words as solid and clear as if I'd written them down.

The answer came swiftly: 'Servum.'

I gasped. I wasn't alone.

'Name…Lisa,' it said. The voice, though alien in its form, was friendly. Human. It wasn't my imagination. It couldn't be. I knew my mind wasn't playing tricks.

'No fear…comfort,' Lisa added.

Tears welled in my eyes. Comfort. That word was almost laughable in the context of my life, but right now, it meant everything. For the first time in what seemed like an eternity, someone was there. Someone who understood.

I clung to that fragile connection, letting the tears flow freely. The sobs returned, racking my body with force again, but this time they weren't just grief. They were a release. Lisa said no more that night, but she didn't have to. Her presence was enough, a faint light in my suffocating darkness.

Eventually, the tears dried up, and exhaustion crept in like a sedative. The quiet air of the room cradled me as I drifted into the most peaceful sleep I'd had in weeks, free from any more nightmares, if only for that night.

Lisa had been a Servum for fifty-three years. That much I managed to piece together, though mindspeak made everything so bloody murky. It wasn't easy to unravel meaning when thoughts sloshed about like water in a leaky jar. But I was getting better at it, improving by leaps in just a few days.

Our conversations filled the dark hours, those voids where nothing existed but each other. What started as monosyllabic exchanges and scattered impressions soon turned into something richer and more intricate. Mindspeak was an odd thing. It came with this constant edge of uncertainty, like catching words through a fog. Images, sensations, flashes of memory – jumbled beyond sense, and yet, somehow, it worked. Lisa's thoughts would hit me like a flash of lightning, full of meaning but impossible to sort out all at once. It was overwhelming at first, but I kept at it. What else was I going to do?

Lisa's life unfolded in snippets, shared through these bursts of connection. Her memories were like holographic reels, playing out for me: silken dresses adorned with pearls, grand receptions echoing with genteel laughter, a husband who was the epitome of kindness and devotion. And her mother – the sight of her! A younger Queen Brynhilda, radiant and commanding. It hit me then. Lisa wasn't just another face in this wretched place; she was royalty. Princess Lisa hadn't died; she was trapped underground, as much a Servum as I now was.

'Servyden,' Lisa called it. A place of the Servums. Their colony. Their prison. Soulless and entirely bot-run.

She'd spent fifty-three years without stepping under an open sky.

'The garden with the sky-screen is nice,' she'd said with some bitterness. 'But it never feels like the real thing. It's like being a fish in a tank, you know?'

'Seen other humans?' I asked, clumsy with my words, still grappling with the mechanics of mindspeak.

'Of course, dear,' she replied. 'And you will too. They have to let us, or we'd all go mad. We're social creatures – they know that. They let us meet, but only just enough to keep us sane. Otherwise, we'd end up like those monkeys they keep caged, rocking back and forth in a corner.'

Her words frightened me. Monkeys in cages. Humans in cages. Not much of a difference.

Lisa described her implant, the way they'd strapped her down and hooked her up to machines. She recounted the physical tests, the mental puzzles, the vomit-inducing exercises. 'It's relentless, my dear. But you learn to endure. You'll see what I mean, soon enough.'

Her memories hit me like punches: the pain, the white rooms, the smell of sterilised air. Flames licking at walls, floors sliding beneath her feet. As vivid as they were, those memories weren't mine. Not yet. But I couldn't stop the terror clawing at my throat.

'This is your life now, dear,' Lisa said, sensing my fear. Her tone was soft but final. 'Don't fight it. The sooner you accept it, the easier it will be.'

'I can't.' The words came out before I could stop them. My body tensed in the darkness. 'I need to believe this will end. I need hope.'

'Hope is dangerous.' Lisa's tone hardened. 'Hope lights fires that will burn you alive. Look at the others – the young ones. Plotting and scheming. What will they achieve? Nothing but a harsh reprimand, I'll tell you that much.'

'Who are they?' I asked.

Images burst into my mind. Black-cloaked figures huddled together in the dirt. Their faces were blurred, indistinct, but the sheer number of them stole the air from my lungs.

'How many?'

'There are thousands of us,' Lisa said, flat with resignation. 'And still, none of their plans will ever succeed. Trust me, dear. Accept your fate. Find solace in what little you have. That's the only way to survive.'

'Can they hear us?' I asked, picturing the Lodgers, their blue gowns and white wigs.

'The Lodgers?' Lisa's laugh was almost bitter. 'They wouldn't waste their time. We're nothing to them – just units. The bots are our masters here. No one else.'

Her words stayed with me long after our conversation ended. Hope was dangerous – a fire that consumed. But what was left without it? Lisa might have found peace in surrender, but I couldn't. Not yet, anyway.

'Sam and I spent some time in Astrin. I used to own a house by the beach. I suppose, in a way, I still do!' I pictured myself laughing. 'Well, it's still there, I imagine...'

I was proud of how far my mindspeak had come. It wasn't anywhere near as good as Lisa's, but I was getting better at it, bit by bit. Through Lisa's thoughts, I'd developed a clear sense of her. Her kind, caring companionship was something I clung to like a lifeline, her affection feeding a part of me starved since my last real human contact.

I'd told Lisa my stories, even the ones I'd never said aloud. I replayed my memories for her, the good and the bad, and she shared hers with the same openness.

'How did you manage today, dear?' she asked at the start of the darkness.

'The voice did something strange,' I said.

'What was it?'

'A lot of talk. Odd sentences... about Servums. A Servum is a seed of life, a beacon of hope. A Servum this...a Servum that...' I replayed the words in my mind for her.

'Oh, they give us plenty of that, darling,' Lisa said, and I sensed something between sarcasm and weariness. 'They think we're creating a new race. The next generation, you see? Generation of what? Nobody knows...with all they've done to our battered bodies. Most Servums aren't seeds, though; that's the real lie. Most of us are just lab rats.'

I rubbed my eyelids, feeling the ache of too many sleepless nights. 'So, those who aren't just lab rats...what are they?'

'The real seeds, I suppose.'

'What does that mean?'

'A seed for the new race,' Lisa said. 'Someone they've decided is fit for procreation. They've got the right attributes – all the gene edits the Lodgers want. You can sometimes tell when you're out on the common. You see them walking around, and you just sort of know who's a seed and who isn't.'

'Were you ever a seed?'

Lisa sent a ripple of laughter through my mind, making me twitch involuntarily. 'Oh, dear, no. Not me. If you could only see me, you wouldn't even ask.'

Her laugh came again, soft but insistent, and I could almost imagine what she might look like.

'What about me?' I asked with unintended caution. 'Am I a seed?'

'You? Are you a seed? Well, I don't know, dear. That's a good question.'

I realised with awful certainty there were still so many ways this could get worse.

For a while, no thoughts passed from either side. The darkness around me thickened, and the pull of exhaustion became harder to resist.

'I'll tell you what, though,' Lisa finally said. 'If they're giving you all that talk now, I reckon it means they'll let you out soon.'

'To meet the others?' Curiosity stirred in me.

'Yes. Out on the common. And when you go there...' Her

thoughts paused with something unsaid. 'There's hardly any surveillance. No bots. No one watching. So you need to stay safe. Some of those people have suffered a great deal, darling. Just remember that. They're not all mean, you know? But it hasn't been easy for many of them. Not easy at all.'

And there I was, standing before the widening gate as the voice announced my release to the common. The words resounded in my mind like a verdict – they meant freedom, but not quite. When I stepped through, the place didn't look exactly the way I'd expected from Lisa's mental imagery. It was wide and barren, just as I'd pictured, but somehow, in person, it appeared less menacing. A small but welcome relief.

Above me arched an illuminated dome, curving like a shield over the common. It was nothing like the sky-screens in Lacunfort. There was no illusion of depth, no blue expanse or drifting clouds. It was just a bleak concrete vault. Beneath my feet, a web of cracks snaked across the parched soil, broken only by the occasional footprint or bump. Small, jagged rocks dug into the soles of my feet. They didn't cut, but they were sharp, turning every step into an exercise in discomfort.

Lisa had said it would take days to walk its entire surface. I squinted into the distance. She wasn't exaggerating. I couldn't even make out the wall at the far end. What struck me most was the energy – the place buzzed with life. Real, human life. Something I'd almost forgotten. Multitudes of Servums were moving about, and something fluttered inside me. I hadn't been with another human in what felt like a long time; the sheer number of them brought a rush of emotions. Anxiety, eagerness, and uncertainty tangled together, making it hard to breathe.

Most wore the same black cloak that I had been given, but others roamed around completely naked, their bodies blackened with dirt as if they'd been dredged from the ground. I stared at the people around me, unable to stop myself. They were talking – real, out-loud talking. It wasn't careful or measured, just messy human chatter. I hadn't realised how much I'd been longing to hear it.

Groups were scattered across the cracked dirt floor. Two teenage girls lay on their backs, propped up on their elbows, their cloaks spread out beneath them like rugs. Nearby, an older group sat in a circle, speaking in turns, their words muffled at this distance. The girls' chatter suddenly turned to shrieks and laughter. One of the older men, a bearded one with his hood pulled low over his face, shushed them with a rough, throaty sound, jabbing a finger at his lips. The girls stifled their giggles, but their eyes sparkled all the same.

A group of five men jogged past, chasing each other like children in a schoolyard. One of them brushed against my cloak with his filthy arm but didn't pause or even glance back. I jolted aside. It was such a strange sensation, to be almost touched, reminding me that I was here, among them.

My breath was just beginning to normalise when a straggler stumbled past, desperate to catch up with the group. He didn't stop or look – just slammed into me, knocking me off my feet. My knees hit the ground hard, and I stayed there, stunned. The man just kept running, leaving me sprawled in the dirt.

'Look where you're going, idiots! May the Saviour break you,' a young woman shouted after them, cupping her hands around her mouth.

'Here.' She extended a hand towards me. 'Get up.'

She looked younger than me. Thick, dark curls framed her face. A pair of expressive eyes met mine as I took her hand; it was rough like sandpaper.

I pulled myself to my feet, brushing the dirt off my cloak.

'You're new, aren't you?' she asked, tilting her head slightly.

I nodded, still catching my breath.

'First time out?'

'Yes,' I said, and my voice wavered slightly. 'How did you—'

'My name is Mona,' she interrupted. 'I'm a dancer.' She fluttered her lashes theatrically, mocking herself.

A genuine smile broke through my hesitation. 'How did you know I was new?'

'Your hair,' she said, her eyes brightening. 'It looks different. Never seen anything like it. I love it.'

'Thank you.'

I instinctively brushed a hand over the strands I could see. Faded remnants of pink still clung to them, though they had long since dulled to pale streaks.

My throat was dry. Only then did I realise how thirsty I was – and how uncertain I felt about when I'd next be back in my room.

'Do you know where I can get some water?' I asked.

'Have you found the fountains yet?'

'Where are they?'

Mona's eyes widened, just a fraction. 'You'll get *really* thirsty. There are many hours until curfew. The fountains are between the section gates.' She pointed to the left, then to the right. 'They can get busy, so don't wait until you're desperate. Just stop by every now and then.'

'Every now and then,' I repeated, trying to take the advice in.

Mona hesitated, studying my face before she asked, 'Are you in section one-sixty-two?'

'I…I'm not sure.'

'You just came out, didn't you? From there?' She gestured behind me.

'Yes, I did.'

She glanced around, lowering her voice. 'Look, I'll show you something. But you can't tell anyone, for the Saviour's sake, or you'll ruin it. Alright?'

'OK,' I said, uncertain but intrigued. She led me a few metres towards a section of the wall.

'This is it.' Her voice dropped to a whisper, but excitement still fizzed beneath it. Her eyes darted to the wall, motioning me closer.

'What is it?' I asked, leaning in.

'A leak!' she said, grinning as if she'd revealed a grand treasure.

It was barely a trickle of water, thin as a thread, seeping from the wall.

'It's not much, I know. But if you press your tongue to it, it's enough to hydrate you after a while.' Demonstrating, she curved her tongue to catch the faint drip, then beamed. 'It's safe to drink. I come here a lot, and I've always been fine.'

'Thank you,' I said, unsure as I glanced at the trickle.

'I'll see you around, maybe.' She flashed a playful grin before turning away. 'Welcome to the common.'

THIRTY

GREN

WHEN THE VEHICLE EASED TO A HALT outside the Rex Royal Hotel, a small crowd descended upon us almost at once. From my seat, they seemed faceless, an undulating sea that seemed to compress the space within the car.

When the door opened, a woman's broad figure loomed into view. She was middle-aged, with a no-nonsense demeanour that matched her build. In her hand, she held a small display bearing the emblem of the Civil Force: an eagle encircled by a cogwheel. The sight of it set my teeth on edge.

'Mr Moritz.' Her tone was formal enough, but she caught herself quickly. 'Chief Minister,' she corrected. 'I'm Officer Belinda Hill. This is my squad team. Can you please follow us inside the building? We have a few questions to ask you.'

I stepped out of the car, drained by the long, sleepless night. It was only when I caught my reflection in the vehicle's window that I registered the absurdity of my appearance. The bellboy uniform hung awkwardly on me, its sleeves too short, the fabric pulling across my shoulders. The trousers, overly narrow and ending just above my ankles, completed the unflattering picture. I looked utterly out of place, the Chief Minister disguised as a hapless hotel staffer.

A pang of embarrassment cut through me. My early morning arrival, unaccompanied and unexplained, would already raise eyebrows. Coupled with this outfit, it was a recipe for speculation I wasn't prepared to answer.

'I have a breakfast appointment in less than an hour,' I said, forcing my voice to remain stable. 'I'm afraid it will have to be quick.'

Officer Hill didn't blink. 'We've cancelled that for you, Chief Minister. A note was sent to the office of the People's Sentinel hours ago. Please, come this way.'

She was polite but firm, leaving no room for negotiation. I glanced at the squad flanking her – thirty officers at least. A show of force that felt pointed. For a split second, I imagined simply walking past them, heading upstairs, and letting the world wait while I buried my face in a pillow. I could almost feel the cool sheets, the welcome darkness behind my eyelids. The temptation to escape was strong but fleeting. I straightened and met Officer Hill's rigid gaze.

'Lead the way,' I said, and followed her into the hotel, leaving the frenzied swarm behind.

'Can you please look at these photographs, Chief Minister?'

The sight was a blow to the chest. Officer Hill's photographs were grotesque. I usually had a strong stomach, but this pushed the limits of what I could handle.

The images showed a body. Slender, female, completely

nude. Her arms and legs were extended as if she'd been arranged deliberately. The face, if one could still call it that, had collapsed inward, leaving a fleshy, blood-filled crater where her features should have been. A maroon stain spread across the sheets beneath her.

Officer Hill tapped the table display, and the photographs expanded, filling the surface with grim definition. She stood next to me, close enough that I could sense her reluctance in the way her fingers lingered on the image. I tried to look away, but my eyes refused to obey.

'Who is she?' I managed to ask, my voice hoarse. 'What happened?'

Hill's expression remained professional, though I caught the tension in her jaw. 'We were hoping you could help us identify her. At this stage, our investigation is constrained by the sensitivity of the case.'

'Constrained how?'

She hesitated before answering. 'Early this morning, hotel security alerted us to an unauthorised entry into your suite. Upon arrival, we discovered an unidentified shell bot had breached the premises. You, of course, weren't present at the time.'

'A shell bot? Are you certain?'

'The security systems picked up its signal. It wasn't autonomous – someone was driving it remotely, likely from Lacunfort. That's our preliminary conclusion based on the data available.'

'And then?'

'The bot entered the Marble Suite, one floor below yours.' She paused, her eyes shaded with sympathy. 'That's where your Chief of Staff, Clara Reza, was staying.'

The world tilted. My knees threatened to buckle, and I had to place both hands on the desk to steady myself.

'Is she...?' The words caught in my throat.

Hill's voice softened. 'We can't confirm yet, Chief Minister. The tests are inconclusive, but...everything we've found so far points to it being Clara. I am deeply sorry.'

My eyes dropped to the photographs again, searching desperately for any sign of a mistake. The disfigured face offered no answers, but the hair – a dull grey clump matted with blood – looked like it could well be hers. My mind flashed with memories of her: Clara pacing hallways, her quick, precise footsteps echoing late into the night; her voice rising above the bustle of campaign trails. She was more than a Chief of Staff. She was my closest ally, my best friend and the closest thing I ever had to a mother. It was impossible to imagine continuing without her.

'She has a birthmark.' The words rushed out of my mouth. 'On her wrist. It looks like a heart-shaped freckle.'

Using a small screen, the officer standing beside Hill quickly flicked through the images until he found one that focused on the victim's hands. He held the device closer. 'Is this it, Chief Minister?'

I stared at the mark. It was faint but unmistakable. The tears came hot and fast, my hands shaking as an overwhelming ache seized me.

'Yes,' I whispered.

Hill's tone turned clinical, retreating behind the shield of procedure. 'The attacker used a corrosive substance, likely acid, to dissolve soft tissues and parts of the skull. The material remains hazardous, which is why we've opted for photographic identification.'

'Water,' I said. 'Could I have a glass of water?'

A young officer left the room to fetch it, and Hill pressed on, her voice kind but probing. 'Chief Minister, do you know of anyone who might have had a motive to harm you or Ms Reza?'

I shook my head, then stopped. 'There are always agitators. Protesters are constantly outside my office.'

'We're aware of that,' Hill said firmly. She hesitated before continuing with a calculating tone. 'I'm afraid I need to ask – where were you last night?'

I straightened. 'Attending to personal matters.'

'You are wearing a hotel staff uniform,' she pressed. 'And your devices were left in your room. Why?'

The water arrived, mercifully interrupting her line of questioning. I drank quickly, the cold liquid offering a brief moment to think.

'I had to leave discreetly,' I replied. 'It was important that I wasn't followed or recognised.'

'And why was that?'

I met her gaze. 'I'm afraid I can't share that information right now.'

Hill opened her mouth to argue, but was interrupted by another officer bursting into the room. 'Officer Hill, a word?' he said, his posture tense.

Hill's frustration was clear as she walked out. When she returned moments later, her tone was all command. 'We need to evacuate this room immediately. Everyone out, now. Except you, Chief Minister. Stay here; you'll receive a call via hologram shortly.'

'Who's calling?'

'I don't know,' she replied. 'Now, please, everyone: out!'

As the room emptied, I stood alone, my thoughts a whirlwind of anger and grief. The revolts should have been a warning – a sign to tighten security. Whoever was behind this had sent a horrific message. Were they about to reveal themselves now?

•••

The Civil Force had placed a small hologram box on the desk beside me. My hands covered my face as I waited, trying to regain focus. Rubbing my eyes, I fought to make sense of the events of the past few hours. Clara. What had she seen before it ended? Had she fought back? Clara, of all people, would have fought back. I hoped the acid had acted swiftly; the thought of her enduring even a moment of that agony was unbearable. I didn't want my memories of Clara tainted by images of her face melting away, turning into a bloody sludge.

'Good morning, Mr Moritz.'

I looked up abruptly. A full-body hologram of Igor Voychenko stood before me.

'Supreme Leader.'

'You've been causing some nuisance, I hear,' Voychenko said, his tone offensively casual.

I didn't respond.

'There is nothing to worry about,' he continued calmly. 'We will clean this up for you. But I hope you'll learn from this experience. It mustn't be in vain.'

'What is there for me to learn?' I tried hard to sound neutral.

Voychenko paused, weighing his response. 'Mr Moritz,' he said, 'I am deeply sorry about the sudden loss of your Chief of Staff. Truly, I am. You worked closely with her for years, didn't you?'

'Yes,' I stated stiffly.

'You must understand, though,' he went on, his voice growing harsher, 'that her fate was not the doing of anyone but yourself.'

'*Me?*' I struggled to contain the rage that surged within me. Once again, my hands pressed against the surface of the desk as I forced myself to remain composed.

'You left us no choice,' he said, shaking his head in apparent disappointment.

My voice rose despite my efforts to control it. 'What did *I* do?'

Voychenko's eyebrows lifted in a gesture that appeared both irritated and condescending. 'Calm yourself, Mr Moritz. You involved her. And Isabel, too. That sorrowful woman. You all call her Doris now, don't you?'

'Clara was not involved. She knew nothing.'

Voychenko regarded me with an impassiveness that only stoked my anger further. 'Is that so?' he asked, almost conversationally. 'Who, then, briefed Doris about your visit? Who arranged the car with a pre-booked destination? Would you have handled that on your own? And who obtained the ridiculous outfit you wore for your clandestine meeting?'

I stared at him, unflinching. I wouldn't let Voychenko break me, but I couldn't stop him from stirring a darkness I hadn't known could rise in me. A thirst for revenge spread through my veins, foul as decay.

'You must know by now,' Voychenko continued, 'the Lodges have ears in every corner, eyes beneath every stone. We take no risks.'

'What will happen to Doris?' My voice had dropped to a tight murmur.

'Doris?' Voychenko's smile was pale and deadly. 'Oh, rest assured, she won't be answering to anyone again.'

THIRTY-ONE

PRIMULA

I HEARD THE SCREAM BEFORE I SAW HER. A raw, ragged sound. A woman.

My head whipped round, and then I spotted her across the common. It was Mona, her cloak dragging along her legs like a ball and chain, hobbling in an attempt to run. Behind her, a man who looked more like a monster moved with horrifying ease. Twice her size, naked, with legs like tree trunks and a chest carved with scars. He looked like a walking nightmare, each stride closing the distance between them like she wasn't even trying to escape.

He reached her before I could process what was happening, grabbing a fistful of her curls and yanking her head back like she was some rag doll. In a flash, she was airborne, her body twisting, before she slammed into the ground. Then came the kicks. His bare foot smashed into her again and again.

Hot fury bubbled up inside me as I stood there, paralysed. It was like the world was collapsing inward, and still, somehow, *I* was growing – my anger swelling until it felt like I could explode.

I didn't plan it. One moment I was watching, teeth grinding, and the next I was charging at him, a scream of war tearing from my throat. My nails sank into his back. Flesh split beneath my fingers like an orange peel, squelching as I kept scratching the skin I'd already torn. I screamed again, louder even. Something primal had burst out of me.

He didn't stop straight away, but he slowed, turning his face to roar at me. I didn't give him the chance to think. My fingers clawed right into his eye, aiming to gouge it out. I wanted him blind and broken. If he could attack someone so easily, he deserved the same. Somehow, this small act of justice might make the world a little less cruel.

His arm swung wide, and I was thrown back, hitting the ground with a brutal impact. I gasped, struggling to suck air into my lungs. Fear shot through me then, but it was drowned out almost instantly by the feeling of his fists and feet smashing against my body. Blow after blow after blow.

Then, suddenly, he stopped, as if he had only just noticed his injuries, as if the pain had only just set in. His hand flew to his face, clutching his eye, blood seeping through his fingers. He stumbled back, moaning. The onlookers clapped – mockingly, I gathered – though, to my surprise, their derision wasn't for me. It was for him. He turned and lumbered off with heavy footsteps until he disappeared into the distance.

As the dust settled, I lay there heaving. My chest screamed with every shallow breath. Voices floated around me.

'Brave woman, that one,' a man said.

'Or brainless,' another said, laughing. 'Fresh Servum, no doubt.'

I forced myself to sit up, clutching my ribs with one hand. Mona was dragging herself towards me, blood trailing down her face. Her lip was split, her teeth red.

'Thank the Saviour,' she whispered, collapsing beside me. 'He would've killed me, you know. He's harmed me bad before. They're always worse after the hormones.' She coughed, then spat blood onto the ground. 'Always remember this – you can't outrun them in a cloak.'

My hands were sticky and raw. Blood pooled under my nails. His blood. Bits of skin clung to the edges. The sight should've revolted me, but instead, I discovered a strange satisfaction.

Mona's laughter startled me. She was shaking her head, incredulous. 'You got him, though. I mean, *really* got him. He'll be a cyclops now.' She covered one eye and burst out laughing again. The sound was coarse and unhinged, but there was joy in it.

'What's your name?' she asked, grinning.

'Primula.' The effort of talking sent a fresh wave of pain through my ribs.

'Well, Primula…' Mona's voice turned affectionate. 'You'll be sore for a while, but you'll be fine.' She paused, wiping blood from her chin. 'Come on, let's get up. I'll show you around. You should meet my family.'

I nodded, though moving felt impossible. Somehow, with her help, I got to my feet. Every step throbbed with pain, but I followed her. Because I had to. Because staying still wasn't an option any more.

The old woman's eyes landed on Mona. 'Your mouth!'

'I'm fine, Ma,' Mona replied, then raised her voice to make an announcement. 'Ma, everyone, this is Fibula.'

'It's Primula.' I forced a polite smile, though each breath came with a tug of pain.

The group of cloaked figures stirred, looking at me like I'd just grown a second head. Then, a ginger man with a straw-coloured beard grunted, 'Primula Zhang.' He said my name like it was some kind of riddle. Arms crossed, his beard swayed as he spoke.

'Oh, Grotto's met her already,' Mona huffed, frowning.

'Not exactly,' he muttered. 'She…'

The old woman's voice broke through in an excited pitch, her tone climbing higher. 'Oh my days, it's like a flash from another life. The fashion model! You haven't aged one bit, love. Bless you. So sorry they've dragged you down here.'

Mona squinted at me. 'Fashion model?'

'Used to work in fashion,' I said, keeping my words short. The less I stood out, the better.

'Like, clothes and things?' Mona said.

'Yes…' I replied, wondering how long Mona had lived in this place. There was something in her ways that suggested she was more of a Servum than anything else.

'I still remember some of it,' she said eagerly. 'Mad, really, to think I once wore proper clothes. Different colours and all. I had this dress, see, blue with little straps here.' She motioned to her filthy collarbone, then tapped her shoulders, trying to help me picture it. Her fingers looked like they hadn't been washed in a lifetime. 'It was beautiful.' Mona beamed, looking directly into my eyes, marking the truth of what she'd said. She hadn't just made that up – she had once owned a dress.

'Anyway!' She clapped her hands. 'This is my family. My Ma, Marydit – she's my Servyden mother – and these are Ronnie, Julian, Grotto and Jose. The others aren't out today.'

A shuffle of noises emerged from the group – barely a

greeting. I gave a weak wave, my best attempt at friendliness. Though the stabbing in my ribcage made it hard to hold a smile. 'Nice to meet you all. You're the first people I've spoken to since I got here.'

'She saved my life!' Mona burst out, though her family barely blinked. It was obvious this lot was well practised in tuning out her stories.

Mona's version of events tumbled out, painting me as some kind of hero – going for the bloke's eyes like a bloody lion. She finished with a laugh, looking to me for validation. 'Didn't you, Primula? Tell them!'

I nodded faintly, keeping my movements small.

'Could this one be the Saviour, then?' one of the young men asked, quietly but with clear curiosity.

The group exchanged uncertain glances.

'No Saviour will ever come,' another said. 'There's no such thing.'

'Well, she saved *me*,' Mona said brightly. 'But the legend says the Saviour isn't meant to have human legs. Is that right?' Her gaze dropped pointedly to my legs, as if closing the case.

'Well, thank you ever so much,' Marydit said, kind and motherly. 'Not many would risk themselves like that for a stranger. You're one of us now, love. Stick close when you're out on the common – it's not always safe to be alone.'

The others started talking among themselves again, scratching careful lines in the dirt with sticks. The way they leaned in and murmured to each other left no doubt that every mark was important to them. Whatever their game was, it clearly mattered more than me. I turned my gaze back to Marydit, drawn to her strange golden eyes. They looked almost inhuman, with oversized pupils and bright irises. When she caught me staring, I looked away too quickly, trying to hide the heat rising in my cheeks.

'Oh, don't be embarrassed, love,' she said. 'It must all seem foreign to you.'

'Ma's got bird eyes,' Mona said as if unveiling a marvellous fact.

'They did that for a while, years ago,' Marydit explained. 'I can see ultraviolet now. Not much use, really, but it's become normal to me after all this time.'

Her calmness unnerved me, but my curiosity wouldn't let go. 'Do you know how they did it?' I asked, instantly regretting the question.

'Not a clue. You wake up one day with patches on your eyes, and next thing you know, you're looking at a rainbow where there isn't one.' She chuckled to herself.

Something about her laughter twisted my insides. It wasn't the sight of her strange eyes or her story – it was the way she seemed so resigned to it all. Like this bleak existence had swallowed her, and she'd just accepted it.

Mona turned back to me. 'How long have you been here?'

'Fifty-one days,' I said. Each one a bloody eternity.

Marydit's face softened into something that bordered on pity. 'Have they done anything to you yet, love?'

'Yes,' I said. 'They cut into the back of my head. Made me stare at pictures for hours.' My fingers brushed the spot behind my ear. 'I don't know exactly what they're doing to me.'

Mona gasped loudly. 'You're not serious!' Her eyes widened. Even Marydit's mouth fell open, the lines of her face deepening in surprise.

'I am,' I said, instantly regretting my honesty. Was it too much to share?

'They'll use you for mindspeak,' Mona said, almost reverent. Then her face crumpled into something between disbelief and excitement. 'You've no idea how lucky you are. I can't believe it. All the new ones are getting the best enhancements. Julian's doing arithmetic, and now Primula is doing mindspeak.' She paused. 'I'm not jealous, though. I'm not. I swear. Primula, you have to tell us everything – every single detail, please.'

My hesitation must have shown, because she leaned in, wide-eyed and hopeful, and whispered, 'Don't leave anything out.'

The urge to hold back wrestled with my need to connect, to be understood. I began recounting the endless hours spent staring at images, following orders from a disembodied voice. Told them about the dark hours, about connecting with someone named Lisa, and the strange conversations we'd shared. As the words spilled out, a strange relief swept through me, though I kept glancing at their faces for signs I'd gone too far.

'Lisa,' Marydit murmured. 'Of course. Princess Lisa had it done, too.'

My heart skipped at the casual familiarity in her tone. 'You know her?' I asked with both hope and caution.

'Ma knows everyone,' Mona said, puffing up like a rooster. 'From sections one-fifty to one-seventy-five, at least. And even more.'

Marydit laughed softly, her golden eyes glinting. 'I know Lisa,' she said. 'I thought she'd be out today.' She scanned the crowd in the distance, then pointed her out. 'There she is.'

Lisa had somehow managed to find a large rock on the bare surface of the common. By the looks of her, if anyone deserved to use a rock as a backrest, that person was Lisa. Her cloak was folded neatly beneath her like a cushion, and she sat on it with both legs bent to one side.

The first thing I noticed was her arms, or what was left of them. The skin hung loosely around the bones. Stripped of any covering, her ribs stood out like bars of a cage, each one distinct, broken only by the vertical lines of her breasts – long, deflated things that drooped towards the ground.

Lisa's eyes were shut, as though even looking at the world might drain her of the tiny reserves of energy she had left.

'Lisa,' Marydit called softly.

Her eyelids fluttered, and she stirred. It took a moment for her to fully return, her consciousness sluggishly emerging from wherever it had been.

'Ah?' The sound that escaped her was like a ghost of a voice.

'Someone is here to see you,' Marydit said gently. 'Her name is Primula.'

Lisa tilted her head, squinting. Her face creased into a frown. 'Who is it?' she asked.

I took a breath and shut my eyes, reaching for focus. Then, switching to mindspeak, I greeted her.

Her eyes snapped wide open, and her brows lifted in surprise. 'Primula! Dear!' She pushed herself up, trying to stand, but her legs faltered beneath her. When both Marydit and I moved to help, Lisa waved us off, leaning back against the rock with a shaky hand.

'It's lovely to see you.' Her voice was brittle. When she smiled, it revealed a single, yellowed incisor in a mouth otherwise barren of teeth. 'My dear, I can see you're in pain.'

'I am,' I admitted, but tried to keep my voice steady. 'There was a man… I saw him hurting a girl – Mona.' I glanced in Mona's direction before continuing. 'And rage just…took over. I didn't think.'

Lisa shook her head slowly. Her grey hair, long and thin,

dragged along the dirt with the movement.

'You need to be careful, dear,' Lisa said. 'This isn't the outside. The rules are different here. Justice is merely a dream. Here, the strongest always win.'

'But you should've seen it,' I said. For once, I was glad to share a story in person, to have Lisa here in the flesh. 'I jumped on his back and scratched him with everything I had. Tore his skin to shreds.'

'Do you know who the man was?' Lisa's face darkened.

'No idea. Over seven feet tall, covered in scars. I suppose I might've added a few more.' I laughed faintly, pressing the back of my hand to my mouth. Telling the story awakened something in me – a liveliness I thought I'd lost. Even the pain in my ribs faded.

But Lisa didn't share my amusement. Her face twisted with anguish. 'Oh, my darling, he'll come back.' She shook her head again, the skin around her neck swaying with the motion. 'He'll come back, and then...what will we do?'

'We'll fight him, that's what,' Marydit said firmly, stepping forward. 'I'll gather the boys. We'll show him. Who knows what would've happened to my Mona if it weren't for Primula? We owe her. Let him come.'

Lisa suddenly lifted her chin, and something in the way she looked at me became frightening. A yelp broke from her throat; quick, startling. Her eyes seemed to stare beyond us, seeing something we couldn't.

'Run,' she said, low and urgent. Then louder, more desperate: 'Primula, run! You have to run now!'

THIRTY-TWO

SAM

NO MORE THAN ONE SEIZURE a day, Mum had said.

As I held her hand in mine, I couldn't believe how rapidly she had gone downhill. Dr Khan had warned me for weeks about the speed of it all, but I kept fooling myself, thinking there'd be more time. Watching her now, so small, lying in that bed, I understood it. That point of no return.

I'd taken the day off work. The morning had been quiet but tense. Mum had insisted on a lavish breakfast, savouring every bite with that deliberate way she'd always eaten – a tortoise-like patience that had become more pronounced with age. Even in her state, there was a grace about her, a kind of dignity that just wouldn't fade.

The sanatorium was like a second home by now, with its cold walls and the faint hum of life-support machines that you stop noticing after a while. But this morning it all seemed different. By tomorrow, this place would start slipping into memory, growing distant over time. Mum was either here or she wasn't. Simple as that. The thought of it being so black and white made me feel sick.

Past the sadness, there was something worse – a kind of numbness that had taken hold over the prior days. It left me feeling empty, like I wasn't even breathing any more. Sadness, at least, was something. But *this* was like all the grief had been wrung out of me, leaving nothing in its place. What are you meant to hold onto when there isn't anything left – not even the hurt?

The mortuary nurse arrived promptly. Her blonde hair was pulled back in a tight bun, her face wrinkled and unadorned. She carried herself with the kind of confidence that could only come from years of practice.

'Are you comfortable?' she asked Mum.

Mum answered with a faint, almost imperceptible huff, her eyes flicking to mine for reassurance. I squeezed her hand gently. She'd been clear – no fuss, no dramatic goodbyes.

The nurse laid out a small table next to the bed, arranging two vials and a delicate porcelain plate with precise movements. A tiny slab of chocolate sat on the plate like a final offering.

'The first drink is an antiemetic,' the nurse explained. Her tone was polite but detached. 'It will numb the insides to prevent nausea.'

Mum took the vial in her unsteady hand. The effort to keep it still just long enough to swallow its contents was clear in the shake of her fingers. I was torn between wanting to say something and knowing it was too late for words.

The second vial was darker, thicker. 'Enhanced hemlock and herbs,' the nurse said. Mum took it like it was nothing, pausing only to glance around the room.

'To a life well lived,' she said, in a voice that was faint but resolute. Then she lifted the vial and drank its contents.

The nurse placed the chocolate to her lips, and Mum accepted it. 'It helps with the bitterness,' she said to me.

Mum reclined into her pillow, her eyes drifting closed, her right hand still clasped in mine. We waited. Every second dragged heavier than the one before. My mind spiralled, thinking about what was happening inside her. Her heart, which had kept going for decades, would finally give out. Her lungs would go still, and her blood would settle wherever it could. She'd change colour. Her body, the thing that had been Mum, would turn into something hollow. Just a thing. Where would she go? What about her laughter, her sharp tongue, her restless way of being – would it all just vanish into the air?

'Time of death: eleven hours, twenty-three minutes,' the nurse announced in her medical voice.

I gasped. The numbness cracked then, letting the sadness flood in. That familiar pain wrapped around my insides. I welcomed it. Feeling it again, however terrible, was better than the void. My shoulders slumped as I let the tears come, my grip on her hand tightening one last time before I let go.

What are you meant to do when something like this happens to you? How are you supposed to keep going after that? I finally got it – why so many people just walked straight into those Express Passing Centres. One quick step, and it's all over. Why not? It made sense in a way it never had before. And honestly, I might've done the same if it weren't for that tiny thread of hope. That slim chance that Primula might still be out there.

If the Lodgers had taken her for losing the game, then losing was all I had left to try. Either I'd lose and see her again, or I'd finally know for sure that this life wasn't worth holding onto.

The dates from our predictions started spinning in my head, and an idea began to take shape – a way to hand Gren an instant win. It was just a glimmer at first, but soon enough, it took over everything.

When people said healthcare bots were easy to hack, I thought they were exaggerating. But after a few hours glued to my screens, digging into some networks, I had everything I needed. The model, the operating system – it was all laid out in forums and manuals that no one bothered to secure. From there, it wasn't hard to program a patch that looked like a routine anti-bug update. Simple. Once I sent it through, I was in.

Didn't take long to realise the access I had was half-useless, though. I could read data, tweak a few parameters; nothing serious. I needed full control.

I worked at it through the night. Full-on obsessed. Couldn't stop. So I called in sick. Didn't care what people at the Agency thought any more. I kept going.

A few more hours and all I'd cracked was a mess of old documents from the bot security network. I flicked through them, yawning, until one caught my eye. It mentioned a nine-digit code, split into three. Each chunk had to be computed separately. But the instructions were right there. Too good to be true. A master passcode? Looked exactly like one. Only way to know was to try.

I spent the rest of the afternoon building an algorithm to crunch the three parts and stitch them together. It didn't work at first. Tried it ten times, then ten more, then kept trying until I lost count. By early evening, I found myself staring at the screen in disbelief – I'd hit the right digits. The whole network was mine. It was more control than I'd ever expected. Every bot in the palace. Every function, down to the most obscure line in their code.

I went for the head bot, Yunnia D. Sleek bit of kit, but under all that polish, her software was as exposed as an open door. I could've had her march through the palace corridors or spin around like she was part of a performance. But I wasn't here to muck about. This was a matter of getting what I needed, fast and quiet, without tripping any alarms.

It all unfolded in the darkness of the Royal Palace, between eleven o'clock and midnight, and I saw it all through Yunnia D's eyes. The feed on my monitor was sharp enough, but the colours were muted and cold. I was seeing the world through the lens of something not alive. The grand stairwell came into view, its red carpet stretching endlessly upwards, plush enough that her white shoes sank with every step. The movement was unnervingly smooth – no hesitation, no adjustment – just one calculated step after another.

My breathing quickened as the feed followed her gloved hand, which didn't so much as touch the bedroom door. Instead, the door slid open as though it had been waiting for her. A living person might've paused there, taking a moment to adjust to the pitch-black room ahead, but not Yunnia D. Her lenses adjusted instantly, giving me a view so clear it was disorienting, every item picked out in detail, like it was broad daylight.

The queen lay still, bundled in thick covers, the faint sound of her breathing whistling through the oxygen mask strapped to her face. Yunnia D approached the bed, her steps careful and deliberate. My hands lingered above my control console. Should I intervene? My stomach churned, but I couldn't bring myself to revert my programming.

The oxygen mask was the first to go. Her hands worked swiftly, disconnecting the central board with a flick. I didn't need to understand the intricacies of the queen's medical set-up to know what came next.

My mind was in chaos. I had full control of Yunnia D. I could stop what I'd started. But I sat, paralysed, watching her hand hover above the queen's face. Then it closed in. Her rubbery fingers pinched the queen's nostrils. The feed jolted slightly as the queen stirred, her mouth gaping open in a desperate gasp for air. Yunnia D moved with terrifying efficiency, slapping her other hand over the queen's lips, sealing them shut. It felt unreal, like watching a film.

The queen's legs kicked under the blankets, her movements wild and erratic at first. But Yunnia D's grip didn't loosen. My breath hitched as she struggled, her motions slowing until, finally, they stopped altogether.

The feed froze on my screen. My stomach was in knots, my palms sweaty. What on earth had I just done? I tapped at the console's controls, desperate to make sense of what I was seeing. Was this the bot's programming? Or had I lost control somewhere? A warning flashed across my screen: *Connection Unstable.*

'No, no, no,' I muttered, hammering the keys, trying to re-establish the link. The feed flickered; the picture warped into jagged lines, then cut out completely.

'Yunnia,' I whispered, as if the machine could somehow hear me. The connection was gone. All I had left was the certainty of what I'd just seen and the haunting question of what might have happened.

Within a couple of hours, the news holograms began to shimmer in front of me, their wavering light bouncing off the walls. I sat hunched over my console, my leg jittering uncontrollably as I fumbled with the controls. The Royal Palace was a hive of activity. Civil Force officers and private security bots swarmed the grounds, their movements precise, purposeful. The press had already descended, a sea of lenses and microphones thrust against the gates, surrounded by anxious civilians desperate for answers.

Rumours poured through the feed: bot violence, an attack before midnight, the queen's safety unconfirmed. The Royal Office stayed silent, which fuelled the fire. I flipped through the holograms, each one spinning another layer of speculation. 'An attempted assassination?' one reporter posited, while another hinted at 'a grave malfunction among the palace's healthcare bots.'

A little over an hour later, the waiting turned restless across Rivennia. Streets emptied. Crowds packed into public squares, their eyes glued to holographic projections, faces strained. Good or bad, the monarchy was tradition, and now people were properly rattled.

A cold tingle spread across my chest as it all settled in. I'd done this. Me.

Sitting in this dim room, shaking so hard I could barely keep my finger steady on the console, I realised just how far this could spiral. The entire world was holding its breath, and I'd lit the match that could burn it all down.

I shifted in my chair and scanned the palace feed, noting that several of the healthcare bots were still connected. Through their eyes, I caught glimpses of the grand vestibule. Staff members huddled in small groups, looking exhausted. Butlers, clerks, cooks and cleaners dragged out of their rooms by the emergency alarms. They sat on chairs that looked like they belonged in a museum. Their fancy cushions that probably had never been used were now starting to sag under the weight of the people on them. Some were standing and others were sitting on the cold marble floor, their knees tucked up to their chest.

The bots' lenses tracked everything: the flicker of the crowd's torches outside the palace gates, the shuffle of feet as Civil Force officers swept the corridors, issuing commands. Through one bot's eyes, I followed an officer inspecting a velvet-draped window. He pulled back the heavy fabric and peered into the crowd beyond, murmuring something into his comm. The officers seemed convinced someone inside the palace had tampered with Yunnia D. Their search was methodical, room by room, leaving no drawer or cupboard unchecked.

I became impatient as I scrolled through the feeds. I needed Yunnia D's eyes. I needed to see what had happened. I hammered at the controls, trying to re-establish the connection I'd lost earlier. The screens blurred and refreshed as I kept scanning. Finally, the feed from Yunnia D snapped back to life.

The view caught me off guard. The royal bedchamber looked even grander in the light, but the atmosphere stripped all that away in a second. I gathered from the angle that Yunnia D was lying on the floor. Queen Brynhilda sat on the edge of the bed, her hunched back silhouetted against the light spilling from the open door. Her elbows dug into her thighs, her hands clasped together. Her face was ashen, the angry bruises on her chin and nose standing out like smudges across her skin.

On a separate screen, I pulled up a diagram of Yunnia D's body and saw her position. She was crumpled, joints twisted in ways they shouldn't be. She'd been tossed aside like rubbish. Without thinking, I zoomed in, my heart thumping as I scanned for any sign of life. It didn't take long to realise that, even though I still had access to her lenses, her motion systems had been manually shut down.

'Her Majesty is in good condition,' someone was saying. 'Apart from the bruises, no damage was inflicted.'

A Royal Sergeant stepped into the frame, moving closer to the queen, and sighed.

'We'll remove Yunnia D from the premises immediately,' a nasal voice from the corner interjected. 'The bot will be incinerated once the Civil Force completes their investigation.'

'Thank you.' The Sergeant whispered something else, but her voice was barely audible.

Then the queen spoke. 'Burn all of them.'

The room went still. Both the Sergeant and the doctor turned to her, caught somewhere between confusion and fear. Even through Yunnia D's distorted feed, the Queen's eyes burned with wrath. She spoke with an unmistakable finality. 'All the bots.'

The Sergeant's tone was cautious. 'Your Majesty, if I may... it was the other bots who stopped Yunnia D. They sounded the alarms, restrained her, separated her from you. If not for them—'

'All the bots.' The queen's words came hard and fast. Her gaze locked on the Sergeant, daring her to argue. The Sergeant straightened, her lips pressing into a thin line.

'Yes, yes, Your Majesty,' the man in the corner said, his voice trembling. 'Of course.'

My hands shook as the feed stuttered and blurred. The signal wavered again, and Yunnia D's view narrowed as her systems continued to fail. I pushed at the console, desperate to hold on for just a moment longer. But then the screen blinked and went black.

I sat back, staring at the empty monitor, breathing hard. A sour wave climbed up my throat, and I barely made it to the paper basket before it all came up in choking spasms.

•••

There were five of them when I opened the door, their faces stiff as iron, wearing crisp, black uniforms. Bots? Maybe. I couldn't tell. Their eyes, though – there was something in them. Too human. Too cold. Staring at the spread-eagled crest stamped on their coats, my heart pounded. Could they hear it? The cool silence of dawn made everything feel louder, like the world had emptied just for this moment.

The man at the front raised a hand display, holding it for me to see. Another eagle, wings stretched inside the cogwheel.

'Samuel Rosendale?'

It was odd to think that the last time I'd slept, my mother was still alive.

'Yes.' It came out wrong; a sound between a croak and a quiver. I swallowed hard, but my throat was still tight, like I couldn't get enough air.

'Civil Force,' he said. 'You're under arrest on suspicion of the attempted murder of Her Majesty, Queen Brynhilda of Rivennia. You will come with us to the Civil Force quarters on Lacunfort Platform 62.'

Just for a second, I had clung to a sliver of hope – a tiny, pathetic belief that maybe they'd come for something else. A misunderstanding. A mistake. Perhaps just a few questions. But their words tore that away, leaving nothing to grasp.

How had they found me? I'd been careful. Ultra careful. I'd used Agency methods to calculate the master passcode, sure, but no one could've guessed that just by looking at the digits. I couldn't think where I'd slipped up. But then again, I was so knackered I could barely think at all.

'It is necessary to arrest you, Mr Rosendale, so the Civil

Force can conduct interrogations. During this time, you will not be free to leave or contact anyone outside the quarters. Do you understand?'

I nodded, but it was like I wasn't really there. My mind had wandered somewhere else, back to a nice, soft memory. Primula, resting in my arms, her skin warm against mine, her voice mixed with that rich, unguarded laugh of hers. What was she saying? I couldn't hear it any more; just the echo of that laugh weaving through the words, pulling a smile from me no matter what.

'Mr Rosendale.' The officer's voice yanked me back. 'I need to hear it. Do you understand?'

'Yes,' I said, the word barely scraping out of my throat. 'I understand.'

There were no handcuffs. No roughness. Just five men carrying this out with the dispassionate efficiency of something they probably did every day. When I asked if I could pack a bag – just some clothes, anything – they shut me down. 'No time,' they said. It had to be now.

So I kept my head up and walked past the few prying neighbours who'd somehow suspected something was going on, until I reached the pneuduct gate, where the capsula waited, its doors yawning open. Inside, the place was as grim as I expected: three rows of black seats, the walls scratched and stained, the cream paint beaten down by years of use. It wasn't hard to picture the others who'd sat here before me – real criminals, people who'd broken the world's rules. Was I one of them now? I didn't think so; my case felt different. But how many of them had told themselves the same thing?

As the capsula whirred through the ducts, my hands stiffened, heat spreading through my palms. I pressed them into my legs, trying to force some calm, but it didn't work. My breath came faster, shallow at first, then strained. The air was too thin, like it wasn't reaching my lungs properly. The walls of the capsula seemed to close in, and my heart began pounding harder than before. I fought the dizziness as my head spun. The world around me started to fog as though I were floating just outside of myself. But it wasn't until the door of my cell slammed shut that everything collapsed. I pressed my hands over my eyes, trying to hold back the tears. My breath jerked uncontrollably as I struggled to get a grip.

I lay down, wrecked, knowing there was no undoing any of this. No rewinding, no escaping. It was over. All the hope I'd clung to had dissolved, crushing the last shred of spirit I had left.

When the ceiling lamps clicked off with a metallic snap, the cell plunged into darkness.

I had never felt more alone.

THIRTY-THREE

GREN

AT FORTY-THREE, I THOUGHT I understood tears. But a body doesn't just mourn with the heart; it grieves with its bones, its muscles. I didn't know about the ache that settles in your ribs from crying so deeply.

I sat motionless on the bench, wrestling with the fraying threads of my thoughts. The pond mirrored the sparse moonlight of the sky-screen. My sorrow had left nothing but a husk, a man who spoke only when necessity demanded.

Every time Lorelei tried to approach me, I retreated. I had the clarity to know this wasn't her fault, and I could see, too, that she was isolated. Any sensible person would have pointed out the irony: two people, husband and wife, meant to safeguard each other from life's evils, yet both miserable and unable to keep one another company. She was painfully lonely, but I couldn't bring myself to take that on; the burden of solving it seemed too great. Being honest about my disinterest always seemed the most compassionate option.

Compassion, however, was in short supply in this world – a world whose government I had chosen to lead. I had walked into this office wearing a blindfold.

There was a distant sound of footsteps, but I didn't look up. I could tell it was Fredrica. Her silhouette approached – a tall figure wrapped in a long coat, graceful but hesitant, as though afraid to step fully into my shadow.

She sat beside me without a word. Then she reached out and rested her hand on my back.

'I truly am sorry,' she whispered.

I didn't want her sympathy. Didn't want anyone's.

I bristled under her touch. 'How many Servums?'

Fredrica blinked and drew her hand back. 'Gren, please.'

It was all the answer I needed.

'How many?' My voice cracked.

She exhaled, defeated. 'Thousands.'

I turned my head, locking eyes with her, searching for who she really was. 'They're being experimented on…and you knew. You've always known.'

Calm and resigned, she didn't answer straight away. 'We don't always choose what we know. Or what we can do about it.'

'Your choices are clear enough to me.'

Her posture tensed, and she turned her face away. I could see the unease rippling through her, though she kept her voice level. 'You need to focus on the game, on winning. That's all that matters now.'

And how do you suggest I do that?' I shot back, standing abruptly. I moved slowly around the bench, my shoes scuffing against the loose stones of the path.

'We have Lodgers in Grawledinn and Hyender losing their

minds over what happened with Samuel Rosendale,' she continued, hardened. 'If Samuel had succeeded in…his attempt, he'd have lost, and you would've won. Why would he want that? It makes no sense.'

'Maybe your Lodgers don't understand as much as they think they do.' I stopped at the edge of the pond, staring into its surface at my reflection.

Fredrica made a sound, somewhere between a sigh and a growl. 'I wish we could talk honestly.'

I turned back to her. 'Don't we always?'

There was something in her face – doubt, perhaps, and fear.

'What do you care, Fredrica? If Sam had succeeded, I would've had the closest prediction. I would've won. Isn't that what you want?'

'I want to see you take control,' she said, standing to face me. She crossed her arms and her lips tightened, but her eyes gave her away – she was worried.

'Then get him out.' I kept my gaze on her.

'Get *who* out?'

'Sam. Get him out of prison.'

Fredrica's brows shot up. 'I can't do that.'

'You've always found a way to bend the rules when it suits you. With all the changes you've made to the system, I'm sure you can work something out.'

'It's not that simple.' She shook her head. 'The entire world knows what happened. He's the main suspect in an assassination attempt. Public perception—'

'Forget perception.' I took a couple of steps away, the anger now breaking through, uncontrolled. 'What if he loses the game today? What then?'

'Gren—'

'What are you afraid of, Fredrica? That I'll lose too?' My

voice dropped to a bitter murmur. 'Or is it something else?'

Her mouth opened as though she might argue, but she quickly pressed her lips shut and looked away.

'If you can't get him out, then let me see him,' I said. 'That much, at least, you can arrange.'

She stared at me for a long moment before saying, reluctantly, 'Give me a day or two.'

'Not good enough.' I kept my voice firm. 'You want me to win? Then I need your help.'

Fredrica ran a hand through her hair, then tucked a loose strand behind her ear, fingers lingering for a moment. 'Do you want to just stroll into the prison?'

'I want him out of there for a few hours. A clean space. No bugs. No devices. Full privacy.'

Her face stiffened as she considered my request. Then she sighed. 'Fine. I'll see what I can do. But don't expect miracles.'

I turned back towards the path, calling to my security bots with a flick of my wrist. 'Let me know when you have it ready.'

As I walked off, the night was somehow darker. This time, I didn't look back at Fredrica, repelled by the truth of who she'd always been.

THIRTY-FOUR

PRIMULA

WAKING UP WAS LIKE CLAWING my way out of a cave. My mind was sluggish, slow to piece together where I was, what had happened. Pain flared immediately, as though my body had been shattered and barely put back together. I couldn't move. I tried, but nothing worked. My limbs felt foreign and disconnected. Both of my legs had been amputated. I didn't need to see them to know. Still, sometimes they ached in full, both the parts that remained and the parts that were gone.

What cut deeper than the pain was something far worse – I had lost track of time. Days, maybe weeks, gone; snatched away while I lay useless and unconscious. My body might heal eventually, but I would never get that sense of time back. It was like someone had severed the only thread keeping me connected to the world outside. Without knowing what day it was, I couldn't picture Saturdays in Lacun Park, Sam sprawled on his bed, sleeping in. I couldn't feel the stillness that made

Sundays beautiful. The tenth day of every month, the anniversary of our first meeting, would vanish now. Sam would still remember – I was sure of that – but I wouldn't know when that day had come. How could I hold onto that connection when time had been ripped away from me?

If I tried to explain this to anyone, they'd call me irrational, maybe superstitious. It didn't matter. The days had melted into a haze – just cycles of darkness and light. I had nothing.

It took time for the memories to catch up. At first, they came in flashes, fractured and messy, but then they neatened and became real. The common. Lisa's voice, tight with panic. 'Run.' The big man had come back – armed now, with a metal rod in one hand and a rock in the other. Mona's words echoed in my head: 'You can't outrun them in a cloak.'

I let the cloak fall without a pause and ran. For a second, I thought I might escape. Then a rock cracked against my skull – the sound rang in my head like a gunshot. My face hit the dirt hard. Dust clung to my lips with a bitter, gritty taste. I didn't even have time to scream before he was on top of me. His fists rained down like hammers, one after the other, until the world spun and lost its shape.

I flipped over and raised my legs, trying to kick him away. A stupid move. His face twisted, veins bulging red-hot beneath his skin, and his single eye locked onto my shaking feet. The rod swung down, whizzing through the air. The crack of bone breaking filled my ears, almost as loud as my scream. A sound I'll never forget. My feet became a mess of splintered bone and torn flesh, like a pair of socks full of gravel. But he wasn't done. He stomped on my legs, again and again, his heels crushing what was left of me into the soil.

I didn't know when the others had arrived. Voices. Screams. A thud as the man fell beside me. The sound of fists landing.

Four, maybe five men, taking turns beating him down on the ground. Somewhere in the tumult, I caught glimpses of faces. Mona's family, Marydit's wailing. And the blood. My blood. Dark, spilling into the dirt. The ground itself was drinking me dry.

The blackness came as a relief, wrapping me up and pulling me under. A small mercy of nature – numbing the senses when it all becomes too much to bear.

The bots that entered the room at intervals throughout the day were unlike any I had seen before. I wouldn't have called them humanised, nor could they be mistaken for real people. But they weren't shapeless machines either. There was a clear difference between these bots and the ones that had pushed needles into my spine when I first arrived in Servyden. These were near-humanoids, with flat, featureless faces atop torsos and shoulders.

I studied them once I was lucid enough. Their bodies were smooth and rubbery, shining under the icy light. Cylindrical arms and legs – like bleached pythons without the natural bend of human joints – twisted in whatever direction they needed. Parts of their bodies would light up as they moved, a flickering array of bars and squares in a single, shifting colour. The purpose of the displays remained indecipherable, though I stared long enough to try and make sense of them.

They weren't designed with empathy in mind; that much was clear. Their purpose was simple: care and healing. And they did it efficiently, without pretence.

When they spoke, their voices matched their appearance: basic, mechanical, stripped of anything resembling humanity. The orders were clear: 'Drink. Do not move. Or, as they applied pressure, 'How much pain, one to ten?'

On three occasions, I tried to reach them through mindspeak, desperate to find some trace of connection. Each time, all I received was a harsh crackle, scattered with an endless stream of numerals. The digits swarmed over one another, leaving me with a sensation like I'd stumbled into the guts of a malfunctioning circuit board. There was no pattern to follow, no meaning to latch onto. Still through mindspeak, I tried a greeting, and got a response immediately. A flat, negative buzz, like I'd given some system the wrong answer. I tried again. Then again. Same buzz, every time. I gave up, shaken.

Had it been these bots that severed my legs above the knee? The stumps ached constantly, and the swelling had only just begun to ease.

Only the injections brought relief. The bots would push amber-coloured fluids into my veins, and I'd drift away into a dreamless sleep. Or perhaps I did dream. It was hard to tell when wakefulness and sleep merged so seamlessly. I wouldn't question it if I weren't awake, I reminded myself. But even that reassurance felt shallow.

Lisa was gone. There were no more whispered talks at night, no more comforting words to hold onto. I didn't know if she'd been moved or if the beating had stolen my ability to mindspeak. The silence was almost as unbearable as the pain, the loneliness nearly as harrowing as the thought of returning to the common. That day would come. I could feel it waiting, looming at the edge of my recovery.

When it did, there would be no impulsive attacks, no reckless decisions. I would not make the same mistakes again. I would be measured. I would be tamed. The lesson had been seared into me. I had learned it well.

•••

The prostheses appeared out of nowhere. One morning after the dark hours, they were just *there*, seamlessly attached to what remained of my thighs. I stared at them. They looked so much like the legs I'd lost, it was almost grotesque. Smooth shins. Perfectly arched feet with toenails, and even that sand-coloured freckle just above my left ankle. Almost perfect. Almost human. How the fuck had they done that?

It was the twitches that gave them away. The calves would tighten on their own. A sudden jolt, and the toes would curl like something had pricked them with an electric needle.

Despite the likeness, they were heavy and awkward. I'd grown used to the absence, to the weightlessness of the stumps. Now, these things dragged at me, as foreign as slabs of stone bolted to my bones.

Once my strength returned and the fog in my head cleared, a restlessness took hold of me with a vengeance. Staying in that bed, day after day, was unbearable. It made my skin itch. I had to move.

I waited, watching the bots, tracking their routine. There were twelve visits during the light hours – I'd counted them all. Lisa had once mentioned that the darkness lasted eight hours, which left me roughly an hour between checks, though I had no way of knowing how quickly the minutes passed. I'd just have to be cautious. But it was time.

Careful not to make a sound, I moved to the edge of the bed, swinging what was left of my body into position. My feet – if I could call them mine – touched the floor. The prostheses felt cold and lifeless. I gripped the mattress for balance, heart hammering as I leaned forward. Then, slowly, one hand lifted. And then the other.

I was standing.

My breath caught as a wave of disbelief crashed over me. I didn't think I'd ever stand again. It had been too cruel to let myself hope. I blinked hard, my vision misting.

The tremor in my body returned. I swayed, but I steadied myself quickly.

I could do this.

One step. I pushed one foot forward, then dragged the other behind me. The thing jerked stiffly as my thigh strained to pull it along. Awkward, but I was moving.

By the second step, I was already off balance. I collapsed. The fall left me gasping for air, and pain flared across my side as I hit the floor.

I groaned, twisting awkwardly. The prosthetic legs moved, twitching as though they had a mind of their own, bending at the joint when I didn't want them to. I shoved them, furious. Tears burned my eyes again.

Getting up took an eternity. The legs wouldn't cooperate, flailing at odd angles, and the effort left me trembling. By the time I hauled myself back to my feet, sweat was dripping down my forehead. My heart was beating fast.

I couldn't risk another fall. I funnelled every bit of energy into moving – one slow step, then another – always keeping one leg firmly planted, using it to anchor myself. When I reached the bed, I collapsed onto it, burying deep under the blanket just as the bots rolled back into the room.

I forced my breath to slow, my pulse still pounding as if I'd run a mile.

Not bad for a first try.

My thighs shuddered beneath the covers, but I smiled. I just needed more practice.

•••

So much for carefully timing the bot check-ups to practise walking in secret. As it turned out, the bots had plans of their own.

'Get up,' one said, blue dots flickering where its face should have been.

Two parallel handrails had appeared in the room overnight. I had to admit, they made relearning how to walk a lot easier. But as the days wore on, walking became less of an achievement and more of a chore. Every session dragged on as long as the bots decided, regardless of pain or exhaustion. It wasn't an adventure any more. No thrill of breaking the rules. Now it was an order.

When my breath came short and the backs of my arms burned from heaving myself forward, all I wanted was to lie down and sink into the mattress like before. Still, there were moments, small ones, where I could see progress. My steps were slow, but each one stretched my ability. The bots didn't miss a beat. My movements weren't seamless yet, but I could move forward steadily.

The old voice returned, delivering its instructions without a hint of care. The first shock came one afternoon when I took too long to reach the end of the rail. It was sudden, biting, and gone just as quickly. And to my surprise, it was reassuring. They hadn't shocked me when I was bleeding. Back then, my body wouldn't have survived it. But now it could.

A shock had come and gone, and now my wounds were just a memory. I was stronger.

The shivers started the moment the voice announced that I was to be let out on the common that morning.

I paced the room. Could my body endure another beating? Surely not. Not like the last time.

Cold sweat. Acid welling in my stomach.

I would run faster. Even with the prosthesis, I could do it. He wouldn't catch me. Not again. But if all else failed, I would fight. I had hurt him once – I could do it again. That dark spot inside me, the one where fury simmered like hot coals, was still there. I'd learned how to reach it and fan it into flames. It just had to be controlled. I would hold it back, then let it build until it couldn't be contained a second longer. Controlled fury was the key.

It was all a haze as I left the room. The long corridor stretched ahead, followed by a series of latches that led to the metal gate. Beyond it waited the common, its desolate ground, its menacing crowd, and all the dangers I now knew too well. How ignorant I had been before. How naive to have been fearless.

I wanted to turn and run back to my bed, to hide under the covers. But I stopped myself. I knew better now. Any disobedience would trigger a shock. I had no choice but to obey.

The thought calmed me. None of this was my choice. It wasn't liberating – not exactly – but it was something I could hold on to.

I picked up my pace, steeling myself as the metal gate groaned, lifting inch by inch with the clink of chains. The smell hit me first – dry soil, dust – and in an instant, the memories came flooding back. Pain. The rod breaking my bones. The dust clogging my throat as I screamed.

But when the gate rose fully, I froze. This wasn't what I'd expected.

A crowd unlike any I'd seen on the common had gathered in a semicircle around the gate. Dozens of heads. Maybe hundreds. They stared at me as I stood there, feeling frail and insignificant in my cloak. For a second, it seemed like an ambush. My instinct urged me to turn back, but something stopped me. I looked again.

There was a strange light in their faces. They weren't menacing. There was something soft, almost welcoming. The men and women at the front grinned, a glint of admiration in their eyes, like proud parents watching a child.

'It's her!' someone shouted. 'She's alive. She's standing.'

The crowd erupted. Cheers and claps broke out. I barely knew how to react before someone dashed towards me and pulled me into a hug. It was Mona.

'Look at you,' she said, breathless as her eyes scanned me from head to toe.

Marydit appeared next, looking concerned. 'Oh, love, you look so thin.'

Mona grinned, her eyebrows raised high. 'Everyone's been talking about you,' she said. 'More and more people gathered here every day, waiting for you to come back.'

'The word spread,' Marydit added. 'What you did to protect Mona... You're *the woman who took the eye of the giant*. You've inspired hundreds of Servums, love. So many look up to you now.'

'We weren't sure you'd make it,' Mona said. 'You looked so bad...so bad.'

Marydit placed her hand on her heart. Her large eyes shone, pupils wide like black gems. 'A living legend, resurrected.'

I swallowed hard. 'They cut my legs off.'

Marydit's shoulders sagged slightly. Her eyelids dropped as she glanced down, inspecting my feet. 'Oh, darling. I'm so sorry. So sorry to hear that.'

Mona tilted her head, thoughtful, and exchanged a glance with Marydit.

'You're alive,' she said at last, 'and it looks like you got new ones, alright. That's something to celebrate.' She turned to the people beside her. 'She's one of us now, isn't she? Nothing bad will happen to her. We'll see to that.'

There was a muffled chorus of agreement. Emotion rose in me, and I clenched my jaw to keep it down. 'I'm very grateful,' I managed, my voice quivering as I pressed a hand to my collarbone.

'Grotto finished him off, didn't he?' Mona asked, tipping her chin towards the ginger-haired man.

Grotto looked at me, his eyes serious and deep beneath a heavy brow like matted straw. His golden beard rested against his chest, blending with the coarse hair beneath.

'He didn't survive.' His voice was a low rumble. 'We gave him five times what he did to you.'

I held his gaze for a moment longer, then looked back at the crowd. Their cheers still rippled around us, mixed with laughter and chatter.

'And Lisa?' I asked.

There was a brief hesitation before Marydit spoke. 'We haven't seen her. Not since that day. Have you talked to her in your enclosure?'

I shook my head. 'No. Not since then.'

Marydit sighed and took a moment to think. 'It's hard to know. Some people disappear and come back. Some are sent to faraway sections. Servyden is a big place. Some people disappear... and that's the end of it.' She paused again. 'I wish her well. She's a strong woman, she is. But she's also old. Those experiments can take a real toll.' Then she looked at me carefully. 'I wish her well.'

•••

The first row of people marked the edge of the ring. They were mostly men, kneeling with cloaks folded beneath their knees. Rhythmic clapping echoed, hands striking bare legs in a constant beat.

At the centre was Mona. Her cloak lay discarded on the ground, dust swirling up like a curtain of smoke as her body twisted and leapt in a frenzied dance.

More people joined the clapping, and the sound transformed into something less like noise and more like music. It was rough, primal, but the closest thing to a song I'd heard in months.

Clap. Clap. Clap.

Clap. Clap. Clap.

Mona's curls bounced in time, a mimicry of the crowd's pulse.

'Come on, love,' Marydit said, her eyes flicking down to her own clapping hands. It was a signal, a push for me to join in.

Marydit's voice rose above the commotion. The sound, soft and clear, was unexpected in its beauty.

'Parched and blood-stained, my arid land,' she sang.

The crowd answered, their voices rising in unison. 'My home is Servyden.'

'Our wishes shortened, our futures banned.'

'My home is Servyden.'

Grotto stood to my left, his heavy arms thumping along with the collective beat.

'Heirs of Rivennia, seeds of the new strand.'

'My home is Servyden.'

A man and a woman joined Mona in the centre. The three of them danced like they were possessed, backs arched, arms stretching up towards the vaulted ceiling. The ring collapsed as others flooded in, swept up in the beautiful chaos. Bodies moved together in a tangle of cloaks and bare skin.

It was there, in the scramble of dancers, that I felt him. Grotto. The brush of his skin against mine jolted something awake, something long forgotten. His hands found my hips, creeping under my cloak with a surreptitious boldness that he masqueraded as part of the dance.

I let my muscles loosen. No point fighting against fate. And it was that very helplessness that fanned a strange fire inside me, a fire that burned hotter with every movement of his hands.

One hand slid down. The other cupped my breast, fingers pressing in, firm and persistent. A pinch followed, firm enough to draw a gasp from me. His lips grazed my neck, then my cheek, teasing my mouth as I threw my head back.

I turned, looking him directly in the eyes. My voice became a murmur as I leaned close to his ear.

'Let's go somewhere else,' I said.

But I didn't know then how little decorum mattered in Servyden, how ridiculous it was to hold onto propriety when life was slipping away. That evening, a truth revealed itself: if the only comfort left to an enslaved body lies in the pleasures of the flesh, the body will claim what it deserves without shame.

Grotto was the first. Ronnie and Jose followed. As for the rest, I didn't know their names, and I couldn't be bothered to ask. My mind was elsewhere, far away, somewhere better. Between the ebb and flow of thrusts, I almost laughed at the absurdity of everything I used to care about. That previous life...

I returned to my enclosure just minutes before the darkness, a shadow of a smile on my lips as I sank into a peaceful sleep.

Last time I'd visited the common, my body had been broken. This time, it had been made whole.

I was a Servum.

My home was Servyden.

THIRTY-FIVE

SAM

THE LIGHTS CLICKED ON, blinding white. I squinted against the glare, eyes stinging as every crack and corner of the cell came into focus. Dust swirled in the air.

'Get up,' came the bark of a stocky bloke standing at the door. 'Get dressed.' His voice was all sharp edges and no patience.

I lay there, letting the world catch up to me. The hard mattress dug into my back as I breathed in the damp smell of concrete. I rubbed my eyes, slowly dragging myself upright, and slumped on the corner of the bed. My fingers pressed into my eyelids as I tried to push away the stupor.

'You deaf?' The officer's shout made me flinch. 'I said get dressed.'

I shot him a hateful look. 'Alright, alright, I'm coming.' I yawned, stretching out the ache in my neck. 'Where am I going?'

'A little trip.' He didn't bother to look at me properly, just jerked his head towards the pile of clothes he had dumped on the floor.

I slipped on the trousers and shirt provided. My mind was spinning, trying to piece together what this 'trip' might be about, but I came up empty. They didn't tell you much in places like this, just enough to keep you wondering.

As I stepped alone into the capsula, the world outside was still pitch black. We moved for what seemed like hours, though my sense of time had blurred. The hum of the vacuum system pulsed around me, giving my thoughts far too much room to wander.

The door slid open, and I breathed in a salty tang that reminded me of old seaside trips. But the nostalgia didn't last. The ground was a mess of soggy grass and muck, and up ahead was a barn. A proper relic, all slanted beams and peeling wood, one wide door thrown open. Light spilled out, throwing long shadows across the dirt.

I stepped out hesitantly, my shoes squelching into the mud. The sea roared in the distance. Somewhere south of Lacunfort, I guessed. My mind spun with possibilities – escape routes, hiding spots, anything that might lead to freedom. But the odds were stacked. Trying to run would only land me back in a cell.

And then there was the box. I'd found it in the capsula, sitting there like it had been waiting for me. Inside was yet another set of clothes: linen trousers, a jumper, slip-on shoes – all exact replicas of things I'd worn before. My throat closed up at the sight. Gren. It had to be Gren. This was either a lifeline or a noose. But after what I'd been through, I figured I'd take either one gladly.

I forced myself forward, my feet heavy as I trudged towards

the barn. The closer I got, the louder my heartbeat became, thudding against my ribs like it wanted out. I drew a deep breath and stepped through the open door.

The space was cold and smelled of rust. In one corner, steel beams were draped with filthy sheets, and a bed of bolts and tacks lay scattered across parts of the floor. But it was the figures near the centre that caught my attention.

Gren slouched on a chair like he hadn't slept in days. His hair was a mess, his suit creased. And beside him, sitting impossibly straight on a floating slate, was Queen Brynhilda. Her cream robe hung loosely over her frame, and her alert eyes held mine with an intensity that left me paralysed.

'Sam,' Gren said, clearing his throat. He stood abruptly, and before I knew it, his arms were around me. I stood stiffly, giving him a couple of pats on the back, unsure of what else to do.

'Are they treating you alright in there?' His hands gripped my shoulders as he looked me over.

I couldn't speak. The queen – the woman I'd tried to kill – was watching us. She looked regal and untouchable, but still, at the same time, just like any other human. My mouth was dry, my head light. All I managed was a polite nod at her.

'You won't be going back to that prison,' she said.

My lips parted to speak, but she didn't give me the chance.

'I will grant you a royal pardon, Mr Rosendale,' she continued. 'But it comes with conditions. Tonight, we must decide whether we can trust you.'

Trust me? I didn't know if I could trust myself.

Gren gestured to a chair nearby. 'Sit down, Sam. There's a lot we need to discuss.'

The chair creaked beneath me as I sat. My hands trembled despite my efforts to keep steady. Sitting there, flanked by Gren and Her Majesty, I felt ridiculously out of place – like I'd stumbled into a story far too grand for someone like me.

'I have long been concerned about the future of humanity in this modern era,' the queen said. Her voice carried authority despite the faint whistle of her breath. 'For years, I have supported Mr Moritz's ideology and commended his fight against ultrahumanism. But I do agree that we have reached a point where peaceful attempts and mere legislation will do little to stop those determined to create an enhanced race.' As she paused, the sound of her laboured breathing was all I could hear, and I adjusted myself in my seat, resisting the urge to fidget.

'And for many years longer than I have supported Mr Moritz,' she went on, gaining a strength that startled me, 'I have observed Igor Voychenko and his underground project, an enterprise that has stripped so many of their freedom and their most basic human rights.'

The mention of Voychenko and his prisoners hit me like a blow. I dragged a hand across my forehead, as if I could wipe away the pressure building there.

'So…it's true,' I stammered. My voice wavered more than I'd meant it to, and I hated the weakness it revealed. But questions began to form in my mind. Could this confirm that Primula was still alive? And if the queen knew all this about the Lodgers, why hadn't she done anything to stop them?

The queen's eyes fell on me. 'Now, I will need your full attention.'

Beside me, Gren's composure seemed unshaken, even as his shoulders sagged and his movements slowed. I envied him for that.

'By now, you will have learned of the Liffdom Lodges and their motives,' the queen continued. 'These prominent citizens share an ideal: the enhancement of human potential. They believe that humanity must enter a new phase in which evolution is shaped not by nature, but by our own hand. Arguing that natural selection no longer suffices to advance our species, they envision a future of perpetual enhancement – one they claim will reveal life's ultimate meaning. But it will also yield considerable profit for those leading the efforts. More troubling still, they are willing to accept experimentation on human subjects as the cost of such progress.'

Her words sank in, twisting inside me. I found my voice, though it sounded low and thin. 'Has the Royal Palace been… watching Liffdom in secret?'

She shook her head slightly. 'In their quest for domination over Rivennia's institutions, which they believe will allow them the freedom to pursue their evolutionary practices, the Lodgers sought to incorporate me into their clandestine ranks. I was approached by Igor Voychenko over five decades ago. At first, the Lodges portrayed themselves as a force for good, focused on humanity's betterment.'

She lowered her voice and spoke with what sounded like a mix of disdain and regret. 'Voychenko spoke of Liffdom's secrecy as merely a preference for staying out of the public eye. According to him, their members were brilliant but private individuals, unwilling to risk the attention or scrutiny that could hinder their work. He framed their hidden nature as a virtue, a mark of their selflessness in pursuing progress without seeking recognition or applause. I was told that their methods, though unconventional, were rooted in altruism and that their success depended on discretion.'

Her expression tightened as she took a pause. 'I soon realised that was all a lie. Their secrecy wasn't about virtue – it was about securing power and concealing crimes against humanity.'

She cleared her throat and placed a hand on her chest. Gren

and I sat frozen.

'The day after I expressed my desire to disassociate from their activities,' she said, her voice breaking for the first time, 'the oldest of my daughters, Princess Lisa, disappeared. Voychenko later confirmed she was under the custody of the Lodges. He warned me her life would be at risk if I revealed anything.'

I tried to process the enormity of what she was saying, but it was like the ground was shifting beneath me. I glanced at Gren, searching for some anchor, but he was staring straight ahead, his face unreadable.

'I spent decades powerless. Five more of my children followed. The official record claims they chose death through euthanasia, just like Princess Lisa, followed by immediate cremation. But I cannot believe that – I refuse to accept it. The Lodgers could not come for me directly, but they have held me hostage in every way that mattered.' Her eyes closed as she drew a shaky breath.

I sat forward, compelled to speak. 'Your Majesty, may I ask… Why not the queen herself? Why not target you directly?'

Her eyes opened, meeting mine. This was not a monarch but a mother burdened by unimaginable grief. 'Simulating my death was not feasible. By Rivennian law, the monarch's euthanasia must be publicly witnessed. The Lodgers knew that holding my children hostage was their most effective weapon. It silenced me. It forced my compliance.'

I swallowed hard. This was a labyrinth of manipulation and control that I could hardly wrap my head around. And here I was, pulled into its depths.

'The war between the Royal Office and the Liffdom Lodges is, in fact, older than both of you,' the queen said. 'It is no coincidence that my death has become the subject of their current Game of Wagers. Regardless of the dates, the Lodgers know that one of you, their chosen players, will eventually make sure the event unfolds as predicted. Many atrocities in our history can be traced back to the Lodgers and their ritualistic games.

'In the year 464, when a surge of radical conservatism in your native Varcega, Mr Moritz, threatened to disrupt their interests, a series of explosions – still unresolved to this day – wiped out many of the so-called Ultracons, instilling fear in anyone daring to veer so blatantly towards conservatism. When the Lodgers deemed the people of Glossden to be a lesser race, an ethnic cleansing ensued, leaving thousands of Glossdenians either massacred or vanished. That was only twenty years ago. And just a year after that, the Lodgers orchestrated the destruction of the Corin water dam – the largest of its kind. The devastation brought death and rationing to the nation's population for years, all while enriching corporations in Lacunfort, owned and controlled by the Lodgers, who profited from the rebuilding and supply efforts.'

My head began to cloud. As much as the pieces started to fit together, I couldn't comprehend how such evil could exist, led by fellow humans. These were people I had seen, been in rooms with, even spoken to.

'If we are to save humanity,' the queen continued, her voice rising, 'all three of us must be prepared to make sacrifices. Significant ones. In matters of such gravity, there is no room for selfishness.'

I couldn't stop myself. 'If the Lodgers fear Your Majesty will denounce them,' I said, my voice unsteady but earnest, 'perhaps the Chief Minister and I could take that step instead. Let them accuse us of treason – it wouldn't matter. We'd pay the price for those arguments. It's a fight worth having.'

The queen raised a hand and shook her head. 'The Lodgers indeed fear my revealing their existence to the world,' she said.

'But, contrary to them, I no longer believe that exposing them would lead to their end. You've both seen the unrest in our streets, the fractures in our society. If the world learns of the Liffdom Lodges, it is more likely to tear itself apart than to come together. Some would rally to oppose them, of course, but just as many would rise to support their vision of engineered evolution. The resulting chaos would plunge humanity into its greatest conflict yet, with no clear path to peace. The only way to defeat the Lodges is from within.'

She adjusted her posture in her cushioned seat, her delicate build radiating a quiet but unshakable resolve. Then she turned to me, her eyes piercing. 'Alongside your royal pardon, Mr Rosendale, I will announce the date of my euthanasia. Since I will not sacrifice my children, I have decided to sacrifice myself.'

I couldn't breathe. I turned to Gren, hoping for some sign that I'd misheard her, but his silence carried the answer. Pressure built in my head as though my skull might crack. Before I could stop myself, I began to weep silently.

'Do not pity me, Mr Rosendale,' the queen said firmly. 'My health declines rapidly. This is something I have long considered, and something I probably should have done sooner. If a queen cannot offer herself in the gravest of times, then perhaps it is just that doom falls upon her people.'

'Yes. I'll do it,' I stammered, the words rushing out before I could weigh them. 'I'll become a Servum. I'll go underground and join the others. We will fight them from the inside. Gren can work among the Lodgers from his position as a peer. It won't be in vain.'

Gren's voice was calm, though the faint tremor in it betrayed his emotions. 'Sam,' he said, his eyes fixed on mine, 'there's a chance…that you won't have to become a Servum.'

'It has to be me, Gren.' I hesitated, my mind tangled in conflicting thoughts. Then, against all sense, I admitted the selfish truth. 'I need to find Primula.'

Gren nodded, thoughtful. 'We'll find a way to make that happen and ensure her safety. But there's a chance – however slim – that we both end up as Lodgers.'

'How?'

He explained with care, pacing himself. 'There's a point equidistant between both our predictions. If the event occurs on that exact date, in theory, we'll both have won.'

'I have agreed to schedule my death for noon on the sixth day of the tenth month, in alignment with this plan,' the queen said.

'A tie...' I whispered. 'But what if it doesn't work? What if we both lose? We'd miss our chance to have at least one of us inside the Lodges.'

Gren's response was restrained but firm. 'It's a risk worth taking.'

The queen's voice softened. 'You will both wield greater influence if you are recognised as Lodgers. The future of humanity may rest on your success.'

I forced myself to inhale as I tried to calm the storm churning within me. My eyes settled on the queen's hands, gnarled with veins, her crooked fingers resting lightly on her lap. So serene. So at peace with her fate.

'There is one last matter,' she said. 'The Lodgers are confident they can corrupt you. They wouldn't have considered you for this game otherwise. Especially you, Chief Minister, given your staunch opposition to ultrahumanism. Igor Voychenko believes he can turn anyone into an ally. The Lodges see your upcoming pro-human legislative agenda as an obstacle to their ambitions. Having you, Mr Moritz, on their side, willingly or not, would be a monumental victory. I need your promise – both of you – that no matter what, you will devote your life to this mission, and that you won't yield to their influence.'

'I promise to devote my life to defeating the Lodges and preserving humanity,' Gren said without hesitation.

Their eyes turned to me, expectant.

I drew a long breath, feeling their trust settle on my shoulders. 'You have my promise,' I said. 'Both of you.'

THIRTY-SIX

PRIMULA

THE CLOAK BARELY DID ANYTHING to shield me from the ground at the common. Small rocks pressed into me no matter how I angled myself. Beside me lay Grotto, in nothing but his skin and utterly at ease, as if this world wasn't an arid wasteland. His breathing was fast, sweat still clinging to his skin in tiny beads.

'We need to be careful,' I said.

He turned his head towards me, just slitting one eye open. 'Careful about what?'

'About me getting pregnant,' I said.

That got his attention. His brow furrowed, then he let out a low, gravelly laugh. 'No one gets pregnant in Servyden. They don't let anyone breed unless they've decided it's worth it. That's what the seeds are for. But even then, it never happens naturally.'

Seeds. Lisa had mentioned them once. Her caring voice returned to me in fragments, reminding me of how much I missed her. I wished I could speak to her again.

'Who are the seeds?'

'They're taller. That's how you spot them. But it's more than that,' he said, dragging a hand lazily over his forehead to wipe the sweat away. 'They've got whatever traits the handlers are after. Health, beauty, intelligence. All the things you would expect.'

'So, the taller ones are always seeds?'

'No, not always.' He coughed twice, as though clearing dust from his throat. 'There are seeds with the traits they're looking for, so they get bred straight away. They like them tall, sure. But then there are others – unaltered humans – they use their eggs and sperm to make embryos. Those embryos are treated early on to get the right traits.'

'What traits?'

'We don't know everything, but people have ideas about what they like. The obvious ones I mentioned. Symmetry's a big one – faces, bodies, the lot. They've got this thing they call enhanced sensory perception, or something like that. Those are the brainy ones, the real super-smart types. They can memorise hundreds of digits in seconds, multiply them all together like living computers.' A wry smile formed on his lips. 'Pompous idiots, though. The smarter they get, the less likeable they are. Julian, the new guy, is being trained on that.'

I straightened up and pulled my knees to my chest.

'Mona mentioned you're a mindspeaker,' Grotto said. 'Is that true?'

'I don't know if I can do it any more,' I said, glancing at the ground. 'I used to talk to Lisa, the older lady...that was mind-speak for sure. But I think it might be broken now, whatever it was.'

'What was it like?'

'Strange at first. Like talking, but freer. You don't just use words – you can share everything. Words aren't enough to express yourself, not really. You understand that once you start mindspeaking.'

'If you can still do it, I could use your help,' he said in an uncharacteristically cautious tone.

'What kind of help?'

'I'll explain when the time comes.' He stretched out on the ground with a groan, his arms splayed wide before he folded them back on his chest.

'Are you a seed?' I asked.

'No, not me. I don't think so, anyway. Most of us get used for their trials. But they have taken my sperm a few times, so who knows?'

'Oh, really? And how do they do that exactly?' I couldn't help the edge of sarcasm creeping into my voice.

'They've got bots for that,' he said with a smirk, raising his head to meet my eyes. 'They're good.'

I chuckled, shaking my head. 'You're not serious.'

He gave a smug little grin, and I glanced down, realising he was already firm again.

'I think I'm ready to go once more,' he said, flicking his head towards me in invitation.

The next day, Grotto and I walked along the wall with the metal gates. He'd worked it all out – said we could get to section one-seventy and back before curfew if we kept a fast pace. He was already warning me about it before we set off, like I didn't know how to walk fast.

'Can your legs handle it?' He threw me a sideways glance.

'They can,' I said, trying not to sound too irritated. I hadn't told anyone, but the prostheses had grown a fine layer of hair. Sometimes I could even feel my fingers pinch my new legs like they were flesh and bone. Walking felt normal now, almost like the amputations had never happened.

'None of them are out today,' he muttered as his eyes darted over the common.

'Who are we looking for?' I asked, though I had an idea where this was heading.

'Mindspeakers,' he said. 'We're going to test you and see if you can still do it.'

'Right,' I said, like it was no big deal.

It took us about half an hour to walk between the gates. They all looked the same: rusted iron slabs, two or three metres wide and at least twice as tall. Some were bent out of shape, with deep scratches as though someone had taken a heavy swing at them. Thrown rocks at them, maybe, though there weren't many big ones lying around. The thought of what else might've been smashed against them slipped into my mind – bodies, flung with desperate force. I shoved the image away. Pointless. Just keep walking.

The sections we passed were no different from the rest. People hunched over in their groups, shouting at one another. Sudden laughs cracked through the noise. But the stench was stronger in some areas. I didn't even try to fight it any more; it was baked into the dust. Apart from the daily food given to all Servums only within their enclosures, bodily needs were met openly on the common, without any regard for others. Privacy or shame were luxuries the Servums couldn't afford. By now, I understood that better than I wanted to.

At the midpoint between the gates, a thin trickle of water spilled from the fountains. Long queues snaked around the mud, faces gaunt with thirst. The same fights played out in every section as we walked. People argued over whose turn it was to slurp at that miserable dribble of liquid and how long they could drink.

'Are you thirsty?' Grotto asked.

I shook my head. 'Let's keep going.' I hadn't told anyone about Mona's leak. It had sounded mad at first, but I was glad she'd trusted me with it.

'Good,' he said.

We hadn't gone much further when a scream stood out from the noise. I turned sharply, my pulse jumping. An older woman, about Marydit's age, was at the centre of the scene. A man grabbed her face with one hand, digging his fingers into her cheeks, her mouth twisting into a grotesque shape. She was trying to speak while saliva bubbled at her lips, but he wouldn't let her. Instead, he bawled something at her – words I couldn't make out. Then he made a rasping sound in his throat as he gathered phlegm and spat a thick gob across her face. He laughed, loud and harsh, like he thought it was the funniest thing imaginable.

I stopped. My whole body went rigid. I couldn't look away. The sheer apathy of everyone around them made my blood boil. How could they just stand there and watch?

'Leave them,' Grotto said.

'We can't.' My fists clenched at my sides. 'We can't just...' The words stuck in my throat. I wanted to charge in, grab the bastard by the neck, and rip him off her. What I'd seen made me sick, but the indifference of the onlookers made it worse.

'Keep walking,' Grotto said, his tone now edged. 'You can't save them one by one, not like this. We'll save them all at once.'

I didn't move. My feet were rooted to the ground, my mind screaming at me to do something.

Grotto grabbed me by the shoulders and spun me around to

face him. His eyes locked onto mine, dead serious.

'All at once,' he said, low but forceful. 'If you help me.'

'How?'

'I'll explain when we find the mindspeakers. For now, we walk.'

I swallowed hard, the taste of bile in my throat, and forced my heavy and unwilling legs to start moving. I didn't look back. I couldn't, if I wanted to carry on.

The first one hit me out of nowhere, just after we passed section one-sixty-nine.

I stopped and took a shallow breath. At first, I thought it was just my overactive mind playing tricks, conjuring some overblown image to distract me. But no, this was too vivid. It didn't have the haze of a dream. It was real.

'Grotto...'

He stopped and turned.

'They're here,' I said, closing my eyes to block out everything else. 'I can see images.'

'What images? What do you see?' He walked towards me. His voice now had a touch of excitement he failed to hide.

'Servums,' I said, eyelids pressed shut as I let the pictures come. 'Hordes of them. They're furious...breaking into the enclosures.'

'It's them!' Grotto's voice had turned hushed, though the enthusiasm was evident. 'They're talking about Rise Day.'

His words went almost unnoticed. The images wouldn't stop. The enclosures collapsing in chaos. People screaming, charging, tearing through the gates. I held my breath as the fury on their faces got imprinted on my mind.

'What else?' Grotto asked, leaning closer. 'What do you see?'

'They're destroying everything,' I said, raising a hand, trying to grasp the fleeting images. 'Wait...'

'What? What is it?'

'They're talking now.'

The voices were faint but urgent – whispers speeding past too quickly to catch.

'What are they saying?' Grotto pressed.

I strained to listen, but the words moved too quickly, slipping away just as I reached for them. I shook my head, frustrated. 'I don't know. It's too fast.'

'Try harder,' he said through clenched teeth.

The voices were foreign, like a language I didn't understand. But suddenly, a few words broke through the rustle: 'Wheeled bots... Shafts... 7,000... Section one-fifty... Section four-sixty-five...'

'What are they saying?' Grotto repeated. He was close to shouting now.

'I told you, I don't bloody know,' I said, exhaling. 'I can only catch pieces. Sections. Numbers. There are a lot of numbers.'

'Do they know you're listening?'

'I don't think so.' But I had no way of knowing.

The voices kept pouring in, a stream of syllables I couldn't quite make sense of. Grotto was slowly scanning the people around us now.

He flicked his eyes toward a small group nearby and whispered, 'Is it any of them?'

I opened my eyes and looked. A pair of teenagers caught my attention, chasing each other in circles, their laughter light and carefree. One of them stretched out an arm, tagging the other with a triumphant shout of, 'I got you!' The sound of their giggles felt strange – unexpected here. I couldn't help but envy them. Did they know how precious this little moment was?

Did they understand how fleeting it might be? Or were they like I'd been once, too blind to recognise happiness until it had already faded?

'Is it them?' Grotto asked.

'No,' I said. 'The voices aren't coming from them.'

'Talk to the voices.'

I hesitated. 'What do I say? Is it safe?'

'Please,' he said, and for once, his tone wasn't commanding. It was almost pleading.

I shut my eyes and focused, pushing through the noise. I threw out a simple greeting, adding my name at the end.

The voices stopped.

My heart leapt into my throat. They'd noticed me.

'What's happening?' Grotto asked.

I raised my hands slightly, motioning for him to wait. I shut my eyes tighter, trying to focus.

Then, finally, a single voice: 'Primula?'

'Yes,' I said. Adrenaline prickled under my skin.

'Are you the woman who killed the one-eyed giant?' The voice had slowed to a pace I could follow. It was like I was speaking to someone right in front of me.

'I didn't kill him myself,' I said. 'He almost killed me.'

'Have they moved you to a new enclosure?' The tone was friendly.

'No,' I said, glancing briefly at Grotto.

'Where are you?'

'Are you talking to them?' Grotto asked.

I nodded, then repeated the question aloud.

Grotto's face grew intense as he said, 'Tell them...tell them we have the maps. Outside section one-fifty-nine. And tell them I am with you.'

I relayed the message as clearly as I could, and the voice

repeated it: 'Maps. Section one-fifty-nine. Grotto by your side. Is that correct?'

'Yes,' I said. 'That's correct.'

'We will run early in the morning. Next time we're out. Be there, both of you.'

When I translated their words to Grotto, his face lit up like I'd just handed him the keys to the bloody world. He grinned, glancing up at the ceiling. 'Yes,' he said, almost laughing. 'Tell them we'll be there.'

We met three days later.

The day after my first exchange with the mindspeakers, I wasn't let out. Instead, they shoved me into one of the white cubes. The flat voice, the glaring lights, the suffocating sterility – it was all so painfully familiar by now, along with the experiments they loved to throw at me.

That day, it was puzzles again. Numbers on a wall display. Adding sums, arranging multiples. It wasn't difficult, but near the end, I slipped up twice and got the shocks. They always came in the same way – searing pain that shot through my spine like molten wire, making me gasp for air. No matter how many times I'd been through it, the agony never dulled.

The next day, they let me out onto the common, as if everything was back to normal. Except it wasn't. I couldn't find Grotto or anyone else I recognised. I tried counting the gates, thinking I could find section one-fifty-nine, but there was no sign of the mindspeakers. I wandered until the curfew bells rang, dragging myself back to my enclosure with a sinking feeling.

We met the following morning. Grotto was there waiting, and for once, luck seemed to be on our side. A few hours after we reached the agreed spot, the mindspeakers arrived.

While we waited, Grotto taught me how to read the maps. I never would've guessed what those lines on the ground meant; to the untrained eye, they looked like messy scratches and scattered pebbles. But when Grotto explained it, I could see it. They were careful, deliberate markings; maps of everything the Servums had learned. They recorded the experiments, the schedules of surveillance bots, the population of Servyden. They had even documented the Lodges and their members. Every bit of knowledge gathered over years, written out on patches of soil.

Most Servums seemed to know where the maps were, and they treated them with reverence. A rotating group of watchmen guarded the area to make sure no one accidentally trampled over the marks. 'Years of work would be ruined if someone walked over them,' Grotto said.

In the distance, Jose and Ronnie were bent over the dirt, sticks in their hands. They moved with precision, tracing careful lines into the ground. Beside them, Julian crouched awkwardly, his stick trembling as he tried to mimic their movements. Jose leaned over, guiding Julian's hand with firm patience, while Ronnie gestured at the ground, explaining something I couldn't hear. Julian nodded, his brows furrowed in concentration, and slowly, his lines became steadier.

When the mindspeakers arrived, they towered over everyone. I had to crane my neck to meet their eyes. They were the tallest Servums I'd ever seen – seeds, probably. They were drenched in sweat, panting from their run, their cloaks discarded to reveal bare, muscular bodies. Grotto gave them a small bow, and they returned the gesture, still catching their breath.

There were three of them: a woman and two men.

'How long do we have?' The woman seemed calm despite

the exertion.

'How long was the run?' Grotto asked.

'Three hours, maybe.'

'Then no more than an hour,' Grotto said. 'It might take longer on the way back. We'll have someone start a count to keep track.'

He turned to me, motioning with his chin. 'This is Primula.'

Each of them introduced themselves: Ula, Hugo and Denzin. I did my best to copy the bow they'd given Grotto. To my surprise, all three of them returned it in perfect coordination.

'How long have you had it?' Ula asked me, speaking plainly so Grotto could hear.

'I don't know,' I admitted, embarrassed that I'd lost track of something that now seemed so important. 'A few months... maybe four? I was unconscious for part of it, so I can't be sure.'

'Your mindspeak is clear,' Ula said. She looked impressed. 'Quite advanced for only four months.'

Her kindness caught me off guard. 'Thank you,' I said, my voice lower than I wanted it to be. Her words were a small gesture, but they were sincere.

'This way,' Grotto said, leading us to another section of the ground.

'Here.' He pointed to what looked like faint bird tracks in the dirt. Everyone gathered around as he explained. 'We've only got reports from two sections, but they match perfectly. It seems like every section has the same layout: a main corridor, cubes on the sides, enclosures – at least ten levels – and an exit shaft at the back.'

Denzin, the dark-skinned mindspeaker, exchanged a glance with the others. His voice was deep and raspy. 'We've had a similar account from section two-eleven.'

I found myself staring at the man's chest, level with my eyes.

His height was unnatural, and the forest of black curls on his torso only made him seem even larger.

'That's excellent news,' Grotto said, lighting up. 'If it's all consistent, we're close to finalising the blueprints.'

'Do we know where the shafts lead?' Hugo asked.

'Not exactly,' Grotto admitted. 'There's a theory that they connect to somewhere under the Human Order temple. Maybe even pneuduct gates in Lacunfort. But it could be anywhere.'

'We can't properly prepare for Rise Day until we know,' Ula said.

Everyone voiced their agreement.

'We need a way to follow a bot,' Ula continued, 'or to extract their data. There are no service stations in Servyden. The bots must go up the shafts at some point, but we'll never know unless we try something new.'

I hesitated but then blurted out, 'What if...we mindspeak?'

All eyes turned to me.

'Go on?' Grotto said.

'With the bots,' I added quickly. 'Or at least listen to them.'

'That's impossible,' Denzin said. 'Our implants only allow communication between humans.'

I hesitated, lowering my eyes. Maybe I was wrong. Maybe it was stupid to suggest. But I pushed on. 'We might not understand at first,' I said, carefully, 'but we could write down what we hear and look for patterns.'

'Bots can't respond to mindspeak,' Ula said. 'They're inert. Only Servums can mindspeak.'

'I think I'm different then,' I said quietly, glancing at Grotto. 'When I was recovering, bots came to my room every hour. I tried to tune in to them, and I couldn't make sense of it, but... I definitely got something. It started as a rustle, and then I saw numbers. Long sets of numbers. Then I tried to speak to them, but only got a buzz, like a rejection signal.'

Ula's jaw dropped, and her hand flew to her mouth. Grotto spun about to face the others, eyes round with disbelief.

'Is that true?' Hugo asked, stepping closer. His lip trembled slightly.

'Yes,' I said, straightening. For the first time in a long while, I experienced a spark of the confidence I used to have.

'It must be a new kind of implant,' Hugo murmured.

'This could change everything,' Ula said.

Grotto looked like he might cry. 'Yes,' he said. 'Yes, it could.'

They began to cheer, laughing and embracing each other in celebration.

A glimmer of happiness. This was a moment to cherish.

'You know, on those maps...' I said as we walked back to our section. 'Do they say what day it is?'

Grotto gave me a look, lifting one brow. 'What day it is?'

'Yes. In Rivennia.'

'Why does it matter?'

'It matters to me.'

He shrugged. 'Today's the second day of month ten. Soon we'll have clocked another year in here.'

I swallowed hard and didn't say anything, but right then, I made myself a promise: I wasn't going to lose track of time again.

A couple of minutes passed before I asked, 'What day of the week?'

'Not sure,' Grotto said.

My feet kept moving. They were dry, cracked, covered in dust and scabs.

'I was right,' I murmured. 'It's been nearly four months.'

•••

'Are you alright?' I asked. 'Should we keep going?'

'Yes,' Hugo said, his voice holding together despite the weariness in his eyes. 'A little tired, that's all. Let's continue.'

Grotto and the others stayed silent, just as they had the previous days, watching us like they were afraid a single word might break the flow. I shut my eyes again, breathing in deeply before I let the characters come through me, clear as day, one after the other. 'Seven... Two... Two... Letter X... Letter D... One... Double Zero... Two...'

Marydit and Mona had joined the group this time. They sat on the floor nearby, legs crossed and chins propped on their hands, looking more curious than anything. The whole thing must've seemed strange to them – a bunch of people sitting around, reciting nonsense like it was gospel. It felt strange to me, too, if I was honest.

I opened my eyes just a sliver and looked at Hugo. He sat stiffly, his face scrunched up in focus, his eyes clamped shut the way mine always were when I had to block out the noise of everything else. The cryptic characters kept trickling in like a drop of water carving its way into rock. We'd been at it for hours with no breaks, and I could feel the curfew creeping closer. Still, I hoped the bits of information were sticking, finding their way into some corner of Hugo's mind where they'd stay safe.

'Did you get that?' I asked.

Hugo gave me the smallest nod, barely more than a twitch. 'Just keep going,' he said.

•••

Ronnie and Jose explained the latest breakthrough: there were pneuduct gates in the strings. I had decoded the numbers during the data reaping, and Hugo had memorised them, reciting them back after each trip to the maps while Ronnie and Jose wrote everything down. As Hugo and I gathered more information from nearby sections, Ronnie and Jose spent every minute on the common, trying to decipher the code.

'How confident are you about this?' Grotto asked, his arms folded across his chest.

'There are too many repetitions for it to be a coincidence,' Ronnie said, pointing to the ground where the latest notes were scrawled. 'Look here. Section one-sixty corresponds to pneuduct gate zero-six-five K. The first three digits mark the platform in Lacunfort, and the district follows with one or two letters.'

'It can't be that simple,' Denzin said. 'Say we reach the shafts and go up. What then? Do we pop out onto the streets of Lacunfort like we're just out for a stroll?'

'Where else?' Jose said. 'Think about it. It's not easy to house and feed this many Servums. They couldn't keep us without being tied into Rivennia's supply infrastructure. They're bringing in stock and disposing of refuse through the shafts. Those shafts are our way out.'

'How many have you mapped so far?' Grotto asked.

'Only two,' Jose replied.

'Well, we will need more than *two* before we can start planning anything serious,' Grotto said.

Jose's head snapped up, and he narrowed his eyes. 'Of course we will, Grotto. Everyone here knows that. What exactly are you trying to say?'

Grotto stared at him without answering.

'Come on, do tell us,' Jose said, flicking the hair out of his eyes as he leaned closer. His pointed nose was nearly touching Grotto's face. 'Because while Ronnie and I have been working every hour to get this far, what have you been doing? Watching Primula mindspeak while stroking your chin, waiting for your next chance to shag her? Is that it, Grotto? You've been *so* helpful, haven't you? And now you think you're in a position to demand we go faster?'

Before I could even register it, Grotto's fist shot out, striking Jose's cheek with a dull, heavy thud. A spray of spit burst out as Jose staggered back.

'Enough!' Marydit's voice lashed out. 'Enough! Look at you two... Do you realise how your attitude could ruin everything for us? How are we supposed to convince anyone else in Servyden to cooperate if we ourselves are acting like a pack of wild animals?'

Jose raised a hand to his face, gingerly touching the red mark blooming on his cheek. Tears – not from pain, but pure rage – glistened on the edge of his lashes.

'What's wrong?' Grotto asked. 'Wasn't even that hard a blow.' He cleared his throat, spat onto the ground, and walked away without looking back.

The crowd thickened as we made our way towards section one sixty-five for another exhausting day of what Hugo had started calling 'data reaping'.

I couldn't remember the dates of Gren's and Sam's predictions any more. I wasn't even sure which one of them had come first. If I'd known, back then, how important that information would become, I'd have etched it into my mind like a carving on wood. But it was too late for that now. I kept my eyes alert, scanning faces. Everyone looked the same after a while: hollowed-out and anonymous.

Servyden was so vast that Sam could be here somewhere, and I'd never know. Sadness swept over me at the thought of him trapped in a white cube, beaten, cut open, electrocuted like the rest of us. The faint hope of finding him, of freeing him if he was here, gave me just enough fuel to keep going.

'Come on,' Grotto shouted. 'Walk faster.'

I tried to pick up my pace, but my legs didn't want to cooperate. With every step, their weight seemed to grow.

Dry soil crusted across my feet, and I couldn't summon the energy to kick it off. All I could manage was to keep shuffling forward, one foot in front of the other, my legs moving like they were stuck in someone else's rhythm.

My hips, thighs, knees and every joint screamed in protest, worn thin by endless days of walking. The prostheses had fused into me so seamlessly that they didn't feel like attachments any more. They were part of me now, grafted in such a natural way that I sometimes doubted my memory. Had my legs really been amputated? The pain I recalled proved it had happened – the throbbing cramps, the raw, healing stumps, those agonising first steps along the handrail. It was all too vivid to be imagined.

'Grotto,' I called, my voice strained as I lagged a few steps behind him.

He stopped, turned to look at me, and waited for me to catch up.

'All these numbers...' I said between breaths.

'Yes?'

'There's more to them than pneuduct gates, isn't there?'

He put his hands on his hips. 'We've all seen that.'

'What kind of information do you think that is?'

'I don't know, and I don't care,' he said flatly. 'As long as it's enough to plan our way out of this place, that's all that matters.'

'But imagine if we could decode their experiments,' I said. 'We could find out what they're after, what they've learnt. Maybe we could interpret the code. Ronnie and Jose could use some help—'

'No.' Grotto shook his head. 'You've lost it. Don't even think about it.'

When I didn't reply, his voice hardened. 'This isn't some research project. What makes you think we've got time to play scientist? Rise Day is about getting out of here, breaking free; nothing else.'

'But my legs…' I faltered. 'We can still plan the breakout and—'

'Stop it!' His voice snapped like a whip. 'No more talking. You know what you need to do.'

I bit back the words rising in my throat and gave him a quick nod. He turned and strode ahead, and I followed.

Far off, a small figure appeared. It was Hugo, waiting for us to begin another session. His silhouette blurred slightly as I pressed on, forcing my legs to keep moving.

'There are lifts,' I said.

'Inside the shafts?' Grotto asked. 'You'd expect so.'

I closed my eyes, trying to shut out the noise. 'I can picture them,' I said, 'going up and down.'

'Are you actually seeing them?'

The question made me pause. *Seeing* wasn't the right word. It was like trying to describe colour to the blind.

'No,' I said finally. 'Not with my eyes, anyway. It's more

like...a dream. Flashes in my mind.'

'How do you know it's not a dream then?'

I frowned. 'Because I'm awake, Grotto.' My voice grew tight with irritation. 'I'm trying to explain this the best I can.'

'Alright, alright...' he said, holding his hands up. 'Well, focus then. What else can you see?'

I took a deep breath and once again tried to block out the bustle around me. It wasn't easy, but eventually, I managed to focus entirely on the lifts. One was descending slowly towards Servyden. It was a walled platform, empty inside but large enough to hold a few dozen people standing shoulder to shoulder. As I concentrated, the lift came to a stop, hovering a few metres above the ground. I let out a quick breath, trying to relax my mind, and in that moment, the lift clonked heavily against the ground, landing with a jarring thud.

I gasped as a sudden tension coursed through me.

'Anything else?' Grotto asked, and his voice broke my concentration.

'Please,' I said, more forcefully than before, 'don't talk to me right now. Just give me one bloody minute of silence, will you?'

I turned my attention back to the lift, forcing myself to stay calm. This time, I tried to raise it. The weight of it was there immediately, heavy and cold against the floor. Then there was a creak, and to my utter shock, the structure began to slide upward. I could barely believe it, but there it was, moving.

Carefully, I lowered it again, inch by inch, making sure to avoid another crash. The tension lifted from my body when it landed gently. I didn't stop there, though. I lifted it again, higher this time, before bringing it back down. Each movement was cautious and controlled.

When I opened my eyes, Grotto and Hugo were both staring at me. I exhaled slowly, stretching my shoulders as I straightened. I'd thought mindspeak was only about sharing information. But really – what moved machines, if not information?

'I think…' I said, taking a moment to clear my thoughts. 'I think I just moved the lift with my mind.'

'I agree with Ronnie,' Marydit said. 'We can keep reaping all we want, but to move fast, we need to start bringing the others in.'

'This is a dangerous plan,' Hugo said. 'Do you really think the Lodgers haven't anticipated that something like this could happen? My guess is they have, and they'll know exactly how to handle insurgents.'

The group fell silent, everyone's eyes flitting around as though someone might hold a spark of hope in the face of Hugo's grim words. We stood beside the newest section of the maps, an area spanning over five hundred square metres where Jose and Ronnie had scratched out thousands of numbers in their secret code. The enormity of it should have been impressive, but instead, it just felt daunting.

'They're not prepared for this,' Grotto said. 'We have thousands. If we all rise at once, we'll break the enclosure. That's how we win.'

'Not everyone would escape,' Ula said. 'Not everyone would survive.'

'Every war has its casualties,' Grotto shot back. 'And what's the alternative? Dying one by one in their white cubes? I'd rather die fighting.' His words were more like a roar. His nose wrinkled, the skin on the bridge glistening as fury rippled through his features.

'Me too,' Jose said.

'How long would it take?' Ula asked. 'How many sections do we need to map before we can trigger Rise Day? How many Servums?'

'All of them,' Grotto said.

Jose exchanged a look with Ronnie, then rolled his eyes, blowing air through his lips in what looked like pure exasperation.

'Every Servum we bring in gives us a better chance of winning,' Grotto said. 'And every day we delay gives the Lodgers more time to stop us.'

'That's right,' Julian said, his words broken by a light stutter. 'There are already stories going around. People are asking questions. Just this morning, two women stopped me. They wanted to know where the new maps were and asked if they could see them.'

'That's not entirely a bad thing,' I said. 'Isn't that what we want, eventually? Those Servums aren't going to fight for us unless they understand the plan...and how we arrived at it.'

'Or a version of it, at least,' Grotto said, looking towards Hugo. 'You knew about Primula before she even spoke to you.'

'I knew *of* her,' Hugo said, his tone cautious, like he wasn't sure where this was heading. 'Not from before Servyden, though... Everyone's heard of the woman who killed the one-eyed giant. They think she is the Saviour.'

'Everyone?' Marydit asked while a faint laugh rippled through the group.

'I didn't kill him—' I started, but Mona cut in before I could finish.

'You nearly did,' she said, brimming with enthusiasm.

'That isn't the point,' Grotto said, silencing us with a glance before turning back to Hugo. 'How many people in Servyden do you think have heard the story of the Saviour?'

Hugo hesitated. 'Hard to say... It's spread far, though. It's a good story, and it resonates with what most Servums are desperate for. It showed them that one of us could rebel against oppression, even if that oppression was from our own kind, in this case. All the same, it's given people hope.'

I caught Marydit exchanging a glance with Grotto. 'The Saviour...' she murmured, almost to herself.

THIRTY-SEVEN

GREN

STANDING NAKED IN THAT GLASS CUBE, the chill of the room sank into my skin, though I refused to shiver. The walls were about three metres long on each side, offering a bleak view of the countless faces staring back at me.

As the lights surged to full brightness, the space resolved into a familiar setting. Behind rows of figures in blue gowns and white wigs, stood the enormous windowpanes, where a white shape twisted sluggishly. We were in the Beluga Room.

'Today, we welcome our players from the Lodge of Grawledinn and the Lodge of Hyender,' announced a voice I recognised instantly – deep and menacing, belonging to none other than Igor Voychenko.

I crossed my arms, keeping them firm against my chest. Every instinct urged me to shield myself, to fold inward, but I would not yield to vulnerability. Dignity was all I could claim in this moment, and I clung to it fiercely.

Not everyone in the room was focused on me, however. A few of the Lodgers had their attention fixed elsewhere, their heads tilted, eyes wide and glinting like predators catching a scent.

Turning slightly, I caught sight of another glass cube, positioned a few metres from mine. Inside stood Sam, trembling. A strong feeling rose in me – not quite pity, more a sense of guardianship. But we were caught in the same trap, each as powerless as the other.

Sam's face was pale, eyes shut. His body swayed as he struggled to stay upright. The increasing light inside the cube exposed his secret for all to see. The indignity of it shook me, but I fought to remain impassive. This was their intent – to break us, to strip us bare in every possible sense.

Before I could dwell on the thought, Voychenko's voice returned, booming across the room. 'We are gathered here today following the solemn death of Queen Brynhilda of Rivennia.' He sounded eerily calm. 'The event chosen for our current Game of Wagers has come to pass, intersecting the final two predictions. Consequently, we have no winner as of yet.'

A ripple of murmurs moved through the crowd. Fidgeting hands, shifting feet. People buzzed with a restlessness that bordered on impatience.

'Silence!' Voychenko's command lashed through the air. 'When we leave this room today,' he continued, 'we will know the result of our Game of Wagers.'

This time, applause broke out, loud and jarring. I stood firm, my gaze fixed on Sam. A hint of emotion passed over his face, though I couldn't tell if it was hope or despair.

'Let us see if we can break this tie,' Voychenko said.

It was then that the pigeon appeared. It materialised in the far corner of my cube, a grey mass ruffling its feathers. I thought it was a hologram at first, but it was real. Its plump chest glimmered faintly in the light, streaked with hues of iridescent green and pink that merged into the black of its nape.

'Humans have dominated this world for centuries,' Voychenko's voice rose again. 'In our domination, much has been forgotten, including the wildness that defined our ancestors and the tools they wielded to survive.' He glanced around the room. 'Today is a reminder of what we are no longer. A testament to the science that keeps us from savagery. Advancement is our aim – the price of it, sacrifice. And so, we revisit our past and honour it through ritual.'

Approving shouts answered him.

'At the sound of the bells,' he announced, 'our players will hunt their pigeons, using only what nature has given them: hands, teeth, nails. No tools but their bodies. The first player to consume their bird entirely, leaving no trace, shall claim victory.'

The world seemed to spin around me. This was not a test of skill. It was humiliation. I forced myself to meet Sam's eyes through the glass. The mix of disbelief and dread in his face mirrored my own. His palms pressed flat against the transparent wall of his cube, rigid with an anxiety I could almost feel.

'Inactivity,' Voychenko added, 'will be punished with electric shocks. If neither player succeeds, both shall become Servums.'

Murmurs stirred around us. Would people really believe the Chief Minister had died at an Express Passing Centre?

'Those who consume others thrive,' Voychenko said loudly.

'Those who consume others thrive,' the crowd responded as one.

Bells chimed, and the room erupted into a cacophony of cheers. The pigeon shifted its wings, its beady eyes meeting mine for the briefest of moments. I exhaled, preparing myself.

It began to strut with a peculiar rhythm, its small head jerking forward with each step.

My first attempt to grab it resulted in a flurry of feathers battering my fingers as the bird leapt to the opposite corner of the cube.

The pigeon was calm, tracking me with faint suspicion, but no real fear. When I advanced slowly, hoping to catch it off guard, the result was the same: another burst of frantic flapping, and the bird was back where it started, cooing softly.

The glass walls amplified every sound. Laughter seeped in from the Lodgers outside. My teeth pressed together, rage seething at their derision, but I could not let their ridicule break my focus. Exhausting the pigeon was pointless; its stamina far outmatched mine. These creatures could cross nations, and no amount of chasing would wear it down. I needed a different approach.

I lunged again, this time throwing my hands upward in a crude arc as the pigeon launched itself into flight. My wrists slammed together, and for an instant, there was nothing but chaos – the violent batter of wings against my grip, the furious energy of the bird's struggle. I tightened my hold, sliding one hand up cautiously until my fingers clamped around its chest. The feathers were soft and dry. The rapid thud of the pigeon's heart pulsed against my palm.

With a deep breath, I gripped the neck and twisted. I didn't hear the crack so much as I felt it. Then I kept twisting until something gave way. Warm blood spurted from the severed head, narrowly missing my face, but drenching my hands in sticky red. The bird's body convulsed briefly, then stilled. I stood there, stunned, as cheers burst from the Lodgers.

Voychenko's words resounded in my mind: 'The first player to ingest the bird in its entirety…' A cold rush swept through me. Every drop of blood, every feather. There could be no trace.

Suppressing the revulsion curling in my stomach, I brought the bird's neck to my lips and sucked the blood from its torn arteries. The warmth was sickening, a grotesque blend of brine and iron, but I forced it down. I squeezed the carcass to drain as much as I could, each gulp tightening the knot of nausea in my gut.

The head was next. I shoved it in, the beak scraping the roof of my mouth as I bit down. A nauseating crack cut it in two, the bone brittle yet stubborn. I chewed as quickly as I could, grinding the fragments into pieces small enough to swallow. Each crunch of the skull sent a jolt of revulsion, but I didn't stop. There was no room for hesitation, no time to falter.

The body was worse. The feathers clung to the meat like needles, and they were impossible to swallow on their own. I had to mix them with chunks of flesh, chewing them down together in a bitter, greasy mess. My hands tore at the remains, separating sinew from bone, pulling apart the innards and stuffing them into my mouth. The taste was a sickening blend of shellfish and red meat. My throat burned with each swallow, and every breath threatened to bring it all back up.

By the time the bird was gone, my hands were shaking. Blood had soaked into every crevice of my skin, and I could feel the beginnings of a retch building. I pressed my lips together, holding my breath as my stomach churned. To vomit would ruin everything. When a quiet burp escaped, it relieved some of the pressure, but the taste lingered, acrid and foul.

There was no time for respite. I dropped to all fours and began licking the floor clean. Blood, feathers, even the sickly yellow bile. I swept it all with my tongue, scraping every trace from the glass. The bitterness clung to my palate, and I fought back another wave of nausea, focusing only on the task.

Then the bells chimed again.

The room exploded in uproar, and the Lodgers' ovation rumbled like thunder against the glass. I sat back, panting, my limbs shaking from exertion. Across the room, Sam had collapsed on the floor of his cube. Pale vomit frothed at his lips and dripped down his chin, his chest heaving weakly. Black and grey feathers were strewn around him. His bird was likely dead, but barely touched.

A rush of air drew my attention. One wall of my cube began to rise, tilting slowly until it folded into the ceiling. Voychenko stood outside, his applause slow and deliberate. A grin stretched across his face. Beside him, Fredrica mirrored his expression.

'The Lodge of Grawledinn welcomes its newest member!' Voychenko declared. 'Gren Moritz, now of the Liffdom Lodges!'

As I stepped out of the cube, someone draped a blue gown over my shoulders. A white wig was fitted onto my head, brushing against my ears. My legs were unsteady, but I stood tall, meeting Voychenko's eyes, then Fredrica's.

'Congratulations, Gren,' Fredrica said. Something in her expression was different – there was pride, maybe, and relief, but also a faint trace of sadness she couldn't quite hide. In that look, I saw what I'd become.

I had survived. I had won. And now, I was one of them.

THIRTY-EIGHT

PRIMULA

THE NIGHTMARES WERE different this time. I saw clouds of dust, the hammering of metal, the screech of something buckling under pressure. Blood splattering. But I still woke up the same – panting and drenched in sweat.

Sleep-deprived and dragging my feet, I walked with Grotto and Marydit towards the maps. We moved slowly, conserving what little energy we had, knowing it would take time for the mindspeakers to meet us at the destination. Fate seemed to have smiled on us lately; for several days, we'd managed to gather as a full group, often joined by Ronnie and Jose, and occasionally by Mona and Julian.

Today, we were supposed to agree on a date for Rise Day. I dreaded it. It was bound to end in another clash of opinions, a heated debate that would almost certainly spiral into a fight.

When we reached the area near section one-fifty-nine, the sight struck me like a physical force. Marydit and Grotto hesitated, twisting their faces in denial, but I understood immediately.

'We've walked too far,' Marydit said.

Grotto spun in a full circle, scanning the surroundings like he could will the maps back into existence. 'No, we're not there yet,' he muttered, pressing a hand to his head.

'But we just passed the gate...' I said. 'That's one-fifty-nine right there.'

We stood paralysed while the silence pressed in on us, broken only by the sound of our laboured breaths. Grotto took a few slow steps, locking his gaze on the ground.

'They're gone,' he said finally. 'They wiped them all out.'

I clutched my arms across my chest as the reality of it sank in. The painstaking work, the endless numbers we'd decoded together – all of it reduced to dust.

To an ordinary Servum, the dirt floor might have looked normal – dry soil with the usual cracks and scratches, scattered with a few pebbles. But for Grotto, Marydit and me, it was like looking at a blank sheet where a vital text had been erased.

'It's all over,' Marydit said, her lips pressed as she lowered her head. 'So many years of work. All gone. How can we expect anyone to carry on without the promise of freedom?'

'What about the watchmen?' I asked. 'Why didn't they stop this?'

'They must've done it during the dark hours,' Grotto said, but his voice sounded unsure. 'The watchmen can't all be gone...'

A strangled cry from Marydit made us turn. 'It's them!' she wailed, her voice breaking with horror. Grotto and I, both still searching the wide expanse for any trace of the scribbles, rushed to her side.

She pointed with a trembling finger to a raised patch of

earth a couple of metres away. Tears streamed down her cheeks, but she didn't speak. She didn't need to.

We moved closer, and the moment we saw it, a pang of pain gripped me. There they were: the watchmen, as well as Hugo, Ula and Denzin. Their faces half-buried in the dirt, their heads lying flat and still, as though they'd been caught mid-scream. The soil around their contours was raised like a grotesque frame, a layer of dust coating their open eyes.

It wasn't a failed burial. It wasn't a mistake. It was a message.

'Why not just kill us all and be done with it?' Grotto's voice quivered, the graveness gone, leaving only a faint, frightened sound.

'Maybe they will,' I said quietly.

I turned my back on the grisly display and took a few steps away.

'Yes,' Marydit said between hiccupped sobs. 'We're all heading to the same place.'

'The maps are gone,' Grotto said, firmer now. He straightened his back, his hands curling into fists. 'But we haven't forgotten what we learned. We can still do Rise Day. We *will* do Rise Day. We must break out and go up those shafts. But we need to act soon.'

Early the next day, three nervous boys approached us. I studied them, noticing how young they were. The little waifs with wide eyes and restless hands couldn't have been older than twelve.

'Can we see them?' one asked, his voice barely holding. The other two looked down, scuffing the dirt with their toes.

'What are you looking for, dear?' Marydit asked.

'The maps,' the boy chirped.

'Oh, the maps.' She beamed at them despite the pain in her

eyes. 'The maps are very safely guarded, of course. I'm afraid you won't be able to see them today, my dears.'

The boys exchanged bashful glances, as if they'd already known the answer but needed to ask anyway. Then, one of them – a freckled boy on the left – raised a bony finger and pointed straight at me.

'Is she...' he began hesitantly. 'Is that the Saviour?'

Grotto let out a dry snort of laughter. 'That's the one, boys. The woman who killed the one-eyed giant.'

Their faces lit up. 'We thought she'd be here!' said the tallest one, his gangly limbs shifting excitedly. 'We'd like to offer her...' He stepped forward and opened his palm, revealing three coloured objects, sticky and slightly misshapen, about the size of grapes. 'Sweets!' he exclaimed, beaming.

'Oh dear.' Marydit shook her head gently. 'That's very kind, but you need that sugar for yourselves. There's a good reason it was on your trays.'

'We want her to have it,' the boy insisted.

I glanced sideways, unsure how to react. 'I can't possibly accept that, but thank you. Truly. That's very generous of you.' I looked closer at the sweets and saw their half-dissolved surfaces clung together. Knowing how food was smuggled into the common – tucked inside cheeks or hidden under tongues – I could only imagine the effort these boys had gone through to save them.

'You'll need the energy,' the boy said, 'when you fight for us.'

'That's right!' Grotto said. 'Primula, take the sweets.'

'I don't think I...'

'Just eat them,' Grotto cut me off.

I hesitated before stepping forward. My right hand stretched out, fingers closing around the sticky pellets. Without a second thought, I popped them into my mouth all at once. The rush of sweetness flooded my tongue.

'Thank you,' I said, looking at the boys. 'That was very kind of you.'

The flavour was rich as the sweets began to dissolve.

'Now, you go tell everyone,' Grotto said, commanding. 'The Saviour will finally free us all. Rise Day is tomorrow.'

The boys gasped, faces bright with enthusiasm. 'Is that true?' the tallest one asked, a touch of reverence in him.

'Yes,' Grotto said. 'Go tell the others. The Saviour will lead us with her strength, and together, we'll bring down the gate at section one-sixty. First thing tomorrow. Can you repeat that for me?'

'Section one-sixty. First thing tomorrow,' they said together.

'That's it.' Grotto agreed. 'Now listen carefully: every person you tell must pass it on to at least ten others before curfew, and they, in turn, will have to do the same. Understood?'

The boys gave a loud affirmation.

'Go, then,' Grotto urged. 'Now. There's no time to waste.'

They sprinted off, their scrawny legs kicking up little clouds of dust with every step.

'Tomorrow?' Marydit's mouth hung open.

'We have no time.' Grotto's tone was grim. 'Let's spread the word, and hope they don't kill us all before we get the chance to do this.'

The nightmares kept getting worse. As soon as I drifted into deep sleep, they dragged me under, suffocating me with visions of hissing gas and black thorns glinting in the dark. The images were disjointed, grotesque, and they vanished before I could make sense of them. They meant something – a warning – though their message remained out of reach.

I wanted to tell Grotto and the others that rushing into Rise Day was a terrible idea. But when we reached section one-sixty, my determination crumbled. My knees weakened at the sight of the crowd gathered there. It was too late to turn back. A mass of Servums shouted over one another, their arms raised high, their cries full of fervour. I couldn't begin to estimate their number. They jostled, impassioned and drunk on the promise of freedom.

Fear clawed at my insides as the enormity of what was about to happen sank in. The sea of bodies stretched out like a blanket over the common, with no end in sight.

Grotto's voice boomed as he addressed the crowd. 'Servums, are you ready to claim what is yours?'

I flinched at the roar that answered him.

'By the power of the Saviour, the woman who killed the one-eyed giant,' Grotto continued, 'we will rise as one, and we will break our enclosure. Today, the Saviour has given her power to *you*.'

The front rows cheered loudly; even those too far away to hear him were shouting just as passionately. Clusters of Servums nearest to Grotto were repeating his words loudly for those further back. The message rippled outward in waves, spreading through the sea of people until it reached even the most distant edges.

'All of us, together, will walk the streets of Lacunfort this evening.'

The ovation surged again, full of fury. It wasn't just a scream of hatred – this was years of repressed rage boiling over. They were like frenzied cattle, moments away from breaking loose, ready to smash through everything in their path.

Grotto turned to me, his face flushed, his breath short. 'We need to act quickly. Can you manage the lifts once the gates are down?'

'Yes,' I said stiffly. Around us, the crowd was simmering, ready to explode.

Then, like the shot of a starter pistol, Grotto gave his final instruction. The Servums surged forward in a stampede, and their bodies slammed against the gate at section one-sixty. Thick dust rose in clouds, choking the air. The metal groaned under the onslaught as wave after wave of Servums hurled themselves at it.

Those at the front screamed in pain as the sheer weight of the bodies behind them crushed them against the gate. Their faces twisted in agony. Their mouths opened in soundless cries. Some tried to shout, 'Stand back! Stand back!' but no one was listening.

A two-metre-wide stretch was clogged with bodies, piled high against the gate. The ground was strewn with wounded Servums – and others who looked dead, limbs twisted like broken dolls. Young men and women quickly organised, dragging the bodies away by their feet. Blood turned the dirt into sticky patches of mud, pooling around crushed skulls and severed limbs. My stomach dropped as a horrifying truth became clear – the furious crowd was tearing itself apart.

'Stand back!' Grotto shouted, dragging me to the side of the gate. The crowd obeyed, retreating to form a semicircle, the ground now almost clear.

With the path open, Servums threw themselves one by one at the gate, bodies colliding like darts against the metal. A rhythm emerged, almost orderly, as shoulders, hips, and heads hammered the gate. At first, the metal seemed unyielding, but soon it began to bend and stretch under the pressure. The groaning intensified until, with a final, ear-splitting screech, the gate gave way.

A shout of victory erupted. Dozens of Servums poured into the corridor beyond, their war cries bouncing off the walls. The echoing sound was overwhelming, magnified by the enclosed space.

Then came a loud thud that resounded in the air. I turned my head towards the broken gate, and terror struck me.

From the ceiling, a new gate had descended like a guillotine, slamming shut and cutting off all access to the tunnel. The barricade split the crowd in two. It wasn't a solid gate like the one the Servums had just destroyed; this one was a metal mesh, its bars covered in clusters of sharp thorns that gleamed under the white light.

Grotto pressed his hand to his forehead. Every Servum who tried to touch the barrier recoiled instantly, crying out in pain. The scrambling crowd outside the tunnel pushed us in every direction. People lurched with red faces, slick with sweat. Desperate cries surrounded us. Some stared at the closed tunnel with tears glistening in their eyes, others lost in anguish.

I craned my neck, trying to see through the meshed barricade and into the tunnel. On the other side of it, the mass of Servums trapped inside came into view. They were still shouting, still pushing through.

'They're trying to reach the lift,' I said to Grotto, though I wasn't sure he heard me over the commotion.

At the far end of the hallway stood the second gate, leading to the shaft – the only thing now separating Servyden from Lacunfort. In my mind, I saw it clearly: the lift sitting idle at the bottom of the shaft, waiting.

'Crush, crush, crush!' the crowd chanted. Their voices were now hoarse. Servums hurled themselves at the second gate with the same frenzied energy. Those near the front knelt and pushed at the edges of the gate with bare hands, while the ones behind them thrust their feet forward, kicking above to widen the gaps.

Finally, I spotted it – barely visible from where I stood. A small opening had emerged, just big enough for a body to squeeze through. One by one, Servums wriggled their way into the lift, their movements frantic and desperate, until the last one slipped inside.

'Do it,' Grotto shouted. 'Lift them up!'

My heart pounded against my ribs, the noise of the crowd fading into a distant hum as I tried to focus. The lift felt impossibly heavy. I had to concentrate. I closed my eyes, sealing my ears with my palms.

The image of the lift came into focus: its metal frame, the bodies teeming on its floor. Slowly, it wiggled an inch off the ground, then slammed back down. I opened my eyes and shook my head at Grotto.

'Try again,' he said. 'They'll stop us soon. You need to get them out. Now.'

'It won't happen unless you let me concentrate,' I said. My voice was strained with fear.

This time, the lift rose higher, loaded with Servums, sliding upwards through the shaft. It moved at a constant pace and looked like it might reach the top. But just below the midpoint, the strain became too much. The lift trembled, and then, like a raincloud bursting, it plummeted.

The crash was deafening. When I opened my eyes to see the aftermath, a shock of horror invaded me. There was no way anyone could have survived. Tears blurred my vision as the reality of what I'd done struck me. How many had I just killed?

Then the alarm blared – a shrill, stabbing sound that sent fresh waves of panic through the crowd. The Servums scattered, cries breaking out as they ran in every direction.

Through the noise came something new: a deep, hissing noise.

'Gas!' someone shouted. 'It's gas!'

'Run,' Grotto said, grabbing my arm. My mind blanked. I was too weak, too shaken to move. He lifted me into his arms and carried me. Then we ran with the others as the low whistle of gas followed behind us.

PART THREE

Month Ten, Year 500 to Month Six, Year 501

THIRTY-NINE

LORELEI

My dear sister,

Yesterday was one of those exhausting days, filled from dawn till late evening. I'm meant to slow down now that the pregnancy is nearly at its end, but it's so hard to say no. When I woke up early this morning, I looked at my schedule and thought: I don't want to do any of this. Not a single task seemed appealing. Your letter arrived just then, lifting my spirits in a way I can't quite describe. And please, stop apologising for not being able to hologram with us. I understand completely. I'd never hold it against you for staying true to yourself. Honestly, I admire that about you. I wish I had some of your courage. It's my fault we've not seen each other, and the moment I can escape these First Lady duties, I'll come to Varcega.

Another bright spot in my week was Sara and Rosa's wonderful news – they're twelve weeks along! We're all overjoyed, including the father-to-be, Mr Otto Schmidt, the DC Director. They haven't decided on the baby's surname yet, as there are three parents and three surnames to choose from, but they have time to sort that out.

Otto has been an interesting acquaintance. He asked me to call him by his first name, and now it feels perfectly natural. There's something about him that puts people at ease. The day we spoke about the grant, I felt his kindness straight away. Though the DC could use the funds, he assured me he'd understand if the grant went elsewhere. 'You don't always get your own way in life,' he said. It struck me then how his signing changes, depending on whether he's speaking directly to a person or through a hologram interpreter. I prefer watching his hands; they are strong and elegant. There's something oddly reassuring about them.

That day, I brought up Sara and Rosa's plan. When I mentioned they were seeking a congenitally deaf donor, he practically lit up. 'I've always dreamed of being a father,' he said. 'Do you think they'd consider me?' I could barely contain my excitement and replied, 'Yes, I think they would.'

I asked him how he felt about being chosen as a donor specifically because he is deaf, and whether he thought it was right to deliberately bring a child into the world with that limitation. His response surprised me, offering a perspective I hadn't considered before. He doesn't see his deafness as a limitation. In fact, he believes it has helped him, much like Sara and Rosa, to form some of the most meaningful connections in his life.

Then he said something that's really stayed with me: 'There is infinite beauty in our differences.' Isn't that a lovely thought? Infinite.

I keep picturing how he signs the word 'beauty' – starting with his hand forming a loose circle near his face, then opening it outward, as if releasing a burst of light. It's such a small, graceful gesture, but it warms my heart.

Later, Rosa and Sara told me everything was arranged. They've been thanking me endlessly, but I keep saying I did very little.

Anyway, their joy is contagious, and I can't wait to meet their baby.

It all left me thinking – so much so that I told Dr Greenville I wouldn't be going ahead with her suggested treatments. Otto's words wouldn't leave me, turning over in my mind until I saw the truth in them. How could I look at my child and see anything less than perfection, no matter what? And so, why would I want to turn my unborn baby into an ultrahuman?

As much as I consider myself a devout believer, I must confess that this is the first time my faith has truly been tested. It takes a certain courage to surrender to God's will. And still, at the same time, I see God's plan in my meeting Sara, Rosa and Otto. In ways they are unaware of, they have taught me things I needed to learn. I know I haven't found my calling yet, but this experience has left me feeling a little closer to it. Who would have thought I'd come to embrace Gren's ideology – and from such a different path?

When I spoke to Dr Greenville, her reaction was so intense it startled me. She insisted I reconsider, and her tone turned almost rude. But that only made me more certain I'd made the right decision. In the end, I had to tell Gren. He was furious, of course, but within hours, they'd assigned me a new doctor. Problem solved.

Now, I must get going, my sweet sister. I'm making Mum's chicken casserole tonight to see if I can cheer Gren up. Real Varcegian food! It's obviously not legal to eat farmed animals in Lacunfort, but apparently, there are no rules against cooking them. So, the plan is to prepare everything here and then set a nice dining table inside a capsula to take us out to the open sea. In less than forty-five minutes, we'll be tucking into our chicken like the barbarians everyone thinks we are. Yum! And don't you dare laugh at me – this is the extent I have to go to, honestly.

Right, I'd better go; that bird won't jump in the pot on its own.

Lots of love, as always,

Lorelei

FORTY

GREN

Few things could transport me back to Varcega like the flavours of a chicken casserole. The blend of spices – cumin, cinnamon, smoky peppers – brought memories to life with every mouthful. As I ate, I couldn't help but compliment Lorelei on her cooking, which seemed nothing short of magical.

She looked pleased, but her focus seemed to waver. Her eyes kept drifting. She adjusted her position, stood for a moment, then sat again as if unsure why she'd risen at all.

'Is everything alright?' I asked.

'Yes – all good,' she replied. 'I'm so glad you liked it.' Her tone was light but unconvincing. 'I think I ate too much,' she added.

Then she got up again, stretching, her steps slow as she moved around the cramped space of the capsula. The growing restlessness in her movements put me on edge. I tried to dismiss it at first, but when she stopped, her hand braced against the wall.

'Something feels off,' she said.

A flush crept up her neck; her face looked clammy.

I was just calling for assistance when there was a gasp behind me. I turned to find her staring at me, wide-eyed, as a gush of fluid spilled from beneath her skirt.

The capsula began its high-speed journey back to Lacunfort, but time seemed to slow. I lined up the chairs and guided Lorelei to recline. Her breathing had grown deep and erratic.

'I wasn't feeling great earlier,' she murmured, clutching her abdomen. 'But I assumed I was just tired, and—' She faltered mid-sentence, gripping her belly tighter, her face twisting in pain.

The hours that followed were a whirlwind of action and waiting. By the next morning, I was finally called into the room, where the bustle had given way to an almost surreal stillness. Lorelei lay there, her cheeks a vivid red. Her face was as tired as it was radiant. In her arms, swaddled in soft cloth, was our baby girl.

'Would you like to hold her?' the nurse asked.

The question made me feel suddenly big and clumsy, but I wanted nothing more. As I took her in my arms, the feelings surged all at once. Nothing about it was gradual. This was something entirely new.

She was tiny, fragile, and I had an overwhelming compulsion to protect her, to provide for her, to give her the best life possible in this bewildering world. Holding her, I saw with fresh clarity the miracle of birth: our capacity to create life. Never before had I been so conscious of the sheer wonder of humanity. Wasn't this miracle worth devoting one's life to?

As strong as my convictions were and as committed as I was to my cause, in that precise moment, there was nothing I could put into action. All I could do was stand there and hope. I hoped for better things for this child and for the rest of humanity. I hoped the world might be kinder to her than it had been to so many others. I hoped for the future of our species, with all its flaws and wonders.

Hope, I realised, was one of humanity's most admirable traits and our most powerful weapon.

Why do we do that? Why do we stubbornly hold on to the belief that the future will be better? Perhaps it's the only way to move forward.

And so we hope. And we move forward.

I knew I would. I was ready.

Lorelei broke into a weary smile. 'Sophia,' she said.

'Sophia,' I repeated the name, looking down at her little face.

She was perfect.

FORTY-ONE

PRIMULA

The dust. The distant bustle. The roughness of the cloak against my skin.

Another day on the common, painfully indistinguishable from the countless others before it. Servyden had settled back into its old rhythms, and Rise Day had faded into a distant, almost forgotten memory for those of us who survived.

But Grotto had changed. The guttural imperiousness that once defined him was gone. He'd turned quiet, withdrawing so deeply into himself that he barely seemed present. Weeks had passed since the tragedy, and the most anyone had got from him were monosyllables. There was a chance he might come back from it one day – might even return to the man he'd been. But it wouldn't be with my help. I'd made myself a promise: whatever life I had left, Grotto would be the last man ever to control me.

No one had seen Marydit or Mona. I had stopped trying

to convince myself they might still be alive. They had probably been inside the tunnel, their bodies either crushed to pulp when the lift hit the ground or suffocated by the gas. Gone, either way.

I avoided everyone now. The human contact I'd once craved had turned into something I dreaded. When they let me out, I wandered alone, deliberately keeping my distance from other Servums. My feet dragged, shuffling with a slow persistence only slightly less dreary than sitting completely still. Hours stretched blankly, the numbness a constant that had begun to feel normal.

That morning, I sat down to rest, leaning my back against a rock near my section. Lisa had used this same rock as a backrest the day we met in person. The memory flared, brief, but still clear.

And then I saw him.

His head was shaven, his frame was thin and fragile, and his face held the disoriented look of someone new to this place. But it was him.

My heart jumped. Suddenly, I was awake, just like that. The fog I'd been drowning in for weeks was gone in an instant.

'Sam…' My voice came out faint and rough, but I forced myself to shout loud enough to reach him. 'Sam!'

His head snapped towards me. He seemed gaunt and weary. Then his face lit up, brighter than I could have imagined. I staggered to my feet, and Sam launched into a sprint.

We collided in an embrace that knocked the air from my lungs, his arms crushing me so tightly I felt it in every bone. Tears welled up before I could stop them. Then something gave way, and we both broke into sobs.

'My lovely Prim,' Sam said as he pulled me even closer, wrapping me in that sweet, manly scent I thought I'd forgotten. 'It's fine. It's all fine. I'm here now.'

I pulled back just enough to take his wrists in my hands and press my forehead to his.

'I vow to stand by you, in moments of light and shadow,' I said, my voice cracking.

His sobs deepened as he gripped my wrists in return. He repeated, 'I vow to stand by you, in moments of light and shadow.'

'I hold dear all that makes you who you are,' I continued.

'I hold dear all that makes you who you are.'

'Together, we are unbreakable, through all that life may bring.'

'Together, we are unbreakable, through all that life may bring.'

FORTY-TWO

SAM

Primula had warned me the shocks would never get easier. She'd been right so far. The anticipation was nearly as bad as the pain itself. Nearly. Because when the shock did hit, it was like the world was trying to rip me in two.

The puzzles were harder that morning, but if I kept my nerves steady, I could still find the solutions.

'Multiples of three,' the voice said.

A grid – the biggest one yet – glowed in front of me. Some numbers were filled in, boxed in black, and the rest I had to figure out. I had to place the right digits so that, when the rows and columns were multiplied together, they matched the command. Get it right, and the wall would light up. Get it wrong, or take too long, and the shock would come.

I was close to filling the last cell when the hum in the background – one I'd barely noticed till now – cut out, and the white light dimmed. At first, I wondered if it was a power failure. A panel behind me slid open, and I turned, blinking against the change in light. My pulse jumped as the shape of a person in a blue gown was revealed. But my tension faded when I saw who it was.

Gren – only he looked drained, greyer, like the fight had been wrung out of him.

'What took you so long?' I muttered.

'We don't have much time,' he said, quickly glancing at me and the cube. He hardly paused before firing off his questions.

He winced as I told him everything. I described the enhanced, the deformed, the whole brutality. I painted it as best I could, and when my memories fell short, I repeated what Primula had told me.

My Primula. She had suffered so much, and no matter how I tried to convince her we'd get out, I could see that hope had left her. To her, it was better that way – to expect the worst, so when it came, it wouldn't hurt as much. She didn't believe my promises of a better life elsewhere. She wasn't waiting to be saved any more. She was just waiting for the end.

But I could see patterns where others couldn't. Even though they had destroyed the maps, some things still survived through stories. And when Primula spoke of the failed uprising, the bot network, the numbers they'd stored, I saw the outline of something familiar. It was a structure I recognised.

'My turn for questions,' I said.

Gren looked taken aback but focused quickly.

'How much do you know about surveillance? Who's watching?'

'Not the Lodgers,' Gren said. 'They've never been ones to get their hands dirty. They know what this place is. They know the numbers. But they care more about product than process. The cost in lives is just part of the overhead.'

'Do they know you're here?'

'Only one other Lodger does. No one else.'

'I see. So most things are automated?'

'Seems that way.'

'I think I know how the security works. I'm sure there are nine digits,' I said. 'They give full control of the bot network. The digits change daily, so what we need isn't a specific number – we need the criteria to generate it.'

'And then what?'

'Then we have options. First, we get the code.'

Gren nodded, silent. His sigh was heavy.

'I've got less than a minute before an alarm triggers,' he said, checking his wrist.

'Go back and get the passcode,' I said. 'Then we can talk some more.'

'We can't...' His words trailed off. He looked over his shoulder, checking the opening he'd come through.

'What?'

'We can't let them all out.'

I stared at him. 'Why not?'

'What's happened here is horrific, but it's contained. If we release these mutations into the population, the human genome may never recover. I know we want to protect the Servums, but we have to think about the greater good.'

'So you're just leaving us here?'

He pressed his lips together, avoiding my eyes. 'I have to go.' Another glance at his wrist, then he turned and rushed back the way he'd come.

I stood there as the opening sealed shut behind him. And that was it – he was gone. Like we hadn't made promises – to the queen, to each other.

The puzzle reappeared, glowing in front of me, waiting.

FORTY-THREE

GREN

The Lodgers' ways were never blatant or vulgar, but it didn't take long for any of them to steer a conversation towards their own greatness. Stories of achievement were always told in the first person, but rarely finished before someone else interjected with a larger feat to their credit. The exclusivity and secrecy of Liffdom evidently fed their need for validation, not just reminding them how much they mattered, but reinforcing their sense of importance by keeping them high above the world. Other people were worthless, mere vehicles to deliver their obsessions: growth, endless growth, and profit stretched so far that the Lodgers lost all connection to what it meant to be human.

Despicable as Voychenko was, I could see how deftly he played his Lodgers, luring them with the promise of what they craved most. If I looked at it coldly, the average Lodger wasn't intrinsically evil. There was none of Voychenko's sinister nature in them – just an oversized ambition and an indifference to others that made them perfect candidates to be recruited, granting their leader yet another extension of control in whatever they ruled over in their daily lives.

Fredrica, however, stood at a crossroads between the loyalty she believed she owed her family and her conscience. The more time we spent together, the more I recognised the conflict within her – a conviction so firm it seemed rehearsed, too forceful to be real. At times, I caught glimpses of scorn; other times, regret. And in those moments, I saw an opening in what had once seemed an impenetrable organisation.

I began visiting her flat more often, even after Sophia was born. Some nights I stayed over, lying awake, thinking about the world – not just what it had become, but what it had always been. Whatever happened, I knew one thing: if there was a solution, Fredrica's help might be the key.

That night, she turned over to find me awake. 'Is everything alright?' she asked – a question as absurd as asking whether a burning house was warm enough.

'Is it your mother who runs the network in Servyden?' I asked.

She sighed. 'Get some sleep, Gren. Forget about Servyden. At least for now.'

'Is it her who runs it?'

'The bot network runs itself.'

'I know that. But someone designed it. Someone governs it.'

She rubbed her eyes. 'My mother, of course. Who else?'

'There's a master passcode.'

'Yes, there should be one.'

'We need to find out how to derive it.'

'We do? What for?'

I sat up and leaned against the headboard. 'This can't go on.

You know that. We can't ignore that there are people trapped, suffering every day. Their families believe them dead.'

'But we didn't create this. It wasn't us.'

'It doesn't matter. If we know about it, doing nothing is the same as being complicit.'

'But there's nothing to do. What are you planning? Handing them the passcode? How will that change anything?'

'I'm asking you to give the passcode to *me*.'

'I don't have it.'

'But you can get it.'

She shook her head. 'You need to be careful. People are anxious after the last uprising. My parents more than ever. If anyone hacks the network and tries something reckless, they won't hesitate to take drastic action. They already doubt they can guarantee security long-term with this many Servums. I've heard talk of a mass culling. I don't think anyone's taking it seriously yet, but another escape attempt will definitely change that. Is that something you want on your conscience?'

'Do you want to spend the rest of your life knowing that hundreds of people suffered while you stood by and did nothing?' I asked. 'How could you live with that?'

'My hands are tied,' she said. 'And so are yours. There's nothing we can do.'

'Offer to help.'

'Help with what?'

'If they're so worried about another uprising, tell them you are too, and offer to strengthen the network's security. Isn't that the kind of work you've done at the prisons?'

'That's different…'

'It doesn't matter!' I shouted, then forced myself to lower my voice. 'All we need is the criteria for generating the passcode.'

'They won't give that to me.'

'You're their daughter. If they trust anyone, it's you.'

Fredrica's breathing quickened. Her gaze drifted. Twice, she seemed on the verge of speaking, but each time, she held back. Then, without a word, she pushed the covers aside, got out of bed, and left the room. I listened as her footsteps trailed down the hall, followed by the sound of a door slamming shut. She didn't return that night.

FORTY-FOUR

PRIMULA

Sam's insistence irritated me. I didn't want to move. I didn't want to think or do anything. But he kept pushing.

'Come on,' he said. 'You need to walk. It'll make you feel better.'

So off we went on a bloody walk – whether to please him or to shut him up, I wasn't sure. Sam kept the conversation going, though I didn't always feel like talking. He still had hope, like I once had. But when he told me that Gren seemed reluctant to help us now, that was the final blow. We were doomed. And it was only a matter of time before Sam accepted that.

He tried to hide it, but every step caused him pain. Walking on the common was harder for him than it was for me now. The soles of my new feet had turned coarse and thick, like everyone else's. But Sam was still new to Servyden. His skin had softened all over. It was drier too. He'd only made a passing comment about it once, saying that the longer he stayed here, the more his body would return to what it once was. He always kept his cloak fastened. I wished I were in a better position, so he didn't always have to be the strong one.

We walked further than I'd expected. It got easier as we went on. Amid the bustle, someone behind me squealed my name. I barely had time to turn before something slammed into my back, arms constricting me.

It was Mona. She held me in a tight hug. 'Oh, thank the Saviour – you're alive.' She pulled back to look at my face before squeezing me again.

'Mona.' My arms tightened around her, warmth surging through me. My hands ran over her back, mostly bare now that she'd tied up her rebel curls in a neat plait.

'I'm glad to finally meet you, Mona,' Sam said, extending a hand.

Mona, visibly confused at first, lifted a limp hand in an awkward imitation of the gesture, then grinned.

'You have to come with me right now.' She grabbed us both and pulled us away from the gates.

A few minutes later, we found Marydit sitting on the floor, legs crossed, with Lisa curled up beside her, head resting in her lap.

My cry of joy startled Lisa awake. I saw the moment she recognised me, and I dropped to the ground to hug her.

Turning to mindspeak, I said, 'I'm so glad to see you well. I've missed you so much.'

'My darling,' she answered. 'How much I've longed to see you again.'

Mona stepped forward to introduce Sam and promptly stood back, beaming, hands clasped near her chin. Then, perhaps to lighten the mood, she drifted around us in a few playful steps, swinging her head from side to side.

'So… what do you think?' she asked, eyes full of expectation.

'About your hair?' I guessed.

'Yes! Do you like it?'

'I absolutely love it!' I peered at her plait. 'How did you do that?'

'Well…' She made a show of glancing around before leaning in and lowering her voice. 'We're not meant to, but no one's noticed. I'm not doing anything bad, really.'

That's when I saw it – the strip of fabric securing her hair, cut from her cloak.

'It's the hem,' she said, as if reading my thoughts. 'It took me forever until I found a little stone with a sharp enough edge. And now…' She tossed her head. 'Ta-da. I'm glad you like it.'

I caught the look on Sam's face – something in his expression told me he'd grown fond of her already.

'Please,' Marydit said, gesturing to the floor. 'Sit with us. We have much to talk about. It's a wonderful gift to have found each other.'

As I lowered myself beside them, I spotted Julian and Grotto among a group of men in the distance. Grotto's gaze flicked to me, then jerked away, too quick to be casual. I wondered if he was plotting something else, but I had more important things in front of me.

Being here with Mona, Marydit and Lisa restored something in me. And now Sam could meet them, too.

He'd promised the walk would make me feel better. Maybe it was that, or maybe it was the comfort of seeing old friends. Either way, for this moment, the world seemed a little less dark.

I hadn't seen Sam in days. That morning, he ran straight for me the second he spotted me across the common – a reckless sprint that nearly sent him sprawling more than once. He clutched at his cloak the whole way, careful not to let it fly open. Something was up. I knew it before he even reached me. But he didn't look distressed or uneasy – quite the opposite. The closer he got, the clearer his excitement became.

He grabbed my shoulders. 'I got it.' He panted. 'The passcode.'

He'd told me about some master passcode before, but no matter how much I wanted to, I couldn't share his optimism. What was a sodding passcode going to do for us? His hope hurt to watch, knowing disappointment would crush him soon enough.

'The master code?' I asked. 'What is it then?'

'Well…' He hesitated. 'I don't have the code itself. The code isn't static. It changes every day. But I have something better. I know how to generate it – any day we need. It's like a recipe.'

What he explained wasn't something I could fully grasp, though after hours of discussion, I managed to scrape together a vague understanding. Sam had nothing written down – only what he remembered from a rushed conversation with Gren inside a cube. His biggest fear wasn't that the code wouldn't work but that he'd misunderstood something, that a crucial detail had been lost or twisted along the way.

Three parts, he said. Three sets of numbers. Nine digits in total. Nine little digits that, according to Sam, would grant us complete control of Servyden. The first set relied on the date, which I always kept track of in my head, even after the maps were destroyed. But, as Sam explained, it wasn't the date itself we needed. It had to be 'hashed' through some mathematical process to turn it into a three-digit number. The second set came from a secret network key we now had, multiplied and hashed with the first three digits. The last set depended on a user-specific code Gren had given us, also multiplied by the previous numbers and hashed down to three digits.

Long days followed. Sam tried and failed to scratch out calculations in the dry earth of the common. He was never satisfied, but he never stopped. 'I'm getting closer,' he'd say, but I couldn't see the difference, and it broke me to watch him so lost in something I didn't believe would work.

After two or three weeks, he was certain he'd cracked it. So we walked to section one-seventy, where I was to input our precious nine digits into the bot network. I would have done anything for Sam, so I helped. What else was I going to do? He was so determined.

When I tuned in through mindspeak, the usual crackle filled my head. The messy numerals gave me the shivers, dragging me back to those long data-reaping sessions. The mindspeakers who were slaughtered. The wreckage of Rise Day. But this time, I wasn't here to listen – I was here to speak.

I fed in Sam's code, one digit at a time. At first, I wasn't sure the system was receiving anything, but the moment I entered the ninth digit, a jarring chime rang out. A wretched, discordant note. There was no mistaking it: an error.

Sam's expectant gaze shattered me. I shook my head lightly, then tried again. And again. And again. Until it was clear – we hadn't got it right.

'Could the criteria have changed?' I asked.

'I doubt it. It's me.' He sighed. 'It's my fault. Without a computer, it's impossible to get all the hashing right. If I make even a tiny mistake at the start, it ruins the whole thing.'

Of course, we kept trying. Every day we had the chance. Every moment on the common belonged to the task. But the long walks were grinding us down. Sam would sit on the ground for hours, silent, thinking.

Then I had an idea.

•••

Grotto's little circus was out in full force – men grunting, flexing, puffing their chests like cockerels in a never-ending contest of virility. A growing pack of brawny Servums, spending their days on the common together, pushing themselves up and down, hoisting each other into the air with bellows and groans, veins snaking under their skin like worms writhing through meat. It seemed to be Grotto's latest obsession: stockpiling brute force, as though rage could be weaponised by sheer numbers. Whether he planned to turn that parade of testosterone into something, I had no idea.

'Isn't that your Saviour girl, Grotto?' one of them called out, setting off a ripple of laughter.

Mona had told me they'd worked out how to trick the bots into thinking they hadn't eaten, just so they could double their rations. More food meant more muscle. As if that brute-force approach hadn't already gone spectacularly wrong on Rise Day.

Grotto, it seemed, had learned nothing.

At least Julian was there. He looked stronger than ever, but I wasn't here for his physique.

'I need your help,' I said as I reached him, Sam trailing behind me. 'Are they still making you do arithmetic?'

'Well, I can't memorise much,' Julian admitted. 'Why?'

'But you can multiply?'

'Yeah, that I can.'

'We need complex matrix multiplications,' Sam said. 'Can you do that?'

'That a man or a woman?' Grotto cut in, eyes narrowing on Sam.

'We're not talking to you right now,' I snapped.

Grotto didn't take kindly to that. His gaze flicked between

me and Sam. 'Julian's one of mine. You can't just show up and put him to work. What's this about?'

'Grotto, please.' I looked him in the eye and let him see I wasn't playing. 'Please.'

Julian looked between us, visibly uncomfortable. 'I mean, I could...give it a go, for sure,' he said, caught between reluctance and a forced cheeriness.

Sam didn't say a word, but I sensed his unease. He knew enough to understand the pecking order here – and that he wasn't in it.

Grotto folded his arms, scowling first at me, then at Sam, then finally at Julian. The moment stretched, taut as a wire, before he gave a stiff jerk of his head. A grudging permission.

'I want him back tomorrow,' he said.

With Julian's help, we generated codes for the next five days.

Sam was buzzing as we walked back to section one-seventy, talking too fast, hands all over the place. His excitement unsettled me. That old fear crept back – the fear of his disillusionment. I just hoped he could take another failure without breaking, that he'd accept it quickly before it had the chance to hurt too much.

As soon as we got there, I fed in the code, just like I had a hundred times before, down to the last digit. And then I heard it. A different sound. Not the usual dull rejection. It was a clean, affirmative beep.

I froze.

And in that moment, I didn't tell Sam. I couldn't. The words wouldn't come.

'What's wrong?' he asked. 'Why are you crying?'

I was crying? I tried to remind myself of the risks of hope, of what happened when you let it in. It was too late, though. I felt it. This time was different.

'Did it work?' Sam asked more urgently. 'Did it?'

My throat was tight, so I nodded, just a little, and I cried some more. Then I was in his arms.

The greyness had lifted. I didn't want it to come back.

This time, we'd get it right.

FORTY-FIVE

SAM

THE MOMENT THE PASSCODE WORKED, a change came over Primula. She was herself again, but with more energy than before. I had to admit, seeing her like that did something to me. Her excitement was catching.

She hesitated before trying the lifts, and I got why. But we needed to be sure that entering the passcode had actually given us the control we expected. I stayed quiet, letting her concentrate. Then her eyebrows jumped, and she drew in a sharp breath before covering her mouth with her hand.

'It's bloody effortless,' she said. 'I can't believe it.'

What had once been like dragging a dead weight had become as easy as breathing, like the lifts had finally caught up with what her mind had been trying to do all along. They moved up and down, governed by her will alone.

She was in charge now. But she said she needed more practice to get familiar with the system, and we had to be careful.

Control meant nothing if we lost it straight away.

Cautiously, we tested a few things. Every time, we ended up more surprised than before. The next day, she raised one of the metal gates a few inches from the ground.

'I could take it all the way up if I wanted,' she said. But we weren't ready for bold moves yet.

'Can you dim the lights in the common?' I asked, almost teasing.

She shut her eyes for a second. The lights softened to mid-strength. Around us, murmurs of confusion spread among the Servums. A second later, the lighting snapped back to normal, quickly enough to be dismissed as nothing. Primula turned to me and winked.

We'd agreed – no sudden actions. This was our only shot, and we knew it. There was no room for mistakes or sloppy attempts at rebellion. So, we planned. The passcode didn't need to be re-entered every day to maintain control, but the longer we waited, the more likely it was that someone in Liffdom would notice. We couldn't sit on this forever.

Soon, the way forward became clear.

Primula took control, her voice carrying an authority I hadn't heard before. I'd always known she had fire in her, but this was another level.

Grotto and his men took some time to get on board, but when Grotto turned obedient overnight, I asked Primula how she'd managed it. She gave me a knowing look.

'I had no choice,' she said.

'What?'

'I can give any Servum shocks now.'

She wasn't proud of it, but I agreed – we didn't have time to ask nicely.

With Grotto as her loyal subordinate, Primula stood in front of his men. They sorted themselves by strength and speed, something that seemed to appeal to their competitive streak. They were enjoying it. A large, restless crowd, eager to follow someone who led with conviction.

Later, we went to check on Marydit and Mona. They'd laid out a few cloaks for Lisa to lie on. They looked raised, puffed up – like something was cushioning them from beneath. I understood when a couple of middle-aged women arrived, handing Mona the hems they'd cut from their own cloaks, and she tucked them under Lisa.

'Thank you, my lovelies,' Marydit said.

'That makes one hundred and fifty so far,' Mona said to Primula. 'We should have double that by this time tomorrow.'

Primula glanced at me then. 'We're nearly ready,' she said.

Gren had given us the exact time of the meeting, and Primula could now track every second with precision. The Lodgers would be gathered in the Beluga Room, draped in their blue gowns, wigs perched atop their heads. I could almost see them – their laughter elegant, their mannerisms refined – but it was all gloss over rot. How had it come to this? How had this disease survived, embedded itself so deeply in the world, until it grew into the monstrosity around us?

'Any moment now,' Primula murmured, squeezing my hand.

She shut her eyes, and when they opened again, I could tell. No words; no signal. Just a look that meant the power in the Beluga Room was out.

It was time to move.

We stepped aside as Grotto's men stormed into the tunnel, advancing the second Primula raised the metal gate. The lift awaited us at the far end. For days, I'd wondered what this moment would feel like – whether fear would creep in, whether my nerves would betray me. But as we followed Grotto's men inside, the adrenaline turned into something cold, less flimsy and more certain. This wasn't about proving anything. It was about survival. There was no time for hesitation. The most important task of our lives lay ahead.

The lift doors opened into absolute darkness. A murmuring void. Then Grotto's men moved, stomping along the perimeter of the room, bare feet hitting the floor, letting the Lodgers know they were no longer alone. When the first screams broke out, the panic followed fast.

Primula let a faint light rise, just enough to outline the shapes before us. Bodies scrambled in every direction. Chaos, just as we'd anticipated.

I couldn't make out one Lodger from the next, but they were mostly old, frail and unprepared. They had no chance against the Servums, who moved with brute efficiency, their strength fuelled by the hunger for revenge. And this was just the first wave – two more groups waited below, ready to be brought up the lift shaft.

The cries grew wilder, more frantic. Some Lodgers dropped to the floor, curling up, hoping to disappear. Others bolted around the room like rats on a sinking ship, their panicked movements making them easy targets. A few fought back with weak kicks and feeble punches, slowed by the folds of their robes.

'Don't kill; just restrain!' Primula commanded in an almost unrecognisable manner.

The Servums moved fast, unravelling the thick hems from their arms and legs, using them to bind hands and feet, pulling a third strip tight to gag the Lodgers' mouths.

'Wrists, ankles, mouth,' Primula ordered.

'Wrists, ankles, mouth,' the Servums kept repeating in a guttural chant.

By the time the last group of Servums entered, the room was nearly silent. The Lodgers lay bound on the floor, writhing like overturned insects. Muffled screams had turned into uneven, choked howls. Wigs, torn garments and shattered jewellery littered the space – a grotesque mess of what they'd been just a short while ago.

Then the lights came on fully, revealing their fear. Eyes bulging, darting from one of us to the next, searching for mercy that would never come. For the briefest moment, something inside me stirred – something dangerously close to pity. But there was no other way.

I found Gren easily, near the edge of the room, like we'd planned. Kneeling, I untied the restraints on his limbs and pulled out the gag, then stepped back as he stood. Around us, the bound Lodgers groaned, seething. Now they had someone to blame – the traitor in their midst. But what did it matter? The hatred in their eyes changed nothing.

Primula paced, counting as the Servums hauled the Lodgers one by one into the lift.

'Ninety-eight,' she said, stopping in front of us. 'We're missing one.'

'It should be all of them,' Gren said, frowning. 'Everyone was here.'

'We'll count again in Servyden,' I said. 'Let's go.'

FORTY-SIX

GREN

THE NOISE DIED THE MOMENT I stepped into the press room. A sea of lenses stared back at me as I began to speak.

'Today, we mourn the deaths of Igor Voychenko, Supreme Leader of the Human Order, and his family, along with so many other distinguished citizens of Lacunfort who, like countless before them, chose to end their lives by euthanasia at an Express Passing Centre. I share the grief of millions across Rivennia who search for solace in the wake of these events. Yet even in mourning – and while further investigations continue – we must act. The scale and suddenness of these deaths have made one thing clear: the last amendments to the Right to Die Act evidently went too far. This must be a reckoning – for our government and for our people. I am pleased to announce that, as of this morning, all Express Passing Centres have been closed by congressional order.'

Ignoring the commotion that followed, I left without taking

questions. With the world reeling in shock, I instructed my team to hold all engagements for the afternoon. Two hours later, my capsula opened to the warm breeze of Liffdom Island. The ancient palace was quiet. Lorelei greeted me, looking efficient and happy, as I stepped into the vestibule.

'All the Servums are settled across the island,' she said. 'Medical bots are conducting check-ups and providing necessary assistance. They have access to the finest meals and amenities. Many of them want to stay here permanently.'

'Of course,' I said.

For those who want to return to the world…we're working on new identities and ensuring their genetic mutations are contained before we find their families and reunite them. It will take years, but I believe we'll get there.

'I'll find someone to organise the work.'

She frowned.

'No,' she said. 'I'll do it. There is no greater privilege – no truer way to honour my brothers and sisters. Do you not see? It is clear to me now. This is the reason God placed me in your path. How blessed I am. This is it. This is my calling.'

She was no longer the unworldly Varcegian she had once been. She believed herself fortunate, but the greater fortune belonged to the hundreds of Servums who now held her devotion – a life of service dedicated to restoring meaning to theirs.

At the end of the great hallway, I walked under a carved arch and opened a heavy door to find Princess Lisa – the sole survivor among the late queen's abducted children – comfortably tucked under a duvet. Her backrest was reclined three-quarters down. She was watching an old romantic comedy projected as a hologram.

Noticing me, she grinned.

'One from my youth,' she said with a playful shrug.

She had made her wishes clear. The world outside was too much to adapt to at her age. Now, she longed for rest, surrounded by the Servums who had become her family.

I smiled back and bowed. 'Your Highness.'

As she became entranced by the story once more, I turned to the window. Below, the walled garden was alive with activity. A large group of Servums in colourful clothes talked animatedly. I recognised many of them – the men who had broken into the Beluga Room – alongside women and youngsters. Several stood around a ginger man with a thick beard, following his instructions as they applied the final touches to a mural. At its centre, unmistakable, was the portrait of Primula. There was warmth in her expression, and a quiet resolve beneath it. Squinting, I read the inscription painted on a ribbon-like strip waving under her chin: *OUR SAVIOUR*.

I walked back down the hallway, glancing at the entrance hall below, where Sam, Primula, Mona and Marydit sat on a sofa, deep in conversation. Their laughter echoed through the space, igniting a kind of happiness in me that I hadn't realised I craved.

Then I made my way to the basement – the place I kept hidden from the rest.

As soon as I stepped inside, dozens of screens flickered to life. It was my own surveillance system, monitoring the ninety-eight Lodgers who now inhabited Servyden.

Ninety-eight; no more. The number remained unchanged, despite our repeated recounts.

Among the screens, one message stood out – a letter I had read so many times I knew every word by heart.

My dear Gren,

By the time you read this, the world will believe all the

Lodgers are dead by euthanasia. In truth, that fate will be mine alone.

I sided with you for the greater good, but I cannot go on, knowing I betrayed my fellow Lodgers and my own blood.

As a Lodger myself, it was only right that I should spend my remaining days in Servyden – a fate I could not bring myself to endure.

I hope you see, as I do, that your conviction has given humanity another chance.

Yours in essence and memory, always,

Fredrica

The largest screen at the centre claimed my full attention. Beneath it, a single button waited. On the display, Igor Voychenko sat within his Servum enclosure – frail and thin, but still clinging to a strength that would take time to fade. His dignity, however, had already withered, replaced by the desperation of survival.

It was feeding time.

I pressed the button, activating the metal flap.

'Those who consume others thrive,' announced the automated voice, as a pigeon fluttered onto the floor.

AUTHOR'S NOTE

Rivennia is a work of fiction. While it explores themes of biotechnology and gene editing, the science presented in this story is speculative and should not be taken as a reflection of current medical practice.

At the time of writing, approved gene therapies are designed to treat specific cells and tissues in the body. These therapies do not target reproductive DNA and therefore do not alter traits that can be passed on to future generations. Heritable modifications remain a subject of ethical debate and are not part of licensed clinical treatments.

Printed in Dunstable, United Kingdom

79885102R00234